Praise for *New York Times* bestselling author Diana Palmer

"Palmer proves that love and passion can be found even in the most dangerous situations."
—*Publishers Weekly* on *Untamed*

"You just can't do better than a Diana Palmer story to make your heart lighter and smile brighter."
—*Fresh Fiction* on *Wyoming Rugged*

"Diana Palmer is a mesmerizing storyteller who captures the essence of what a romance should be."
—*Affaire de Coeur*

"The popular Palmer has penned another winning novel, a perfect blend of romance and suspense."
—*Booklist* on *Lawman*

"Diana Palmer's characters leap off the page. She captures their emotions and scars beautifully and makes them come alive for readers."
—*RT Book Reviews* on *Lawless*

Dear Reader,

I can't believe that it has been thirty years since my first Long, Tall Texans book, *Calhoun*, debuted! The series was suggested by my former editor Tara Gavin, who asked if I might like to set stories in a fictional town of my own design. Would I! And the rest is history.

As the years went by, I found more and more sexy ranchers and cowboys to add to the collection. My readers (especially Amy!) found time to gift me with a notebook listing every single one of them, wives and kids and connections to other families in my own Texas town of Jacobsville. Eventually the town got a little too big for me, so I added another smaller town called Comanche Wells and began to fill it up, too.

You can't imagine how much pleasure this series has given me. I continue to add to the population of Jacobs County, Texas, and I have no plans to stop. Ever.

I hope all of you enjoy reading the Long, Tall Texans as much as I enjoy writing them. Thank you all for your kindness and loyalty and friendship. I am your biggest fan!

Love,

Diana Palmer

DIANA PALMER

LONG, TALL TEXANS:
Donavan
Emmett

Previously published as
Donavan and *Emmett*

ISBN-13: 978-1-335-62184-9

Long, Tall Texans: Donavan/Emmett

Copyright © 2019 by Harlequin Books S.A.

First published as Donavan by Harlequin Books in 1991 and Emmett by Harlequin Books in 1992.

The publisher acknowledges the copyright holder of the individual works as follows:

Donavan
Copyright © 1991 by Diana Palmer

Emmett
Copyright © 1992 by Diana Palmer

Recycling programs for this product may not exist in your area.

Printed in U.S.A.

HARLEQUIN®
www.Harlequin.com

CONTENTS

A prolific author of more than one hundred books, **Diana Palmer** got her start as a newspaper reporter. A *New York Times* bestselling author and voted one of the top ten romance writers in America, she has a gift for telling the most sensual tales with charm and humor. Diana lives with her family in Cornelia, Georgia. Visit her website at www.dianapalmer.com.

Books by Diana Palmer

Long, Tall Texans

Fearless
Heartless
Dangerous
Merciless
Courageous
Protector
Invincible
Untamed
Defender
Undaunted

The Wyoming Men

Wyoming Tough
Wyoming Fierce
Wyoming Bold
Wyoming Strong
Wyoming Rugged
Wyoming Brave

Morcai Battalion

The Morcai Battalion
The Morcai Battalion: The Recruit
The Morcai Battalion: Invictus
The Morcai Battalion: The Rescue

Visit the Author Profile page
at Harlequin.com for more titles.

DONAVAN

For a special reader—Peggy

CHAPTER ONE

FAY FELT AS if every eye in the bar was on her when she walked in. It had been purely an impulse, and she was already regretting it. A lone female walking into a bar on the wrong side of town in south Texas late at night was asking for trouble. Women's lib hadn't been heard of this far out, and several pairs of male eyes were telling her so.

She could only imagine how she looked in her tight designer jeans, her feet encased in silk hose and high heels, a soft yellow knit sweater showing the faint swell of her high breasts. Her long dark hair was around her shoulders in soft swirls, and her green eyes darted nervously from one side of the small, smoke-filled room to the other. There was a jukebox playing so loud that she had to yell to tell the bartender she wanted a beer. That was a joke, too, because in all her twenty years, she'd never had a beer. White wine, yes. Even a piña colada down in Jamaica. But never a beer.

Defiance was becoming expensive, she thought, watching a burly man separate himself from his companions with a mumbled remark that made them laugh.

He perched himself beside her at the bar, his narrow eyes giving her an appraisal that made her want to run. "Hello, pretty thing," he said, grinning through his beard. "Wanta dance?"

She cupped her hands around the beer mug to stop them from shaking. "No, thank you," she said in her soft, cultured voice, keeping her eyes down. "I'm... waiting for someone."

That was almost true. She'd been waiting for someone all her life, but he hadn't shown up yet. She needed him now. She was living with a mercenary, social-climbing relative who was doing his best to sell her to a rich friend with eyes that made her skin crawl. All her money was tied up in trust, and she was stuck with her mother's brother. Rescue was certainly uppermost in her mind, but this rowdy cowboy wasn't her idea of a white knight.

"You and me could have a good time, honey," her admirer continued, unabashed. He smoothed her sweater-clad arm and she withdrew as if his fingers were snakes. "Now, don't start backing away, sweet thing! I know how to treat a lady."

No one noticed the dark face in the corner suddenly lift, or saw the dangerous glitter in silver eyes that dominated it. No one noticed the look he gave the girl, or the colder one that he gave her companion before he got gracefully to his feet and moved toward the bar.

He wore jeans, too. Not like Fay's, because his were working jeans. They were faded and stained from work, and his boots were a howling thumbed nose at city cowboys' elegant footwear. His hat was blacker than his thick, unruly hair, a little crumpled here and there. He was tall. Very tall. Lean and muscular and quite well-known locally. His temper, in fact, was as legendary as the big fists now curled with deceptive laxness at his sides as he walked.

"You'd like me if you just got to know me—" The pudgy cowboy broke off when the newcomer came into his line of vision. He became almost comically still, his head slightly cocked. "Why, hello, Donavan," he began uneasily. "I didn't know she was with *you*."

"Now you do," he replied in a deep, gravelly voice that sent chills down Fay's spine.

She turned her head and looked into diamond-glinted eyes, and lost her heart forever. She couldn't seem to breathe.

"It's about time you showed up," he told Fay. He took her arm, eased her down from the bar stool with a grip that was firm and exciting. He handed her beer mug to her, and with a last cutting glare at the other man, he escorted her back to his table.

"Thank you," she stammered when she was sitting beside him. He'd left a cigarette smoking in the dented metal ashtray, and a half-touched glass of whiskey. He didn't take off his hat when he sat down. She'd noticed that Western men seemed to have little use for the courtesies she'd taken for granted back home.

He picked up his cigarette and took a long draw from it. His nails were flat and clean, despite traces of grease that clung to his long-fingered, dark hands. They were beautiful masculine hands, with no jewelry adorning them. Working hands, she thought idly.

"Who are you?" he asked suddenly.

"I'm Fay," she told him. She forced a smile. "And you…?"

"Most people just call me Donavan."

She took a sip of beer and grimaced. It tasted terrible. She stared at it with an expression that brought a faint smile to the man's hard, thin mouth.

"You don't drink beer, and you don't belong in a bar. What are you doing on this side of town, debutante?" he drawled.

"I'm running away from home," she said with a laugh. "Escaping my jailers. Having a night on the town. Rebelling. Take your pick."

"Are you old enough to do that?" he asked pointedly.

"If you mean, am I old enough to order a beer in a bar, yes. I'm two months shy of twenty-one."

"You don't look it."

She studied his hard, suntanned face and his unruly hair. With a little trimming up and proper dressing, he might be rather devastating. "Are you from around here?" she asked.

"All my life," he agreed.

"Do you…work?"

"Child, in this part of Texas, everybody works." He scowled. "Most everybody," he amended, letting his eyes linger pointedly on her diamond tennis bracelet. "Wearing that into a country bar is asking for trouble. Pull your sleeve down."

She did, obeying him instantly when she was known for ignoring anything that sounded like a command at home. She flushed at her instant deference. Maybe she was drunk already. Sure, she mused, on two sips of beer.

"What do you do when you aren't giving orders?" she taunted.

He searched her green eyes. "I'm a ranch foreman," he said. "I give orders for a living."

"Oh. You're a cowboy."

"That's one name for it."

She smiled again. "I've never met a real cowboy before."

"You aren't from here."

She shook her head. "Georgia. My parents were killed in a plane crash, so I was sent out here to live with my uncle." She whistled softly. "You can't imagine what it's like."

"Get out," he said simply. "People live in prisons out of choice. You can always walk away from a situation you don't care for."

"Want to bet? I'm rich," she said curtly. "Filthy rich. But it's all tied up in a trust that I can't touch until I'm twenty-one, and my uncle is hoping to marry me off to a business associate in time to get his hands on some of it."

"Are you for real?" he asked. He picked up the whiskey glass and took a sip, putting the glass down with a sharp movement of his hand. "Tell him to go to hell and do what you please. At your age I was working for myself, not for any relatives."

"You're a man," she pointed out.

"What difference does that make?" he asked. "Haven't you ever heard of women's lib?"

She smiled. At least one person in the bar had heard of women's lib. "I'm not that kind of woman. I'm wimpy."

"Listen, lady, no wimpy girl walks into a place like this in the middle of the night and orders a beer."

She laughed, her green eyes brilliant. "Yes, she does, when she's driven to it. Besides, it was safe, wasn't it? You were here."

He lifted his chin and a different light came into the pale, silvery eyes. "And you think I'm safe," he murmured. "Or, more precisely, that you're safe with me?"

Her heart began to thud against her ribs. That was a very adult look in his eyes, and she noticed the corresponding drop of his voice into a silky, soft purr. Her lips parted as she let out the breath she was holding.

"I hope I am," she said after a minute. "Because I've done a stupid thing and even though I might deserve a hard time, I'm hoping you won't give me one."

He smiled, and this time it was without mockery. "Good girl. You're learning."

"Is it a lesson?" she asked.

He drained the whiskey glass. "Life is all lessons.

The ones you don't learn right off the bat, you have to repeat. Get up. I'll drive you home."

"Must you?" she asked, sighing. "It's the first adventure I've ever had, and it may be the last."

He cocked his hat over one eye and looked down at her. "In that case, I'll do my best to make it memorable," he murmured dryly. He held out a lean, strong hand and pulled her up when she took it. "Are you game?"

She was feeling her way with him, but oddly, she trusted him. She smiled. "I'm game."

He nodded. He took her arm and guided her out the door. She noticed a few looks that came their way, but no one tried to distract him.

"People seem to know you in there," she remarked when they were outside in the cool night air.

"They know me," he returned. "I've treed that bar a time or two."

"Treed it?"

He glanced down at her. "Broken it up in a brawl. Men get into trouble, young lady, and women aren't always handy to get them out of it."

"I'm not really handy," she said hesitantly.

He chuckled. "Honey, what you are is written all over you in green ink. I don't mind a little adventure, but that's all you'll get from me." His silvery eyes narrowed. "If you stay around here long enough, you'll learn that I don't like rich women, and you'll learn why. But for tonight, I'm in a generous mood."

"I don't understand," she said.

He laughed without humor. "I don't suppose you

do." He eyed her intently. "You aren't safe to be let out."

"That's what everybody keeps saying." She smiled with what she hoped was sophistication. "But how will I learn anything about life if I'm kept in a glass bowl?"

His eyes narrowed. "Maybe you've got a head start already." He tugged her along to a raunchy gray pickup truck with dents all over it. "I hope you weren't expecting a Rolls-Royce, debutante. I could hardly haul cattle in one."

She felt terrible. She actually winced as she looked up at him, and he felt a twinge of guilt at the dry remark that was meant to be funny.

"Oh, I don't care what you drive," she said honestly. "You could be riding a horse, and it wouldn't matter. I don't judge people by what they have."

His pale eyes slid over her face lightly. "I think I knew that already," he said quietly. "I'm sorry. I meant it as a joke. Here. Don't cut yourself on that spring. It popped out and I haven't had time to fix it."

"Okay." She bounced into the cab and he closed the door. It smelled of the whole outdoors, and when he got in, it smelled of leather and smoke. He glanced at her and smiled.

He started the truck and glanced at her. "Did you drive here?" he asked.

"Yes."

He paused to look around the parking lot, pursing his lips with faint amusement when he saw the regal blue Mercedes-Benz sitting among the dented pickup trucks and dusty four-wheel-drive vehicles.

"That's right, you don't need to ask what I drove here in," she muttered self-consciously. "And yes, it's mine."

He chuckled. "Bristling already, and we've only just met," he murmured as he pulled out into the road. "What do you do when you aren't trying to pick up strange men in bars?"

She glared at him. "I study piano, paint a little and generally try to stay sane through endless dinner parties and morning coffees."

He whistled through his teeth. "Some life."

She turned in the seat, liking the strength of his profile. "What do you do?"

"Chase cattle, mostly. Figure percentages, decide which cattle to cull, hire and fire cowboys, go to conferences, make financial decisions." He glanced at her. "Occasionally I sit on the board of directors of two corporations."

She frowned slightly. "I thought you said you were a foreman."

"There's a little more to it than that," he said comfortably. "You don't need to know the rest. Where do you want to go?"

She had to readjust her thinking from the abrupt statement. She glanced out the dark window at the flat south Texas landscape. "Well… I don't know. I just don't want to go home."

"They're having a fiesta down in San Moreno," he said with an amused glance. "Ever been to one?"

"No!" Her eyes brightened. "Could we?"

"I don't see why not. There isn't much to do except dance, though, and drink beer. Do you dance?"

"Oh, yes. Do you?"

He chuckled. "I can when forced into it. But you may have trouble with the beer part."

"I learned to like caviar," she said. "Maybe I can learn to like beer."

He didn't comment. He turned on the radio and country-western music filled the cab. She leaned her head back on the seat and smiled as she closed her eyes. Incredible, she thought, how much she trusted this man when she'd only just met him. She felt as though she'd known him for years.

The feeling continued when they got to the small, dusty town of San Moreno. A band of mariachis was playing loud, lively Mexican music while people danced in the roped-off main square. Vendors sold everything from beer to tequila and chimichangas and tacos. The music was loud, the beer was hot, but nobody seemed to mind. Most of the people were Mexican-American, although Fay noticed a few cowboys among the celebrants.

"What are we celebrating?" Fay asked breathlessly as Donavan swung her around and around to the quick beat of the music.

"Who cares?" He chuckled.

She shook her head. In all her life, she couldn't remember being so happy or feeling so carefree. If she died tomorrow, it would be worth it, because she had tonight to remember. So she drank warm beer that tasted better with each sip, and she danced in Donavan's lean, strong arms, and rested against his muscular chest and breathed in the scent of him until she was more drunk on the man than the liquor.

Finally the frantic pace died down and there was a slow two-step. She melted into Donavan, sliding her arms around him with the kind of familiarity that usually came from weeks of togetherness. She seemed to fit against him, like a soft glove. He smelled of tobacco and beer and the whole outdoors, and the feel of his body so close to hers was delightfully exciting. His arms enfolded her, both of them wrapped close around her, and for a few minutes there was nobody else in the world. She heard the music as if through a fog of pure pleasure, her body reacting to the closeness of his in a way it had never reacted before. She felt a tension that was disturbing, and a kind of throbbing ache in her lower body that she'd never experienced. Being close to him was becoming intolerable. She caught her breath and pulled away a little, raising eyes full of curious apprehension to his.

He searched her face quietly, aware of her fear and equally aware of the cause of it. He smiled gently. "It's all right," he said quietly.

She frowned. "I… I don't quite understand what's wrong with me," she whispered. "Maybe the beer…"

"There's no need to pretend. Not with me." He framed her face in his lean hands and bent, pressing a tender kiss against her forehead. "We'd better go."

"Must we?" she sighed.

He nodded. "It's late." He caught her hand in his and tugged her along to the truck. He was feeling something of the same reckless excitement she was, except that he was older and more adept at controlling it. He knew that she'd wanted him while they were dancing, but things were getting ahead of him. He didn't need a rich society girl in his life. God knew, one had been the ruin of his family. People around Jacobsville, Texas, still remembered how his father had gone pell-mell after a local debutante without any scruples about how he forced her to marry him, right on the heels of his wife's funeral, too. Donavan had turned bitter trying to live down the family scandal. Miss High Society here would find it out eventually. Better not to start something he couldn't finish, even if she did cause an inconvenient ache in his body. No doubt she'd had half a dozen men, but she might be addictive—and he couldn't risk finding out she was.

She was pleasantly relaxed when they got back to the deserted bar where she'd left her Mercedes. The spell had worn off a little, and her head had cleared. But with that return to reality came the unpleasantness of having to go home and face the music. She hadn't told anyone where she was going, and they were going to be angry. Really angry.

"Thank you," she said simply, turning to Donavan after she unlocked her car. "It was a magical night."

"For me, too." He opened the door for her. "Stay out of my part of town, debutante," he said gently. "You don't belong here."

Her green eyes searched his gray ones. "I hate my life," she said.

"Change it," he replied. "You can if you want to."

"I'm not used to fighting."

"Get used to it. Life doesn't give, it takes. Anything worth having is worth fighting for."

"So they say." She toyed with her car keys. "But in my world, the fighting gets dirty."

"It does in mine, too. That never stopped me. Don't let it stop you."

She lowered her eyes to the hard chest that had pillowed her head while they danced. "I won't forget you."

"Don't get any ideas," he murmured dryly, flicking a long strand of hair away from her face. "I'm not looking for complications or ties. Not ever. Your world and mine wouldn't mix. Don't go looking for trouble."

"You just told me to," she pointed out, lifting her face to his.

"Not in my direction," he emphasized. He smiled at her. The action made him look younger, less formidable. "Go home."

She sighed. "I guess I should. You wouldn't like to kiss me good-night, I guess?" she added with lifted eyebrows.

"I would," he replied. "Which is why I'm not going to. Get in the car."

"Men," she muttered. She glared at him, but she got into the car and closed the door.

"Drive carefully," he said. "And wear your seat belt."

She fastened it, but not because of his order—she usually wore a seat belt. She spared him one long, last look before she started the car and pulled away. When she drove onto the main highway, he was already driving off in the other direction, and without looking back. She felt a sense of loss that shocked her, as if she'd given up part of herself. Maybe she had. She couldn't remember ever feeling so close to another human being.

Her father and mother had never been really close to her. They'd had their own independent lives, and they almost never included her in any of their activities. She'd grown up with housekeepers and governesses for companionship, and with no brothers or sisters for company. From lonely child to lonely woman, she'd gone through the motions of living. But she'd never felt that anyone would really mind if she died.

That hadn't changed when she'd come out to Jacobsville, Texas, to live with her mother's brother, Uncle Henry Rollins. He wasn't well-to-do, but he wanted to be. He wasn't above using his control over Fay's estate to provide the means to entertain. Fay hadn't protested, but she'd just realized tonight how lax she'd been in looking out for her own interests. Uncle Henry had invited his business partner to supper and hadn't told Fay until the last minute. She was tired of having Sean thrown at her, and she'd rebelled, running out the door to her car.

It had been almost comical, bowlegged Uncle Henry rushing after her, huffing and puffing as he tried to match his bulk to her slender swiftness and lost. She hadn't known where she was going, but she'd wound up at the bar. Fate had sent her there, perhaps, to a man who made her see what a docile child she'd become, when she was an independent woman. Well, things were going to change. Starting now.

Donavan had fascinated her. She tingled, just remembering how he hadn't even had to lift a hand in the bar to make the man who'd been worrying her back down. He was the stuff of which romantic fantasies were made. But he didn't like rich women.

It would be nice, she thought, if Donavan had fallen madly in love with her and started searching for her. That would be improbable, though, since he didn't have a clue as to her real identity. She didn't know his, either, come to think of it; all she knew was what he did for a living. But he could have been stretching the truth a little. He hadn't sounded quite forceful when he'd said he was a foreman.

Well, it didn't really matter, she thought sadly. She'd never see him again. But it had been a memorable meeting altogether, and she knew she'd never forget him. Not ever.

CHAPTER TWO

THE FEEDLOT OFFICE was quiet, and Fay York was grateful for the respite. It had been a hectic two weeks since she started this, her first job. She was still faintly amazed at her own courage and grit, because she'd never thought she'd be able to actually do it. She'd surprised her uncle Henry as much as herself when she'd announced her plans to get a job and become independent until her inheritance came through.

It had been because of Donavan that she'd done it. Her evening with him had changed her life. He'd made it possible for her to believe in herself. He'd given her a kind of self-confidence that she hadn't thought possible.

But it hadn't been easy, and she'd been scared to death the morning she'd walked into the office of the gigantic Ballenger feedlot to ask for a job.

Barry Holman, the local attorney who was to handle her inheritance, had suggested that she see Justin Ballenger about work, because his secretary was out having a baby and Calhoun Ballenger's wife, Abby, had been reluctantly filling in.

She could still remember her shock when she'd

gone to Mr. Holman to ask for a living allowance until her inheritance came through, something that would give her a little independence from her overbearing uncle.

That was when the blow fell. "I'm sorry," Holman said. "But there's no provision for any living allowance. According to the terms of the will, you can't inherit until you're twenty-one. Until that time, the executor of your parents' estate has total control of your money."

She gasped. "You mean I don't have any money unless Uncle Henry gives it to me?"

"I'm afraid so," he said. "I realize it probably seems terribly unfair to you, Fay, but your parents must have thought they were doing the right thing."

"I can't believe it," she said, feeling sick. She wrapped her arms around her body. "What will I do?"

"What you originally planned. Go ahead and get a job. You'll only need it for a couple of weeks, until you get your inheritance."

The statement helped her fight out of her misery. Involuntarily, she smiled, liking the blond attorney. He was in his early thirties, very good-looking and successful. He was married, because on his desk was a photograph of a young woman with long, brown hair holding a baby.

"Thank you," she said.

"Oh, it's my pleasure. Don't worry, you won't even have to look far for a job. I just happen to know of an opening. Know anything about cattle?"

She hesitated. "Not really."

"Do you mind working around them?"

"Not if I don't have to brand them," she murmured dryly.

He laughed. "It won't come to that. The Ballenger brothers are looking for a temporary secretary. Their full-time one was pregnant and just had a complicated delivery. She'll be out about two months and they're looking for someone to fill in. Calhoun Ballenger's wife has been trying to handle it, but you'd be a godsend right now. Can you type?"

"Oh, yes," she said. "I can handle a computer, too. I took several college courses before my parents died and I had to come out here to comply with the terms of their will."

"Good!"

"But surely they've found someone…"

"There aren't that many people available for part-time work," he said. "Mostly high-school students, and they don't like the environment that goes with the job."

She grinned. "I won't care, as long as I make enough to pay my rent."

"You will. Here." He scribbled an address. "Go and see Justin or Calhoun. Tell them I sent you. Trust me," he added, rising to shake hands with her. "You'll like them."

"I hope so. I sure don't like my uncle much at the moment."

He nodded. "I can understand that. But Henry

isn't a bad man, you know. And there could be more to this than meets the eye," he added reluctantly.

That statement gave her cold chills. The way Uncle Henry had been throwing her headlong at a rich bachelor friend of his made her uneasy. "I suppose so." She hesitated. "Do you know just how my uncle's been managing my affairs in the past two months?"

"Not yet," Barry Holman replied. "I've asked for an accounting, but he's refused to turn over any documents to me until the day you turn twenty-one."

"That doesn't sound promising," she said nervously. "I understood my father to say he had at least two million dollars tied up in trust for me. Surely Uncle Henry couldn't have gone through that in a few weeks, could he?"

"I hardly think so," he assured her. "Don't worry. Everything will be all right. Go and see the Ballengers. Good luck."

"I think I'll need it, but thanks for your help," she said as she left the office.

THE BALLENGER FEEDLOT was a mammoth operation. During the short time she'd been in Jacobsville, Fay had never gotten a good look at it. Now, up close, the sheer enormity of it was staggering. So was the relative cleanliness of the operation and the attention to sanitation.

It was Justin Ballenger who interviewed her. He was tall and rangy, not at all handsome, but kind and courteous.

"You understand that this would only be a temporary job?" he emphasized, leaning forward. "Our secretary, Nita, is only going to be out long enough to recuperate from her C-section and have a few weeks with their new baby."

"Yes, Mr. Holman told me about that," Fay said. "I don't mind. I only need something temporary until I get used to being on my own. I was living with my uncle but the situation was pretty uncomfortable." Without meaning to, she went on to explain what had happened, finding in Justin a sympathetic listener.

Justin's dark eyes narrowed. "Your uncle is a mercenary man. I think you did the right thing. Make sure Barry keeps a close watch on your holdings."

"He's doing that." She gnawed her lower lip worriedly. "You won't mention it to anyone...?"

"It's nobody's business but yours," he agreed. "As far as we know, you're strictly a working girl who had a minor disagreement with her kin. Fair enough?"

"Yes, sir," she said, smiling. "I'm not really much more than a working girl, since everything is tied up in trust. But only for a few more weeks." She smiled. "Money doesn't really mean that much to me. Honestly I'd rather marry someone who loved me than someone who just wanted an easy life."

"You're a wise girl," he replied quietly. "Shelby and I both felt like that. We're not poor, but it wouldn't matter if we were. We have each other, and our boys. We're very lucky."

She smiled, because she'd heard about Shelby Ballenger and the circumstances that had finally led to her marriage to Justin. It was a real love story. "Maybe I'll get lucky like that one day," she said, thinking about Donavan.

"Well, if you want the job under those conditions, it's yours," he said after a minute. "Welcome aboard. Come on and I'll introduce you to my brother."

He preceded her down the hall, where a tall blond man was poring over figures on sheets of paper scattered all over his desk.

"This is Fay York," he said, introducing her. "Fay, my brother, Calhoun."

"Nice to meet you," she said sincerely, and shook hands. "I hope I can help you keep things in order while Nita's away."

"Abby will get down and kiss your shoes," Calhoun assured her. "She's been trying to keep one of our boys in school and the other two in day care and take care of the house while she worked in Nita's place this week. She's already threatened to open all the gates if we didn't do something to help her."

"I'm glad I needed a job, then," she said.

"So are we."

Abby came barreling in with an armload of files, her black hair askew around her face, her blue-gray eyes wide and curious when they met Fay's green ones.

"Please be my replacement," she said with such fervor that Fay laughed helplessly. "Do you take bribes? I can get you real chocolate truffles and mocha ice cream…"

"No need. I've already accepted the job while Nita is out with her baby," Fay assured the other woman.

"Oh, thank *God!*" she sighed, dropping the files on her husband's desk. She grinned at Calhoun. "Thank you, too, darling. I'll make you a big beef stew for dinner, with homemade rolls."

"Don't just stand there, go home!" he burst out. He grinned sheepishly at Fay. "She makes the best rolls in town. I've been eating hot dogs for so many days that I bark, because it's all I can cook! This has been hard on my stomach."

"And on my stamina." Abby laughed. "The boys have missed me. Well, I'll show you what to do, Fay, then I'll rush right home and start dough rising."

Fay followed her back to the desk out front and listened carefully and made notes while Abby briefed her on the routine and showed her how to fill in the forms. She went over the basics of feedlot operation as well, so that Fay would understand what she was doing.

"You make it sound very easy, but it isn't, is it?"

"No," Abby agreed. "Especially when you deal with some of our clients. J. D. Langley alone is enough to make a saint throw in the towel."

"Is he a rancher?"

"He's a..." Abby cleared her throat. "Yes, he's a rancher. But most of the cattle he deals in are other people's. He's general manager of the Mesa Blanco ranch combine."

"I don't know much about ranching, but I've heard of them."

"Most everybody has. J.D.'s good at his job, don't get me wrong, but he's a perfectionist when it comes to diet and handling of cattle. He saw one of the men use a cattle prod on some of his stock once and he jumped the man, right over a rail. We can't afford to turn down his business, but he makes things difficult. You'll find that out for yourself. Nobody crosses J.D. around Jacobsville."

"Is he rich?"

"No. He has plenty of power because of the job he does for Mesa Blanco, but it's his temperament that makes people jump when he speaks. J.D. would be arrogant in rags. He's just that kind of man."

Abby's description brought to mind another man, a rangy cowboy who'd given her the most magical evening of her life. She smiled sadly, thinking that she'd probably never see him again. Walking into that bar had been an act of desperation and bravado. She'd never have the nerve to do it twice. It would look as if she were chasing him, and he'd said at the time that there was no future in it. She'd driven by the bar two or three times, but she couldn't manage enough courage to go in again.

"Is Mr. Langley married?" Fay asked.

"There's no woman brave enough, anywhere," Abby said shortly. "His father's marriage soured him on women. He's been something of a playboy in past years, but he's settled somewhat since he's been managing the Mesa Blanco companies. There's a new president of the company who's a hard-line conservative, so J.D.'s toned down his playboy image. There's talk of the president giving that job to a man who's married and settled and has kids. The only child in J.D.'s life, ever, is a nephew in Houston, his sister's child. His sister died." She shook her head. "I can't really imagine J.D. with a child. He isn't the fatherly type."

"Is he really that bad?"

Abby nodded. "He was always difficult. But his father's remarriage, and then his death, left scars. These days, he's a dangerous man to be around, even for other men. Calhoun leaves the office when he's due to check on his stock. Justin seems to like him, but Calhoun almost came to blows with him once."

"Is he here very often?" Fay asked with obvious reluctance.

"Every other week, like clockwork."

"Then I'm very glad I won't be around long," she said with feeling.

Abby laughed. "Not to worry. He'll barely notice you. It's Calhoun and Justin who get the range language."

"I feel better already," she said.

HER FIRST DAY was tiring, but by the end of it she knew how many records had to be compiled each day on the individual lots of cattle. She learned volumes about weight gain ratios, feed supplements, veterinary services, daily chores and form filing. If it sounded simple just to feed cattle, it wasn't. There were hundreds of details to be attended to, and printouts of daily averages to be compiled for clients.

As the days went by and she fell into the routine of the job, Fay couldn't help but wonder if Donavan ever came here. He was foreman for a ranch, he'd told her. If that ranch had feeder cattle, this was probably where they'd be brought. But from what she'd learned, it was subordinates who dealt with the logistics of the transporting of feeder cattle, not the bosses.

She wanted badly to see him, to tell him how big an impact he'd had on her life with his pep talk that night she'd gone to the bar. Her horizons had enlarged, and she was independent for the first time in her life. She'd gone from frightened girl to confident woman in a very short time, and she wanted to thank him. She'd almost asked Abby a dozen times if she knew anyone named Donavan, but Abby would hardly travel in those circles. The Ballengers were high society now, even if they weren't social types. They wouldn't hang out in country bars with men who treed them.

Her uncle had tried to get her to come back to his house when word got out that she was working for a living, but she'd stood firm. No, she told Uncle Henry firmly. She wasn't going to be at his mercy until she inherited. And, she added, Mr. Holman was going to expect an accounting in the near future. Her uncle had looked very uncomfortable when she'd said that and she'd called Barry Holman the next morning to ask about her uncle's authority to act on her behalf.

His reply was that her uncle's power of attorney was a very limited one, and it was doubtful that he could do much damage in the short time he had left. Fay wondered about that. Her uncle was shrewd and underhanded. Heaven knew what wheeling and dealing he might have done already without her knowledge.

Pressure of work caught her attention and held it until the early afternoon. She took long enough to eat lunch at a nearby seafood place and came back just in time to catch the tail end of a heated argument coming from Calhoun's office.

"You're being unreasonable, J.D., and you know it!" Calhoun's deep voice carried down the hall.

"Unreasonable, hell," an equally deep voice drawled. "You and I may never see eye to eye on production methods, but while you're feeding out my cattle, you'll do it my way."

"For God's sake, you'd have me out there feeding the damned things with a fork!"

"Not at all. I only want them treated humanely."

"They *are* treated humanely!"

"I wouldn't call an electric cattle prod that. And stressed animals aren't healthy animals."

"Have you ever thought about joining an animal rights lobby?" came the exasperated reply.

"I belong to two, thanks."

The door opened and Fay couldn't drag her eyes away from it. That curt voice was so familiar...

Sure enough, the tall, lithe man who came out of the office in front of Calhoun was equally familiar. Fay couldn't help the radiance of her face, the softness of her eyes as they adored his lean, dark face under the wide brim of his hat.

Donavan. She could have danced on her desk.

But when he turned and saw her, he frowned. His silvery eyes narrowed, glittered. He paused by her desk, his head cocked slightly to one side, a lit cigar dangling from his fingers.

"What are you doing here?" he asked her bluntly.

"I'm filling in for Nita," she began.

"Don't tell me you have to work for a living now, debutante?" he asked in a mocking tone.

She hesitated. He sounded as if he disliked her. But she knew he'd enjoyed the fiesta as much as she had. His behavior puzzled her, intimidated her.

"Well, yes," she stammered. "I do." And she did. For the time being.

"What a hell of a comedown," he murmured with patent disbelief. "Still driving the Mercedes?"

"You know each other?" Calhoun asked narrowly.

Donavan lifted the cigar to his mouth and blew out thick smoke. "Vaguely." He glanced at Calhoun until the other man sighed angrily and went back to his office with a muttered goodbye.

"You've been driving by the bar fairly regularly," he remarked curtly, and she blushed because she couldn't deny it. She'd been looking for him, hoping to have a chance to tell him how he'd helped her turn her life around. But he seemed to be putting a totally different connotation on her actions. "Is that where you found out I did business with the Ballengers?" He didn't even give her time to deny it. "Well, no go,

honey. I told you that night, no bored debutante is
going to try to make a minor amusement out of me.
So if you came here hoping for another shot at me,
you might as well quit right now and go home to your
caviar and champagne. You're not hard on the eyes,
but I'm off the market, is that clear?"

She stared at him in quiet confusion. "Mr. Holman
told me about the job," she said with what dignity she
had left. "I don't have a dime until my twenty-first
birthday, and I'm living on my own so I have to pay
rent. This was the only job available." She dropped
her gaze to her computer. "I drove by the bar a time
or two, yes. I wanted to tell you that you'd changed
my life, that I was learning to stand on my own feet.
I wanted to thank you."

His jaw tautened and he looked more dangerous
than ever. "I don't want thanks, teenage adulation,
hero worship or misplaced lust. But you're welcome,
if it matters."

He sounded cynical and mocking. Fay felt chas-
tised. She'd only been grateful, but he made her feel
stupid. Maybe she was. She'd spun a few midnight
dreams about him. Except for some very innocent
dates with boys, she'd never had much attention from
the opposite sex. His protective attitude that night
in the bar, his quiet handling of what could have become a bad incident, had made her feel feminine
and hungry for more of his company. He was telling her that she'd made too much of it, that she was
offering him affection that he didn't want or need.
It was probably a kindness, but it hurt all the same.

She forced a smile. "You needn't worry. I wasn't planning to follow you around with a wedding band on a hook or anything. I just wanted to thank you for what you did."

"You've done that. So?"

"I...have a lot of work to get through. I'm only temporary," she added quickly. "Just until Nita comes back. When I get my legacy, I'll be on the first plane back to Georgia. Honest."

His dark eyebrows plunged above the straight bridge of his nose. "I don't remember asking for any explanations."

"Excuse me, then." She turned her attention back to her keyboard; her hands were cold and numb. She forced them to work. She didn't look up, either. He'd made her feel like what came out of a sausage grinder.

He didn't reply. He didn't linger, either. His measured footsteps went out the door immediately, leaving the pungent scent of cigar smoke in their wake.

Calhoun came back out five minutes later, checking his watch. "I have to be out of the office for an hour or so. Tell Justin when he comes back, will you?"

"Yes, sir," she said, smiling.

He hesitated, his narrowed eyes registering the hurt on her face that she couldn't hide. "Listen, Fay, don't let him upset you," he added quietly. "He doesn't really mean things as personally as they sound, but he rubs everybody the wrong way except Justin."

"He saved me from a bad situation," she began. "I only wanted to thank him, but he seemed to think I had designs on him or something. My goodness, he thought I came to work here because he did business with you!"

He laughed. "Can't blame him. Several have, and no, I'm not kidding. The more he snarls, the harder some women chase him. He's a catch, too. He makes good money with Mesa Blanco, and his own ranch is nothing to laugh at."

"Mesa… Blanco?" she stammered, as puzzle pieces began to make a pattern in her mind.

"Sure. Didn't he introduce himself before?" He smiled ruefully. "I guess not. Well, that was J. D. Langley."

CHAPTER THREE

FAY GOT THROUGH the rest of the day without showing too much of her heartache. She'd had hopes that Donavan might have felt something for her, but he'd dashed those very efficiently. He couldn't have made it more obvious that he wanted no part of her or her monied background. He wouldn't believe that she had to work. Well, of course, she didn't, really. But he might have given her the benefit of the doubt.

It hadn't been a terrible shock to learn that he was J. D. Langley. He did live down to his publicity. Later, she'd found out that Donavan was his middle name and what he was called locally, except by people who did business with him. She certainly understood why the Ballengers hated to see him coming.

She was sorry about his hostility, because the first time she'd ever seen him, there had been a tenderness between them that she'd never experienced. It must have all been on one side, though, she decided miserably.

Well, she told herself as she lay trying to sleep that night, she'd do better to stop brooding and concentrate on her own problems. She had enough, without adding the formidable Mr. Langley to them.

But fate was conspiring against her. The next day, she tried a new cafeteria in Jacobsville and came face-to-face with J. D. Langley as she sat down with her tray.

He gave her a glare that would have stopped traffic. He'd obviously just finished his meal. He was draining his coffee cup. Fay turned her chair so that she wasn't looking directly at him and, with unsteady hands, took her food off the tray.

"I told you yesterday," Donavan said at her shoulder, "that I don't like being chased. Didn't you listen?"

The whip of his voice cut. Not only that, it was loud enough to attract attention from other diners in the crowded room.

Fay's face went red as she glanced at him apprehensively, her green eyes huge as they met the fierce silvery glitter of his.

"I didn't know you were going to be here…" she began uneasily.

"No?" he challenged, his smile an insult in itself. "You didn't recognize my car sitting in the parking lot? Give it up, debutante. I don't like bored little rich girls, so stop following me around. Got that?"

He turned and left the cafeteria. Fay was too humiliated by the unwanted attention to enjoy much of her meal. She left quickly and went back to work.

Following him around, indeed, she muttered to herself while she fed data into her computer. She didn't know what kind of car he drove. The only vehicle she'd seen him in was a battered gray pickup truck, had he forgotten? Perhaps he thought she'd seen his car when he'd come to the feedlot, but she hadn't. The more she saw of him the less she liked him, and she'd hardly been hounding him. She certainly wouldn't again, he could bank on that!

Abby came in the next afternoon with an invitation. "Calhoun and I have to go to a charity ball tonight. I know it's spur-of-the-moment, but would you like to come?"

"Will my uncle be there, do you think?" Fay asked.

"I hardly think so." Abby grinned. "Come on. You've been moping around here for two days, it will be good for you. You can ride with us, and there's a very nice man I want to introduce you to when we get there. He's unattached, personable and rich enough not to mind that you are."

"Uh, Mr. Langley...?"

"I heard what happened in Cole's Café." Abby grimaced. "J.D. doesn't go to charity balls, so you aren't likely to run into him there."

"Thank God. He was so kind to me the night I met him, but he's been terrible to me ever since. I only wanted to thank him. He thinks I have designs on him." She shuddered. "As if I'd ever chased a man in my life...!"

"You're not J.D.'s kind of woman, Fay," the older woman said gently. "Your wealth alone would keep him at bay, without the difference in your ages. J.D.'s in his early thirties, and he doesn't like younger women."

"I don't think he likes *any* women," Fay replied with a sigh. "Especially me. But I wasn't chasing him, honestly!"

"Don't let it worry you."

"You're sure he won't be there tonight?"

"Absolutely positive," Abby assured her.

PROPHETIC WORDS. ABBY and Calhoun picked Fay up at her apartment house, and drove her to the elegant Whitman estate where the charity ball was already in progress. Fay was wearing a long, white silk dress with one shoulder bare and her hair in a very elegant braided bun atop her head. She looked young and fragile…and very rich.

They went through the receiving line and Fay moved ahead of Calhoun and Abby to the refreshment table while they spoke to an acquaintance. She bumped into someone and turned to apologize.

"Again?" J. D. Langley asked with a vicious scowl. "My God, do you have radar?"

Fay didn't say a word. She turned and went back toward Abby and Calhoun, her heart pounding in her chest.

Abby spotted J.D. and grimaced. "I didn't know," she told a shattered Fay. "I swear I didn't. Here, you stick close to us. He won't bother you. Come on, I'll introduce you to Bart and that will solve all your problems. I'm sorry, Fay."

"It wasn't your fault. It's fate, I guess," she said dryly, although her eyes were troubled.

"Arrogant beast," Abby muttered, sparing the tall,

elegant man in the dinner jacket a speaking glance. "If he were a little less conceited, you wouldn't have this problem." She drew Fay forward. "Here he is. Bart!"

A thin, lazy-looking man with wavy blond hair and mischievous blue eyes turned as his name was called. He greeted Abby warmly and glanced at Fay with open curiosity and delight.

"Well, well, Greek goddesses are back in style again, I see. Do favor me with a waltz before you set off for Mount Olympus, fair damsel."

"This is our newest employee, Fay York," she introduced them. "Fay, this is Bartlett Markham. He's president of the local cattlemen's association."

"Nice to meet you," she said, extending a hand. "Do you know cattle?"

"I grew up on a ranch. I work for a firm of accountants now, but my family still has a pretty formidable Santa Gertrudis purebred operation."

"I don't know much, but I'm learning every day," Fay laughed.

"I'll leave her with you, Bart," Abby said. "Do keep her away from J.D., will you? He seems to think she's stalking him."

"Do tell?" His eyebrows levered up and he grinned. "Why not stalk me instead? I'm a much better catch than J.D., and you won't need preventive shots if you go out with me, either."

Insinuating that she would with J.D., she thought. Rabies probably, she mused venomously, in case he bit her. She smiled at Bart, feeling happier already.

"Consider yourself on the endangered species list, then," she said.

He laughed. "Gladly." He glanced toward the band. "Would you like to dance?"

"Charmed." She gave him her hand and let him lead her to the dance floor, where a live band was playing a bluesy two-step. She knew exactly where J. D. Langley was, as if she really did have radar, so she was careful not to look in that direction.

He noticed. It was impossible not to, when she was dancing with one of his bitterest enemies. He stood quietly against a wall, his silver eyes steady and unblinking as he registered the fluid grace with which she followed her partner's steps. He didn't like the way Markham was holding her, or the way she was responding.

Not that he wanted her, he assured himself. She was nothing but another troublesome woman. A debutante, at that, and over ten years his junior. He had no use for her at all, and he'd made sure she knew it. Their one evening together had sent him tearing away in the opposite direction. She appealed to him terribly. He couldn't afford an involvement with a society girl. He knew he was better off alone, so keeping this tempting little morsel away from him became imperative. If he had to savage her to do it, it was still the best thing for both of them. She was much too soft and delicate for a man like himself. He'd break her spirit and her heart, because he had nothing to give. And his father's reputation in the community made it impossible for him to be seen in public with her in any congenial way. He'd accused her of stalking him, but gossip would have it the other way around. Another money-crazy Langley, critics would scoff, out to snare himself a rich wife. He groaned at just the thought.

He didn't like seeing her with Markham, but there was nothing he could do about it. He shouldn't have come tonight.

He turned away to the refreshment table and poured himself a glass of Scotch.

"You aren't really after Donavan, are you?" Bart asked humorously.

"He flatters himself," she said haughtily.

"That's what I thought. Like father, like son," he said unpleasantly.

"I don't understand."

He made a graceful turn, carrying her with him as the music's tempo increased. "After Donavan's mother died, Rand Langley got into a financial tangle and was about to lose his ranch. My aunt was very young then, plain and shy, but she was filthy rich and single, so Rand set his cap for her. He kept after her until he seduced her, so that she had to marry him or disgrace her family. She was crazy about him. Worshiped the ground he walked on. Then, inevitably, she found out why he really married her and she couldn't live with it. She killed herself."

Fay grimaced. "I'm sorry."

"So were all of us," he added coldly, glaring at J. D. Langley's back. "Rand didn't even come to the funeral. He was too busy spending her money. He died a few years later, and believe me, none of us grieved for him."

"That wasn't Donavan's fault," she felt bound to point out.

"Blood will tell," came the unbelieving reply. "You're well-to-do."

"Yes, but he can't stand me," she replied.

"I don't believe that. I can't imagine J.D. passing up a rich woman."

"How many has he dated over the years?" she asked with faint irritation.

"I don't keep up with his love life," he said tersely, and all his prejudices showed quite clearly. Fay could see that he wouldn't believe a kind word about J. D. Langley if he had proof.

"The two of you don't get along, I gather."

"We disagree on just about everything. Especially on his ridiculous theories about cattle raising," he added sarcastically. "No. We don't get along."

She was quiet after that. Now she understood the situation. It couldn't have been made clearer.

She danced with several eligible bachelors and several married men before the evening ended. It surprised her that J. D. Langley was still present. He remained on the fringes of the dance floor, talking to other men. He asked no one to dance. Fay was sadly certain that he wouldn't ask her.

But in that, she was surprised. The band was playing a soft love song and she watched Bart glance in her direction. But before he could get across the room, Donavan suddenly swung her into his arms and onto the dance floor.

Her heart skipped wildly as she felt the firm clasp of his hand on her waist, his fingers steely as they linked her own.

"This is not a good idea," she said firmly. "I'll think you're encouraging me."

"Not likely. By now Bart's filled you in, hasn't he?" he replied with a mocking smile.

She averted her eyes to the white ruffled shirt he wore under his dinner jacket. On another man it might look effeminate. On Donavan, it looked masculine and very sexy, emphasizing his dark good looks. "I got an earful, thanks," she replied.

He shook her gently. "Stiff as a board," he mused, looking down at her. "Are you afraid to let your guard down? There's very little I could do to you on a dance floor in front of half of Jacobsville."

"You've made your opinion of me crystal clear, Mr. Langley," she said without looking up. "I haven't been stalking you, as you put it, but you're free to think what you like. Do try to remember that I didn't ask you to dance."

"That was the whole purpose of the exercise," he said carelessly. "To make sure you didn't set your cap for me."

"Then why are you dancing with me?"

His lean arm whipped her close on a turn, but he didn't let her go afterward. His dark face was all too close, so that she could smell his tangy aftershave, and his silver eyes bit into hers at point-blank range. "Don't you know?" he asked at her lips.

Her heart tripped as she felt his breath. "Oh, I see," she said suddenly. "You're trying to irritate Bart."

He lifted his head and one eyebrow quirked. "Is that it?"

"What else?" she asked with a nervous laugh, averting her eyes to a fuming Bart nearby. "Listen, I'm not going to be used for any vendettas, by you or your hissing kin."

His fingers curled into hers and drew them to his broad chest. It rose and fell heavily, and he stared over her dark head without seeing anything. "I don't have any vendettas," he said quietly. "But I won't be accused of following in my father's footsteps."

She could feel the pain in those terse words, but she didn't remark on it. Her eyes closed and she drank in the delicious masculine scent of him. "I won't be rich for another week or two," she murmured. "Until the legal work goes through, I'm just a temporary secretary."

He laughed in spite of himself. "I see. For two weeks you're on my level. No Mercedes. No mansion. No padded checkbook."

"Something like that." She sighed and snuggled closer. "How about a wild, passionate affair? We could throw the coats on the closet floor and you could have your way with me under somebody's silver fox stole."

He burst out laughing. His steely arm drew her

close as he made a sudden turn, and her body throbbed with the sensations it caused in her untried body.

"Hasn't anyone told you yet that I belong to two animal rights groups?"

"So you're one of those people who protest lab animal experiments that save little children's lives and throw paint on people who wear fur coats?" she asked, her temper rising.

"Not me. I'm no fanatic. I just think animals have the right to humane treatment, even in medical facilities." His arm tightened. "As for throwing paint on fur coats, a few lawsuits should stem that habit. The idea is to stop further slaughter of wild animals. A fur coat is already a dead animal."

She shivered. "You make it sound morbid."

One silver eye narrowed. "Do you wear fur?"

She chuckled. "I can't. Fur makes me break out in hives."

He began to smile. "A rich girl with no furs. What a tragedy."

"I have plenty of velvet coats, thanks very much. I think they're much more elegant than fur and they don't shed." She moved closer, shocked when his hand caught her hip and contracted painfully. "Ouch!" she protested.

He moved her back an inch. "Don't push your luck," he said, his voice low and faintly threatening, like his glittery eyes. "You're pretty sexy in that little number you're wearing, and I'm easily aroused. Want me to prove it?"

"No, thanks," she said quickly. "I'll take your word for it."

He laughed as he spun her around in a neat turn. "For a sophisticated debutante, sometimes you're a contradiction. Is that a blush?"

"It's hot in here."

"Ah. The conventional excuse." He leaned close and brushed his cheek against hers. "Too bad you're rich."

"Is it? Why?" she asked in a tone that sounded, unfortunately, all too breathless.

He nibbled gently on her earlobe. "Because I'm dynamite in bed."

"Do tell?" She hid her face against him. "Are you?" she whispered shakily.

His lean hand slid up her back and into the coiled hair at her nape. He caressed it gently while he held her, the music washing over them in a sultry silence.

"So I've been told." His chin rubbed softly against her temple, his breath coming roughly. "But why take someone else's word for it?"

She forced a laugh. "Isn't this a little sudden? I mean, just a day ago you were giving me hell for eating lunch in the same restaurant with you."

"I'm sure Bart told you the problem. Rich, you're right off my Christmas list. Poor, you're an endangered species." His hand contracted, coaxing her face up to his glittery eyes.

"Should I cut and run?" she asked, her voice husky.

"Do you really want to?" he whispered.

As he spoke, he moved closer, and his powerful thighs brushed hers. Even through all the layers of fabric, she felt the imprint of them, the strength. His hand slid down her back to her waist and pulled, very gently, so that she was pressed right up to him, welded from breast to thigh. He watched her eyes and something masculine and arrogant kindled in his gaze as he felt the faint shiver of her soft body.

"Do you like Chinese food?" he asked.

She nodded.

"I like to drive up to Houston for it. There's a good restaurant just inside the city limits. How about it?"

Her heart jumped. "Are you asking me out?"

"Sounds like it," he mused. "Don't expect steak and lobster. I make a good salary, but it doesn't run to champagne."

She colored furiously. "Please, don't," she said quickly. "I'm not like that."

He touched her face gently. "Yes, I know. It makes it harder. Do you think I enjoyed hurting you?" he asked harshly, and for an instant something showed in his eyes that startled her. He looked away. "There's no future for us, little one."

She felt him hesitating. Any second, he was going to take back that supper invitation.

"Just Chinese food," she prompted, one slender hand poking him gently in the ribs.

He started, and she grinned at him. "And no moonlight seduction on the way home," she added. "As you said, it isn't wise to start things we can't finish."

"I could finish that," he murmured dryly.

She cleared her throat. "Well, I don't take chances. I'll risk my stomach with you, but not my heart."

He cocked an eyebrow. "Does that mean that making love with me might enslave you?" he teased.

"Exactly. Besides, I never sleep with a man on the first date."

There was the faintest movement of his eyelashes. He averted his gaze to a point beyond her head. He couldn't admit that it bothered him, thinking of her with other men. She was a debutante and filthy rich, surely there had been a steady stream of suitors. She might have more experience even than he did. He'd never thought about a woman's past before. It had never occurred to him to wonder how experienced his lover of the evening actually was. But with Fay, he wondered.

"What's wrong?" she asked curiously.

He glanced down at her. She looked very innocent until she smiled, and then her eyes crinkled and there was a sophistication in them that made him feel cool. "Nothing."

"That's usually the woman's line, isn't it?"

"Equal rights," he reminded her. "Friday night. I'll pick you up at six."

"I don't live with Uncle Henry anymore," she began.

"I know where you live," he replied. "We'll eat Chinese food and you can show me what you know. It should be quite an experience…"

LONG AFTER THE dance was over and she was back in her apartment, she worried over that last statement. She felt as if she were about to get in well over her head.

She wanted Donavan more than she'd ever wanted anything in her life. A date with him was the gold at the end of the rainbow. But she'd pretended to be something she wasn't, and she didn't know what she was going to do if he took her up on it.

ABBY NOTICED FAY'S preoccupation the next day when she stopped by to see Calhoun.

"You're positively morose!" Abby exclaimed. "What's wrong?"

"Donavan asked me out."

Her eyebrows went up. "J.D. asked you out? But he hates rich women."

"Yes, I know. I told him I was going to be poor for two more weeks, so I guess he thought it was safe enough until my inheritance comes through."

"I see." Abby didn't say anything, but she began to look worried herself. "Fay, I never thought to mention it, because J.D. was giving you such a hard time, but he's something of a womanizer..."

"I figured that out for myself," she murmured with a smile. "It shows."

"He's a gentleman, in his way. Just don't give him too much rope. He'll hang you with it."

"I know that, too. I'll be careful."

Abby hesitated. "If it helps, I know how you feel. I was crazy about Calhoun, but he liked a different kind of woman altogether. We had a very rocky path to the altar."

"He's crazy about you, though. Anyone can see that."

Abby smiled contentedly. "Of course he is. But it wasn't always that way."

"Donavan already said that he doesn't want commitment. I'm not going to get my hopes up. But an evening out with him… Well, it's going to be like brushing heaven, you know?"

"I do, indeed." Abby smiled, remembering her first date with Calhoun. She glanced back at Fay, her eyes wistful. She only hoped their newest employee wasn't going to be badly hurt. Everyone locally knew that J. D. Langley wasn't a marrying man. But Abby would have bet her prize bull that Fay was as innocent as Abby herself had once been. If she was, she had a lot of heartache in store. When J.D. found out, and he would, he'd drop Fay like a hot rock. Innocents were not his style.

FAY WENT THROUGH the motions of working like a zombie for the next week, with a dull and tedious weekend in between that did little for her nerves. Donavan didn't come by the feedlot at all, and when she left the office the next Friday afternoon, she still hadn't heard from him. For all she knew, he might have forgotten all about her.

The phone was ringing even as she got in the door, and she grabbed up the receiver as if it were a life preserver.

"Hello?" she said breathlessly.

"I'll be by in an hour. You hadn't forgotten?" Donavan drawled.

"How could I?" she asked, adding mischievously, "I love Chinese food."

He chuckled. "That puts me in my place, I guess. See you."

He hung up and Fay ran to dress. The only thing in her closet that would suit a fairly casual evening out was a pale green silk suit and she hated wearing it. It screamed big money, something sure to set Donavan's teeth on edge. But other than designer jeans and a silk blouse, or evening gowns, it was all she had. The cotton pantsuit she'd worn to work today was just too wrinkled and stained to wear out tonight. It wouldn't have been suitable anyway.

She teamed the silk suit with a nice cotton blouse and sat down to wait, after renewing her makeup. She only hoped that he wasn't going to take one look at her and run. If he didn't throw her over entirely, she was going to have to invest in some medium-priced clothing!

CHAPTER FOUR

Just as Fay had feared, Donavan's first glimpse of her silk suit brought a scowl to his face.

"It's old," she said inadequately, and looked miserable. She locked her fingers together and stared at him with sadness all over her face.

He shoved his hands into the pockets of his gray slacks. He was wearing a white cotton shirt and a blue blazer with them, a black Stetson cocked over one eye and matching boots on his feet. He looked nice, but hardly elegant or wealthy. Her silk suit seemed to point out all the differences between the lifestyle she was used to, and his own.

"You look very nice," he said quietly.

"And very expensive," she added on a curt laugh. "I'm sorry."

"Why?"

"I didn't want you to think I wore this on purpose," she said, faltering.

He lifted an eyebrow and smiled mockingly. "I'm taking you out for a Chinese dinner. A proposal of marriage doesn't come with the egg roll."

She blushed furiously. "I know that."

"Then why bother about appearances?" He

shrugged. "A date is one thing. A serious relationship is something else." His silver eyes narrowed. "Let's settle that at the outset. I have nothing serious or permanent in mind. Even if we wind up as the hottest couple in town between the sheets, there still won't be anything offered in the way of commitment."

"I knew that already," she said, steeling herself not to react to the provocative statement.

"Good." He glanced around the apartment, frowning slightly. "This is pretty spartan, isn't it?" he asked, suddenly realizing how frugally she seemed to be living.

"It's all I could afford on my salary," she told him. She wrapped her arms across her breasts and smiled. "I don't mind it. It's just a place to sleep."

"Henry doesn't help you financially?" he persisted.

"He can't," she explained. "He's got his own financial woes. I'll be fine when he turns over my affairs to Mr. Holman and I can get to my trust."

Donavan didn't say a word, but suddenly he was beginning to see things she apparently didn't. If Henry was having money problems, surely his control of Fay's estate would give him the means of solving them, even if he had to pay her back later. The fact that he was suffering a reversal didn't bode well for Fay, but she seemed oblivious. Perhaps like most rich women she didn't know or care much about handling money.

He was aware that he'd been silent a long time.

He took his hands out of his pockets and caught her slender fingers in his. They were cold, like ice. "We'd better go," he said, drawing her along with him.

Fay had never realized how exciting it could be to hold hands with a man. He linked her fingers into his as they walked, and she felt the sensuous contraction all the way to her toes. It was like walking on a cloud, she thought. She could almost float.

Donavan was feeling something similar and fighting it tooth and nail. He hadn't really wanted this date at all, but something stronger than his will had forced him into it. Fay was a delicious little morsel, full of contradictions. He'd always liked puzzles. She was one he really wanted to solve, even if his inclination was to get her into the nearest bed with all possible haste.

She had to be experienced. He'd never denied that. He wondered if pampered rich boys were as anemic in bed as they seemed when he saw them at board meetings. His contempt for the upper classes was, he knew, a result of his father's ruthless greed.

He could still barely believe the whole episode, his father running pell-mell after a woman half his age when his wife of twenty years was just barely in her grave. It had disgusted and shocked him, and led to a confrontation of stellar proportions. He hadn't spoken to his father afterward, and his presence at his father's funeral two years later was only a nod to convention. It wasn't until much later that he'd learned why Rand Langley had been so ruthless. It had been to save the family ranch, which had been

Langley land for three generations. Not that it excused what he'd done, but it did at least explain it. Rand had wanted Donavan to inherit the ranch. Marrying money had been the only way he could keep it.

"You're very quiet," Fay remarked on the way to Houston. "Are you sorry you asked me out?"

He glanced at her. "No. I was remembering."

"Yes?"

He was smoking one of the small cigars he favored, his gray eyes thoughtful as they lingered on the long road ahead. "My father disgraced himself to marry money, to keep the ranch for me and my children, if I ever have any. Ironic, that I've never married and never want to, because of him."

She folded her hands primly in her lap. It flattered her that he was willing to tell her something so personal.

"If you don't have children, what will happen to your ranch?" she asked.

"I've got a ten-year-old nephew," he said. "My sister's boy. His father's been dead for years. My sister remarried three years ago, and she died last year. Her husband got custody. But he's just remarried, and last month he stuck Jeffrey in a military school. The boy's in trouble constantly, and he hates his stepfather." He took a long draw from the cigar, scowling. "That's why I was sitting in that bar the night you walked in. I was trying to decide what to do. Jeff wants to come out here and live with me."

"Can't he?"

He shook his head. "No chance. His stepfather

and I don't get along. He'd more than likely refuse just to get at me. His new wife is pregnant and he doesn't seem to care about Jeff at all."

"That's sad," she said. "Does he miss his mother?"

"He never talks about her."

"Probably because he cares too much," she said. "I miss my parents," she added unexpectedly. "They died in a plane crash. Even if I never saw much of them, they were still my parents."

"What do you mean, you never saw much of them?"

She laughed softly. "They liked traveling. I was in school, and they didn't want to interrupt my education. I stayed at home with an elderly great-aunt. She liked me very much, but it was kind of lonely. Especially during holidays." She stared out the window, aware of his curious stare. "If I ever have kids, I'll be where they are," she said suddenly. "And they won't ever have to spend Christmas without me."

"I suppose," he began slowly, "there are some things money won't buy."

"An endless list," she agreed. "Beginning and ending with love."

He chuckled softly, to lighten the atmosphere. He glanced sideways at her. "Money can buy love, you know," he murmured.

"Well, not really," she disagreed. "It can buy the illusion of it, but I wouldn't call a timed session in bed 'love.'"

He burst out laughing. "No," he said after a minute. "I don't suppose it is. They say that type of experience is less than satisfying. I wouldn't know. I couldn't find any pleasure in a body I had to pay for."

"I can understand that."

There was a pleasant tension in the silence that dropped between them. Minutes later, Donavan pulled up in front of a Chinese restaurant and cut off the engine.

"This is it," he said. He helped her out of the car and escorted her inside.

It was a very nice restaurant, with Chinese music playing softly in the background and excellent service.

Donavan watched her covertly as he sampled the jasmine tea the waitress had served. "Tell me about your job. How does it feel to work for a living?"

Her eyes brightened and she smiled. "I like it very much," she confessed. "I've never been responsible for my own life before. I've always had people telling me what to do and how to do it. The night I met you at the bar really opened my eyes. You made me see what my life was like, showed me that I could change it if I wanted to. I wasn't kidding when I said you turned my world around."

"I thought the job was a means to an end," he confessed, smiling at his own folly. "I've been chased before, and by well-to-do women who saw me as a challenge."

"You're not bad looking," she said demurely, averting her eyes. "And you're very much a man. But I meant it when I said I wasn't chasing you. I have too much pride to behave that way."

Probably she did. He liked her honesty. He liked the way she looked and dressed, too. She wasn't beautiful, but she was elegant and well-mannered, and she had a big heart. He found himself wondering how Jeff would react to her.

They ate in a pleasant silence and talked about politics and the weather, everything except themselves. All too soon it was time to start back for Jacobsville.

"How are you and your uncle getting along?" Donavan asked on the way back.

"We speak and not much more. Uncle Henry's worried about something," she added. "He gets more nervous by the day."

He'd never thought of her uncle as a nervous man. Perhaps it had something to do with Fay's inheritance.

"Suppose you inherit only a few dollars and an apology?" he asked suddenly.

She laughed. "That isn't likely."

"But if it was?"

She thought about it seriously. "It would be hard," she confessed. "I'm not used to asking the price of anything, or denying myself a whim purchase. But like anything else, I expect I could get used to it. I don't mind hard work."

He nodded. That would make her life easier.

He turned off onto a farm road just at the outskirts of Jacobsville.

"Where are we going?" she asked, glancing around at unfamiliar terrain.

"I'm going to show you my ranch," he said simply. His eyes lanced over her and he smiled wickedly. "Then I'm going to shove you into the henhouse and have my way with you."

"Do you have a henhouse?" she asked excitedly.

"Yes. And a flock of chickens to go with it. I like fresh eggs."

He didn't add that he often had to budget in between cattle sales, even on the good salary he made.

"I guess you have your own beef, too?" she asked.

"Not for slaughter," he replied. "I like animals too much to raise one to kill. Mesa Blanco has slaughter cattle, but I don't spend any more time around them than I have to."

The picture she was getting of him didn't have a lot to do with the image he projected. An animal lover with a core of steel was unusual.

"Do you have dogs and cats?"

He smiled slowly. "And puppies and kittens," he said. "I give them away when the population gets out of control, and most of mine are neutered. It's criminal to turn an unneutered animal loose on the streets." He slowed as the road curved toward a simple white frame house. "Ever had a dog or cat of your own?"

"No," she said sadly. "My parents weren't animal lovers. My mother would have fainted at the thought of cat hair on her Louis Quinze furniture."

"I'd rather have the cat than the furniture," he remarked.

She smiled. "So would I."

His heart lifted. She wasn't at all what he'd expected. He pulled up in front of the ranch house and cut off the engine.

There were flowers everywhere, from shrubs to trees to beds of them right and left around the porch. She could see them by the fierce light of the almost-full moon. "How beautiful!" she exclaimed.

"Thank you."

"You planted them?"

"Nobody else. I like flowers," he said defensively as he got out and helped her out of the car.

"I didn't say a word," she assured him. "I like flowers, too."

He unlocked the front door while she glanced covetously along the long front porch at the old-fashioned swing and rocking chair. Somewhere nearby cattle made pleasant mooing noises.

"Do you keep a lot of cattle here?" she asked.

"I have purebred Santa Gertrudis," he told her. "Stud cattle, not beef cattle."

"Why doesn't that surprise me?" she teased.

He laughed, standing aside to let her enter the house.

The living room was done in Early American, and it looked both neat and lived-in. For a bachelor, he was a good housekeeper. She said so.

"Thanks, but I can't take all the credit. My foreman's wife looks after things when I can't."

She was insanely jealous of the foreman's wife, all at once.

He saw her expression and smiled. "She's fifty and happily married."

She blushed, moving farther into the room.

"Look out," he warned.

Before the words went silent, her foot was attacked by a tiny ball of fur with teeth.

"Good heavens!" she exclaimed, laughing. "A miniature tiger!" she kidded.

"I'm training her to be an attack cat. I call her Bee."

"Bee?"

He grinned. "Short for Beelzebub. You can't imagine what she did to the curtains a day or so ago."

She reached down and picked up the tiny thing. It looked up at her with a calico face and the softest, most loving blue-green eyes she'd ever seen, with black fur outlining them.

"Why, she's beautiful!" she exclaimed.

"I think so."

The kitten's eyes half closed as it began to purr and knead her jacket with its tiny paws.

"She'll pick that silk," he said, reaching for the kitten.

She looked at him curiously. "That doesn't matter," she said, surprised by his comment.

His silver eyes registered his own surprise as they looked deeply into hers. "That suit must have cost a small fortune," he persisted. He extricated the kitten, despite her protests, and carried it into the bedroom, closing the door behind him.

"Want some coffee?" he asked.

"That would be nice."

"It will only take a minute or so." He tossed his hat onto the hat rack and went into the kitchen.

Fay wandered around the living room, stopping at a photograph on the mantel. It was of a young boy, a studio pose. He looked a lot like Donavan, except that his eyes were dark, and he had a more rounded face. He looked sad.

"That's Jeff," he told her from the doorway. He leaned against it, waiting for the coffee to brew. His long legs were crossed, like his arms, and he looked very masculine and sexy with his jacket off and the top buttons of his shirt unfastened over a thicket of jet black hair.

"He favors you," she remarked. "Did your sister look like you?"

"Quite a lot," he said. "But her eyes were darker than mine. Jeff has his father's eyes."

"What does he like?" she asked. "I mean, is he a sports fan?"

"He doesn't care much for football. He likes martial arts, and he's good at them. He's a blue belt in tae kwon do—a Korean martial art that concentrates on kicking styles."

"Isn't that a demonstration sport in the summer Olympics?"

He smiled, surprised. "Yes, it is. Jeff hopes to be able to participate in the 1996 summer games in Atlanta."

"A group of Atlantans worked very hard to get the games to come there," she recalled. "One of my

friends worked in the archives at Georgia Tech—
a lot of the people on campus were active in that
committee."

"You don't have many friends here, do you?" he
asked.

"Abby Ballenger is a friend," she corrected. "And
I get along well with the girls at the office."

"I meant friends in your own social class."

She put the picture of Jeff back on the mantel. "I
never had friends in my own social class. I don't like
their idea of fun."

"Don't you?"

He moved closer. His hands slid around her waist
from behind and tugged her against him. His cheek
nuzzled hers roughly. "What was their idea of fun?"

"Sleeping around," she said huskily. "That's...
suicidal these days. All it takes is the wrong partner
and you can die."

"I know." His lips slid down her long, elegant
neck. His tongue tip found the artery at her throat
and pressed there, feeling it accelerate wildly at his
touch. His fingers slid to her slender hips and dug
in, welding her to his hard thighs.

"Donavan?" she whispered unsteadily.

His hands flattened on her stomach, making odd
little motions that sent tremors down her long legs
and a rush of warmth into her bloodstream.

She didn't act very experienced. The camouflage
was only good at long range, he thought as he drank
in the gardenia scent of her skin. He should have
been disappointed, because he'd wanted her badly

tonight. But something inside him was elated at his growing suspicion that she was innocent. He had to find out if it was true.

"Turn your mouth up for me, Fay," he whispered at her chin. "I want to taste it under my own."

The words sent thrills down to her toes and curled them. Blind, deaf, she raised her face and turned it, feeling the sudden warm pressure of his mouth on her parted lips.

It wasn't at all what he'd expected. The contact was explosive. He'd been in complete control until he touched her. Now, suddenly he was fighting to keep his head at all. He turned her in his arms and caught his breath as he felt her body melt hungrily into his.

It shouldn't have happened like this. He could barely think. His hands bit into the backs of her thighs and lifted her, pulled at her, needing the close contact as he'd never needed anything. His legs began to tremble as his body went taut and capable, and his hands became ruthless.

Fay moaned. Never at any time in her life had she felt such a sudden, vicious fever of longing. She could always pull back, until now. With a tiny gasp, she lifted her arms around his neck and gave in completely. She felt him against her stomach, knew that he was already painfully aroused. She couldn't manage enough willpower to deny him, whatever the cost, whatever the risk. He was giving her a kind of pleasure she'd never dreamed of experiencing.

He invaded the silk jacket and the blouse she wore

under it. He unbuttoned them and drew the fabric aside seconds before his mouth went down against the bare curve of her breast above her lacy bra. She'd never been touched like that. She clung to him, shivering as his lips became ruthless, his face rubbing the bra strap aside so he could nuzzle down far enough to find the hard, warm nipple.

She cried out. It was beyond bearing, sensation upon hot sensation, anguished joy. Her fingers tangled in his thick, dark hair and pulled at it as he suckled her in a silence throbbing with need.

"You taste of gardenias," he breathed urgently. "Soft and sweet... Fay...!"

His hands were as urgent as his voice. He unfastened her bra and slid it, along with her half-unbuttoned jacket and blouse, right down to her waist. His glazed eyes lingered for one long minute on the uncovered pink and mauve beauty of her naked breasts with their crowns hard and tip-tilted. Then his mouth and his hands were touching them, and she was glorying in his own pleasure, in the sweet delight of his ardor.

"So beautiful," he whispered as he drew his face over her soft breasts. "Fay, you make my body throb. Feel it. Feel me..."

One hand went to gather her hips close to his, to emphasize what he was saying. She moaned and searched blindly for his mouth, inviting a kiss as deep and ardent as the hand enjoying her soft breasts in the stillness of the room.

"Little one," he said huskily, "do you know what's going to happen between us now? Do you want me?"

"Yes!" she whispered achingly, hanging at his lips.

His body shivered with its blatant need. It had never been so urgent before, with any woman. He bit at her mouth. "Do you have anything to use? Are you on the pill?"

She hesitated. "No."

No. The word echoed through his swaying mind. No, she wasn't protected. He could have her, but he could also make her pregnant. Pregnant! He said something explicit and embarrassing, then he put his hands on her upper arms and thrust her away from him. He went blindly toward the kitchen and slammed the door behind him.

Fay sat down on the sofa, fastening hooks and buttons with hands so unsteady that she missed half the buttons and had to start over. It was a long time before she was back in order again, and only a few seconds after that, Donavan came in with a tray of coffee.

She couldn't look at him. She knew her face looked like rice paper. She was still trembling visibly, too, her mouth red and swollen, her breathing erratic and irregular.

He put a cup of black coffee in front of her without saying anything.

She didn't raise her eyes when she felt the sofa depress near her. She reached for the cup, barely able to hold it for the unsteadiness of her icy fingers.

A big, warm hand came to support hers, and when

she looked up, his eyes weren't angry at all. They were faintly curious and almost affectionate.

"Thank you," she stammered as she sipped the hot, black liquid.

He smiled. A real smile, not the mocking ones she was used to. "You're welcome."

"I'm so sorry…!" she began nervously.

He put a long finger over her soft lips. "No. I am. I shouldn't have let it go so far."

"You were angry," she said hesitantly, her eyes glancing with sheer embarrassment off his before they fell to her cup.

"I was hotter than I've been in years and I had to stop," he said simply, and without anger. "It doesn't put a man in a sparkling mood, let me tell you."

"Oh."

He leaned back and sipped his own coffee, his eyes quiet and faintly acquisitive. "Why are you still a virgin?" he asked suddenly.

The coffee cup made a nosedive, and she only just caught it in time. Her gaze hit his with staggering impact. "What did you say?"

"You heard me," he accused softly. "You can't even put on an act, can you? The second I touch you intimately, you're mine."

She flushed and looked away. "Rub it in," she invited.

"Oh, I intend to," he said with malicious glee. "I'm not sure I've ever made love to a virgin in my life. It was fascinating. You just go right in headfirst, don't you? There's not even a sense of self-preservation in you."

She glared at him. "Having fun?"

"Sure." He rested his arm over the back of the sofa and his gaze was slow and thorough as it fell to her breasts and watched their soft rise and fall. "Pretty little creature," he mused. "All pink and dusk."

"You stop that, J. D. Langley," she muttered hotly. "It isn't decent to even talk about it."

One eyebrow went up. "This is the nineties," he reminded her.

"Wonderful," she told him. "Life is liberal. No more rules and codes of behavior. No wonder the world's a mess."

He leaned back, chuckling. "As it happens, I agree with you. Rules aren't a bad thing, when they prevent the kind of insanity that's gripping the world today. But periodically, people have to find that out for themselves. Ever heard of the Roaring Twenties?" he added.

"Gin flowed like water, women smoked, sexually transmitted diseases ran rampant because everybody was promiscuous..."

"You're getting the idea. But it's nothing new. People had cycles when rules were suspended even back in the Roman Empire. There were orgies and every evil known to man thrived. Then society woke up and the cycle started all over again. The only certain thing in life, Miss York, is change."

"I suppose so. But it's discouraging."

"Maybe you haven't heard, but the majority of

people in this country feel exactly the same way you do," he said. "America is still a very moral place, little one. But it's what's different that makes news, not what's traditional."

"I see." She smiled. "That's encouraging."

"You come from wealth. Odd that you don't have an exaggerated sense of morality to go with it."

"You mean, because I was rich, I should be greedy and pleasure-loving and indifferent to my fellow man?" she teased. "Actually, that's a stereotype."

"I get the picture." He stared at her silently, his eyes growing dark with memory. "I wanted you like hell. But in a way, I'm glad you aren't on the pill."

She eyed him curiously. "You didn't sound glad."

"Wanting hurts a man when he can't satisfy it," he explained matter-of-factly. "But you weren't on the pill and I didn't have anything with me to protect you from pregnancy. That's one risk I'll never take."

She smiled at him. "I feel the same way."

His eyes warmed. "We'd better not create any accidental people," he said softly. "That's why I stopped. That," he added, "and the fact that I'm too old-fashioned to dishonor a chaste woman. Go ahead. Laugh," he invited. "But it's how I feel."

"Oh, Donavan, you and I are throwbacks to another time," she said heavily. "There's no place for us on earth."

"Why, sure there is, honey," he disagreed. "I'll carry you to church with me one Sunday and prove to you that we're not alone in the way we think. Listen, it's the radicals who are the minority." He leaned closer. "But the radicals are the ones who make news."

She laughed. "I guess so. I'd like to go to church with you," she said shyly. "I haven't been in a long time. Our housekeeper used to let me go to services with her, but when she quit I had no way to get there. It was before I was old enough to drive."

"Poor little rich girl," he said, but he smiled and the words sounded affectionate.

She smiled back. Everything had changed, suddenly. She looked at him and knew without question that she could love him if she was ever given the chance.

He reached out and tapped her cheek. "Let's go. And from now on, stay out of lonely ranch houses with amorous bachelors. Got that?"

"You were the one who dragged me here," she exclaimed.

"That's right, blame it all on me," he agreed after he'd put the coffee things away and then escorted her out the door. "It's always the man who leads the sweet, innocent girl into a life of sin."

She frowned. "Isn't it the woman who's supposed to lead the innocent man into it?"

He raised both eyebrows as he locked the door. "There aren't any innocent men."

"A likely story. What about priests and monks?"

He sighed. "Well, other than them," he conceded.

"I like your house," she said.

He opened the car door and put her inside. "I like it, too." He got in and started the engine, pausing to glance her way. "We may be heading for a fall, but I'm game if you are."

"Game?" she asked blankly.

He slid a lean hand under her nape and brought her face under his, very gently. He bent to kiss her, with tenderness and respect. "In the old days," he whispered, "they called it courting."

She felt a wave of heat rush over her. Wide-eyed, she stared helplessly up at him.

He nodded, his face solemn. "That's right, I said I didn't believe in marriage. But there's always the one woman who can make a man change his mind." His eyes dropped to her mouth. "I want Jeff. If I'm married I have a good chance of getting him. But you and I could give each other a lot, too. If you're willing, we'll start spending time together and see where it leads."

"I'm rich," she began hesitantly.

"Don't worry. I won't hold it against you," he whispered, smiling as he kissed her again. What he didn't mention was that he had his own suspicions about her future. He didn't think she was going to inherit anything at all, and that would put her right in his league. She'd be lost and alone, except for him, when the boom fell. She was sweet and biddable and he wanted her. Jeff needed a stable environment. It wouldn't hurt his chances with the new president of Mesa Blanco to be a settled family man, either, but that was only a minor consideration. Jeff came first.

He'd worry about the complications later. Right now, he was going to get in over his head for once without looking too closely at his motives.

CHAPTER FIVE

IT WAS ALL Fay could do to work the next day. She was so lighthearted that she wondered how she managed to keep both feet on the floor.

Her dreams of being with Donavan honestly hadn't included marriage because he'd said that he didn't believe in it. In fact, he'd given her hell for chasing him. How ironic that she'd landed in his orbit at all.

Probably, she had to admit, he needed a wife so that he could gain custody of his nephew, and to help him get ahead in his job. He didn't want a rich wife.

But why, then, was he paying her any attention at all? She'd been honest with him. She'd told him that in a couple of weeks she stood to inherit a fortune. Hadn't he believed her?

Work piled up and she realized that she was paying more attention to her own thoughts than she was to her job, so she settled down to the job-related problems.

"How's everything going?" Abby asked when she came by to meet Calhoun for lunch.

"Great!"

Abby lifted a curious eyebrow. "Really?"

She glanced around her and leaned forward. "Donavan's taking me out."

"J.D.?"

"Don't look so horrified," Fay laughed. "He's serious. He was the perfect gentleman last night and he actually talked about a commitment."

"J.D.?"

Fay nodded. "J.D. Did you know he had a nephew and there's a custody suit in the offing?"

"Yes," Abby said, sobering at once. "The poor little boy's had a hard time. I don't like J.D. a lot, but I'll give him credit for caring about Jeff. He really does." She frowned. "Is that why he's talking seriously?"

"Probably," Fay said, then she smiled. "I don't have any illusions that he's suddenly discovered undying love for me. But he might learn to love me one day. Love takes time."

"Yes," Abby said, remembering. "But you're still rich."

"He said it wouldn't matter."

Abby didn't say another word, until she was alone with Calhoun. "I'm afraid Fay's heading for a bad fall," she told him when they were sharing a quick lunch. "J.D. doesn't seem to mind about her inheritance, but you know how he is about rich women."

"I think he's got some suspicions that her uncle Henry isn't telling her everything. I have some of my own," he added. "I wonder if Fay has anything left to inherit."

"I had the same feeling. Poor Fay. J.D. doesn't love

her, I know he doesn't. He's too much of a womanizer to feel anything deep for a woman."

Calhoun lifted an eyebrow and pursed his lips. "He may be a reforming womanizer." He covered her hand with his and clasped it affectionately. "We all meet our Waterloo eventually. God, I'm glad I met mine with you!"

"Oh, so am I, my darling," she said softly. She leaned forward and kissed him tenderly, despite the amused looks from other diners. "You and the boys are my whole life."

"We've had a good beginning," he agreed. "And the best is still yet to come. We're very lucky."

"Very. I hope Fay fares as well," she added before she concentrated on her food instead of her sexy husband.

FAY DIDN'T SEE Donavan again for a few days. He'd phoned just to say that he was going out of town on business and that he'd call her when he got back. He hadn't sounded anything like an impatient lover, although he had sounded impatient, as if he hadn't wanted to call her in the first place. She'd been morose ever since, wondering if he'd had second thoughts. Her joy deflated almost at once.

From the day Donavan left, her life went downhill. Two days later she had to go to see Barry Holman about her inheritance. A nervous Uncle Henry was in the office when she got there, and Mr. Holman didn't look very happy.

"Sit down, Fay," Barry said quietly, standing until she was seated.

"It's bad news, isn't it?" she asked, looking from one of them to the other with quick, uneasy eyes.

"I'm afraid so," Barry began, and went on to tell her the bad news. She was penniless.

"I'm sorry, honey," Uncle Henry said heavily. "I did my best, honest to God I did. I pushed you at Sean because I hoped the two of you might hit it off. Sean's rich." His shoulders moved helplessly. "I thought if you married him, you wouldn't have to give up so much."

"Why didn't you tell me?" she asked miserably.

"I didn't know how," he replied. "Your father was a speculator, but for once, he picked the wrong thing to speculate on. I didn't know until a few weeks ago myself, when I tried to liquidate the stock. It fell almost overnight. There's nothing left. Just nothing." He spread his hands. "Fay, you can always come back and live with me…"

"I have a job," she said thinly, remembering almost at once that it was only a temporary job and would soon end. She felt like crying.

"You still have the Mercedes," Barry said surprisingly. "Your father had the foresight to take out insurance that would pay it off if he died. That's yours, and it has a high resale value. I could handle that for you, if you like. Then you'd have a little ready capital and enough over to buy a smaller car."

"I'd appreciate that," she said dully. "I'll get the

papers together and bring them by in the morning, if that's all right."

"That will be fine. There are just a few more details, and I'll need your signature in several places..."

Fay hardly heard anything else that was said. She felt numb. In shock. Just a week ago, she'd been in Donavan's arms with a whole future to look forward to and an inheritance to fall back on. Now she had nothing at all. Even Donavan had seemed to have second thoughts, because he'd certainly dropped her flat.

What if he'd only wanted her for the money in the first place? she thought with hysteria. Or to help him provide a settled home so that he could get custody of his nephew?

The more she worried it in her mind, the worse it got. Donavan hadn't wanted her when she was rich, he'd made sure she knew it. Then all at once, about the time he decided to fight for custody of his nephew, he became suddenly interested in her.

It all fit. The only thing that didn't was his abrupt lack of interest. Had he decided he didn't need her after all? Well, she wouldn't do him much good now, she thought wildly. She was just another member of the working class, and what was she going to do when her job folded?

She went through the motions of her job for the rest of the day, white-faced and terrified. Calhoun noticed, but when he asked what was wrong, she only smiled and pretended it was a headache.

That didn't fool him. He knew too much about

women. He picked up the phone and called Barry Holman.

"I know it's all confidential and you can't tell me anything," Calhoun said. "But you can pause in significant places. I only want to help. Fay didn't get a damned thing did she?"

There was a long pause.

"That's what I thought," Calhoun said quietly. "Poor kid."

"She really needs that job," Barry replied. "Knowing it's only temporary is probably eating her up. She's never had to depend on herself before."

"No problem there," Calhoun returned, smiling. "Fay's got a job here as long as she can type. We'll find a niche for her. Damn Henry!"

"Not his fault," Barry said. "A bad investment gone sour, that's all. The old story, but a tragic one for Fay. All she's got left is the Mercedes. And you didn't hear this from me," he added firmly.

"Of course not! I'll just sort of mention that she's working out too well to let go and we want to keep her on."

Barry chuckled. "She'll appreciate that."

"We appreciate her. For a debutante, she's a hell of a hard worker." His eyes narrowed. "See you," he said, and hung up. He had another call to make.

He dialed J. D. Langley's number.

"Hello?" came the abrupt reply.

"I thought you were out of town," Calhoun said curtly.

"I was. I just got in fifteen minutes ago. I was

having a cup of coffee. What's wrong?" he asked. "Something about the cattle?"

"Something about Fay York," Calhoun said.

There was a deathly hush. "Has anything happened to her?" he asked, feeling as if the ground had been cut out from under him. "Is she all right?"

Calhoun felt relieved. That was genuine concern in the other man's voice. Of course, and he hated himself for thinking of it, it could be that J.D. was counting on Fay's money to help him get his nephew. If he was, he was going to do Fay a big favor.

"I'm going to tell you something I'm not supposed to know," he said. "You aren't supposed to know it, either, so don't let on."

"What?"

"Fay didn't get a penny. Her father lost everything. All she inherits is the Mercedes."

J.D. didn't say anything, and Calhoun felt sorry for Fay. Until the sound of soft laughter came over the line and eased his mind.

"So she's busted," Donavan said warmly. "I had a feeling it would work out like that. I'm sorry for her, but I'm damned glad in a way. I wouldn't want people to think another Langley was taking the easy way out with a rich wife."

"You're really serious about her?" Calhoun asked, surprised.

"Why is that so hard to believe? You must have noticed that she's got a heart as big as all outdoors," he replied. Then he spoiled it all by adding, "She's just the kind of foster mother Jeff needs."

"You aren't going to marry her over a custody suit?"

"Whatever it is, is none of your business, Ballenger," J.D. said with icy politeness. "If Fay wants to marry me, that's her affair."

"And if she loves you, what then?"

"She isn't old enough to love anyone yet," Donavan said carelessly. "She's infatuated with me, and she needs a little security. I can give her enough to make her happy."

Calhoun called him a name he wouldn't have wanted Abby to hear. "You're lower than I gave you credit for," he added coldly.

"And it's still none of your damned business. I'll be in to check on the Mesa Blanco stock in the morning." He hung up, leaving Calhoun furious.

AFTER HANGING UP on Calhoun, Donavan sipped his coffee without really tasting it. He was fond of Fay, and physically she appealed to him as no other woman had. She was innocent, and that alone excited him. He could make her happy.

But the thing was to get Jeff, to rescue the boy who was his sister's only child from the hell he was living in. It had taken all his powers of persuasion and a lot of tongue-biting to get his venomous brother-in-law to let Jeff come up here just for the spring holidays. Possession was nine-tenths of the law. He had Jeff and he was going to keep him. He'd already talked to the lawyer he shared with

Mesa Blanco about filing for custody, so the wheels were turning.

"Are you sure you won't mind having me around, Uncle Don?" Jeff asked from his sprawled position in the armchair. With his crewcut and husky physique, he looked the very picture of a boy who was all boy.

"No, sport, I won't," Donavan said. "We get along pretty good most of the time."

Jeff smiled. "Sure we do. Can we go riding tomorrow?"

"Maybe. First we have to go to the feedlot and check up on the feeder cattle. There's someone I want you to meet."

"Fay, right?" he asked, smiling again at his uncle's surprise. "She was all you talked about on the plane," he added.

Donavan lit a cigar and didn't look at the boy. He hadn't realized that he'd been so transparent. He'd missed Fay, but he didn't like admitting it even to himself. He'd been footloose all his life. Even if he married Fay for Jeff's sake, he didn't intend giving up his freedom.

"Aren't you going to call her?" Jeff asked.

"No," Donavan said, frowning. He did want to, but he wasn't going to give in to his impulse. Better to start the way he meant to go on, and acting like a boy with a crush wasn't going to keep him in control of his life.

"It's nice here," Jeff said after a minute. "I hate military school. You can't do anything without permission."

"Don't expect to be able to run wild here," his uncle cautioned.

"No, I don't. But you like me, at least. My step-father hates my guts," he added coldly. "Especially now that he's married *her* and they're expecting their own child. He didn't even love my mother, did you know?"

Donavan's face hardened. "I knew," he said. He didn't elaborate on it, but he knew very well that his brother-in-law's blatant affairs had all but killed his sister. She'd loved the man, but his womanizing had depressed her to the point of madness. A simple case of pneumonia had taken her out of this world, out of her torment, leaving a heartbroken brother and son behind to mourn her. Donavan had hated Jeff's stepfather ever since. Better his sister had stayed in mourning for her first husband than pitch head-long into a second marriage that was doomed from the start.

"What did she see in him?" Jeff asked miserably. "He drinks like a fish and he's always off some-where. I think he's running around on his new wife already."

It wouldn't surprise Donavan. After all, he thought viciously, he was running around with his current wife while he was still married to Donavan's sister.

"Let's forget he exists for a few days," he told Jeff. "How about a game of chess?"

"Super!"

WHILE DONAVAN AND Jeff were playing chess, Fay was trying to come to grips with her new situation.

She'd always secretly wondered how she would cope if she ever lost everything. Now was her big chance, she thought with black humor, to find out. If she could conquer her fear of having her livelihood depend on her own efforts, she could manage. Thank goodness Donavan had made her take a good look at herself and start learning independence. If she'd still been living with Uncle Henry now, she really would have been terrified.

She understood now why her uncle had been so eager to push her at his business associate, Sean. It had been out of a misplaced protective instinct. He'd hoped she'd marry Sean and be secure when she found out there was nothing left of her parents' estate.

Even though she was grateful for his concern, she wished he'd told her sooner. She put her face in her hands. Well, she could always write to Great-Aunt Tessie and beg for help if things got too bad. She and the old lady had always kept in touch. In fact, there was no one else who loved Tessie just because of her sweet self and not her money. Fay always remembered the elderly woman's birthday. She wondered if anyone else ever had. Certainly not her parents.

She wiped the tears away and wondered when Donavan was coming back. He might not want her now. She had to face the fact that without her wealth, despite what he'd said about not wanting a wealthy woman, he might walk away without looking back.

Time would tell. For now, she had enough to keep her busy. She got up from her chair and went to find the paperwork on the Mercedes. At least it would bring a tidy sum, and give her a badly needed nest egg.

The next morning after she'd dropped the papers off at Barry Holman's office, she was working away when the office door opened and Donavan Langley came in with a dark-haired boy at his side.

So he was back. And that had to be Jeff. Her heart ran wild, but she pinned a polite smile to her face as he approached her desk.

"Good morning," she said politely.

"This is Jeff," he replied without answering her. "Jeff, this is Fay York."

"Nice to meet you," Jeff said. He was watching her with open curiosity. "You're pretty."

She flushed. "Thank you."

Jeff grinned. "My uncle likes you."

"That's enough," Donavan drawled. "Go out and look at the cattle. But don't get in the way, and stay out of the pens."

"Yes, sir!"

He was off at a dead run, barely missing one of the amused cowboys. "Keep an eye on him, will you, Ted?" Donavan called.

"Sure thing, Mr. Langley," the cowboy replied, and turned on his heel to follow Jeff.

"He's impulsive and high tempered," Donavan told her. "I have to watch him like a hawk so that he doesn't hurt himself." He searched her eyes with no particular expression on his lean face, but his silver eyes were glittery with contained excitement. She stirred him up. He'd missed her more than he wanted to admit. But she wasn't receptive today. That smile was as artificial as the ficus plant in the pot beside her desk.

"Did you have a nice trip?" she asked for something to break the silence.

He nodded. "Jeff and I got in last night."

And he hadn't called. Well, now she knew where she stood. The fixed smile didn't waver, even if she had gone a shade paler. "He's a nice looking young man."

"He favors his mother. How about lunch? You can go with us to the hamburger joint."

She wanted to, but it was better to break this off now even if it killed her. Things could only get worse, and her life was in utter turmoil.

"I can't today, but thanks anyway."

He started. "Why can't you?"

"I have to see Mr. Holman about selling the Mercedes," she said with stiff pride. "You'll find out sooner or later, so I might as well tell you. I don't have any money. My parents left me without a dime." She lifted her chin and stared at him fearlessly. "All I have is the Mercedes and it's going on the market so that I'll have a nest egg for emergencies."

He didn't like the way she said that. She made it sound as if his only interest in her was what she had. Didn't she know it was her wealth that had stood between them in the first place?

He scowled. "The money didn't matter."

"Didn't it?" she asked bravely.

His gray eyes narrowed. "So you did believe Bart after all. You think I'm as money-crazy as my father." His expression went hard with contained rage. He'd thought she knew him better than that. It hurt to realize that she was just like several other people in Jacobsville who tarred him with the same brush they'd used on his father. "All right, honey. If that's the kind of man you think I am, then take your damned Mercedes and go to hell with it," he said cuttingly. He turned and went after Jeff.

Fay couldn't believe she'd said such a thing to him. Not that it would make any difference, she kept assuring herself. He didn't want her in the first place, so all she'd done was save herself a little more heartache.

Donavan didn't come back through the office on his way out. He took Jeff with him the back route, stormy and unapproachable, smoking his cigar like a furnace all the way to the car.

"What's eating you?" Jeff asked curiously.

"Nothing. What do you want for lunch?"

"A cheeseburger. I thought you said Fay was coming with us? Didn't she want to?"

"She was busy," he said curtly. "Get in."

Jeff shrugged. He wondered if he was ever going to understand adults.

Calhoun paused by Fay's desk, noticing her worn expression and trembling hands.

"J.D.'s been by, I gather," he said dryly.

She lifted her miserable eyes to his. "You might say that. He had Jeff with him."

"And left you here?"

She sat up straighter. "I told him I didn't have any money. He left."

He whistled. "Not a wise move, Fay," Calhoun said gently. "Donavan's touchy about money. You knew that his father—?"

"Yes, I knew," she cut him off gently. "It's for the best," she said. "He didn't really care about me. If he wanted me at all it was because he had a better chance of keeping Jeff if I was around. I'm not stupid. I know he doesn't love me."

Calhoun wanted to deny that, to reassure her, but it was patently obvious that she was right, J. D. Langley wasn't the hearts-and-roses type, but he sure didn't act like a man in love.

"It's early days yet," he told her, wanting to say something positive. "Give him time. J.D.'s been a loner ever since I've known him. He's a lot like Justin. Maybe that's why they get along so well. I have to admit, he and I have never been particularly friendly, but that doesn't have anything to do with you."

"I guess I should apologize," she began.

"Oh, not yet," he said, smiling. "Let him sweat for a while. It will do him good to be on the receiving end for once."

"You mean, he's usually the one who does the jilting," she said, sighing as she remembered how experienced he was. "I guess he's done his share of breaking hearts."

"Be careful of yours," Calhoun said seriously. "There's something I want to mention to you. I told you that this job was temporary, just until Nita came back." He hesitated, noticing her depressed look as she nodded. "Well, I want to offer it to you permanently. I need a secretary of my own, and Nita works a lot better with Justin than she does with me. What do you say? We've been thinking of adding a secretary, but until you came along, we weren't sure exactly what we wanted. You suit me and we seem to work pretty well together. Besides," he added on a chuckle, "Abby might divorce me if I let you go. She thinks a lot of you."

"I think a lot of her." Fay brightened magically. "You really mean it?"

"I mean it. If you want the job permanently, it's yours."

"And Nita won't mind working just for Justin?"

"I've already asked her. She almost kissed my feet. It seems that she's only been putting on a brave face about handling the workload for both of us. Getting some relief has given her a new lease on life. She said she was actually thinking of staying home with the baby just to get away from the work."

"Then I'd love the job, thank you," she said brightly. "You have no idea how much I enjoy working here. Besides," she confessed, not realizing that he already knew her situation, "I'm afraid I'm going to have to work for the rest of my life. My parents didn't leave me anything. I'm flat broke."

"In that case, we'll be helping each other out," he said. "So welcome aboard."

"Thanks, Calhoun," she said, and meant it. "Thanks very much."

"My pleasure."

She turned her attention back to her computer with an improved outlook. At least she had a job, even if she didn't have J. D. Langley. But that might still be for the best. She'd only have been letting herself in for a lot of heartache. It was better not to even begin something that was blighted from the start. And it wasn't as if he loved her. She had to keep remembering that.

THE MAN DRIVING back toward home was trying to keep it in mind himself, while he fumed inwardly at Fay's attitude. He wasn't mercenary, but she thought he was. Like father, like son. He groaned inwardly. Would he never be free of the stigma?

Jeff hadn't said a word, and Donavan couldn't bring himself to tell the boy why Fay wouldn't come to lunch with them. She thought he'd only been keeping company with her because of her money, when he'd already told her he didn't like rich women.

But in all honesty, he had to admit that he'd given her no real reason to think she was of value to him as a person. He'd talked much more about getting custody of Jeff than of wanting her for herself. He'd made love to her lightly, but even that could have convinced her that it was desire mingled with the need for a woman to aid his case to keep Jeff.

He frowned. He hadn't given her any chance at all. To compound it, he'd told her that he'd been back in town for almost a whole day and hadn't even bothered to phone her. He groaned inwardly. He'd made so many mistakes.

Worst of all, he hadn't considered her feelings. She'd just been told that she'd lost everything. All she had to her name was a Mercedes-Benz that she was going to have to sell. It was more than an inheritance she'd lost—it was her whole way of life. She had to be terrified at being responsible for herself. She was only twenty-one, and so alone, because she and her uncle weren't close. She'd needed comfort and help, and he'd told her to go to hell.

"You look terrible, Uncle Don," Jeff broke the tense silence. "Are you sure you're okay?"

"Not yet. But I will be," he said, and abruptly turned around in his own front yard and headed right back toward town. It was quitting time, so Fay would most likely be at home. He didn't know what he was going to say to her. He'd think of something.

CHAPTER SIX

FAY HAD THOUGHT about staying late at the office, just to keep her mind busy, but in the end she decided she would be equally well-off at home. She said good-night to her coworkers and drove the short distance back to her apartment house.

The Mercedes felt uncomfortable now that she was a working girl. It was just as well that Mr. Holman was going to help her sell it. There would be no more luxury cars, no more shopping sprees that didn't include looking at price tags. There would be no more designer clothes. No bottomless bank account to fall back on. She could have cried. She would make it. She knew she would. But getting used to her circumstances was going to take a little time.

She got out of the car and was walking onto the front porch when she heard the roar of a vehicle and saw Donavan driving up next to the Mercedes with Jeff beside him.

Not another fight, she prayed silently, her wan face resigned and miserable even if her eyes did light up helplessly at the very sight of him when he got out and approached her.

He stopped just in front of her, his own expression

somber. She looked bad. The camouflage she'd hidden her fears behind had vanished now, because she was tired and her guard was down. He reached out and touched her mouth, dry and devoid of lipstick.

"I'm sorry," he said without preamble. "I didn't think about how you must feel until I was back home."

The unexpected compassion, on top of the emotional turmoil she'd been through, cracked inside her. Tears poured down her cheeks.

"I'm sorry, too," she managed brokenly. "Oh, Donavan, I didn't mean it…!"

His breath caught at her vulnerability, and he was glad he'd made the decision to come back. Without a word, he bent and lifted her in his hard arms and started back toward his car, kissing the tears away as he went, whispering comforting things that she didn't quite hear.

Jeff saw them coming and, with a grin, moved into the backseat. Donavan winked at him before he slid Fay into the passenger seat and trussed her up in her seat belt.

"Stay put," he told her. "We're kidnapping you."

"What will my landlord think?" she asked with a watery smile.

"That you're being kidnapped, of course. We'll take her home and hold her prisoner until she cooks supper for us," he told Jeff, who was smiling from ear to ear. "If she's a good cook, I'll marry her right away."

Fay was trying not to choke. "But you told me to go to…!" she began.

"Not in front of the boy," he said with a mock glower. "He isn't supposed to know words like that."

"What century is *he* living in?" Jeff asked, rolling his eyes. "Gimme a break, man!"

"Too much TV," Donavan said. "We'll have to take a plug out of the set."

Fay's head was whirling. "But, Donavan, I can't cook. That is, I can," she faltered, wiping at her eyes. "But only omelets and bacon."

"No problem," he said as he started the car. "I like breakfast. Don't you, Jeff?"

"Sure!"

She gave up. In the scant minutes it took them to get to the ranch, she'd dried her tears and managed to gather her composure. She still didn't understand what had prompted Donavan to come after her, despite the way she'd insulted him, but she wasn't going to question a kindly fate.

Jeff was in a flaming rush to get to the living room for one of his favorite TV programs, leaving Donavan to escort a worn Fay into the kitchen.

"Mind Bee," he murmured, stepping around the kitten as she rushed toward them.

"I'll take care of her, Uncle Don," Jeff interrupted. He scooped up the kitten, popped back into the living room and closed the door behind him. The blare of the television could be heard even through it.

"The noise takes a little getting used to," Donavan said slowly. He studied Fay, whose hair was straggly as it came loose from its neat chignon. "Why do you wear it like that, anyway?" he asked gently, moving far too close to her. His lean hands deftly separated hairpins from upswept strands, loosening the dark cloud of her hair around her shoulders. "That's better," he whispered. "Now you look like my Fay again."

A tiny sob broke from her lips at the tenderness. Somehow she'd never associated it with him until now.

"I said such terrible things to you," she whispered back, her eyes eloquent.

"I said such terrible things back," he murmured, smiling. "We had a lovers' quarrel. Nothing to lose sleep over. Everything's all right now."

"We aren't lovers," she protested.

His eyes searched hers. "We're going to be, though."

She flushed. "I'm not like that."

He bent and drew his lips with aching tenderness over her own, gently parting them. His hands went to her hips and brought them firmly into the cradle of his, so that she could feel every vibrant muscle and tendon of him close, close against her softness.

"Come on, baby," he breathed into her open mouth. "Don't make me fight for it…"

She lost the will to protest the second she felt his tongue going past her lips, into the darkness beyond. A white-hot flash of sensation rippled her body in his arms, stiffened her. She caught her breath and then released it in a long, shuddering sigh that he could feel and taste.

"Yes," he said huskily. "That's it. That's it!"

He lifted her by the waist, turning her deftly to the wall. He pinned her there with his body, his long legs pushing between her thighs as he penetrated her mouth with quick, hard thrusts that simulated a kind of joining she'd never experienced.

When he finally lifted his head, she couldn't see anything except his swollen mouth. Her body was throbbing, like the tiny breaths that pulsed out of her, like her heart in her throat.

He leaned closer and bit her lower lip, not hard enough to hurt, but quite hard enough to make her aware of the violence of his passion.

She couldn't move. He had her pelvis completely under his, her legs supported by his, her breasts pinned beneath the heavy pressure of his chest. Behind her, the wall was cold and hard, not warm and alive like the man who had her helpless.

"I think you'd better marry me, Fay," he said huskily. "I don't know how much longer I can protect you."

"Protect me from what?" she asked, dazed by passion.

"Do you really need to ask?" he murmured against her bruised mouth.

"Marriage is a big step," she said weakly.

"Sure it is. But you and I are getting more explosive by the day. I want you like hell, honey, but not in the back seat of my car or some out-of-the-way motel when time permits. You're a virgin. That puts you right off-limits."

"I'm poor," she said. "No, don't look like that," she pleaded, touching his thick eyebrows where they clashed to smooth away the scowl. "I mean, I'd be a burden on you. I'll work, but I can't make much…"

"How do you think other couples manage?" he asked. "For God's sake, I don't care if you're poor! So am I, in a lot of ways. You're much more desirable to me without money than you were with it, and I think you know why."

"Yes. I shouldn't have said what I did. I was so afraid that you wouldn't want me anymore."

He lifted an eyebrow. "Does it feel like I don't want you?" he asked pleasantly.

He hadn't moved, but what he felt was rather blatant and she blushed.

He laughed softly as he let her slide down against him until her feet touched the floor. He loomed over her as he searched her flushed face with indulgent amusement.

"You're priceless," he murmured. "Will you faint on our wedding night, or hide in the bathroom? I'll wager you've never seen a naked man, much less an aroused one."

"I guess I'll get used to it," she replied gamely.

He chuckled. "I guess you'll have to. Yes or no?"

She took a deep breath. "Yes, then," she said, refusing to worry about his motives or even her own. She wanted him and he wanted her. She'd worry about the rest of the problems later.

He didn't speak for so long that she was frankly worried that he was regretting the proposal. Then he lifted her hands to his mouth and kissed them with breathless tenderness, and the look in his silver eyes made her feel humble. Whatever he felt right now, it wasn't reluctance. Her heart lifted and flew.

Jeff was called in minutes later and told the news. He literally jumped for joy.

"When?" he asked them.

Fay hesitated. Donavan didn't. "Next week," he said, his eyes daring Fay to challenge him.

"Then," Jeff said, as if he was reluctant to put it into words, "can I stay for the wedding?"

Donavan studied him in a silence that became more tense by the second. "As far as I'm concerned, you can stay until you're of legal age."

"That goes for me, too," Fay said without prompting.

Jeff looked embarrassed. He colored and averted his eyes. Like his uncle, very little showed in his face unless he wanted it to. But his uneasiness was a dead giveaway.

"I'd like that," Jeff said. "But wouldn't I be in the way?"

"No," Donavan said tersely. "We won't have time for a honeymoon right away, and you'll need to be registered in school here, even though it's almost the end of the school year."

Jeff's eyes widened. "You mean I won't have to go back to military school?"

"Not unless you want to," Donavan told him. "I've already started custody proceedings for you."

"Gosh, Uncle Don," Jeff said enthusiastically. "I don't even know what to say!"

"Say okay and go back and watch television with Bee," Donavan mused, glancing warmly at Fay. "I haven't finished kissing Fay yet."

"Oh. That mushy stuff," Jeff said with a sly grin.

"That mushy stuff," Donavan agreed, smiling at Fay's wild-rose blush. "You'll understand in a few years."

"Don't bet on it," the boy murmured. He reached down to retrieve Bee, who was tangling his shoe-laces. "I'd like to stay here," he said without look-ing at them. "I'd like it a lot. But my stepdad won't ever agree."

"Let me worry about that," Donavan told him. "We'll call you when supper's ready."

"Okay. I won't hold my breath or anything, though," he added dryly, and closed the door be-hind him.

Fay stared up at Donavan and felt as if every dream she'd ever had was about to come true. She had nothing. But if she had Donavan, she had the world.

She said so. He looked briefly uncomfortable. She didn't know that he was unsure of his own reasons for wanting to marry her. He wanted to keep Jeff. He felt a furious physical longing to make love to Fay. But beyond that, he was afraid to speculate.

He'd done without love all his life. He wasn't sure he knew what it was.

"I haven't embarrassed you?" she asked worriedly.

He moved forward and drew her slowly into his arms. "No," he said. His eyes searched hers. "It's going to be hard for you getting used to my lifestyle. I like my own way. I budget like a madman. There's no provision for pretty dresses and expensive cosmetics and a trip to the hairdresser once a week..."

Daringly, she put her fingers against his hard mouth. "I won't miss those things." She traced his lean cheek and his firm mouth and chin, loving the way he tolerated her exploration. "Oh, glory," she said on an unsteady breath. "I'll get to sleep with you every night."

He stiffened at the way she said it, as if being in his arms would lift her right up to heaven. He brought her closer and bent to kiss her with slow, expert thoroughness.

She reached up to hold him back, giving in with exquisite delight pulsing through her body, loving him as she'd never dreamed she could love someone.

He lifted his head feverish seconds later and clasped her shoulders firmly while he looked down at her. "I hope I'm going to be man enough to satisfy you in bed," he said on a husky laugh. "You are one wild little creature, Fay."

She flushed. "I hope that's a compliment."

"It's a compliment, all right," he replied, fighting for enough breath to talk. She confounded him. For an innocent, which he was almost certain she was, there was no reticence in her when he started kissing her. She made his knees weak. In bed, she was going to be the end of his rainbow.

She studied him with soft, worried green eyes. "I haven't ever slept with anyone," she began nervously.

He smiled gently. "I know that. But you've got promise, honey. A lot of it." He leaned close and brushed his lips over her nose. "I'm glad it's going to be with me, Fay," he whispered huskily. "Your first time, I mean."

Her heart ran wild. "So am I."

His lips probed gently at her mouth, teasing it open. "Do you know what to expect?" he breathed.

"I…think so."

His eyes opened at point-blank range, silver fires that burned while she felt his coffee-scented breath on her lips. "I've never been gentle," he whispered. "But I will be. With you."

"Donavan," she breathed, her eyes closing as she pulled him down to her.

He didn't know if he was going to survive the soft heat of her body, the clinging temptation of her mouth. He groaned under his breath as the kiss went on and on, burning into his very soul.

"I can't bear it," he groaned at her lips. "Fay…!"

The tormented sound gave her the willpower to pull gently out of his arms and move away. Her knees felt weak, but he looked as if he was having a hard time standing up straight.

"It's like being thirsty, isn't it?" she asked breathlessly. "You can't quite get enough to drink."

"Yes." He turned away from her and lit a cigar with hands that were just faintly unsteady.

She stared at his long back lovingly, at the body that would one day worship hers. He was going to be her man, her very own. Losing her fortune seemed such a tiny sacrifice to make to have Donavan for the rest of her life.

She smiled to herself. "If you'll show me where the eggs are, I'll make you and Jeff an omelet," she offered. "I'm sorry I can't cook anything else just yet, but I'll learn."

"I know that. Don't worry about it," he added with a fairly calm smile. "I can cook."

"You can teach me," she mused.

"To cook," he agreed. His eyes fell to the visible tautness of her breasts. "And other things."

She smiled with barely contained excitement as she followed him to the refrigerator.

SUPPER WAS A gleeful affair, with Jeff laughing and joking with his uncle and Fay as if he'd never had a solemn, sad day in his life. He rode back with them when Donavan eventually drove Fay home and sat in the car while they walked to the door of Fay's apartment house.

"I can't believe the change in Jeff," he remarked as they paused on the darkened porch. "He's not the same boy who came out here with dead eyes and even deader dreams."

"Does his stepfather care about him?"

"Not so anyone would notice," he replied. "He

was always jealous of the way my sister got along with Jeff, always resentful of him. He made Jeff's life hell from the very beginning. Since my sister died, it's been much worse."

"Will he fight you over custody, do you think?"

"Oh, I'm convinced of it," Donavan said lightly. "That's all right. I don't mind a good fight."

"That's what I've heard," she murmured dryly.

He chuckled. "I grew up swinging. Had to. My father made sure of that." His eyes darkened and the smile faded. "You'll have that to live down, too, if you marry me. Some people won't know that you've lost your inheritance. There will be talk."

"I don't mind," she murmured. "While they're talking about me, they'll be leaving someone else alone."

"You don't get depressed much, do you?" he asked quizzically.

"I used to, before you came along." She toyed with a button of his shirt, loving the feel of him close to her, the warm strength of his hands on her shoulders. She looked up, her eyes shadowed in the darkness of the porch. "I'm much too happy now to be depressed."

He frowned. "Fay... I've been alone a long time. Jeff's taking some getting used to. A wife...well, I may make things difficult for you at first."

"Just as long as you don't have women running through the house in towels or anything," she said with an impish smile.

He chuckled. "No chance of that. I've kept to myself in recent years." He bent and brushed her mouth lightly with his, refusing to let the kiss ignite this time. "Good night, little one. Jeff and I will pick you up for lunch tomorrow."

"Cheeseburgers, right?"

"Right," he murmured. "I wish we were already married, Fay, and that we were completely alone. I'd carry you up those steps and take an hour stripping the clothes off you."

"Hush!" She giggled. "I don't wear *that* many!"

"You don't understand, do you?" he whispered. "You will."

"That first time we went out, you wouldn't even kiss me," she recalled suddenly.

"I didn't dare. I wanted it too much." He smoothed back her hair. "I figured you'd be addictive, Fay. I was right, wasn't I?"

"I'm glad I am," she said fervently.

"So am I. Good night, sweet."

He turned and left her, and he didn't look back, not even when he'd started the car and drove away. Jeff waved, and she waved back. But Donavan hadn't even glanced in the rearview mirror.

It made her nervous, realizing that he didn't seem to look back. Was it an omen? Was she doing the right thing to marry a man whose only feeling for her was desire?

She worried it all night, but by morning, the only thing she was certain of was that she couldn't live without Donavan. She went into the office resolute, determined to make the best of the situation.

"Is it true?" Abby asked the minute she came in the door later that morning, looking and sounding breathless.

Fay didn't have to ask any questions. She laughed. "If you mean, am I going to marry J. D. Langley, yes."

"Fay, you're crazy," Abby said gently. She sat down beside the younger woman. "Listen, he wants custody of Jeff, that's all. I'll absolve him of wanting your money, but if you think he's marrying you for love…"

Fay shook her head. "No, I'm not that crazy," she assured her friend. "But I care too much to refuse," she added quietly. "He may learn to love me one day. I have to hope that he will."

"It's not fair," Abby argued worriedly.

"It's fair to Jeff," Fay reminded her. "He stands to lose so much if he has to go back to live with his stepfather. He's a great boy, Abby. A boy with promise."

"Yes, I know. I've met him." She sat down on the edge of Fay's desk with a long sigh. "I hope you know what you're doing. I can't see J.D. passionately in love. Calhoun said he was actually cussing you when he left here yesterday."

"He was," she replied dryly. "And I was giving as good as I got. But we made up later."

Abby raised an eyebrow at the blush. "So I see."

"I can't say no, regardless of his reasons for wanting to marry me," Fay said urgently. "Abby, I love him."

The older woman didn't have an argument left.

She looked at Fay and saw herself several years before, desperately in love with Calhoun and living on dreams. She knew that she'd have done anything Calhoun had asked, right down to living with him.

She smiled indulgently. "I know how that feels," she said finally. "But I hope you're doing the right thing."

"Oh, so do I!" Fay said with heartfelt emotion.

When Donavan came to pick her up for lunch, the office was empty. Calhoun and Abby had their midday meal together most of the time, and the office girls took an early lunch so that they could be back during the regular lunch hour.

"Where's Jeff?" she asked, surprised that the boy wasn't with him.

"Gone to the movies," Donavan told her, smiling. "He thinks engaged people need some time alone. That being the case," he murmured, tugging her up by one hand, "suppose we buy the ingredients for a picnic lunch and find a secluded spot down by the river where we can make love to each other after we eat?"

She blushed, smiling at him with her whole heart. "Okay."

He chuckled as he pulled her along with him, standing aside to let the first of the office crew back in the building before he escorted her out to his car.

"We're raising eyebrows," he murmured. "Do they know we're engaged?"

"Everybody seems to," she replied.

"Small town gossip. Well, it doesn't matter, does it?"

She shook her head. "Not at all."

They stopped by a grocery store in a nearby shopping center and bought lunch at the take-out deli, adding soft drinks and ice for a small cooler. It wasn't a fancy or expensive lunch, but Fay felt as if it were sheer elegance.

"You look like one of those posed pictures of a debutante at a garden party," he remarked, his eyes on the way her gauzy white-and-green patterned dress outlined her body as she lay across from him on a spot of grass.

"I feel that way, too," she mused, tossing her long hair as she arched her back and sighed. Her eyes closed. "It's so peaceful here."

"If that's a complaint..."

The sound of movement brought her eyes open just in time to find Donavan levering his jean-clad body over hers. He was smiling, but there was a kind of heat in the smile that made her body begin to throb.

His elbows caught his weight as he eased down on top of her, his long legs cradling hers in a silence tense with promise. His eyes dropped to her mouth.

"This is as good a time as any for you to start getting used to me," he whispered. His hips shifted slowly, first to one side, then to the other. The faint movement aroused him and he tensed as the familiar heat shot through him like fire.

Fay watched his face contort slightly even as she felt the changing contours of his body. Her lips parted on a held breath.

"A hundred years or so ago, when I was young and hot-blooded, that was a frequent and worrying occurrence. These days," he mused, watching her flushed face, "it's more of a delightful surprise. I like the way my body reacts to you."

"It doesn't...react to other women like this?" she asked, torn between embarrassment and curiosity.

He shook his head. "Only to you, apparently. I must be getting old. Either that, or a diet of virginal shock is rejuvenating me."

"It isn't shock. Well, not exactly," she faltered.

"No?" He bent and gently parted her lips. One long, powerful leg began to ease its way between hers, parting them and spreading her skirt on the cool ground. He felt her gasp and lifted his head. "We don't have a lot of time for courtship," he breathed. "We need to get used to each other physically before we marry. It will make it easier."

"I've never done this," she said nervously.

"Not even this far?" he asked, surprised.

She shook her head. "My parents were very strict. So were the relatives I used to stay with. They all said it was a sin to let a man do what he liked to a woman's body."

"Perhaps in some respects it is," he replied quietly. "But you and I are going to be married. One day, I'm going to put my seed deep in your body and you're going to have my baby. That won't be a sin of any kind."

The words, so carelessly spoken, had a very uncareless reaction on Fay. Her eyes went wide and watchful, and her face went scarlet.

He felt her sudden tension, saw it in her face. "That excites you, does it?" he whispered huskily. His eyes fell to her breasts, and he watched the nipples go hard with quiet pride before he caught her shocked eyes again. "You have pretty breasts."

The blush exploded and he chuckled. "I shouldn't tease you, Fay. Not about something so profound. But it's irresistible. As irresistible as…this."

And as he spoke, he bent suddenly and put his open mouth over the hard tip of her breast.

CHAPTER SEVEN

FAY THOUGHT THAT if she died and flew into the sun she couldn't have felt any greater explosion of heat. The feel of Donavan's hot mouth on her body, even through the cloth, was incredible.

She arched against him and made a sound, half gasp, half groan, while her nails bit into his hard shoulders.

His teeth nipped her delicately, before his tongue began to swirl around the hard tip and make it unbearably sensitive to the moist heat of his mouth.

"Please," she whispered huskily. "Please, please, please…!"

He barely heard her through his own need. His fingers were quick and rough on her bodice, painful seconds passing before he managed to disarrange the hated fabric that kept her soft skin from his mouth. He found her with his lips and his hands simultaneously, and she clung to him, no thought of protest in her whirling mind as she fed on the feverish tasting of his mouth, the hot sensuality of his hands on her body.

"Don…avan!" she sobbed.

He lifted his head abruptly and looked at her.

"My God, you're beautiful, Fay," he said unsteadily.

"The most beautiful creature unclothed that I've ever seen in my life!"

"I want you," she said weakly.

"I want you, too."

"Here."

He shook his head, fighting for sanity. He had to drag his eyes away from her body to meet her own. "No. Not now. We aren't married, little one."

"It...doesn't matter!" she wept, her body racked with need.

"Yes, it does." Gently he disengaged her hands and put her clothing to rights. When she was dressed again, he rolled onto his back and pulled her down into his arms. He held her while she cried, his voice soothing, his hands gentling her while the storm passed.

"I'm a lucky man, Fay," he said when she was quiet again. "A very lucky man."

"I think I'm the lucky one," she said breathlessly, clinging.

He bent and kissed her, his silver eyes looking straight into hers while his lean hands framed her flushed face gently. "We're taking a big step together," he said then, and looked solemn. "I hope for both our sakes, and Jeff's, that it's the right one."

"It will be," she assured him. Somehow, she knew it. But it didn't escape her notice that he looked unconvinced.

THE NEXT WEEK went by in a pleasant haze. Fay spent every free moment with Donavan and Jeff, taking just time enough to go shopping with Abby for her wedding gown. She chose an oyster-hued suit, which was sensible, because it would go with everything she had left in her wardrobe. She splurged on a hat, too, and a veil to drape over it. She worried about the amount of money she'd spent, because it was no longer possible to buy without looking at price tags. But Donavan only smiled when she mentioned that, and told her that getting married certainly warranted a little splurging.

The ceremony was held at the local church where Donavan was a member, and half the population of Jacobsville turned out for the occasion. Most everyone knew by now that Fay had lost everything, and even Donavan's cousin Bart was civil to him.

Jeff stayed with the Ballengers while Donavan drove himself and his new bride all the way to San Antonio for their two-day honeymoon. They had supper on the Paseo del Rio, where lighted barges went past with mariachi bands and music filled the flower-scented air.

"There can't be any place on earth more beautiful than this," she commented when she finished the last bite of her apple pie à la mode and looked at her new husband with quiet possession.

He cocked an eyebrow, very handsome in the pale gray suit he'd worn to be married in. He hadn't changed. Neither had she. She was still wearing her off-white suit, because they hadn't wanted to take the time to change earlier.

"Aren't you disappointed that I couldn't offer you a week in Nice or St. Tropez?"

She smiled and shook her head. "I'm very happy. I hope I can make you that way, too."

His returning smile became slowly wicked. "Suppose I take you back to our room now? I want to see how many times I can make you blush before I show you what physical love is."

Her heart beat faster. "All right," she whispered with barely contained excitement, and was unable to meet his eyes as he paid the bill and led her out into the sweetly scented night.

"Are you afraid of it, Fay?" he asked in the elevator, where they were briefly alone.

"A little, I think," she confessed with a nervous laugh. She looked up at him. "I don't want to disappoint you. I know you aren't innocent..."

He smiled gently. "I've never been married, though," he reminded her. "Or had a virgin to initiate." The smile faded. "I'll try not to hurt you too much."

"Oh, I'm not worried about...that," she faltered.

"Aren't you?" he mused knowingly as the elevator stopped.

They entered the room and he locked the door behind them, but when her cold hand went toward the light switch, he caught it.

"It will be easier for you in the dark," he whispered as he brought her gently close. "I don't want you to see me just yet."

"Do you have warts?" She laughed, trying to make a joke of it.

"No. You'll understand a lot better in the morning. For now," he said, swinging her up in his arms as he started toward the bed, "let's enjoy each other."

She'd never dreamed that she could lie quietly while a man took her clothes off, but she did. Donavan made what could have been an ordeal into a breathless anticipation, kissing her between buttons and catches, stroking her body gently to relax her while he slowly and deftly removed every stitch she had on. Then he pulled her against him, and she felt the faint abrasion of his suit while he began to kiss her.

"You…you're still dressed," she whispered.

He bit at her mouth with lazy delight. "I noticed. Open your mouth a little more. That's it." He kissed her very slowly and his hand smoothed down over her taut breasts, making her gasp, before it left a warm trail down her flat belly to the soft inside of her thighs. "Don't faint," he whispered as he touched her intimately for the first time and felt her tense. "Relax, Fay," he breathed at her lips as he trespassed beyond even her wildest and most erotic dreams. She cried out and he made a rough sound, deep in his throat. "My God, this isn't going to be the best night of your life. Listen, sweetheart, do you want to wait until you can see a doctor?" he asked, lifting his head. "I don't want to frighten you, but this barrier isn't going to be easily dispensed with. You know, don't you, that I'm going to have to break it before I can take you?"

"Yes." She swallowed. "Will it hurt you, too, if you do?"

"More than likely." He rolled onto his back and pulled her close, his body pulsating with its denied need while he fought his inclination to say to hell with it and go ahead. He needed her, but he didn't want to hurt her, to make intimacy something that would frighten and scar her.

"I didn't know," she said hesitantly. "I've never had any female problems, and I didn't think I needed a prenuptial checkup…"

He smoothed her long hair gently. "I'm not fussing, am I?" he murmured.

"I'll bet you feel like it," she said miserably. She laughed and then began to cry. "I've ruined everything!"

"Don't be absurd." His arms tightened and he rolled over against her, his mouth warm and soft and slow as his hand moved down her body again. Instead of probing, this time it touched, lightly, sensually. She gasped and instinctively caught his hand, but it was already too late. The pleasure caught her by surprise and for minutes that seemed never to end, she was oblivious to everything except her husband.

A long time later, he got up, leaving her wide-eyed and more than a little shaken on the bed. He turned the lights on and looked at his handiwork, from the drowsy, sated green eyes to the pink luxury of her sprawled body. She was too fulfilled to even protest the intimacy now, and his expression was just faintly smug.

"No need to ask if you liked it," he murmured unforgivably and began to take off his clothes.

She watched him with visible pleasure. He had a stunning body, very powerful and darkly tanned, except for a pale band where she imagined his swimming trunks normally rested. He was lightly feathered all over with dark, curling hair, except for his chest and flat stomach, where it was thickest. He turned toward her and she caught her breath, unable to take her eyes off him. Even like this, he was any woman's dream. Especially like this.

He knelt over her, his eyes glittering with unsatisfied desire. "Now it's my turn," he whispered, easing down beside her. "I want what I gave you."

"Anything," she choked. "Teach me...!"

His mouth covered hers, and lessons followed that banished her shyness, her fear, her inhibitions. When he cried out a second time and was still, she lay against him with drowsy pleasure and closed her eyes in satisfied sleep.

They went back home the next morning. Donavan murmured dryly that he wasn't spending another night playing at sex when they could have the real thing after she saw the doctor. She did, first thing Monday morning, although the minor surgery was a little embarrassing. The doctor was pleased at Donavan's care, because, he added, it would have been an unpleasant experience for both of them if her new husband had been impatient. He sent her home with

a smile and she dreamed for the three days it took
for the discomfort to pass.

It was going to be the most exciting night of Donavan's life, Fay promised herself as she got everything ready. She'd already asked Abby to keep Jeff
for that one evening, without telling her why, and
Jeff had agreed with a murmured dry remark about
newlyweds needing some privacy. Nobody knew that
the marriage hadn't been consummated. But tonight
it was going to be.

Fay had a bottle of champagne chilling. She'd
cooked a special meal and made a crepe dessert,
things she'd had Abby show her how to do. Everything looked delicious. Even Fay, who was wearing
one of the only sexy dresses she possessed, a little
strappy black satin number that showed off her full
breasts and her long, elegant legs in the nicest possible way. She'd left her hair loose around her shoulders, the way Donavan liked it, and sprayed herself
with perfume. He'd been exquisitely patient and caring for the past few nights, contenting himself with a
few gentle kisses and the feel of her in his arms and
nothing more. Tonight, she was going to make him
glad he'd been so considerate.

She heard his car pull up in the driveway, very
impatiently, and heard the vicious slam of his door.
Something must have upset him at work, she thought
as she quickly lit the candles on the table. Well, she
had the cure for that.

She turned as he threw open the front door and
came in. That was when she realized that what had

upset him wasn't the job. He was staring at her with undisguised fury, his whole look accusing and violent.

"You didn't tell me you had a great-aunt who could buy and sell Miami Beach."

She blinked and had to think hard. "You mean Great-Aunt Tessie," she faltered. "Well, yes, but…"

His face hardened. His lean hand almost crushed the hat he'd just swept from his damp hair. "Your uncle Henry had a call a few minutes ago. He wanted me to break the news to you." He took a steadying breath. "Your great-aunt died last night. You inherit everything she owned, and that includes millions of dollars."

He was white in the face. Now she knew why. She sat down heavily. "Tessie is dead? But I had a letter from her just last week. She was fine…"

"You didn't tell me," he ground out. "Why?"

She lifted her eyes. "I never thought of it. Honestly," she said dully. Tears stung her eyelids. She'd been very fond of Tessie. "I loved her. Her money never made any difference to me. I expected she'd leave it to charity. She knew I didn't need it."

"Didn't, as in past tense." He nodded. "But now you're not a woman of property. Or are you?"

"I can always refuse it," she began.

"Don't bother. I assume you'll want to fly down there," he said shortly. "Your uncle will go with you. He said he'd make the travel arrangements and let you know later." He tugged at his tie, glaring at her.

"It's not my fault," she said huskily, tears pouring down her cheeks.

"Don't you think I know that?" he replied, his eyes cold and dark. "But it changes everything. I won't stay married to you. Not now."

"What about Jeff?" she gasped. "The custody suit?"

"I don't know..."

He was uncharacteristically hesitant. She went closer to him. "We don't have to tell anyone," she said. "I'll swear Uncle Henry to secrecy. We can stay married long enough for you to get Jeff away from his stepfather. Then we can get a...a divorce."

"Divorce?" he asked with a curt laugh. "An annulment." She flushed. "Had you forgotten, baby?" he asked mockingly. "We played at sex, but we never had it. Now it's just as well that we didn't. No harm done. You can find yourself some society boy in your own circle and get married again."

"And you?"

He shrugged indifferently and turned away before she could see his face. "I'll have Jeff."

"You don't want me?"

"What I want or don't want doesn't enter into it anymore," he said coolly, careful not to let her see his face. "The last thing I can afford is to have Jacobsville start gossiping about another Langley marrying for money, especially when I've got Jeff's future to think about."

"Oh, I see."

She did, painfully. Donavan would never want her

with millions. He was a proud man. Much too proud to withstand the snide remarks and gossip. Even if he was less proud, there was Jeff. The boy shouldn't have to suffer for things he'd never done.

"I'll...just phone Uncle Henry," she said, but Donavan didn't answer her. He went out and closed the door.

THE NEXT MORNING, he drove her and her uncle to the airport and put them on a plane. The Ballengers had been very understanding about her absence from work for a couple of days, and Abby was glad to fill in for her under the circumstances. They all put down Fay's apathy to her fondness for her great-aunt, so it was just as well they didn't see her with Donavan. His fierce scowl might have changed their minds.

"Thanks for driving us here," Henry said uncomfortably. "Fay, I'll wait for you on the concourse."

"Yes." She watched him go with dull eyes before she lifted her own to Donavan.

"You haven't slept, have you?" he asked formally. And he had to ask, because he'd moved out of her bedroom the night before without a word.

She shook her head. "I was fond of Great-Aunt Tessie. We were good friends."

"I wasn't very sympathetic last night," he said stiffly. "I'm sorry..."

Her chin lifted proudly. "I haven't asked for anything from you, have I, Donavan?" she asked with expression. "And I won't. I'll stay with you until the custody hearing. Then, as you suggested, we can get an annulment."

"What will you do?" he asked.

She only laughed. She felt a million years old. "What do you care?" she asked without looking at him. She picked up the case he'd been carrying for her. "I haven't told the Ballengers about what I'll inherit, and I hope you won't," she said over her shoulder. "Until I talk to her lawyers, nothing is really certain."

"Don't make some stupid decision about that money out of misplaced loyalty to me," he said coldly, forcing himself to smile as if he didn't give a damn about her. Letting her give up millions to live a modest lifestyle with him, out of nothing but desire, would be criminal. "I only married you to get Jeff. Maybe I wanted you, too," he added when she looked at him. "But bodies come cheap, honey. I've never gone hungry."

Her face went, if possible, a shade paler. "It's nice to know that I'll be leaving you heart-whole and unencumbered. Goodbye, Donavan."

"Not goodbye," he said carelessly. "So long."

She shook her head. "No, I meant it. I'll come back. I'll stay, for Jeff. But in every other way, it's goodbye." Her eyes fell away from his and she tried not to feel the bitter wound of rejection that made her insides hurt. Every step was one less she'd have to repeat. She thought about that as she counted them. She didn't look back, either. She was learning, as he apparently already had, not to ever look back.

THE TRIP TO Miami was long and tiresome. She and Uncle Henry spent two days dealing with Great-Aunt Tessie's possessions, saving keepsakes and arranging for disposal of everything else. The very last stop was the lawyer's office, where Fay sat beside her uncle with dead eyes, hardly aware of her surroundings.

"I know the will seems cut-and-dried," the attorney said apologetically, glancing at Fay and grimacing, "but I'm afraid it was altered just recently without my knowledge. Tessie's maid found the new will in her bedside table, witnessed and properly signed."

Henry's eyebrows raised. "Did she leave the whole shooting match to her cats?" he asked with a chuckle.

"Oh, it's a little better than that," the attorney returned, reading over the document. "She left it to open a chain of hostels that would house the families of children with incurable cancer. It seems her housekeeper's sister had a child with leukemia and was having to drive a hundred miles a day back and forth because she couldn't afford to stay in a hotel... Mrs. Langley, are you all right?"

Fay was aghast. Delighted. Unbearably pleased. She looked at the attorney. "You mean, I don't have to take the money?"

Her wording shocked him, when very little ever had. "You don't want it!"

"Oh, no," she agreed. "I'm quite happy as I am."

"Well, I'm not," Henry muttered. "She could have left me a few sticks of furniture or something."

"But she did," the attorney recovered himself enough to add. "There's a provision for the contents of her apartment to be sold at public auction and the proceeds split between the two of you. I should say it will amount to very nearly a quarter of a million dollars. There is, too, her jewelry, which she wanted to go to Mrs. Langley—provided none of it is sold. Heirlooms, you know."

Fay smiled. "Some of the pieces date back three hundred years to European royal houses. I'd never sell it. It should go to descendants." She realized that she wouldn't have any now, and her face fell.

"At least we got something," Henry told her once they were outside. "I don't feel so bad that your inheritance didn't come through, now."

"There was nothing you could have done," Fay assured him. "I don't have any hard feelings."

He stared at her curiously. "You didn't want Tessie's money?"

She shook her head as they walked back to the rented car. "Not at all. Donavan would never have married me in the first place if I'd been rich."

"Yes. He does have a sore spot about his father." He glanced at her. "Well, this slight in Tessie's will should make your marriage a little more stable. I can imagine what J. D. Langley would have thought if you'd inherited all that money."

"Yes. Can't you, though?" Although she was thinking that if he'd loved her, money wouldn't have mattered at all. He'd tossed her out on her ear because he thought she was inheriting Tessie's money.

He didn't want her rich. Well, that was all right with her. A relationship based on money—no matter if it was too much or too little—wasn't the right kind. She'd go on with her job at the feedlot and tell him that her inheritance was going to be tied up for a time. Beyond that, he didn't really need to know anything else. He'd thrown her out. She had to consider that maybe he'd done her a favor. She was falling more in love with him by the day. But aside from his need to keep Jeff and his desire for her, there was nothing on his side worth fighting for. As he'd already said, he could have all the women he needed. What would he want with Fay?

She did feel somewhat responsible for Jeff, though, since she'd agreed to the marriage in the first place partly to help rescue him from his stepfather. She liked the boy. For his sake, she wasn't going to walk out on J. D. Langley. She'd stick with them until the court case was settled one way or the other. Then she'd make whatever decisions had to be made.

It was ironic, though, that she'd gone to her marriage bed a virgin and left it still a virgin, even if she had learned quite a lot about pleasure in the process. She wondered if she could get into *The Guinness Book of Records?*

She packed her things and got ready to head back to Jacobsville. She didn't seem fated to be rich anymore, and she was rather glad about it. It was one thing to be born into money, quite another to learn to make it in the world without a big bankroll to fall back on.

If Donavan had loved her, she'd have had everything. She remembered so many good times with him, so much sweetness and pleasure. He'd genuinely seemed to like her at times, and his desire for her had been quite unmistakable. But desire wasn't love.

She couldn't settle for a man who looked at her as an infrequent dessert that he could live without. She wanted to be loved as well as wanted, to be cherished just for herself. Donavan had put conditions on their relationship that she couldn't meet. Be poor and I'll want you, he'd as good as said. If he'd loved her, whether she was rich or poor wouldn't have mattered. And all the gossip in the world wouldn't have made any difference.

Donavan had never loved, so he couldn't know that. But Fay did. She had to go back to him now and pretend that she didn't love him, that they were simply two people living together for the sake of a child. They weren't even legally married, because the marriage hadn't been consummated. She laughed bitterly. Jeff's stepfather could have had plenty of fun with that charge in court, but nobody knew except Donavan and herself, thank God.

She closed the case she'd been packing and went to phone the bellhop station. She had to go home and face Donavan, and the future.

CHAPTER EIGHT

WHEN FAY AND her uncle arrived at the airport, it was a shock to find Donavan waiting for them.

She shot a curious glance at her uncle, but he looked as surprised as she did.

"We could have gotten a cab," she began, her very calm voice belying the turmoil that the sight of Donavan engendered in her.

"It was no hardship to pick you up," he said easily. He was smoking a cigar, wearing working clothes that were clean if not new. His Stetson was cocked over one eye so that it wasn't possible to see the expression on his lean face. Just as well, too, he thought, because he wasn't ready for Fay to find out how glad he was to see her. The days had been endless since she left, and his conscience was hurting him. He'd been unkind to her at a time when she'd needed compassion and a shoulder to cry on.

"This is decent of you, Donavan," Henry said as he shouldered cases and followed Donavan out to the car. "I hate cabs."

Fay didn't comment. She clutched her purse and her overnight bag tightly, not returning Donavan's quiet, close scrutiny. She didn't care what he did or said anymore, she told herself. He'd hurt her for the very last time.

He dropped Henry off and not a word was spoken until he escorted Fay into the house.

"Jeff's in school," he told her when she noticed the sudden hush in the house. Only Bee, the kitten, was in evidence when Donavan came back from depositing her bags in her room. He picked her up with a faint smile and deposited her in a chair.

"You enrolled Jeff in school here, then?" she asked.

"Yes." He stopped just in front of her, his silver eyes probing as he looked down at her in the off-white suit she'd been married in. It brought back painful memories.

"How are you?" he asked.

"Still kicking," she replied dryly. "I'm not bleeding, Donavan, so you don't need to worry over me. I won't be a problem. Now, if you'll excuse me, I'll unpack and change. Then I'll see about starting something for supper."

"You don't have to…" he began irritably.

"I don't mind." She turned away, cutting him off before he could sway her resolve. "You've said it all already," she added without turning. "Let's just leave it alone. Have you heard from your lawyer about the custody hearing?"

"Yes," he said after a minute. "It's scheduled for next week."

She didn't know what else to say, so she nodded and left him there. It was some small consolation that he seemed as ill at ease as she felt. Their marriage was over before it had even had a chance to begin. She wished they could start again. But she doubted that Donavan believed in second chances any more than she did herself.

It was a silent meal. Jeff looked from one of them to the other with curiosity and faint uneasiness.

"I'm sorry about your great-aunt, Fay," Jeff said when they were eating the pudding she'd made for dessert. "I guess you're still sad."

"Yes," she agreed without argument. "Great-Aunt Tessie was special. She was a renegade in a day and age when it wasn't popular."

"Was she really rich?"

Fay hated the question, but she couldn't very well take out her wounds on the boy. "Yes, Jeff, she was. Very rich. But money isn't the most important thing in the world. It won't buy good health or happiness."

"Yeah, but it sure would buy a lot of Nintendo games!" he enthused.

She laughed despite herself. But Donavan was silent all through the meal, and afterward.

While Fay was washing dishes, he came into the room. His hands were dangling from the thumbs in his jeans pockets, his silver eyes watchful in a face like a carving in a stone cliff.

"I heard you call Abby Ballenger just before supper. Why? Did you tell her you were resigning?" he asked slowly.

"I'm not resigning. You do realize that paperwork and so forth takes time?" she added, playing for time. "I don't automatically inherit. Neither does Uncle Henry."

"You wouldn't have known that by the way he was talking on the way to his house," he reminded her with a calculating smile. "He's already got his money spent. Or he will have, by the time he actually gets it."

She didn't speak. He made her nervous. It was impossible to be in the same room with him and not remember how it had been between them that one night of their honeymoon. Even without the ultimate intimacy, she'd had a taste of Donavan that still could make her head spin. She loved him with all her heart. It wouldn't have mattered if he'd owned several multinational corporations or only a rope and an old horse. She loved him so much that his circumstances would never have made any difference. But he didn't feel the same about her, and she didn't need him to put it into words. She had money—or so he thought—and he didn't, so he didn't want her. Nothing would alter his opinion one iota, and she knew that, too.

"I should have stayed there with you, shouldn't I?" he asked unexpectedly. "You look worn to a nub, Fay. All that grief and your uncle to deal with at once. I suppose all the details were left up to you."

It was a question, she supposed. "Yes," she replied. "Uncle Henry was able to make the funeral arrangements, though, with the attorney's help. I sorted out the things in the apartment—" She stopped, blinking to stay the tears. She washed the same plate again, slowly. "It was so empty without her."

He hesitated. "So was this house, without you in it," he said gruffly.

She swallowed. She didn't dare turn around. "Thanks, but you don't have to pretend. I haven't lived here long enough to make any real difference in your life, or Jeff's. You're a better cook than I am, and you've had people to help you straighten up. I'm just a temporary convenience. Nothing more."

He was conscious of a terrible wounding in her and in himself. Had he made her feel so inadequate that she thought he was better off without her than with her?

"The boy wants to see that new adventure movie that just came out. It's playing at the Longview. Want to come with us?"

"Oh, no, I don't think so," she forced herself to say. "I'm very tired. You two go ahead, and enjoy yourselves. I just want to go to bed and sleep the clock around."

He hesitated. "Fay, we can wait until you're rested."

"I don't like movies, honestly," she said quickly. "But thanks all the same."

He moved closer, his eyes narrow and concerned. "You've had a rough time lately, and I haven't been much help. Listen, Fay…"

"I don't need pity," she said, her voice steady despite the turmoil his nearness aroused. She dried her hands and sidestepped away from him. "I'm learning to stand on my own two feet. I won't pretend it's easy, but I think I'm finally getting the hang of it. After the custody hearing next week, I may see about moving back to my apartment house."

"You're assuming that I'll win it," he said formally. "There's a good chance that I won't. And if you tip out the front door hours later, Jeff's stepfather may appeal the court's decision even if I do win. Proof of an unstable home life would cost dearly."

Incredible that he sounded so determined to keep her with him, when she knew that wasn't what he wanted at all. Of course, it was for Jeff's sake. He loved the boy, if he loved no one else.

"All right," she said, sounding and feeling trapped. She sighed deeply. "I'll stay as long as you need me."

"If you stay that long, you'll never leave," he said curtly.

He turned and left the room, with Fay staring after him in a daze, not quite sure that she'd really heard him right. Probably, she thought later, it was only wishful thinking on her part.

THEY FELL INTO a routine as the days passed. Fay went back to work, despite Donavan's comment that she was taking a job that someone else might really need, and Jeff went to school each day and began to look the very picture of a happy boy.

Fay worked harder than she ever had before, deliberately putting in late hours and paying more attention to detail than ever. Calhoun and Justin Ballenger were complimentary and appreciative of her efforts. Donavan was not.

"You do nothing but work!" he complained one evening when she wasn't working late—a rarity in recent days. "Don't Jeff and I count with you?"

"Uncle Don, Fay has to do her job right," Jeff pointed out. He grinned. "Besides, Mr. Ballenger says she's saved them plenty with all that hard work."

Donavan finished his dessert and reached for the carafe, to pour himself a second cup of coffee. "So I hear."

"You don't work any less hard yourself," Fay accused him. "And I don't complain."

His silver eyes met hers with cold impact. "Most brand-new wives would."

He was making an insinuation that, fortunately, went right over Jeff's head. But Fay knew what he was really saying, and she flushed.

"Yes, well, ours is hardly a normal situation."

"It could be," he said, startling her into looking up. There was no teasing, no mockery in his expression. He was deadly serious.

Fay flushed. "There's no time."

He lifted an eyebrow. "I beg your pardon?"

The flush grew worse. Jeff finished the last of his dessert and excused himself. "I want to get out of the line of fire," he said dryly, and closed the door into the living room. Seconds later, the TV blared out.

"Turn that damned thing down!" Donavan raged.

"You bet!" Jeff said irrepressibly and barely touched the knob.

Donavan, placated, was still glaring at Fay. "We're husband and wife," he reminded her. "There's no reason on earth that you can't share a bed with me."

"There's a very good one," she differed. She put down her napkin. "When Jeff's situation is resolved, I don't plan to stay here any longer than I have to. I won't risk getting pregnant."

His face drained of color. He looked...wounded. Cut to the bone. Fay felt sick at the careless comment when she saw its results. She hadn't even meant it. She loved him, but he only wanted her. She was fighting for her emotional survival, with the few weapons she had left.

"I didn't mean that," she said stiffly, averting her eyes. "Not like it sounded. But you must realize I'm right. A baby right now would...would complicate things."

"You don't think children can be prevented?" he asked with cutting sarcasm.

She lifted her eyes to his. "I won't be around that much longer," she said quietly. "I realize I must be stifling your sex life, and I'm sorry, but very soon I'll be gone and you can... Your life can get back to normal."

He grew colder in front of her eyes. He threw down his napkin and slowly got to his feet. "So that's what it's come down to in your mind. I'm hot for a woman and you're someone I can use in the meantime, until I'm free."

She went scarlet. "You can't pretend you feel anything other than desire for me," she said proudly. "After all, I'm rich."

His gaze averted to the table. He stared at it for a long moment. "Yes." He'd almost forgotten. Memories came back, of his father's greed, the censure after Rand Langley's second wife had committed suicide.

He left without another word. After a few minutes, Fay got up and cleared away the dishes. Well, what had she expected him to do, deny it? She laughed at her own folly and then had to bite back tears.

THE COURT HEARING was only two days away now, and both Jeff and Donavan were looking as if the pressure of it was giving them some problems.

Fay went by the video rental store and found three movies that would probably appeal to the two men in her life—both of whom were adventure fans—and presented them after supper.

"Wow!" Jeff enthused. "I've wanted to see these for ages! Thanks, Aunt Fay!"

"I didn't think you liked adventure films," Donavan remarked.

She shrugged. "I can take them or leave them. But I thought they might take Jeff's mind off court." She looked up at him curiously. "Have you heard anything from his stepfather, even through the lawyer?"

He shook his head. "It wouldn't surprise me to find that he's having us watched, though."

"Why?"

"Looking for anything to further his case." He laughed coldly. "It would be like him."

"Neither of us has been indiscreet," she reminded him primly, but with a nervous glance.

He glared at her. "I told you, I don't have women on the side. As long as we're married, you're it."

She averted her face. "Thank you."

"I hope that I can expect the same courtesy?"

Her eyes on his face were explosive and expressive. "You don't have to worry about that. I don't attract too many men now that I'm not rich anymore!"

The slip caught Donavan's attention. "You just inherited a fortune," he reminded her.

"Oh. Oh, yes," she faltered. She turned away quickly. "Nevertheless, I'm not going to break my wedding vows."

"I never thought you would, Fay," he said unexpectedly. He moved close behind her and caught her waist gently in his lean hands. "You needn't flinch like that." His voice was quiet, tender. "I may be a 14-karat heel, but I wouldn't hurt you physically."

"I know that," she said breathlessly. "And I don't think you're a heel. You love Jeff very much, don't you?"

He heard the jerky sound of her breathing and moved even closer, his powerful body all but wrapping around hers from behind. His face eased down so that his cheek was against hers, his warm breath sighing out at the corner of her mouth.

Her cold hands rested uneasily atop his, tremulous as the spell of his nearness made her pulse race wildly.

"It's easy to love a child," he said heavily. "Even a neglected, temperamental one. A child accepts love and returns it. Adults know better than to trust it."

"I see."

His hands tightened and his mouth dropped to her soft neck, pressing there hotly. "You see nothing," he said huskily. "Lift your mouth. I want it."

She started to protest, but the stark need of his mouth silenced her. His lips parted hers ruthlessly. He whipped her around against him, his body hardening as he held her possessively to it. He groaned softly, and the sound made her even weaker.

With a tiny sigh, her mind let go and made her vulnerable in his arms. She reached up, opening her mouth to the rough, insistent probing of his tongue. The sensations he was causing made her knees tremble, and eventually it was only the crush of his arms that kept her on her feet at all.

The sudden silence in the living room was as blatant as a gunshot. Donavan reluctantly lifted his head just as Jeff's footsteps impinged on the silence.

Fay tried to pull back, but Donavan wouldn't let go.

"He isn't blind," he said unsteadily. "Stay put."

She didn't quite grasp what he meant until he moved deliberately against her, making her realize at once that his hunger for her was blatant and easily seen.

She subsided and laid her cheek on his broad

chest, relaxing against him as Jeff pushed open the kitchen door, and made an embarrassed sound.

"Sorry," he faltered. "I needed a soft drink."

"Help yourself," Donavan said, chuckling. "We are married, you know," he added, lightening the atmosphere.

"It's about time you started acting like you were," Jeff murmured with a grin. He got his soft drink and closed the door behind him with a faint wink at Fay.

"I'll remind you of the same thing," he told her when he stepped back and her face flamed before she was able to avert her eyes. "And you've seen me with a hell of a lot less on, in this condition."

"Will you stop?" she moaned.

"You're very easily embarrassed for an old married woman." His eyes narrowed as he paused long enough to light a cigar. He watched her closely. "I'll keep you from getting pregnant. I want you in my bed tonight. Hear me out," he added when she started to speak. "Sophistication is the one thing you can't fake. If even Jeff realizes we aren't living like married people, his stepfather might realize it as well. We could still lose Jeff."

She hesitated. "I realize that."

"You can pretend all you like," he added, "but you want what I can give you in bed. You're as excited right now as you were in the motel room the night after we married. The difference," he said sensually, "is that now we can experience each other totally, Fay. I can satisfy you totally."

Her lips parted. She could still feel him on them,

taste him on them. He looked at her and knew, at once, that she was totally at his mercy.

Slowly he put out the cigar. He opened the door. "Jeff, we're going to have an early night. Bed by eleven, got that?"

"What? Oh, sure, Uncle Don," he said distractedly, his eyes on the TV screen. "Sleep well."

"You, too."

He closed the door and caught Fay's cold hand in his. He tugged her with him to the hall door, opened and closed it behind them and then led her into the darkness of his own bedroom.

He closed that door, and locked it. Seconds later, in the warm dark, Fay felt him lever down completely against her, pushing her back against the cool wood of the door as the heat of his muscular body overwhelmed her.

While he kissed her, his hands slid under the dress she was wearing and played havoc with her aroused body. Long before he began to take her clothes off, she was barely able to stand alone.

Later, she lay quietly, trembling, in his bed while he removed his own clothes. She could barely see him in the faint light from the window, but what she saw was devastating, and her breath caught.

"You know what to expect already," he whispered as he eased down beside her and began to arouse her all over again. "Except that this time," he whispered into her mouth, "I'm going to fill you…"

She cried out. His mouth hurt, his body was hard and heavy, but she didn't notice, didn't care. She welcomed the warm weight of him, the fierce passion of his mouth and hands. She even welcomed the faint flash of pain when he came into her, her body arching up to receive him, her eyes wide with shock and awe as he slowly completed his possession and then paused, hovering with her on the brink of some sensual precipice.

One lean hand had her hip in its steely grasp. He looked at her, breathing unsteadily, his silver eyes glistening with excitement, beads of sweat on his lean, swarthy face.

His hand contracted and he moved, sensually, just enough to make her feverishly aware of how intimate their embrace was.

She caught her breath and he laughed, deep in his throat.

"Yes," he whispered roughly. "You didn't realize just how intimate it was going to be, did you, little one?"

"N-no," she got out. She looked at him in astonishment, feeling him in every cell of her body. It was embarrassing, shocking, to talk to a man in the throes of such intimacy. And he was laughing. "It isn't funny," she choked.

"I'm not laughing because I'm amused," he whispered, and bent to nibble with barely contained hunger at her softly swollen lips. His hips curled down into hers and lifted, creating a sudden sensual vortex that coaxed a cry of shocked pleasure from her lips. "I'm laughing because you're the most sensual little virgin in the world, and because despite the newness and fear, you're giving yourself to me without a single inhibition. Lift your hips. Let me feel you as close as you can get."

She obeyed him, her body on fire. Her dreams had never been so explicit. Her nails bit into his broad shoulders as he began to move with exquisite delicacy.

"I may be a little rough with you now," he whispered into her mouth. "Don't be afraid of my passion. If you give yourself to it, to me, I'll give you a kind of pleasure you can't even imagine. Match me. Match my rhythm. Don't pull back. That's it." His teeth clenched and he groaned as his body stiffened. "Oh, God, I'm losing it…!"

He did. He lost it completely, before he could give her the time she needed to experience fulfillment. He arched above her, his face contorted and terrible in its unearthly pleasure, and he bit off something explicit and harsh as he gave in to the silky convulsions.

"I'm sorry," he whispered, lying drained and heavy over her. "My God, I'm so sorry!"

"Sorry that you made love to me?" she asked in a curious whisper.

"Sorry that I didn't satisfy you!"

"Oh." She stroked his dark hair gently. "You mean, the way you did the night we were married?" She smiled. "Now you can, can't you?"

He stared at her poleaxed. "You think that what just happened was only for my benefit?"

She frowned. "Wasn't it?"

He pulled her close and his arms tightened. "You're

one in a million, do you know that? Lift this leg… yes!"

She gasped as his body suddenly became part of hers. She hadn't expected this again so soon. Weren't men supposed to be incapable for several minutes after intimacy?

He moved slowly, exquisitely, and her breath caught. She clung to him, as the most astounding sensations worked through her tightening body.

"Donavan," she began, and suddenly cried out at the unexpected spasm of staggering pleasure.

"Be quiet, sweetheart," he whispered at her mouth, his hips moving with more insistence now, more purpose. "Hold on tight. Yes, Fay, feel it, yes… yes!"

She wept brokenly as the pleasure burst inside her like an overfilled balloon. She had no control whatsoever over her body or the vicious contractions that convulsed her under his openly watchful eyes.

He whispered to her, words of encouragement, praise, flattery, while his mouth touched quickly over her flushed, taut face. It went on and on. She shuddered and clung, convulsed and clung, experiencing sensations beyond her wildest dreams of perfection.

At last, the world stopped rocking and whirling around her. She trembled helplessly in the aftermath, drenched in sweat, weeping softly from the onrush of pleasure and its abrupt loss.

Donavan cradled her in his hard arms, smoothing back her damp hair as he comforted her.

"This," he said after a few minutes, "is what intimacy really is."

"I thought…before, at the motel…" She couldn't quite find the words.

"An alternate way of making love," he said quietly. "But nothing like the real thing. Was it, Fay?"

He wasn't mocking, or teasing. His voice was soft and deep and matter-of-fact.

"We…were like one person," she whispered into his cool, hair-roughened chest.

"Yes." His cheek moved against hers and he kissed her, very gently.

Her body felt pleasantly tired. She went boneless against him and slid even closer, her legs tangling with his. "Can I stay with you?" she asked drowsily.

His arms tightened. "Let me put it this way—just try to get away."

She smiled sleepily. "I don't think I want to."

He bit the lobe of her ear softly. "I want you again, right now," he said huskily, feeling her heart jump under his palm. "But we'll wait until in the morning. It didn't hurt? Even the first time?"

"No," she lied, and snuggled closer. It hadn't hurt very much. And the second time had been heaven.

"Fay," he said hesitantly. His fingers threaded through her soft hair. "Fay, I forgot to use anything."

She didn't stir, or answer. He looked down and realized belatedly that she was asleep.

He bent and kissed her closed eyelids. "Maybe it's just as well that you didn't hear me," he whispered. His lean hand found her soft belly and rested there possessively. "You'd love a baby, Fay. So would I. Maybe it's already happened. If it has, perhaps I can convince you that it would be a bonus, not a complication."

Fay was wavering between consciousness and sleep. She heard Donavan say something about a bonus, but her mind was already headed for oblivion. She clung closer and gave in to it.

CHAPTER NINE

FAY WAS HUMMING softly to herself when Donavan
came in from the barn. He'd gone out without wak-
ing her, and she was disappointed. She'd been hoping
that the night before might have coaxed him to want
her again, but obviously that hope had been doomed.

She stopped humming when he walked in, her
eyes a little shy and nervous. "Good morning," she
began, searching for the right words.

He paused in the doorway, and he could have been
playing poker for all the expression in his face. Her
stiff composure told him things he didn't want to
know. He'd pleased her in the night. He'd hoped
that things would change between them now that
she knew what married life could be. But he wasn't
reassured. She looked uncomfortable and poised to
run. If she felt anything for him, it didn't show. And
he needed some reassurance before he paraded his
own feelings in front of her; his pride would take a
mighty blow if she didn't care anymore.

"Good morning," he replied with equal formality.
"Breakfast ready?"

"Almost."

He turned. "I'll call Jeff."

And not a word was said, either about the night before, or about what he felt. Fay watched him surreptitiously, hoping to see some flicker of warmth in those silver eyes. But they never met hers. He was polite, nothing more. Fay left the table resolved not to expect anything from that encounter in the darkness the night before. It was just as well, because that night he didn't come near her.

The next morning, they went to church, and then spent a lazy afternoon in front of the television watching old movies. There had hardly been three words spoken in front of Jeff, who looked worried.

"Something bothering you?" Donavan asked curtly after supper.

Jeff looked uncomfortable. "Yes, sir. Sort of."

"What is it?"

"It's you and Aunt Fay," he said miserably, wincing at Fay's shock and Donavan's quick anger. "I'm sorry, but if you two go into court tomorrow looking like you do right now, I guess I'll be back in military school by the next morning. Could you pretend to like each other, just while we're in court?"

"No problem there," Donavan assured him. "Now you'd better get your bath and go to sleep. We've got a big day ahead tomorrow."

When he left the room, Donavan got up and turned off the television. His eyes lingered on Fay's flushed cheeks for a few seconds before he spoke.

"He's dead right," he told her. "If we don't present a united front, he won't be able to stay here."

"I know." She folded her hands in her lap and

clenched them, staring at her nails. "I don't want him to have to leave, Donavan, whatever you think."

His broad shoulders lifted and fell in an off-hand gesture. He lit a cigar and stared at its tip. "I shouldn't have lost my head night before last," he said tersely. "It made things worse between us."

She didn't know how to answer that. She picked at one of her fingernails and didn't look up. "It was my fault, too."

"Was it? You didn't seduce me, honey," he drawled.

She sighed heavily. "I'm not on the pill," she said.

He hesitated. "Yes, I know."

"And you…well, you didn't do anything…"

"That's right," he replied. "Keep going."

She cleared her throat, glancing up at him. "You might have made me pregnant."

One corner of his mouth curved gently. "There's an old family christening gown around here somewhere. My great-grandmother made the lace it's edged in. There's a high chair and even a cradle that date back to the first settlers in Jacobsville."

Fay's green eyes softened as they met his. Her cheeks warmed as she looked at him. "I… I have a baptismal set, too. The furniture's all gone. But there's one antique that Great-Aunt Tessie kept—a silver baptismal bowl. I saved it from the auction."

The mention of her deceased relative made his expression become grim. He averted his face and smoked his cigar, still pacing slowly. "You inherited a lot of money," he said. "Can't you keep the furniture, or don't you want it?"

"I have no place for it in my apartment," she said simply.

He spun on his heel, glaring at her. "This is your home. There's no way on earth you're leaving here until I know if you're pregnant."

She started. "It's unlikely…"

"Why? Because it was the first time?" he asked with mocking amusement.

His sophisticated attitude angered her. "Can't we talk about something else?" she asked stiffly.

"Sure." He raised the cigar to his firm lips. He felt optimistic for the first time. She still reacted to him. She couldn't hide the way he affected her. It made him feel proud to realize that she was as helplessly attracted to him as he was to her.

Now, if only her heart was involved…

"Why don't you sleep with me tonight?" he asked sensuously. "After all, one more time isn't going to make much difference now."

"You don't want me to stay here," she said. "I don't want a child who has to grow up without his father."

"I didn't say I didn't want you to stay here," he returned.

"You did so!" she raged, standing. "You said that you didn't want me anymore because my great-aunt died and left me rich again! You let me go to Florida all by myself—"

"Not quite. Henry went with you," he pointed out.

She continued as if he hadn't interrupted "—and then you said I could find somewhere else to live!"

"I didn't say that," he murmured dryly. "Surely not?"

"Yes, you did!"

"That was before I slept with you, of course," he pointed out, letting his eyes punctuate the flat statement. "Now I'm hopelessly addicted."

"Any woman would do," she muttered.

"Not really, or I'd have had a few in the past year or so. I'd all but lost interest in sex until you came along and knocked my legs out from under me."

"A likely story, after the things you did to me night before last…!"

She stopped very suddenly, her hand going to her mouth as she realized what she'd said. She sat down again, hard.

"I had experience, Fay," he said softly.

She flushed. "I noticed!"

"You might consider that those early encounters made your life a little easier."

She stared at her feet, still smoldering. "You did things to me that I never even read in books."

"I'll tell you a secret, honey," he mused, putting out his cigar before he came to kneel between her legs where she sat rigidly on the sofa. He was almost on a level with her shocked eyes as he looked into them. "I've never done with anyone some of those things I did to you. And never could."

"C-couldn't you?" she whispered.

"No." His hands caught her waist and pulled gently, suddenly overbalancing so that she landed breathlessly on his chest. He rolled, pinning her under him on the big throw rug. As he held her eyes, one long leg inserted itself between both of hers and he moved slowly.

"I want you again. Now," he told her, his body screaming it in the intimate embrace. His lean hand smoothed blatantly over her soft breast and then began to slip buttons out of buttonholes.

"But the door…" she began.

"Isn't closed. I know." He slid his hand inside her bodice and under her soft bra, to find even softer flesh. His fingers gently caressed it, and she arched, gasping. "I'm going to carry you to bed now," he breathed. "And I'm going to do all those things I did two nights ago. Right now."

He got to his feet and picked her up, shifting her gently as he carried her down the long hall and into his bedroom. He placed her on the bedspread and went to close and lock the door. Then he stood at the foot of the bed, his black hair half in his eyes, his face devoid of expression, his body blatantly aroused.

She eased up onto her elbows, feeling feminine and hotly desired, her green eyes lost in the glitter of his gray ones. He nodded slowly. And then he moved toward her.

But just as he reached her, bent over her, warmed her mouth with his breath in a deliciously tense bit of provocation—the telephone rang noisily on the bedside table.

Donavan stared at it blankly, as if for a moment he didn't even realize what was making the noise.

Impatiently he jerked up the receiver and spoke into it.

A familiar, sarcastic voice came over the line—
Brad Danner, Jeff's stepfather.

"I'm looking forward to tomorrow, Donavan,"
he told the angry man on the other end of the line.
"If you think that sham marriage is going to make
any difference in a custody suit, you're very wrong."

"It isn't a sham marriage," Donavan said tersely,
without looking at Fay, who was sitting shocked and
disoriented beside him now, on the bed.

"I'll let you prove that tomorrow. Take good care
of my stepson, won't you? I'm looking forward to
having him home again."

"Yes, it would be something of a luxury, wouldn't
it?" Donavan asked icily. "When you stuck him in
military school at his first show of spirit."

"One of you in a family is enough," the other man
replied, obviously straining to keep his temper. "All
my married life, Debbie threw you up to me. Nothing
I did was ever right, ever the same thing *you* would
have done in my place. My God, you don't know
how I hated you!"

"Debbie always had a tendency to romanticize everything," Donavan said curtly. "After Dad died, I
was all she had. As for her opinion of you," he added
with mocking amusement, "I had nothing to do with
it. You were a spineless complainer from day one.
And don't tell me the dowry I gave her wasn't the
real inducement to get you to the altar. You spent half
of it the first week you were married to Debbie—on
your mistress!"

The other receiver slammed down. Donavan slowly replaced his, chuckling with bitter amusement.

"Jeff's would-be guardian," he said, nodding toward the telephone. "He fancies himself a man. Imagine that?"

"He might have loved your sister," she began.

"Really? If he did, why was he involved with another woman before, during and after the marriage? The woman he's married to now, by the way. Debbie's insurance money set them up real well. He made sure that Jeff wasn't mentioned as a beneficiary."

"He sounds very mercenary," she said quietly.

"He thinks he can prove that our marriage is a fraud," he said. His eyes narrowed on her face. "It's imperative that we act like lovers. You understand that?"

She nodded. Her eyes fell to his broad chest, where his shirt was unbuttoned over a thick mat of curling black hair.

"I understand." Her lips parted with helpless hunger, but she lowered her eyes so that he wouldn't see how she felt. "That's why you brought me in here, isn't it, Donavan? So that it would show, in court tomorrow, that we'd been intimate."

He hesitated, but only for an instant. "Yes," he said curtly. "That's right. I wanted to make you look loved, so that I wouldn't risk losing Jeff."

"I see."

Her defeated expression made him wild. "He might run away if he gets sent back, don't you see?

He's high-strung. I can't let that happen. He's all the family I have left in the world, Fay!"

She stood up with a long, gentle sigh. "Funny," she said as she turned. "Once upon a time, I thought I was part of your family. It just goes to show how money can warp you. Being rich must have made me stupid."

He rammed his hands into his pockets. He felt guilty, and he didn't like it. She was rich. She had the world. She didn't need a poor husband and a ready-made family, anyway. Even *if* he wanted her for keeps, which he didn't. He had one scandal to live down. He couldn't take another.

He only hoped he hadn't made her pregnant in that feverish coupling. It would make her life impossible, because he knew he'd never be able to turn his back on his own child. She'd be trapped then, and so would he.

"It's just as well that Brad interrupted us," he said tersely, thinking aloud. "I've been unforgivably careless about taking precautions. It's just as well if we don't take any more risks. I'll see you in the morning, Fay."

It was a dismissal. He looked as unapproachable as a porcupine. Fay couldn't understand why he'd bothered trying to seduce her in the first place. Now he seemed concerned about not making her pregnant. She left him there and went to bed, hurt and bitter and totally confused.

She dressed very carefully for court the next morning, in her off-white suit and leather high heels.

She carried the one designer purse she had left, and wore a very becoming and very expensive spring hat. She looked what she was—a young woman with breeding who'd been raised to be a lady.

Donavan, in his pale gray suit, was openly appreciative of the way she looked. In fact, he could hardly keep his eyes off her.

"You look…lovely," he said.

She managed a cool smile. "Why thank you, darling," she said, playing her part to the hilt. Only her eyes gave the show away, because they were like two green pieces of ice. His hot-cold attitude had worn her out. She was giving up all hope of a happy marriage, but first she was going to help Jeff out of his predicament. It was a matter of honor. She'd given her word.

"Very nice," he replied curtly. "You'll convince anyone who doesn't look at your face too closely."

"I can handle that." She pulled the hat's matching veil down over her nose. "Now. One wife, properly accounted for, ready to go on stage."

He stiffened and turned away, his anger evident and blatant.

Jeff came out of his bedroom in a suit. He looked from Fay to Donavan and grimaced. "Well, I guess I'm as ready as I'll ever be, but I'm sure not looking forward to it."

"Neither are we," Donavan said. "All the more reason to get it over with as soon as possible. Try not to worry," he added gently, placing an affectionate hand on the boy's stooped shoulder. "And stand up straight. Don't let him think he's got you buffaloed."

"Yes, Uncle Don."

He herded Fay and Jeff out to the car and drove them to the county courthouse in a silence filled with worried looks and cigar smoke.

BRAD DANNER WASN'T at all what Fay had expected. He was short and redheaded and looked as if he had a massive ego.

"So you're the brand-new Mrs. J. D. Langley," Brad said mockingly, shaking off the firm hand of a suited man who was probably his attorney. "Well, it won't work. You might as well go back to whichever bar he found you at and throw in your chips. You'll never pull this off. I've got too much on you!"

"Have you indeed?" Fay asked, enjoying herself now. "Actually, Donavan did find me in a bar." She leaned closer. "But I didn't work there."

"Oh, of course not," he agreed amiably, and laughed as he turned back to the bleached blonde with the overlipsticked mouth who was obviously pregnant and almost certainly his wife.

Donavan motioned for Fay to sit down at the table with him. Jeff had already been taken away by a juvenile officer for the course of the hearing.

Formalities had to be observed. Once those were out of the way, Donavan's attorney—an elderly man with keen eyes and alarming dignity—offered Brad's attorney the opportunity to present his case first.

Donavan looked nervous, but Mr. Flores only smiled and winked.

Brad's attorney got up and made a long speech about the things Brad had done for his stepson, most recently having enrolled him in a top-flight educational facility, which would lead him to an admirable career.

"We do concede that Mr. Danner has no blood relationship with the boy, as does Mr. Langley. However, despite his hasty marriage in an attempt to present a stable home environment, Mr. Langley overlooked one small detail. He neglected to keep his new wife close to home."

Fay and Donavan exchanged puzzled glances. The opposing attorney opened his briefcase and dragged out several photographs of Fay with her uncle on the way to Florida, and at Tessie's apartment, where they'd stayed until the funeral was over.

"This is the kind of monkey business the new Mrs. Langley gets up to when her husband's back is turned," the attorney said haughtily, glaring at Fay as if she were a fallen woman. "Hardly a moral example for a young boy!"

Donavan chuckled.

"You find these photographs amusing, Mr. Langley? You had been married for only a matter of days, I believe, when Mrs. Langley and her gentleman friend flew to Florida alone?"

"You aren't from here, are you?" Donavan asked the attorney. "And apparently neither is your private detective."

"He isn't a private detective, he's a friend of mine who used to be in intelligence work during the Korean War," Brad said stiffly. "But you won't lie your way out of this. That man in the photographs is...!"

"...my uncle," Fay said. She glanced at Judge Ridley, who was an old friend of her family—and who was also trying not to break up.

"I'm afraid so," Judge Ridley agreed, wiping the unjudicial smile off his face. "I've known Henry for years."

"If he's her uncle, why doesn't he have the same surname she does?" the other attorney argued.

"Henry is Fay's mother's brother," Judge Ridley explained. "Surely your detective checked?"

"He said Donavan had probably found her at a bar," Brad began.

"Mrs. Langley and her uncle went to Florida to make the final arrangements for Mrs. Langley's great-aunt," Donavan's attorney clarified. "As for your friend's assertion that Mrs. Langley worked in a bar, let me assure you that nothing could be further from the truth. In point of fact, she was a debutante. And now, with the death of her great-aunt, she stands to inherit a large share of the estate."

Brad looked sick.

"I am also reliably told," Judge Ridley interrupted, "by the young boy whose custody is in question, that his uncle and Mrs. Langley have a warm, loving relationship, which gives him a much-needed feeling of security. Your accusation that the marriage is fraudulent hardly concurs with the home life the young man describes."

"He'd do anything to get Jeff, even pretending to be happily married. Ask him if he loves her," he challenged the judge. "Go ahead! He never lies. Make him tell her how he really feels about her!"

Fay stood up. "I know how my husband feels about me, Mr. Danner," she said stiffly. "I also know how you feel about him. Jeff is only a pawn to you. But he's a flesh-and-blood boy to Donavan. They're very happy together. Jeff will get a good education and caring company, and it won't be in a military school where he isn't even allowed weekend visits home more than twice a year! If you wanted him so badly, why send him away in the first place?"

"A good question," the judge agreed. He stared at Brad, who was slowly turning red. "Answer it, please."

"My wife is pregnant," Brad said shortly. "Jeff makes her nervous. Isn't that right, honey?"

"I fail to see why you sought custody, Mr. Danner," the judge persisted.

"Oh, tell him, Bradley," the blonde muttered. She sanded a nail to perfection. "He only wants the insurance money. He's afraid if he loses custody, he'll have to give Jeff his share of it, and he's already spent it."

"You idiot!" Brad raged at his wife.

"What's so terrible about the truth?" she asked with careless unconcern. "You were so scared of your brother-in-law finding out. Well, now he knows.

Big deal. It's only a thousand dollars, anyway. If you hadn't bought that stupid boat, you could have afforded to pay it back."

The courtroom erupted. Before the fur stopped flying, Fay got a glimpse of the real Brad Danner, and she was very sorry for his second wife. By the time Fay and Donavan left the courtroom, with custody of Jeff and the promise of repayment of the insurance money Jeff should have had, Fay's head was whirling.

"Aunt Fay, I'm so relieved!" Jeff laughed, and hugged her impulsively. "I can stay, isn't it radical?"

"Just radical," she agreed happily.

"And you and Uncle Don fooled them all," he added. "Everybody thought you were the most devoted couple anywhere!"

"That was the joke of the century, all right," Fay said quietly, and met Donavan's angry eyes over Jeff's head. "Congratulations. You've got what you wanted."

"Yes," he said. "I've got everything I wanted."

She smiled coolly, grateful for the veil that hid her sadness, and put an affectionate arm around Jeff as they walked toward the car.

Donavan walked a little behind them. He didn't know how he felt exactly, but elated wouldn't have covered it. He was glad to have Jeff with him, of course, but in the process he was certain to lose Fay.

That shouldn't bother him. Fay was rich; he wasn't. Their lifestyles would never mix, and everyone would think that he'd married her for her money.

Hell, they probably thought it already. He laughed at his own folly. Even if he divorced her, they'd say he was after a big cash settlement in return for her freedom. They'd say like father, like son.

Suddenly the public censure that had worried him so much before fell into place. If he knew what his motives were, did it really matter what a few small-minded people thought? It was usually the hypocrites who gossiped, anyway—the people who lived public lives of high morality and private lives of glaring impurity. The few friends he had wouldn't sit in judgment on him. So why was he agonizing over his plight?

He glanced at Fay hungrily. Hell, he wanted her. He'd grown used to having her around the house. He enjoyed watching her stumbling attempts to cook edible meals. He liked the smell of her perfume when he stood close to her, and the way she fussed over him and Jeff, as if it really mattered to her that something might happen to one of them. He liked her, most especially, sliding under his body in bed, giving him her warmth and exquisite sensuality, giving him ecstasy that even in memory could make him weak in the knees. He wanted to stay with her. He wanted a child with her. Was it too late? Had he done too much damage?

"Suppose we stop off at the pizza place and get a supreme to go?" Jeff suggested. "After all, we are celebrating."

"Good idea. We'll give Aunt Fay the night off," Donavan agreed.

"He's just tired of bouncing biscuits and black steak," she told Jeff with a sigh. "I guess one well-cooked meal won't kill us all."

Jeff laughed, but Fay didn't. Now that Donavan had Jeff, she wondered how much time she had left until Donavan wanted her out of his life for good.

CHAPTER TEN

THE PIZZA WAS DELICIOUS. Fay enjoyed it as much as the rest of the family seemed to, but her heart wasn't in the celebration. She wanted to stand up and scream that life was unfair, that she'd been shortchanged all the way around. She'd always had money. But she'd never had love. Now it seemed that she didn't have either. Great-Aunt Tessie's legacy would be nice, but it would hardly allow her to give up her job. With some careful investing, it would grow, as long as she could live on what she made.

She worried about that for the rest of the day, trying to put on a happy face for Jeff. But Donavan saw through it. He joined her on the porch swing while Jeff played with one of three new snow-white puppies in the barn.

"We won," he reminded her as he smoked his cigar. Like her, he'd changed into casual clothes—jeans and a cotton shirt. He propped one booted foot on the swing and glanced down at her. "Aren't you glad?"

"Of course," she said absently. "I know how worried Jeff was."

He stared out over the horizon. "There really

wasn't too much to worry about," he mused. "I had a contact of mine feed his Korean War veteran buddy a few scandalous facts about you and Uncle Henry. It's not my fault the man took it for gospel and didn't double check. His loss, my gain."

"Donavan!" she burst out. "That's devious!"

"That's how I am when people I love get threatened." He looked down at her. "I'll fight under the table, any way at all, to win when someone else's life depends on it. I couldn't let that strutting rooster get Jeff. It wasn't a tug of war with me—it was Jeff's whole life."

"I know he appreciates what you've done for him."

"I don't imagine you do. I'm sorry to have made you look, even temporarily, like a fallen angel. But I had no choice."

"I understood. Even the judge was having a hard time keeping a straight face."

"Where do we go from here, Fay?" he asked solemnly.

She listened to the creak as the wooden swing pulled against the chains rhythmically.

"I'll stay until your brother-in-law is safely back home and over his defeat," she said. "We've already discussed where I'll go."

"No we haven't," he disagreed. "You said you were going to move back to the apartment house and I said you weren't. My God, buy yourself a place, why don't you?"

Her hands clasped together painfully. Didn't he know he was tearing the heart out of her?

"I might, later on."

She wasn't giving an inch. He couldn't tell anything by her voice or her expression.

"You could stay on here," he remarked casually. "There's plenty of room. Jeff likes you. So does Bee."

"I've burned up enough good food already."

"We haven't complained."

She smiled to herself. Amazingly they hadn't. Only three days ago, Jeff had complimented her on one small side dish that was actually fit to eat.

"I might get the hang of it one day."

He studied his boot. "How about getting the hang of making formula and changing dirty diapers?" he asked, his eyes on the horizon.

She hesitated. He sounded…serious. "What do you mean?"

He shrugged. He lifted the cigar to his mouth and took a draw from it, blowing out a large cloud of pungent smoke. "I mean, suppose we stayed married. If you'd let me, I think I could make you pregnant eventually. We could raise a family, give Jeff a stable environment to finish growing up in."

She studied his profile. Nothing there. He looked as formidable as he had the first time she'd ever seen him. Just as handsome, too, she thought wistfully.

He glanced down and saw that wistfulness and one eyebrow went up. He looked at her openly now, from her forehead down to her mouth and back up to her eyes. "You're thinner. I've been cruel to you, Fay. Give me a chance to put things right."

"By making me pregnant?" she asked with pretended lightness.

"If it's what you want, yes. If not, we can put it off for a few years. You're still very young, little one. You might like to go to college or do some traveling before you get tied down with children."

"I've already done my traveling, and I don't want to go to college. I have a nice job already."

"You can resign from that," he said. "You don't need it."

She stared at him for a long moment, until he scowled. "Actually," she confessed, "I'm afraid I do."

"If you just want a way to get out of the house…"

She rested her cool fingers atop the lean hand that was propped on his jean-clad knee. "Donavan, I'm not exactly going to inherit a fortune."

"Yes, I know. Henry said you'll only get about a third, when it's all wrapped up. It doesn't matter," he said doggedly, averting his face. "I don't give a damn what people think anymore. I don't know now why I ever did. I'm not like my father. I married you for Jeff's sake, not because I stood to gain a fortune."

She felt the impact of that statement down to her toes. If only he'd married her for love of her. She sighed, audibly.

He tilted her face up to his. "What a wistful little sound," he said quietly. "You don't like thinking that I only married you for Jeff. You liked it even less when you thought it was for money."

"It doesn't bother me," she lied.

"Sure it does," he countered quietly. "I wanted

you," he said softly. "You knew that already, I imagine."

"Yes."

"You wanted me back. I didn't have to coerce you into my bed. You came willingly."

She flushed and looked down at the lean fingers that slowly wrapped around hers in a close embrace. "It was new and…exciting."

"More than just exciting, I think, little one." His voice was soft, deep, sensual. "I lost you for a few seconds just as I fulfilled you. It made me feel pretty good to know I could give you that much pleasure."

"As you said," she swallowed, "you've had a lot of experience."

"I've had a lot of *bodies*," he said with faint cynicism. "Just that, Fay, a lot of bodies in the dark. I went through the motions and learned the right moves. But it was nothing like what I had with you, even on our wedding night, when my hands were all but tied. I knew then that it was more than physical attraction. But I knew it for certain when I put you on that plane to Florida and let you walk away from me. I didn't sleep all night, for thinking how cruel I'd been. You loved Tessie, and I'd given you no comfort, no support at all. I'm sorry for that. I owed you more than that."

"You owed me nothing," she told him dully. "We got married for Jeff, that's all."

His free hand spread against her soft cheek and lifted her face. "Haven't you been listening to me at all?" he asked softly.

"Yes," she said nervously. "You've got me on your conscience."

"Fay, listen with your heart, not your ears," he replied. He searched her face with eyes that adored it. "Can't you see it? Can't you feel it? Fay, can't you put your mouth on mine and taste it…?"

He pulled her lips under his and kissed her with such tenderness that she felt her body ripple with sheer pleasure.

His tongue probed inside her mouth, increasing the heat, making her moan. While he built the kiss, he lifted and turned her, so that she was lying completely in his arms, pressed close against the heat of his muscular chest.

Unseen, his lean hand eased inside her shirt and began to trace the warm, taut contours of her breast until he made the nipple go hard against his fingers.

He lifted his head minutes later, and looked down at her swollen mouth and dazed eyes before his gaze dropped to the taut nipple so evident under the thin fabric.

"You look as out of control as I feel," he said huskily, his gray eyes pure silver in the daylight. "If we were alone, I wouldn't even bother to strip you. I'd just get the necessary things out of the way and I'd take you like a tornado."

She shivered, pressing her hot face into his throat.

"Want it like that?" he whispered at her ear. "Rough and quick and blazing hot?" He glanced over her head at Jeff, who was sprawled in the aisle of the barn playing with the dogs while one of Donavan's older hands watched him.

Donavan stood up abruptly and put Fay on her feet. Catching the older hand's attention, he indicated that he wanted him to keep an eye on Jeff. The cowhand nodded, grinned and waved. Then Donavan turned back to Fay, his eyes glittery with intent.

"Oh…we can't," she faltered as he came toward her and she began backing toward the screen door. "Surely, you were kidding, with Jeff right outside…!"

"Like hell I was kidding," he whispered against her mouth.

He picked her up and carried her straight into his bedroom, pausing just long enough to lock the door before he backed her up against the waist-high vanity and opened the fastening of her jeans.

She gasped and started to protest, but he had her mouth under his, and she couldn't manage speech. She heard the rasp of another zipper, felt him move, and then her jeans slid off her legs. His tongue went roughly into her mouth, in quick, sharp thrusts that were unbelievably arousing.

He lifted her sharply and she felt him suddenly in an intimacy that took her breath. He half lifted her from the vanity, his body levering between her legs while he invaded her with urgent, exquisite mastery. She clung to his neck, feeling the force of his desire with faint awe as she experienced for the first time the unbridled violence of passion.

He wasn't tender, or particularly gentle, but the pleasure that convulsed her was beyond anything he'd given her before. She heard him cry out and felt him tense, then he was heavy in her arms, damp with sweat, trembling faintly from the strength he'd had to exert in the uncomfortable position.

"I like the noises that boil out of you when we make love," he said roughly. "You excite me."

"I can't stop shaking." She laughed shyly.

"Neither can I. We went high this time."

"Yes. Oh, yes!"

He drew back, finally, and looked at her. His face was solemn, his eyes quiet and gentle. He brushed back her damp hair and smiled. "That will have to last us until tonight," he whispered. "Think you can manage?"

"If you can," she teased. His eyes were telling her impossible things, too wonderful for reality. "Am I dreaming?" she asked.

"No, sweetheart. Not at all."

He lifted her, separating his body from hers, and grinned wickedly when she flushed.

"You needn't look so shocked," he chided as he rearranged his own clothing. "Five minutes ago you wouldn't have noticed if we were lying under a table in a restaurant."

"Neither would you!" she accused.

He drew her close and kissed her gently. "That's a fact," he whispered. "God, I love you, Fay."

She stiffened. She couldn't have heard that. She opened her eyes, very wide, and stared at him.

"I haven't given you much reason to believe it, but it's true just the same," he told her quietly. "You're all I want, you and Jeff and however many kids we can have together. If we can't have any, then you and Jeff will more than suffice."

"How long?" she asked gently, desperate now to believe him.

"Since the very first night we met," he replied. "I fought it. God, I did! But in the end, I couldn't do without you. After I made love to you, even light love, I was lost. I knew I'd never be able to let you go."

"Then I inherited Tessie's money," she began.

"I told you. It doesn't matter. I love you. Do whatever you like with your inheritance."

"In that case," she murmured, "I'll put it in the bank for Jeff's education. It should just about cover college."

"Where are we sending him to college—the Waldorf Astoria?"

She smiled warmly, convinced at last that she was awake and aware. "I only inherit part of the proceeds from the sale of her furniture," she told him, and proceeded to explain where the rest of the money was going.

He was surprised, and frankly pleased, that Fay's inheritance wouldn't amount to very much. "She must have been some kind of lady," he remarked.

"She was. A very special one. My share will just about pay for Jeff's college. Now you know why I wouldn't give up my job. I couldn't afford to."

"Just as well the Ballengers made one for you," he murmured. He sighed heavily. "I guess this means that I'll have to start being, ugh, nice to Calhoun."

"That wouldn't hurt," she agreed.

"And your uncle," he added irritably.

"Also a nice touch."

He searched her eyes. "I won't reform completely. You know that. I'm exactly what you see. I won't change."

"Neither will I," she replied. "I might get a little rounder eventually, and have a few gray hairs."

"That's okay," he said pleasantly. "I might do that myself." He pulled her closer. "Fay, I'll never be a rich man. But I'll love you, and take care of you when you need it. If we have nothing else, we'll have each other."

She had to fight tears at the tenderness in his deep voice. She kissed him and then reached up and locked her arms gently around his neck. "I haven't said it," she whispered.

"You said it the night you gave yourself to me completely," he replied, surprised. "Don't you remember? You said it over and over again while you were trembling in my arms at the last."

"I must have been half out of my mind. Loving you does that to me," she whispered with her heart in her eyes.

"And to me," he replied. He bent, fusing her mouth with his in a slow, sweet expression of love.

"Uncle Don!" came a loud voice from below the window.

Donavan groaned. "What now?"

He opened the window and looked down. Jeff was

waiting with two of Donavan's foreman's sons, both of whom were carrying fishing poles and tackle boxes.

"Please?" he pleaded with his uncle. "I haven't gotten to go fishing since the last time you took me. I'll bring home supper, honest, can I?"

"Go ahead." Donavan chuckled. "But you'd better bring home supper."

"We'll make sure he does, sir!" one of the older boys called. "Even if we have to swim under his line and hook the fish on it ourselves."

"Thanks!" Jeff laughed.

The boys were out of sight in no time. Donavan closed the window and took the phone off the hook. He moved toward her with a wicked smile.

"Sometimes," he told a breathlessly excited Fay as he began to caress her out of her clothing, "fate can be kind."

A sentiment that Fay would gladly have echoed, except that Donavan's mouth was hard over her own, and seconds later, she was in no condition to think at all...

THE NEXT MORNING, Fay was hard at work when Donavan showed up unexpectedly at the feedlot.

Calhoun, just coming out of his office, grimaced.

"No need to rush, finding excuses to get out of the office right away," Donavan drawled. "I'm reformed. I didn't come to complain. I actually dropped by to see about moving in some more cattle."

Calhoun's eyebrows went up. "You don't say!"

"I just did. While I'm about it, I might add a word

of thanks about keeping my wife on," he added ruefully. "We figure her inheritance from her great-aunt
will just about put one kid through college. Since we
plan on more than our nephew taking up residence,
every penny is going to count."

"We like the job Fay does. But it's tough luck,"
Calhoun ventured, "about the inheritance."

Donavan smiled lazily. "Not in my book. I like the
idea of working toward something." He glanced at
Fay with his heart in his eyes. "Struggling together
brings two people close."

"Indeed it does," Fay agreed with a sigh.

"If you'd like to take your wife to lunch, we might
be able to let her off a little early," Calhoun said.

"I was hoping you'd say that," Donavan said and
grinned.

He took Fay to the local hamburger joint and they
ate cheeseburgers and drank milkshakes until they
were pretty well stuffed.

"You won't have an easy life with me," he said
when they were outside again. He paused, catching
her hand in his to stop and look down at her. "You'll
probably always have to work. I can take some of
the burden off you at home, because I can cook and
do dishes and sweep. But when the kids come along,
things could get pretty hectic."

"Am I worried?" she asked, smiling. "Am I complaining? I've got you. I don't need promises, as-
surances or anything else. I'm happier than I ever
dreamed of being."

"Are you sure?" he asked, and looked worried. "You've always had everything you wanted."

"I still do."

"You know what I mean," he said irritably.

"Yes. Money was nice, but it wasn't particularly easy to cuddle up to. I don't mind living like ordinary working people. In fact," she said honestly, "I really like the challenge. It's nice to feel independent, and to know that you're earning what you have. I never had to earn anything before."

"You're giving me a lot to live up to, honey," he said quietly. "I hope I won't let you down. I'm not the easiest man to live with."

"Yes, you are," she replied. She put her arms around him and pressed close. "As long as I'm holding you, you're the easiest man in the world to get along with. So suppose I just never let go?"

He laughed and let out his breath in a long, contented sigh as he pulled her close and returned the gentle embrace. "I'll tell you something, sweetheart," he murmured contentedly. "That suits me just fine!"

And she never did.

* * * * *

EMMETT

CHAPTER ONE

THE OFFICE WAS in chaos. Melody Cartman eyed the window ledge with keen speculation and wondered if standing out there might get her a few minutes' reprieve. She glanced toward her newly married third cousin, Logan Deverell, and his beaming wife, Kit, and decided that she couldn't spoil their honeymoon.

"You'll cope," Kit promised in a whisper. "Just tell everyone he'll be back in touch with them next week and that Tom Walker is handling all his accounts until he returns."

"Has he told Mr. Walker that?" Melody asked, acutely aware of Mr. Walker's temper. Tom had started out in New York City, but circumstances had brought him to Houston. Texas, he'd once said, reminded him a little of his native South Dakota. Melody had often wondered if he'd been brought up by a mountain lion there, because on occasion he could give a pretty good imitation of one.

"Honest." Kit put her hand over her heart. "I swear Logan spoke to him first this time. I heard him with my own ears."

"That's all right then. Honestly he seemed like such a nice man when I first met him. But I took

him that client of Mr. Deverell's and found him involved in giving another client the bum's rush out the
door. Our client and the other client both ran for it,
and I was left to face the music. He never used a bad
word or the same word twice, but I was three inches
shorter when I escaped from his office."

"Logan is your third cousin. Can't you call him
Logan?"

Melody glanced toward the big, dark man on the
telephone in his office. "Not without a head start,"
she said finally.

"Anyway, he didn't volunteer Tom without mentioning it to him this time, so you won't get your
ears burned. Think you can handle everything for
a week?"

"If I can't cope by now, I'll never be able to," Melody said, and her brave smile made her look almost
pretty. She was a tall woman, very country-looking
in some ways, with freckles and a softly rounded
face that was framed by long, blond-streaked light
brown hair. Her eyes were brown, with tiny flecks
of gold in them. If she took the time, she could look
very attractive, Kit thought. But Melody wore jump-
ers with long-sleeved blouses, or tailored suits, and
always in colors that were much better suited to the
coloring of someone with dark hair and an equally
dark complexion.

"You'd like Tom if you got to know him," Kit told
her. "He knocked that man out the door for some
pretty blatant sexual harassment of his secretary.
He's only bad tempered when he needs to be, and

he's all alone except for a married sister back home and a nephew. He doesn't even go out with women."

"I can see why…!"

"Not nice," Kit chided. "He's a good-looking, intelligent man, and he's rich."

"I can think of at least one ax murderer with the same description. I read about him in there." She gestured toward one of the supermarket tabloids.

Kit's eyes fell to the tabloid on Melody's desk, its cover carrying color photos of a particularly gruesome murder. "Do you actually read this stuff?" Kit asked with a grimace. "These photos are terrible!"

"I thought you were a detective," Melody said. "Aren't detectives supposed to be used to stuff like that?"

Kit smiled sheepishly. "Well, I don't detect those sort of cases."

"I don't blame you. Actually I didn't buy it for the grisly pictures. I bought it for this nifty reducing diet. Doesn't it look interesting? You don't give up any foods, you simply cut down and cut out sweets."

"You aren't fat, Melody," the other woman pointed out.

"No, I'm just big. I do wish I were slender and willowy," she said wistfully.

"There isn't a thing wrong with the way you are."

"That's what you think! Actually I—"

A sudden commotion in the hall cut her off. She and Kit turned just as Emmett Deverell and his three children walked in. The kids were wearing

costumes left over from their Thanksgiving Day play
last month—Indian costumes.

Guy, the eldest, stood beside his father and glared
at Melody. But Amy and Polk, the younger kids,
made a beeline for their favorite person in the office.

"Hi, Kit!" they said in unison. "Hello, Melody.
Can we sit and watch TV with you for a while?"

"Please?" Amy ventured, looking up at Melody
with eyes that were the same shade of green as her
father's. "We'll be ever so good. Emmett has to get
our airplane tickets and Polk and I don't want to go to
the airport. We got to be in the parade in the rodeo!"

"You all look very nice," Melody told them.

Guy ignored her.

Polk had already turned on the TV and was staring at the screen. "Aw, gee, Big Bird isn't on right
now, Amy," he said miserably.

Melody glanced at the kids, noticing again how
much they all favored their father. Guy came clos-
est. He was tall, too, with a lean face and dark hair.
Amy looked a lot like her mother, Adell, except for
those green eyes. All the kids had them.

The last time Emmett had been in the office, he'd
savaged Melody. The San Antonio rancher hated her
and made no secret of the fact. He didn't approve of
her working for Logan, who was a relative of his as
well, but by blood, not marriage, as Melody was.
Melody had had several days to remember and burn
over his attitude. She was through being intimidated
by him. He might be almost a generation older than

she was, but he wasn't going to walk on her feelings anymore.

"Amy and Polk want to stay with you while I go to the airport," Emmett said icily. He didn't mention leaving Guy, because Guy disliked Melody as much as Emmett did.

Melody cocked an eyebrow, and tried to stay calm. She was melting with fear inside, but she wasn't going to let him know it. "Am I being asked?" she replied formally.

Emmett's pale green eyes glittered at her. "Yes, if you want the whole ten yards."

"In that case, Amy and Polk are welcome to watch TV while you're gone," she said, triumphant with her small victory.

Emmett didn't like the challenge in her dark eyes, or that tiny smirk. If those kids hadn't been giving him hell all morning, he wouldn't even be here. He was surly with bad temper.

"You won't help them run away or anything?" he asked, with a sarcastic, pointed reference to her part in his ex-wife Adell's sudden departure with Melody's brother, Randy.

He wasn't going to do that to her, she promised herself. She wasn't going to let him play on her conscience. Her eyes settled on the tabloid and it triggered a memory; something Kit had elaborated on since her return from Emmett's house in San Antonio. She smiled sweetly and picked up the tabloid. "Have you seen the latest on that ax murder, Mr.

Deverell?" she asked, and stuck the gory front page under his arrogant nose.

He turned green instantly. "Damn you…!" He choked before his mad dash to the restroom.

Melody and Polk and Amy and Kit chuckled helplessly. Guy glared at them and walked out to find his father.

"He has a stomach of glass," Melody pronounced, recalling Kit's revelations about how easily Emmett could be made ill with even talk of gory things. Amazing, for a rancher who was also something of a rodeo star. It was one of many paradoxes about Emmett that would have fascinated a less prejudiced woman. She took the paper and stuck it into her purse. She could use it as a talisman against future attack by Emmett. "Make yourselves comfortable, kids," she told Amy and Polk.

"That was a dirty trick." Kit laughed.

"He deserved it. Nasty, arrogant beast," she muttered, glaring at the door into the hall as if he were hiding there waiting to pounce. "If he can't take it, he shouldn't dish it out."

Kit was trying not to laugh too hard. Logan joined them, affectionately slipping an arm around his wife. "If we can't dish what out?"

"Melody made Emmett sick," Amy volunteered. "Look what's on educational television, Melody! It's Reading Rainbow!"

"Good, good," Melody said absently.

"How did you make Emmett sick?" Logan asked curiously.

"Never mind. We women have to have our secret weapons, especially when it comes to people like your cousin Emmett," Kit told him. "Melody, I've given you a number where we can be reached if you need to contact us."

"I'll only use it if there's an emergency," Melody promised.

Kit smiled at her. "I know that."

"And don't let Tom give you fits," Logan told her. "He's not a bad man. It was my fault. I should have told him he was being volunteered to handle my clients that afternoon, but I was in a rush to get married."

"I remember." Melody chuckled. "It's okay. I'll manage."

"If you can't, you might turn those kids loose on him," Logan suggested.

"Don't give her any ideas. We have to leave, right now," Kit said mirthfully, tugging at her husband's arm. "Take care, Melody."

"Yes, and don't let my cousin walk on you," Logan added. "You're my secretary, not his paid babysitter. Keep that in mind."

"I will."

"So long."

They walked out the door just as a pale, subdued Emmett was coming back in with Guy at his heels.

"That wasn't fair," Guy said angrily, glaring at Melody.

"You kids did it to him," she pointed out. "Kit told me all about it."

"We're family. You're not!"

"Yes, she is," Amy argued. "She's our aunt. Isn't that right, Emmett?"

He looked even worse. "I'll be back for Amy and Polk about three o'clock," he said without answering the question.

"But isn't she our aunt?" Amy persisted.

"She's our stepaunt," Polk told her.

"Oh." She was satisfied and went back to watching TV. "Do take care of Emmett, Guy, and don't let him get run over by any buses."

"I don't need taking care of," Emmett muttered. "But she might," he added with a glare at Melody.

"Watch it," Logan advised sotto voce. "She slipped that tabloid into her purse."

"Turncoat!" Kit gasped, hitting her husband's shoulder.

"We men have to stick together," Logan told her, chuckling. "In today's world, there's nothing more endangered than a male. Any day now, the women's lib movement will start passing out hit lists and organizing death squads to wipe out men."

"Wouldn't surprise me." Emmett sighed. "The way it looks, we're evolving into an Amazon society where men will be used to procreate the species and then efficiently be put to death."

Melody eyed Emmett. "What an interesting idea."

"Shame on you!" Kit chuckled. "Honestly, the radicals just get all the publicity. Most women's libbers just want a fair shake—equal pay and equal rights. What's so terrible about that?"

"And there are men who are just as prejudiced against women." Logan drew Kit close. "Haven't you ever heard of the battle of the sexes? It's been around since time began. It's just getting better press."

"I suppose so." Melody sighed. "Maybe men aren't endangered after all."

"Thank you," Emmett said tersely. "I'm glad to know that I won't have to stand guard at my front door to ward off women death squads."

"Oh, I wouldn't go that far," Melody advised.

"Wouldn't you?" Emmett muttered. "And I thought you were a little shrinking violet."

"More like a Venus flytrap, actually," she replied brightly. "I thought you were going to the airport to get tickets home?"

"Notice how much enthusiasm she put into that question?" Logan asked with pure relish. "And you said women wouldn't leave you alone. This must be refreshing for you."

Emmett didn't look refreshed. He looked as if he might explode momentarily. "Let's go, Guy. Have a nice honeymoon, you two," he added to Logan and Kit. "I don't think much of marriage, but good luck anyway."

"Our mama ran off and left him," Amy volunteered. "Emmett doesn't want to marry anybody."

"But he must," Polk said with a serious frown. "Isn't he always bringing those real glittery, pretty ladies home?"

"Don't be silly," Guy said urbanely. "Those are good-time girls. You don't marry them."

"What's a good-time girl?" Amy asked.

"Just the same as a good-time boy, only shorter," Melody said with icy delight, and she smiled at Emmett.

He went two shades darker.

"Time to go," Kit said quickly. "Emmett, can we give you a lift? We're going straight to the airport."

"Yes," Logan said, taking his tall cousin's muscular arm in a big hand. "Come along, Guy. See you in a week, Melody. If you have any problems, call me. And if you could check on Tansy in the hospital, I'd appreciate it. Chris is watching out for her, but you can't have too many observers where my mother is concerned."

"Certainly I will," Melody agreed. "I don't have much to do in the evenings, anyway."

"I didn't think there would be a man that brave," Emmett agreed.

Melody reached for her purse. Emmett spared her a glance that promised retribution before he made a quick exit with the others.

THE CHAOS BEGAN to calm with Logan's exit. The telephones rang for an hour or two. After that, there were only a few calls and two clients who came in person to ask about their investments. Melody had the figures. It was only a matter of pulling them up—her boss had given her permission before he left—and showing them to the visitors.

The kids were amazingly good. They watched educational programming without a peep, except to ask for change for the soft drink machine. Melody gave it to them and then listened worriedly for sounds of the machine being mugged. Fortunately there was no such noise, and she settled down to the first peace she'd had all day.

She managed to clear her desk of work before Emmett showed up, late, to pick up the kids.

"Aw, do we have to go?" Polk groaned. "Mr. Rogers is coming on!"

"Yes, we have to go. We're leaving for home in the morning, thank God. Only one more event to go tonight—bareback bronc riding."

"Isn't that one of the most dangerous events?" Melody asked.

His eyebrows arched under the wide-brimmed Stetson he hadn't bothered to remove from his dark hair. "Any rodeo event is dangerous if a contestant is stupid or careless. I'm neither."

She knew that already. He was something of a legend in rodeo. He wouldn't be aware that she'd followed his career. She was a rodeo fan, but Emmett's attitude toward her had kept her silent about her interest in the sport.

"Thank you for letting us stay with you, Melody," Amy said, smiling up at her.

Melody smiled back. She liked the little girl very much. She was open and warm and loving, despite her mischievous nature.

Emmett saw that smile and felt it all the way to his toes. He couldn't have imagined even a minute before that a smile could change a plain face and make it radiate beauty. But he saw the reality of it in Melody's soft features. Involuntarily his eyes fell to her body. She was what a kind man would call voluptuous, her form and shape perfectly proportioned but just a tad past slender. Adell had been bacon-thin. Melody was her exact opposite.

It irritated him that he should notice Melody in that way. She was nothing to him except a turncoat. She and her brother had disrupted and destroyed his life. Not only his, but his children's, as well. He could easily have hated her for that.

"I said, let's go," he told the children.

"Okay." Polk sighed.

"I'll wait in the hall," Guy murmured. He avoided even looking at Melody.

"Guy hates you," Amy told her with blunt honesty. "But I think you're wonderful."

"I think you're wonderful, too," Melody replied.

Amy grinned and walked up to her father. "We can go now, Emmett. Can I write to my friend Melody?"

"We'll talk about it," Emmett said noncommittally. "Thanks for watching them," he said as an afterthought.

"Oh, it was my plea…sure!" She tripped over a tomahawk that someone had left lying on the floor and ended up on her back. Guy picked up the weapon, and the kids and Emmett made a circle around her prone body. She glared up at them, trying not to think how a sacrificial victim in an Indian encampment might have felt. In those Indian costumes, the kids looked eerie.

"Whose tomahawk?" Emmett asked as he reached down and pulled Melody up with a minimum of strain. His hand made hers tingle. She wondered if he'd felt the excitement of the contact, too, because he certainly let go of her fast.

"It's mine, Emmett," Amy said, sighing. She looked up at him, pushing back her pigtails, and her green eyes were resigned. "Go ahead and hit me. I didn't mean to make Melody hurt herself, though. I like her."

"I know you didn't mean it," Melody said, and smiled. "It's okay, nothing dented."

"Next time, be more careful where you put that thing," Emmett muttered.

"That's right, Amy," Melody said, nodding. "Between your father's ears would be a good place."

He glared at her. "You didn't hear that, Amy. Let's go, kids."

He herded the children out the door and closed it. Melody sat by herself with no ringing phones, no blaring television, no laughing children. Her life and the office were suddenly empty.

SHE CLOSED UP precisely at 5:00 p.m. and went by the grocery store to get enough for the weekend, which was just beginning. Thanksgiving Day had been quiet and lonely. She'd had a turkey breast, but she and Alistair had finished it off for supper the night before. So she bought ground beef for hamburgers and a small beef roast and vegetables to make stew and, later, soup. She lived on a budget, which meant that she bypassed steak and frozen éclairs. She would have loved to indulge her taste for both. Maybe someday, she thought wistfully...

She fed Alistair, her big marmalade tabby, and then made herself a light supper. She ate it with little enthusiasm. Then she curled up with Alistair on the sofa to watch a movie on television. During the last scene, a very interesting standoff between a murderer and the police, the telephone started ringing. She grimaced, hating the interruption. If she answered it, she'd surely miss the end of the movie she'd been watching for two hours. She ignored it at first. The only people who ever telephoned her were people who were selling things. But whoever was calling wouldn't give up. It stopped, briefly, only to start ringing insistently again. This time she was afraid not to answer it. It might be Kit or Logan or Tansy or even her brother.

She picked up the receiver. "Hello?"

"Is this Miss Melody Cartman?" a crisp, professional voice asked.

"Yes."

"I'm Nurse Willoughby. We have a Mr. Emmett Deverell here at city general hospital with a massive concussion. He's only just regained consciousness. He gave us your name and asked us to call and have you pick up his children at the Mellenger Hotel."

Melody stood frozen in place. The only thing that registered was that Emmett was hurt and she'd become a babysitter. She could hardly say no or argue. Concussions were terribly dangerous.

"The children are…where?"

"At the Mellenger Hotel. Room three hundred and something. He's very foggy at the moment and in a great deal of pain."

"He will be all right?" Melody asked, hating herself for being concerned.

"We hope so," came the crisp reply.

"Tell him that I'll look after the children," she said.

"Very well."

The phone went dead before she could ask another question. She stared around her like someone in a trance. Where in the world was she going to put three renegade children, one of whom hated her? And how long was she going to have them?

For one insane moment, she thought about calling Adell and Randy, but she dismissed that idea at once. Emmett would never forgive her. At the moment, he deserved a little consideration, she supposed.

She got her coat and took a cab to the hotel. It was very late to be driving around Houston, and her little car was unreliable in wet weather. Houston was notorious for flooding, and the rain was coming down steadily now.

She asked at the desk for Emmett's room number, quickly explaining the circumstances to a sympathetic desk clerk after giving Emmett's condition and the hospital's number, so that management could check her story if they felt the need to. In fact, they did, and she didn't blame them. These days, one simply couldn't turn over three children to a total stranger who might or might not intend them harm.

When she got to the hotel room, there were muffled sounds from within. Melody, who knew the kids all too well, knocked briefly but firmly on the door.

There was a sudden silence, followed by a scuffle and a wail. The door flew open and a matronly lady with frazzled hair almost fell on Melody with relief.

"Are you their mother?" the elderly woman asked. "I'm Mrs. Johnson. Here they are, safe and sound, my fee will be added to the hotel bill. You are their mother?"

"Well, no," she began.

"Oh, my God!"

"I'm to take charge of them," Melody added, because it looked as if the woman might be preparing to have a heart attack on the spot.

A wavery smile replaced the horror on the woman's lined face. "Then I'll just be off. Good night!"

"Chicken," Amy muttered, peering around Melody to watch the woman's incredibly fast retreat.

"What have you three been up to?" Melody asked, glaring at them.

"Nothing at all, Melody, dear," Amy said sweetly, and grinned.

"She just wasn't used to kids, I guess," Polk added. He grinned, too.

Behind them there were the remains of two foam-filled pillows and what appeared to be the ropes that closed the heavy curtains.

"We had a pillow fight," Amy explained.

"And then we went skiing in the bathroom," Polk said.

Melody could barely see the bathroom. The door was ajar and the floor seemed to be soaked. She was beginning to understand her predecessor's agile retreat. Days and days…of this. She wouldn't have an apartment left! And all because she felt sorry for a man who had to be her worst enemy.

"Why are you here?" Guy asked belligerently. "Where's Dad?"

That brought her back to her original purpose for being there. Emmett's accident.

She sat down on the sofa, tossing her purse beside her, while she struggled to find the right words to tell them.

"Something's happened," Guy said when he saw her face. He stiffened. "What?"

Even at such a young age, he was already showing signs of great inner strength, of ability to cope with whatever life threw at him. Amy and Polk looked suddenly vulnerable, but not Guy.

"Your father has a brain concussion," Melody told them. "He's conscious now, but in a lot of pain. He'll have to stay in the hospital for a day or so. Meanwhile, he wants you to come home with me."

"He hates you," Guy said coldly. "Why would he want us to stay with you?"

"Because I'm all you've got," Melody replied. "Unless you'd rather I called the juvenile authorities…?"

Guy's massive self-confidence failed. He shrugged and turned away.

Amy climbed onto Melody's lap and clung. "Our daddy will be all right, won't he?" she asked tearfully.

"Of course he will," Melody assured her, gathering her close. "He's very tough. It will take more than a concussion to keep him down."

"Yes, it will," Polk said. He turned away because his lower lip was trembling.

"Let's get your things together and go," Melody said. "Have you had something to eat?"

"We had pizza and chocolate sundaes."

Melody could imagine that the elderly lady in charge of them had agreed with any menu that would keep them quiet. But she'd have to get some decent food into them. That would give her something to work toward. Meanwhile, she found herself actually worrying about Emmett. The first thing she was going to do when they got to the apartment was phone the hospital and get an update. Surely Emmett was indestructible, wasn't he?

She looked at the children and felt a surge of pity for them. She knew how it felt to be alone. When their parents had died, Randy had worked at two jobs to support them, while Melody was still in school. She'd carried her share of the load, but it had been lonely for both of them. She hoped these children wouldn't have the same ordeal to face that she and Randy had.

CHAPTER TWO

THE NURSE ON duty in Emmett's ward told Melody that Emmett would have to be confined for at least two days. He was barely conscious, but they were cautiously optimistic about his condition.

Melody was assured that she and the children would be allowed to see him the next day, during visiting hours. In the meantime, she scoured her apartment to find enough blankets and pillows for three sleepy children. She put two of them in her bed, and one of them on a cot that had belonged to Randy when he was a boy. She slept on her own pull-out sofa bed, and was delighted to find that it wasn't terribly uncomfortable.

It was fortunate that she had the weekend to look after the children. Having to juggle them, along with her job, would have been a real headache. She'd have coped. But how?

They had a change of clothing. Getting them to change, though, was the trick.

"This isn't dirty—" Guy indicated a shirt limp and dingy and smelly from long wear "—and I won't change it."

"I'm all right, too," Polk said, grinning at her.

"We're fine, Melody," Amy agreed. She patted the woman's hand in a most patronizing way. "Now, you just get dressed yourself and don't worry about us, all right?"

Melody counted to ten. "We're going to see your father," she said calmly. "Don't you want him to think you look nice?"

"Oh, Emmett never notices unless we go naked, Melody," Amy assured her.

"And sometimes not even then," Polk said with a chuckle. "Dad's very absentminded when he's rodeoing."

"He sure doesn't seem to notice what the three of you get up to," she said quietly.

"We like our dad just the way he is," Guy said belligerently. "Nobody bad-mouths our dad."

"I wasn't bad-mouthing him," Melody said through her teeth. "Can we just go to the hospital now?"

"Sure," Guy said, folding his thin arms over his chest. "But I'm not changing clothes."

She threw up her hands. "Oh, all right," she muttered. "Have it your way. But if your clothes set off the sprinkler system, I'm climbing into a broom closet so nobody will know who brought you."

AT THE HOSPITAL, Melody herded them off the elevator and down the hall to the nurses' station.

"Look at all the gadgets." Polk whistled, peering over the counter at the computers. "Wouldn't I love to play with that!"

"Bite your tongue," Melody said under her breath.

She smiled at an approaching nurse. "I'm Melody Cartman. You have an Emmett Deverell on this floor with a concussion...?"

A loud roar, followed by, "You're not putting that damned thing under me!" caught their attention.

"Indeed we do," the nurse told Melody. "Are you a concerned relative anxious to transfer him to another hospital?" she added hopefully.

"I'm afraid not," Melody said. "These are his children and they want to see him very much."

"Do you have him tied up in one of those white things?" Amy asked.

"No," the nurse said with a wistful sigh. She turned. "Come on, I'll take you down to his room. Perhaps a diversion will improve his mood."

"I really wouldn't count on it," Melody replied.

"I was afraid you were going to say that. Here we are."

"Dad!" Guy exclaimed, running to his father as a practical nurse laid down a trail of fire getting out the door. "How are you?"

Emmett stared at his eldest blankly. His pale green eyes were bloodshot. His dark hair was disheveled. There was a huge bump on his forehead with stitches and red antiseptic lacing it. He was wearing a white patterned hospital gown and looking as if he'd like to eat half the staff raw.

"It's almost noon," he informed Melody. "Where in hell have you been? Get me out of here!"

"Don't worry, Dad, we'll spring you," Guy promised, with a wary glance toward the nurse.

"You can't leave today, Mr. Deverell," the young nurse said apologetically. "Dr. Miller said that you must stay for at least forty-eight hours. You've had a very severe concussion. You can't go walking around the streets like that. It's very dangerous."

Emmett glared at her. "I hate it here!"

The nurse looked as if she might bite through her tongue trying not to reply in kind. She forced a smile. "I'm sure you do. But you can't leave yet. I'll leave you to visit with your family. I'm sure you're glad to see your wife and children."

"She's not the hell my wife!" Emmett raged. "I'd rather marry a pit viper!"

"I assure you that the feeling is mutual," Melody said to the nurse.

The woman leaned close on her way out the door. "Dr. Miller escaped. When he comes back, I'll beg on my knees for sedation for Mr. Deverell. I swear."

"God bless you," Melody said fervently.

"What are you mumbling about?" Emmett demanded when the nurse left. "And why haven't these kids changed clothes? They smell of pizza and dirt!"

"They wouldn't change," she said defensively.

"You're bigger than they are," he pointed out. "Make them."

She glanced at the kids and shook her head. "Not me, mister. I know when I'm outnumbered. I'm not going to end my days tied to a post imitating barbecue."

"They don't burn people at the stake," he said with

exaggerated patience. "That was just gossip about that lady motorist they kidnapped."

"That's right," Polk said. "Gossip."

"Anyway, she got loose before she was very singed." Amy sighed.

Melody gave Emmett a speaking look. It was totally wasted.

"Are you really okay?" Guy asked his father. He, of the three children, was the most worried. He was the oldest. He understood better than they did how serious his father's injury could have been.

"I'm okay," Emmett said. His voice was different when he spoke to the children; it was softer, more tender. He smiled at Guy, and Melody couldn't remember ever being on the receiving end of such a smile. "How about you kids?"

"We're fine," Amy told him. "Melody has a very nice apartment, Emmett. We like it there."

"She has a cat," Polk added. "He's a big orange tabby named Alistair."

"Alistair?" Emmett mused.

"He was a very ordinary-looking cat," Melody said defensively. "The least he deserved was a nice name."

He leaned back against his pillows and closed his eyes. "Saints deliver us."

"I don't think the saints like you very much, Mr. Deverell, on present evidence," she couldn't resist saying.

One bloodshot pale green eye opened. "The saints didn't do this to me. It was a horse. A very nasty-tempered horse whose only purpose in life is to maim poor stupid cowboys who are dim enough to get on him. I let myself get distracted and I came off like a loose hat."

She smiled gently at the description. "I'm sure the horse is crying his eyes out with guilt."

The smile changed her. He liked what he saw. She was vulnerable when her eyes twinkled like that. He opened the other eye, too, and for one long moment they just looked at each other. Melody felt warning bells go off in her head.

"When can you come home, Emmett?" Amy asked, her big eyes on her father.

He blinked and looked down at her. "Two days they said," he replied. "God, I'm sorry about this!" He glanced toward Melody. "I had no right to involve you in my problems."

That sounded like a wholesale apology. Perhaps the head injury had erased his memory so that he'd forgotten her part in Adell's escape.

"I don't mind watching the children for you," she said hesitantly. She pushed back her hair with a nervous hand. "They're no trouble."

"Of course not, they were asleep all night," he replied. "Don't let them out of your sight."

"Aw, Dad," Polk grumbled. "We'll be good."

"Sure we will," Guy said. He glanced at Melody irritably. "If we have to."

"It's only for a day or two," Emmett said. He was feeling foggier by the minute. "I'll reimburse you, of course," he told Melody. He touched his head with an unsteady hand. "God, my head hurts!"

"I guess it does," Melody said gently. She moved closer to the bed, concerned. "Shall I call the nurse?"

"They won't give me anything until the doctor authorizes it, and he's in hiding," he said. His eyes closed. "Can't say I blame him. I was pretty unhappy about being here."

"I noticed."

He managed a weak chuckle. "If Logan had been at home, you wouldn't be landed with those kids…"

He was asleep.

"Is he going to be okay?" Amy asked. She was chewing her lower lip, looking very young and worried.

Melody smoothed back her hair. "Yes, he'll be fine," she assured the girl. "Come on. We'll go home and I'll make lunch for all of you."

"I want a hot dog," Polk said. "So does Amy."

"I hate hot dogs," Guy replied. "I don't want to stay with you. I'll stay here with Dad."

"You aren't allowed to," Melody pointed out.

He took an angry breath.

"I don't like it any more than you do," she murmured. "But we're stuck with each other. We'd better go."

They followed her out, reluctantly. She stopped long enough to assure the nurse at the desk that she'd bring the kids back the next day to visit their father. She was concerned enough to ask if it was natural for

Emmett to go to sleep, and was told that the doctor would check to make sure he was all right.

GUY'S DISLIKE OF Melody extended to her apartment, her cat, her furniture and especially her cooking.

"I won't eat that," he said forcefully when she put hot dogs and buns and condiments on the table. "I'll starve first."

She knew that it would give him the upper hand if she stooped to arguing with him, so she didn't. "Suit yourself. But we'll have ice cream for dessert and you won't. It's a house rule that you don't get dessert if you don't eat the main course."

"I hate ice cream," he said triumphantly.

"No, he doesn't," Amy said sadly. "He just doesn't like you. He thinks you took our mom away. She won't even write to us or talk to us on the telephone."

"That's right," Guy said angrily. "It's all because of you! Because of your stupid brother!"

He got up, knocking over his chair, and stomped off into the bathroom, slamming the door behind him.

Melody took a bite of her own hot dog, but it tasted like so much cardboard. It was going to be a long two days.

SHE DIDN'T KNOW how true her prediction was going to be. Guy sulked for the rest of the day, while she and the other two children watched television and played Monopoly on the kitchen table. While they

were going past Go for the tenth time, Guy opened
the apartment door and deliberately let Alistair out...

MELODY DIDN'T DISCOVER that her cat was missing
until she started to put his food into his dish.

She looked around, frowning. "Alistair?" she
called. The big cat was nowhere in sight. He couldn't
have gone out the window. The apartment was on the
fourth story and there was no balcony. She searched
the apartment, including under the bed, but she
couldn't find him.

"Have any of you seen my cat?" she asked.

"Not me," Amy murmured. She was watching
cartoons with Polk.

"Me, neither," he said absently.

Guy was staring out the window. He jerked his
head, which she assumed meant he hadn't seen the cat.

But he looked odd. She frowned. Alistair had been
curled up on the couch just before Guy had stormed
off into the bathroom. She hadn't seen the cat since.
But surely the boy wouldn't have done something
so heartless as to let the cat out. Surely he wouldn't!

Melody had found Alistair in an alley on her way
home from work late one rainy afternoon last year.
He'd had a string tied around his neck and was choking. She'd freed him and taken him home. He was
flea-infested and pitifully thin, but a trip to the veterinarian and some healthful food had transformed
him. He'd been Melody's friend and companion and
confidant ever since.

Tears stung her eyes as she searched again, her

voice sounding frantic as she called her pet's name with increasing urgency.

Amy got up from the carpet and followed her, frowning. "Can't you find your cat?"

"No," Melody said, her voice raspy. She brushed at a tear on her face.

"Oh, Melody, don't cry!" Amy said. She hugged her. "It will be all right! We'll find him! Polk, Guy," she called sharply. "Come on. Help us hunt for Melody's cat! She can't find him anywhere!"

"Sure," Polk said. "We'll help."

They scoured the apartment. Guy looked, too, but his cheeks were flushed and he wouldn't meet Melody's eyes.

In desperation, Melody went to the two apartments nearby to ask her neighbors if they'd seen her cat, but no one had noticed him. There was an elevator and a staircase, but there was a door that led to the stairwell and surely it would be closed...

All the same, she checked, and was disturbed to find that the stairwell door was propped open while workmen carried materials to an apartment down the hall that was being renovated.

Leaving the children in the apartment, she rushed down the steps looking for Alistair. She called and called, but there was no answer, and he was nowhere to be found.

DEFEATED, MELODY WENT back to the apartment. Her expression was so morose that the children knew without asking that she hadn't found the cat.

"I'm sorry," Amy said. "I guess you love him a lot, huh?"

"He's all I have," Melody said without looking up. The pain in her voice was almost tangible. "All I... had."

Guy turned up the television and sat down very close to the screen. He didn't say a word.

Melody cried herself to sleep that night. Randy had Adell, but Melody had no other family. Alistair was the only real family she had left. She was so sick at heart that she didn't know how she was going to stand it. Dismal images of Alistair being run over or chased by dogs and children made her miserable.

She got up early and fixed bacon and eggs before she called the children. They were unnaturally quiet, too, and ate very little. Melody was preoccupied all through the meal. When it was over, she went outside to search some more. But Alistair was nowhere to be found.

Later, she took the kids to the hospital to see Emmett. He was sitting up in a chair looking impatient.

"Get me the hell out of here," he said immediately. "I'm leaving whether they like it or not!"

He seemed to mean it. He was fully dressed, in the jeans and shirt and boots he'd been wearing when they'd taken him to the hospital. The shirt was bloodstained but wearable. He looked pale, even if he sounded in charge of himself.

"What did the doctor say?"

"He said I could go if I insisted, and I'm insisting," Emmett said. "I'll take the kids and go back to the hotel."

Melody went closer to him, clutching her purse. "Mr. Deverell, don't you realize what a risk you'd be taking? If you won't think of yourself, do think of the kids. What will they do if anything happens to you?"

"I won't stay here!" he muttered. "They keep trying to bathe me!"

She managed a faint smile even through her misery. "It's for your own good."

"I'm leaving," he said, his flinty pale green eyes glaring straight into her dark ones.

She sighed. "Well, you can come back with us for today," she said firmly. "I can't let you stagger around Houston alone. My boss would never forgive me."

"Think so?" He narrowed one eye. "I don't need help."

"Yes, you do. One more night won't kill me, I suppose," she added.

"Her cat ran away," Amy said. "She's very sad."

Emmett scowled. "Alistair? How could he run away? Don't you live in an apartment building?"

"Yes. I… He must have gotten out the door," she said, staring down at her feet. "The stairwell door was open, where the workmen were going in and out of the building."

"I'm sorry," he said shortly. He glanced at the kids. Amy and Polk seemed very sympathetic, but Guy was surlier than ever and his lower lip was prominent. Emmett's eyes narrowed.

"Have you checked yourself out?" Melody asked, changing the subject to keep from bursting into tears.

"Yes." He got to his feet, a little unsteadily.

"I'll help you, Dad," Guy said. He propped up his father's side. He wouldn't look at Melody.

"Did you drive or take a cab?" he asked her.

"I drove."

"What do you drive?"

"A Volkswagen," she told him.

He groaned. She smiled for the first time that day. As tall as he was, fitting him inside her small car, even in the front seat, was going to be an interesting experience.

And it was. He had to bring his knees up almost to his chin. Polk and Amy laughed at the picture he made.

"Poor Emmett," Amy said. "You don't fit very well."

"First you shove gory pictures under my nose. Then you stuff me into a tin can with wheels," Emmett began with a meaningful glance in Melody's direction.

"Don't insult my beautiful little car. It isn't the car's fault that you're too tall," she reminded him as she started her car. "And you were horrible to me. I was only getting even."

"I am not too tall."

"I hope you aren't going to collapse," she said worriedly when he leaned his head back against the seat. "I live on the fourth floor."

"I'm all right. I'm just groggy."

"I hope so," she murmured. She put the car in gear and reversed it.

GUY HELPED HIM into the elevator and upstairs. Amy and Polk got on the other side, and between them, they maneuvered him into Melody's apartment and onto her sofa.

The sleeping arrangements were going to be interesting, she thought. She could put Emmett and the boys in her bedroom and she and Amy could share the sleeper sofa. It wasn't ideal, but it would be adequate. What wouldn't was managing some pajamas for Emmett.

"I don't wear pajamas," he muttered. "You aren't going to be in the bedroom, so it won't concern you," he added with a glittery green stare.

She turned away to keep him from seeing the color in her cheeks. "All right. I'll see about getting something together for sandwiches."

At least, he wasn't picky about what he ate. That was a mixed blessing. Perhaps it was the concussion, making him so agreeable.

"This isn't bad," he murmured when he'd finished off two egg salad sandwiches.

"Thank you," she replied.

"I hate eggs," Guy remarked, but he was still eating his sandwich as he said it. He didn't look at Melody.

"And me," Melody added for him. He looked up, surprised, and her steady gaze told him that she knew exactly how her cat had managed to get out the door and lost.

He flushed and put down the rest of his sandwich. "I'm not hungry." He got up and went into the living room with Amy and Polk, who were eating on TV tables.

Emmett ran a big hand through his dark hair. "I'm sorry about your cat," he said.

"So am I." She got up and cleared away the dishes. "There's coffee if you'd like some."

"I would. Black."

"I'll bet you don't eat catsup on steak, either," she murmured.

He smiled at her as she put a mug of steaming coffee beside his hand. "Smart girl."

"Why do you ride in rodeos?" she asked when she was sitting down.

The question surprised him. He leaned back in his chair fingering the hot mug, and considered it. "I always have," he began.

"It must be hard on the children, having you away from home so much," she continued. "Even if your housekeeper does look after them."

"They're resourceful," he said noncommittally.

"They're ruined," she returned. "And you know it. Especially Guy."

His eyes narrowed as they met hers. "They're my kids," he said quietly. "And how I raise them is none of your business."

"They're my nephews and niece," she pointed out.

His face went taut under its dark tan. "Don't bring that up."

"Why do you have to keep hiding from it?" she asked miserably. "Randy's my brother. I love him. But he couldn't have taken Adell if she hadn't wanted to go with him…!"

"My God, don't you think I know that?" he asked with bridled fury.

She saw the pain in his face, in his eyes, and she understood. "But, it wasn't because something was lacking in you," she said softly, trying to make him understand. "It was because she found something in Randy that she needed. Don't you see, it wasn't your fault!"

His whole body clenched. He grimaced and lifted the cup, burning his lips as he forced coffee between them. "It's none of your business," he said gruffly. "Let it alone."

She wanted to pursue the subject, but it wouldn't be wise. She let it go.

"There's a little ice cream," she told him.

He shook his head. "I don't like sweets."

Just like Guy, but she didn't say it. Guy hated her. He hated her enough to let her cat out the door and into the street. Her eyes closed on a wave of pain. It was just as well she wasn't mooning over Emmett, because she was certain that Guy wouldn't let that situation develop.

"You should be in bed," she told Emmett after a tense minute.

"Yes," he agreed without heat and then stood

up slowly. "Tomorrow I'll take the kids back to the hotel, and we'll get a flight out to San Antonio. We'll all be out of your hair."

She didn't argue. There was nothing to say.

CHAPTER THREE

EARLIER IN THE DAY, Melody had telephoned the nearest veterinarian's office and animal shelter, hoping that Alistair might turn up there. But the veterinarian's receptionist hadn't heard of any lost cats, and there was only a new part-time girl at the animal shelter who wasn't very knowledgeable about recent acquisitions. In fact, she'd confided, they'd had a fire the week before, and everything was mixed up. The lady who usually ran the shelter was in the hospital, having suffered smoke inhalation trying to get the animals out. She was very sorry, but she didn't know which cats were new acquisitions and which were old ones.

Melody was sorry about the fire, but she was even more worried about her cat. She went out into the hall one last time to call Alistair, in vain because he didn't appear. She just had to accept that he was gone. It wasn't easy. It was going to be similar to losing a member of her family, and part of her blamed Guy for that. He might hate her, but why had he taken out that hatred on her cat? Alistair had done nothing to hurt him.

Melody slept fitfully, and not only because she

was worried about Alistair. The couch was comfortable, as a rule, but Amy was a restless sleeper and it was hard to dodge little flailing arms and legs and not wake up.

Just before daylight, she gave up. She covered the sleeping child, her eyes tender on the little oval face with its light brown hair and straight nose so reminiscent of Adell. Amy's eyes, though, were her father's. All the kids had green eyes, every single one. Adell's were blue, and her hair was light brown. Amy was the one who most resembled her mother, despite her tomboy ways and the temper that matched her father's. That physical resemblance to her mother must have been very painful to Emmett when Adell first left him. Guy seemed to be his favorite, and it wasn't surprising. Guy looked and acted the most like him. Polk was just himself, bespectacled and slight, with no real distinguishing feature except his brain. He seemed to be far and away the brains of the bunch.

She pulled on her quilted robe, her long hair disheveled from sleep, and went slowly into the bathroom, yawning as she opened the door.

Emmett's dark eyebrows levered up when she stopped dead and turned scarlet.

"Sorry!" she gasped, jerking the door back shut.

She went into the living room and sat down in a chair, very quickly. It was disconcerting to find a naked man stepping out of her shower, even if he did have a body that would grace a centerfold in any women's magazine.

He came out a minute later with a towel wrapped

around his lean hips. He had an athlete's body, wide shouldered and narrow hipped, and his legs were incredible, Melody thought. She stared at him pie-eyed, trying to act sophisticated when she was just short of starstruck.

"I'm sorry," he said. "I didn't think to lock the door. I assumed this was a little early for you to be up, and I needed a shower."

"Of course."

He frowned as he stared down at her. She was doing her best not to look at him, and her cheeks were flaming. He was an experienced man, and he'd been married. He understood without words why she was reacting so violently to what she'd seen.

"It's all right," he said gently, and he smiled at her. "There's nothing to be embarrassed about."

She swallowed. "Right. Would you like some breakfast?"

"Anything will suit me. I'll get dressed."

She nodded, but she didn't look as he strode back into the bedroom and gently closed the door.

She got up and went to the kitchen, surprised to find that her hands shook when she got the pans out and began to put bacon into one.

Emmett came back while she was breaking eggs into a bowl. He was wearing jeans and a white T-shirt, which stretched over his powerful muscles. He wasn't wearing shoes. He looked rakish and appealing. She pretended not to notice; her memory was giving her enough trouble.

Melody wasn't dressed because she'd forgotten to

get her clothes out of the bedroom the night before. That had been an unfortunate oversight, because he was staring quite openly at her in the long green gown and matching quilted robe that fit much too well and showed an alarming amount of bare skin in the deep V neckline. She wasn't wearing makeup, but her blond-streaked brown hair and freckled pale skin gave her enough color to make her interesting to a man.

Emmett realized that she must not know that, because she kept fiddling with her hair after she'd set the eggs aside and started to heat a pan to cook them in.

"Where are the plates?" he asked. He didn't want to add to her discomfort by staring.

"They're up in the cabinet, there—" she gestured "—and so are the cups and saucers. But you don't have to…"

"I'm domesticated," he said gently. "I always was, even before I married." The words, once spoken, dispelled his good mood. He went about setting the table and didn't speak again until he was finished.

Melody had scrambled eggs and taken up the bacon while the biscuits were baking. She took them out of the oven, surprised to see that they weren't over-cooked. People in the kitchen made her nervous—Emmett, especially.

"You couldn't get to your clothes, could you?" he mused. "I should have reminded you last night."

It was an intimate conversation. Having a man in her apartment at all was intimate, and after having met him in the altogether in the bathroom, Melody was more nervous than ever.

"That's all right, I'll dress when the boys get up. You could call them…?"

"Not yet," he replied. "I want to talk to you."

"About what?"

He motioned her into a chair and then sat down across from her, his big, lean hands dangling between his knees as he studied her. "About what you said last night. I've been thinking about it. Did Adell tell you that it was loving Randy, not hating me, that broke up our marriage?"

Melody clasped her hands in her lap and stared at them. "She said that she married you because you were kind and gentle and obviously cared about her so much," she told him, because only honesty would do. "When she met Randy, at the service station where she had her car worked on and bought gas, she tried to pretend it wasn't happening, that she wasn't falling in love. But she was too weak to stop it. I'm not excusing what she did, Emmett," she said when he looked haunted. "There should have been a kinder way. And I should have said no when Randy asked me to help them get away. But nothing will change what happened. She really does love him. There's no way to get around that."

"I see."

He looked grim. She hated the wounded expression on his lean face.

"Emmett," she said gently, "you have to believe it wasn't because of you personally. She fell in love, really in love. The biggest mistake she made was marrying you when she didn't love you properly."

"Do you know what that is?" he asked with a bitter smile. "Loving 'properly'?"

"Well, not really," she said. "I haven't ever been in love." That was true enough. She'd had crushes on movie stars, and once she'd had a crush on a boy back in San Antonio. But that had been a very lukewarm relationship and the boy had gone crazy over a cheerleader who was more willing in the backseat of his car than Melody had been.

"Why?" he asked curiously.

She sighed. "You must have noticed that I'm oversized and not very attractive," she said with a wistful smile.

He frowned. "Aren't you? Who says?"

Color came and went in her cheeks. "Well, no one, but I…"

It disturbed him that he'd said such a thing to her, when she'd been the enemy since Randy had spirited Adell away. "Have the kids given you any trouble?"

"Just Guy," she replied after a minute. "He doesn't like me."

"He doesn't like anybody except me," he said easily. "He's the most insecure of the three."

She nodded. "Amy and Polk are very sweet."

"Adell spoiled them. She favored Guy, although he took it the best of the three when she left. I think he loved her, but he never talks about her."

"He's a very private person, isn't he? Divorce must be hard on everyone," she replied. "My parents loved each other for thirty years—until they died. There was never any question of them getting a divorce or separating. They were happy. So were we. It was a blow when we lost them. Randy wound up being part brother and part parent to me. I was still in school."

"That explains why you were so close, I suppose." He cocked his head and studied her. "How did they die?"

"In a freak accident," she said sadly. "My mother was in very bad health—a semi-invalid. She had what Dad thought was a light heart attack. He got her into the car and was speeding, trying to get her to the hospital. He lost control in a curve and wrecked the car. They both died." She averted her eyes. "There was an oil slick on the road that he didn't see, and a light rain…just enough to bring the oil to the surface. Randy and I blamed ourselves for not insisting that Dad call an ambulance instead of trying to drive her to the emergency room himself. To this day I hate rain."

"I'm sorry," he said kindly. "I lost my parents several years apart, but it was pretty rough just the same. Especially my mother." He was silent for a moment. "She killed herself. Dad had only been dead six months when she was diagnosed with leukemia. She refused treatment, went home and took a handful of barbiturates that they'd given her for pain. I was in my last few weeks of college before graduation. I hadn't started until I was nineteen, so I was late getting out. It was pretty rough, passing my finals after the funeral," he added with a rough laugh.

"I can only imagine," she said sympathetically.

"I'd already been running the ranch and going to school as a commuting student. That's where I met Adell, at college. She was sympathetic and I was so torn up inside. I just wanted to get married and have kids and not be alone anymore." He shrugged. "I thought marriage would ease the pain. It didn't. Nobody cares like your parents do. When they die, you're alone. Except, maybe, if you've got kids," he added thoughtfully, and realized that he hadn't really paid enough attention to his own kids. He frowned. He'd avoided them since Adell left. Rodeo and ranch work had pretty much replaced parenting with him. He wondered why he hadn't noticed it until he got hit in the head.

"Do you have brothers or sisters?" Melody asked unexpectedly. She hadn't ever had occasion to question his background. Now, suddenly, she was curious about it.

"No," he said. "I had a sister, they said, but she died a few weeks after she was born. There was just me. My dad was a rodeo star. He taught me everything I know."

"He must have been good at it."

"So am I, when I'm not distracted. There was a little commotion before my ride. I wasn't paying attention and it was almost fatal."

"The kids would have missed you."

"Maybe Guy would have, although he's pretty solitary most of the time," he replied. His eyes narrowed. "Amy and Polk seem very happy to stay with anybody."

So the truce was over. She stared at him. "They probably were half-starved for a little of the attention you give rodeoing," she returned abruptly. "You seem to spend your life avoiding your own children."

"You're outspoken," he said angrily.

"So are you."

His green eyes narrowed. "Not very worldly, though."

She wouldn't blush, she wouldn't blush, she wouldn't…!

"The eggs are getting cold," she reminded him.

The color in her face was noticeable now, but she was a trouper. He admired her attempt at subterfuge, even as he felt himself tensing with faint pleasure at her naiveté. Her obvious innocence excited him. "I have to make a living," he said, feeling oddly defensive. "Rodeo is what I do best, and it's profitable."

"Your cousin mentioned that the ranch is profitable, too."

"Only if it gets a boost in lean times from other capital, and times are pretty lean right now," he said shortly. "It's the kids' legacy. I can't afford to lose it."

"Yes, but there are other ways of making money besides rodeo. You must know a lot about how to manage cattle and horses and accounts."

"I do. But I like working for myself."

She stared pointedly at his head. "Yes, I can see how successful you are at it. Head not hurting this morning?"

"I haven't taken a fall that bad before," he muttered.

"You're getting older, though."

"Older! My God, I'm only in my thirties!"

"Emmett, you're so loud!" Amy protested sleepily from deep in her blankets.

"Sorry, honey," he said automatically. His green eyes narrowed and glittered on Melody. "I can ride as well as I ever did!"

"Am I arguing?" she asked in mock surprise.

He got up from his chair and towered over her. "Nobody tells me what to do."

"I wasn't," she replied pleasantly. "But when those kids reach their teens, do you really think anyone's going to be able to manage them? And what if something happens to you? What will become of them?"

She was asking questions he didn't like. He'd already started to ask them himself. He didn't like that, either. He went off toward the bedroom to call the boys and didn't say another word.

Melody worried at her own forwardness in mentioning such things to him. It was none of her business, but she was fond of Amy and Polk. Guy was a trial, but he was intelligent and he had grit. They were good kids. If Emmett woke up in time to take proper care of them, they'd be good adults. But they were heading for trouble without supervision.

EMMETT CAME BACK wearing a checked shirt and black boots. Being fully dressed made him feel better armored to talk to Miss Bossy in the kitchen.

"They're getting up," he muttered, sitting.

"I'll warm everything when they get in here." She busied herself washing the dishes and cleaning the sink until the boys came out of her room, dressed. Then she escaped into the bedroom and closed the door. Emmett's stare had been provokingly intimate. She'd felt undressed in front of those knowing eyes and she wondered why he had suddenly become so disturbing to her.

Seeing him without his clothes had kindled something unfamiliar in her. She'd never been curious about men that way, even if she did daydream about love and marriage. But Emmett's powerful shoulders and hair-roughened chest and flat stomach and long, muscular legs, along with his blatant masculinity, stuck in her mind like a vivid oil painting that she couldn't cover up. He hadn't even had a white streak across his hips. That was oddly sensual. If he sunbathed, he must do it as he slept: without anything on. He looked very much like one of those marble statues she'd seen photographs of, but he was even more thrilling to look at. She reproached herself for that thought.

She looked at the rumpled bed where Emmett had lain with the boys and her pulse raced. Tonight she'd be sleeping where his body had rested. She wondered if she'd ever sleep again.

After she was dressed, she went to the kitchen and warmed the food before she put it on the table. The kids all ate hungrily, even Guy, although he wouldn't look at Melody. He was just as sullen and uncommunicative as ever.

But now, Melody was avoiding looking at him, too. Guy noticed her resentment and was surprised that it bothered him. He was guilty about the cat, as well. It had been an ugly cat, all scarred and big and orange, but it had purred when he petted it. His conscience stung him.

He had to remember that Melody was responsible for his mother's departure. He'd loved his mother. She'd gone away, so it had to be because of him. He'd given her a hard time, just as he'd been giving Melody one. He'd been much more caring about his father since his mother left, because he knew it was his fault that she'd run away with that Randy Cartman. If he'd been a better boy, a nicer boy, his mother would have stayed. Maybe if he could keep his father single, his mother would come back.

Blissfully unaware of his son's mistaken reasoning, Emmett smiled at the boy. He was a bit curious about Guy's behavior. The boy and Melody were restrained with each other. Melody's eyes were accusing, and Guy's were guilt-ridden. It wasn't a big jump from that observation to the subject of the cat.

He could ask Guy about it, but it would be better to let the boy bring it up himself, when they were away from here. If it was true that Guy really had let the cat out…

He was sorry that he'd spent so much time avoiding his children. Adell's betrayal wasn't their fault. If Adell genuinely loved Randy, and had left only because of that, no one was to blame for what had happened. Least of all the kids.

Emmett felt better about himself, and them. He had a lot of omissions to make up for, and he didn't know where to start.

The kids finished breakfast and went to watch television. Emmett insisted on helping Melody clean up.

He dried while she washed and rinsed. "Tell me about the cat," he said.

Her face stiffened.

"Come on." He prodded gently.

She sighed heavily. "I found him last year in an alley," she said finally. "He had a string tied around his neck. He was thick with parasites, and half-starved. It took him a long time to learn to trust me. I thought he never would." She washed the same plate twice. "We've been together ever since. I'll miss him."

"He may still turn up," he told her.

She shook her head sadly. "It isn't likely. There are so many streets…"

"If he was a street cat when you got him, he's street smart. Don't give up on him yet."

She smiled, but she didn't reply.

"What you said about the kids," he began, glancing toward the living room to make sure they weren't listening. "I guess maybe I've been negligent with them. I thought they were adjusting to my being away so much. But this concussion has made me apprehensive." He stared at her quietly. "Adell isn't

likely to be able to handle all three of them with
a stepfather, even if she wouldn't mind visitation
rights. They'd be split up, with no place to go."

"Adell loves them, you know she does," she replied.

"She gave up when I refused to let her see them.
I never would have given up."

"Adell isn't you," she reminded him. "She isn't
really a fighter."

"That's probably why she said yes when I pro-
posed to her," he said angrily. "I was overbearing, because I wanted her so much. If I'd given her a choice,
she'd probably have turned me down."

"You have three fine children to show for your
marriage," she said softly.

He looked down into her quiet dark eyes and
something stirred deep inside his heart. He began
to smile. "You've been a surprise," he said absently.

"So have you," she replied.

He noticed that she'd thrown away a box of cat
food. "Did you mean to do that?" he asked, lifting it.

She grimaced. "Well, he's gone, isn't he?" she
asked huskily.

She turned to put away the plates and he moved,
but she caught her foot on a chair leg and tripped.

He caught her easily, his reflexes honed by years
of ranch work. His lean hands on her waist kindled
exquisite little ripples on her skin. She looked up into
his eyes and her gaze hung there, curious, a little surprised by the strength of the need she felt to be held
close against him and comforted.

He seemed to understand that need in her eyes, because he reacted to it immediately. Taking the clean colorful plastic plates from her hand in a silence broken only by the blaring television, he set them on the table. Then he pulled her quite roughly into his arms.

She shivered with feeling. Never, she thought, never like this! She was frightened, but she didn't pull away. She let him hold her, closed her eyes and delighted in the security she felt for this brief moment. It made the ache in her heart subside. His shirt smelled of pleasant detergent and cologne, and it felt wonderful to be held so closely to his warm strength.

"The cat will show up," he said at her ear, his voice deep, soothing. "Don't lose heart."

She had to force herself to draw away from him. It was embarrassing to allow herself to be comforted. She was used to bearing things bravely.

She managed a wan smile. "Thanks," she said huskily.

He nodded. He picked up the plates and handed them back to her. "I'll get the kids packed," he said.

He moved out of the kitchen. He was disturbed and vaguely aroused. He didn't want to think about how his feelings had changed since his concussion. That could wait until he was more lucid and out of Melody's very disturbing presence.

Guy had noticed the embrace and he remarked on it when Emmett joined the children in the living room.

"Losing the cat upset her," Emmett said, and that

explanation seemed to satisfy Guy. At the same time, the boy's face went a little paler.

Later, Emmett promised himself, he was going to have to talk to Guy about that cat. He had some suspicions that he sincerely hoped were wrong.

He and Guy weren't close, although they got along well enough. But lately the boy was standoffish and seemed to not want affection from anyone. He bossed the other two around and when he wasn't doing that, he spent his time by himself. He didn't ask for anything, least of all attention. But as Emmett pondered that, he began to wonder if Guy's solitary leanings weren't because he was afraid to get attached. He'd lost his mother, whom he adored, to a stranger. Perhaps he was afraid of losing Emmett, too.

Emmett could have told him that people don't stop loving their children, whether or not they're divorced. He'd done his kids an injustice, probably, by not letting Adell near them. He began to rethink his entire position, and he didn't like what he saw. He'd been punishing everyone for Adell's defection. Perhaps he'd been punishing himself, as well. Melody had said some things that disturbed him. That might not be bad. It was time he came to grips with the past, and his kids. Fate had given him a second chance. He couldn't afford to waste it.

CHAPTER FOUR

IT ONLY TOOK her reluctant houseguests a few minutes to pack and be ready to leave.

"You could stay another day if you need to," Melody told Emmett and her dark eyes were worried. "Concussions can be dangerous."

"Indeed they can," he said. "But the headache is gone and I'm not feeling disoriented anymore. Believe me, I don't take chances. I'm all right. I'd never take the kids with me if I wasn't sure."

"If you're sure then," she said.

"Besides," he added ruefully, "we've given you enough trouble. Thank you for taking care of those kids for me. And for your hospitality." He opened his wallet and put two twenty-dollar bills on the table. "For groceries," he said.

"They didn't eat forty dollars' worth of food," she returned angrily.

"The babysitter cost that much for two hours, much less two days," he said, putting his wallet away. "I won't argue. I don't want to be under any obligation to you. In my place, you'd feel exactly the same," he added with a smile when she started to protest again.

She would have felt the same way, she had to admit. Reluctantly, she gave in. "All right. Thank you," she said stiffly. "I hope you'll be all right," she added. She couldn't quite hide her worry for him.

Her concern touched him. "I will. I've got the world's hardest head." He guided the kids out the door. "We'll get a cab," he added when she offered to drive them.

"I'll miss you, Melody," Amy said sadly. She hugged Melody warmly. "Can't you come with us?"

"I've got a job," Melody said simply. She smiled and kissed the little girl's forehead. "But I'll miss you, too. You could write me, if your dad doesn't mind."

"Me, too?" Polk asked.

She smiled. "You, too."

He beamed. Guy didn't say a word. He stuck his hands into the pockets of his jeans and trailed after Amy and Polk.

"I'll say goodbye, then," Emmett said quietly. He searched Melody's eyes, feeling oddly disconcerted at the thought of not seeing her again. He scowled, his expression steady and intent, and a jolt of pure pleasure seared through him as he let his gaze fall slowly to her mouth. It was silky and soft looking, and he wondered how it would feel to smooth her body against his and kiss her blind.

He dragged his gaze away. He must still be concussed, he decided, to be considering that! Any such thoughts were a road to disaster. She, of all women, was off-limits. He would never forget Adell and

Randy. The past would destroy any thought of a relationship with Melody.

"Goodbye," he said stiffly, and followed the kids
into the elevator. Guy looked over his shoulder,
and there was something in his eyes that mingled
strangely with the hostility. He looked as if he were
about to say something, but Emmett's gentle hand
on his shoulder guided him out the door.

The apartment was quiet and lonely with everyone
gone. Melody got her clothes ready for work the next
day, but she did it without any real interest. With a
sinking heart, she washed Alistair's bowls and put
them out of sight. Tears stung her eyes at the thought
of never seeing him again. She'd never dreamed that
a child could be so vindictive.

BACK AT THE HOTEL, Guy was totally uncommunicative until that night. After Amy and Polk went to bed,
he sat down on the couch next to his father.

"Something's bothering you," Emmett remarked
quietly.

Guy shrugged. "Yeah."

"Want to tell me about it?"

The boy leaned forward, resting his elbows on
his knees in a position that Emmett often assumed.

"I let Melody's cat out."

Emmett's head lifted. He wasn't really surprised.
He'd suspected this because of Guy's behavior. "That
was cruel," he replied, "after she was kind enough
to take care of all three of you. The cat was special
to her. Like Barney is to you," he added, mentioning

the mongrel pup that Guy was fond of back home. "Try to think how you'd feel if someone let Barney out in the streets…"

Guy burst into tears. It was the first time in memory that Emmett had seen that happen. Even when his mother left, Guy hadn't cried.

Awkwardly Emmett pulled the boy against him and patted his back. He wasn't too good at being a parent most of the time. The kids made him uncomfortable with their woes and antics, which was really why he spent so much time away from home. Now he wondered if he'd been needed more than he realized. The kids hadn't had anyone to talk to about their mother in two years, or anybody to lean on. He'd assumed that they hadn't needed that. But they were only children. Why hadn't he realized how young they really were?

"Why did you let the cat out?" Emmett asked Guy gently.

"Because I hate her! She helped Mom leave!" Guy choked. "She's nothing but a troublemaking witch!" He looked up, a little uncertainly. "You called her that!" he added defensively, because his father didn't look pleased about what he'd said.

Emmett groaned. "Yes, I did, but it was because I was hurting. Nobody made your mother leave. She went away because she never really loved me." It was painful to say that, but now that it was out, it didn't hurt so much. "She did fall in love, but with another man, and she couldn't live without him. That's not your fault or mine or Melody's. It's just life."

Guy sniffed, and pulled away, wiping his tears on the back of his hand. "Melody cried all night. I heard her. I thought it would serve her right, because of Mom. But it made me feel awful."

"It made her feel pretty awful, too."

"I know." He looked up at his father. "What'll I do?"

Emmett thought for a minute. "Go to bed. I've got an idea. We'll talk some more tomorrow."

"We're going home, aren't we?"

"Yes. Tomorrow afternoon. But first, in the morning, I want to make a few phone calls."

HE MADE EIGHT phone calls before he got the information he wanted. His head had stopped throbbing and he felt much better. Leaving the kids with a babysitter—not the elderly one of two nights ago—he went downstairs and hailed a cab.

Melody was just hanging up the telephone when she heard the outer office door open. She looked up with a smile ready for the client coming in. But it wasn't a client; it was Emmett. And under his arm was a big, straggly-looking orange tabby cat.

"Alistair!"

She scrambled up from the desk, tears of joy streaming down her face. "Alistair! Oh, Alistair…!"

She took the cat from Emmett and kissed Alistair and hugged him and petted him and stroked him in such delight that Emmett felt even worse than he had when Guy told him what he'd done. Seeing Melody vulnerable like this touched him. It was as shocking as it had been to see Guy in tears.

"Where did you find him?" she choked, big-eyed.

He touched her cheek gently. "At the local pound," he said. He didn't add that the shelter had been in a state of chaos and the cat had inadvertently been scheduled for premature termination. That wouldn't do at all. "I suppose you know that it was Guy who let him out."

"I know," she said.

"It's my fault more than his," he murmured reluctantly. "I've blamed everyone for Adell, especially you. I couldn't stand to admit that she left because of me, because she didn't love me. I stayed away too much. The kids and the loneliness killed our marriage."

"Not the kids," she replied, clutching Alistair. "Adell loves the children. She'd love to have them visit, but…" She paused.

"But I wouldn't let her near them. That's right," he agreed tersely. "I hated her, too. Her, and your brother and you. Everybody."

"You were hurt," she said softly, her eyes searching his. "We all understood. Even Adell."

His jaw went taut. He took a deep breath and looked over her head. "We're flying out this afternoon. I have to go."

"Thank you for my cat," she said sincerely. In a fever of gratitude and without thinking of the consequences, she reached up and touched her soft lips fervently to his chin.

Shocked at the look it produced on his lean, dark face, and not a little by her own behavior, she drew back at once.

He looked down at her curiously, stunned. When she began to step away, his lean hand caught her shoulder and stopped the slow movement.

"No," he said hesitantly, searching her soft, dark eyes while his heart began to race in his chest. "Not yet, Melody."

While she was getting her breath, he let his gaze drop abruptly to her soft, parted mouth and his big hand moved up to her chin, gently cupping it as he tilted her face up.

His thumb moved hesitantly over her full lower lip. "I've...wondered," he whispered as his head began to lower. "Haven't you?"

She didn't get the chance to reply. His mouth slowly closed on hers with tender, confident mastery. It was firm, and hard and a little rough. She let her eyes close and stopped breathing. She'd been kissed, but just the touch of a man's lips had never been quite so vivid. It had to be because of the antagonism they'd felt for each other, she thought dizzily.

But her knees were going weak and her heartbeat went wild when she felt his teeth gently nip her lower lip. She heard his breathing change even as his head lifted a fraction of an inch.

"Open it," he said roughly, his hand sliding into the thick hair at her nape. "Open your mouth...!"

His lips crushed into hers with sudden violence, hunger making him less considerate of her needs and more aware of his own. With a rough groan, he made her lips part to admit his, and his tongue probed insistently between them.

Shocked, her gasp gave him what he wanted—access to her mouth. He made a satisfied sound in his throat and penetrated the soft, warm darkness past her lips with slow thrusts.

She gasped and clutched at him as waves of physical pleasure buffeted her untried body. Her mouth pushed upward, to meet his ardor headlong. And Alistair chose that instant to insist physically on being put down, his claws digging into her arm.

She pulled away from Emmett, breathless and puzzled by the violence in his eyes. His hand let go of her hair. She looked away while she put the battle-scarred old tomcat on his feet and dazedly watched him leap into her chair and begin to bathe himself with magnificent abandon.

She took steadying breaths and slowly looked at Emmett. He seemed as shaken as she felt. Her dark eyes stared up into his turbulent green ones with mute curiosity.

The delight he felt was far too disturbing. He could get in over his head here with no trouble at all. The chemistry was there, just as he'd known it was somewhere in the back of his mind. He was sorry about that. Of all the women he'd ever wanted, Melody was the first one that he absolutely could not have.

He forced himself to breathe normally, to pretend that it was natural for him to feel this aroused from a casual kiss. He had to force back the impulse to drag her against him.

He laughed a little angrily. "I'm glad the cat turned up," he said when he wanted to ask how she felt, if her body was throbbing as madly as his own was. He had to keep his head, talk normally. "Thanks for the hospitality."

"That's all right." She could barely speak. She cleared her throat. "Thank you for finding my cat. He…he really is all I have."

His throat felt tight. He had to stop looking at her mouth. His broad shoulders squared. "Guy's sorry for what he did. I'll make sure he doesn't do it again."

"You won't…be mean to him?"

He cocked an eyebrow. "I don't have a bullwhip."

She flushed. "Sorry," she said sheepishly.

He managed a short laugh. "I don't beat my kids. Can't you tell?"

She smiled at him, her lips still tingling with pleasure from the hunger of his mouth.

He smiled back. She looked delectable when she smiled. He wanted her. No! He couldn't afford to think like that.

"Well…goodbye."

"Goodbye," he said. He hesitated for an instant. She made him want things he'd forgotten he needed. There had been women, but this one touched him in ways no one else ever had. He wanted to tell her that, but he didn't dare. There was no future in a relationship between them. Surely she knew, too, that it had been an impulse, a mad moment that was better forgotten by both of them.

With a tip of his broad-brimmed hat, he turned abruptly and left without looking back.

Melody stroked her cat with a hand that trembled. "Oh, Alistair." She sighed, cuddling him. "I've missed you so much!"

Alistair butted his head against her and purred. She laughed, imagining that he was telling her he'd missed her, too. She murmured a small prayer of thanks and carried him into the bathroom. He'd have to stay there until it was time to go home. Perhaps she could find him part of a sandwich and a saucer of milk later to keep him happy.

EMMETT WAS SET upon the minute he walked into the hotel room.

"Did you find him?" Guy asked impatiently.

Emmett put off telling him long enough to make him sweat. Object lessons stayed in the mind. "Yes, I found him," he said, and watched the young face lose its pallor. "No thanks to you," he added firmly. "He was scheduled to be put down."

"I'm sorry," Guy said tightly. He was trying not to hope for too much. Last night, his father had been approachable for the first time in memory. It had felt good to be cared about. But now Emmett seemed distant again, and Guy was feeling the transition all too much.

Emmett turned away. He didn't see the wounded look on the young face, or the hope that slowly drained out of it. "You got a second chance. Most people don't. Remember how it felt. That way you won't be tempted to do such a cruel thing again."

"You hate her," Guy muttered. "You said you did," he added defensively.

"I know." Emmett hesitated. "I'll try to explain that one day," he told his son, and somewhere in the back of his mind he was remembering the incredible softness of Melody's innocent mouth under his lips.

He paid the babysitter, packed the suitcases and took his kids home. Maybe when he was back in familiar surroundings, he could put Melody out of his thoughts.

MELODY CHECKED ON Tansy Deverell Sunday evening. Tansy had been discharged from the hospital and had been moved to Logan's house where she had a private nurse until Kit and Logan got back so that she wouldn't be in the house alone. Spending the evening with the elderly lady took her mind off her own problems.

"I saw Emmett before they released him," Tansy mused with twinkling eyes when she was in a comfortable bed at Logan's house. "Two nurses threatened to resign, I believe?"

"I heard it was three, and the doctor." Melody chuckled. "Isn't he something? And those kids…!"

"Those kids would settle down if Guy would," Tansy replied. "He's the ringleader. He leads and the other two follow. Guy's said the least about his mother leaving them, but I think it hit him the hardest—

almost as hard as it hit Emmett. They both blame themselves, when it was no one's fault."

"I told Emmett that," Melody remarked. "He actually listened. I don't know if he believed me or not, but he was…well, less volatile after that."

"Emmett's always been explosive," the elderly woman recalled. "He was high-strung and forceful when he was younger, a real hell-raiser. Adell was sheltered and shy. He just walked right over her. He was devastated when his mother committed suicide and he wanted a wife and a family right then. He picked Adell and rushed her to the altar. She never should have married him. He was the exact opposite of the kind of man she needed. She didn't want a fistful of children right away, but Emmett gave her no real choice. He's lived to regret his rashness. I'm sorry for the way things turned out for him. He's a sad, lonely man."

"And a very bitter one," Melody added. "He hated me."

"Past tense?" Tansy fished gently.

"I don't know. He was very different when he left," she replied, frowning in confusion.

"I hope he'll go home and rethink his life after this," Tansy said. "He had a close call that could have ended tragically. The kids deserve a better shake than they're getting. If he doesn't wake up pretty soon, he'll never be able to control them when they get older."

"I think he knows that."

"Then let's both hope he'll do something about it. They're sweet kids."

Melody only nodded. She didn't want to go into any details about why she could have cheerfully excluded Guy from that description.

"IT'S GREAT TO be back." Kit sighed when she stopped by the office Monday morning with a weary-looking Logan. "You really need a vacation from a vacation. We had so much fun!" She stared after Logan, who'd gone into his office to take a telephone call.

Melody stared at her grimly. "I'm glad you did," she said, emphasizing the "you." "Emmett landed himself in the hospital with a concussion over the weekend. Guess who got to look after those kids."

"Oh, Lord," Kit said on a moan. "You poor thing!"

"I kept reminding myself that they're my nieces and nephews," Melody remarked. "But it was a very long weekend." She didn't mention Alistair's adventure or Guy's part in it.

"I'm really sorry. If we'd been in town, all of us could have split them up."

"I shudder to think of the consequences," Melody mused. "I can see them now, trying to get to each other through downtown Houston at two in the morning."

"Hmm. You might have a point there." She glanced at her watch. "I have to get to work, or I may not have a job. Have a nice day," she called, pausing to blow a kiss at her husband through the open door of his office.

Melody wondered at the obviously loving relationship the married couple had, and felt a faint envy. Probably she'd never know anything like that. Emmett had kissed her, but it had been passionate, not loving. She permitted herself to dream for just a moment about how it would have felt to be loved half to death. Then the phone rang and saved her from any more malingering.

DURING THE TIME Logan and Kit had been away, Melody hadn't been forced to call on Tom Walker. That was a blessing. He strolled into the office later on the day Logan came back, a little curious, because he'd expected to have someone to advise in Logan's absence.

"I suppose I had you buffaloed?" he mused in a deep voice with a very faint crisp northwestern accent, his dark eyes twinkling as they met Melody's. "That was just bad timing before, when Logan left town. I'd already had a hell of a day. You caught the overflow. I'm sorry if I've put you off financial advisors for life." There was a faint query in his scrutiny.

"You haven't," Melody said, and smiled back. "But we really didn't have anyone with an emergency this time. Aren't you glad?"

"I guess so," he said wearily. "It's been a long week. How was the honeymoon?" he asked Logan, who joined them in the outer office.

"Nothing like it. Get married and find out for yourself," he said, chuckling as he shook Tom's hand.

The older man's face closed up. "Marriage is not

for me," he said quietly. "I'm not suited for it. Besides, when would I have time for a wife?" he added with a mocking smile. "I work eighteen hours out of every twenty-four. In my spare time, I sleep."

"That will get old one day," Logan told him. He was obviously thinking about Kit and his heart was in his face. "Time can pass you by if you don't pay attention."

Tom turned away. "I've got a client due. I just wanted to stop by and welcome you back. I'll be in touch."

"Don't forget, we're having dinner with the Rowena Marshal people next Saturday at the Sheraton."

"How could I forget? Ms. Marshal herself phoned to remind me," he said with a nip in his tone. "After expressing outrage that her business partner had dared to approach us about changing their investments without her knowledge. If you recall, I was against taking their account in the first place. It's been nothing short of a headache. They should have used one firm, not split their investments between two. I tried to tell them that, too. Ms. Marshal wouldn't listen."

"Mrs. Marshal," Logan corrected.

"Are you sure? When would she find time for a husband and family?" Tom muttered. "That cosmetic company seems to keep her as occupied as investments keep me."

"She and her husband are divorced," Logan replied. "Or so I hear."

Tom didn't say a word, but one eyebrow went up.

"Am I surprised? How could a mere man compete with the power and prestige of owning one of the Fortune 500 companies?"

"I'm sure there's more to it than that," Logan replied.

Tom shrugged. "There usually is. Well, we'll see what they want to do after we talk to them. If you want the account, you can have it with my blessing. Tell her that, would you?"

Logan chuckled. "What have I ever done to you?"

Tom shook his head. "See you."

Logan watched him leave with narrow, curious dark eyes. Tom was a real puzzle even to the people who knew him best. He had a feeling his friend and the lovely Mrs. Marshal were going to strike sparks off each other from the very beginning.

He turned to Melody, who was sorting files. "Anything that can't wait until tomorrow?" he mused.

"Why, no, sir," she said with a mischievous smile. "In fact, I think I can now run the office all by myself, advise clients on the best investments, speak to civic organizations…"

"I can call Emmett and tell him you miss having him and the kids at your apartment, and that you'd like him to come back," he suggested.

She stuck both arms up in the air over her head.

He chuckled and left to pick up Kit at her office.

EMMETT WAS WONDERING if his age was beginning to affect him. He was noticing things about his kids that had escaped him for months. They didn't take regular baths. They didn't have new clothes. They didn't do their homework. They played really nasty jokes on people around the ranch.

"You haven't noticed much, have you?" the housekeeper, Tally Ray, remarked dryly. "I've done my best, but as they keep reminding me, I don't have any real authority to order them around."

"We'll see about that," he began irritably.

"Why don't you see about that? Because I'm retiring. Here's my notice. I didn't mind doing housework, but I draw the line at being a part-time mother to three kids. I want to enjoy my golden years, if you please."

"But you've been here forever!" he protested.

"And that's why I'm leaving." She patted him on the shoulder. "One week is all you get, by the way. I hope you can find somebody stupid enough to replace me."

Emmett felt the world coming down on his shoulders. Now what was he going to do?

He phoned Tansy, supposedly to check on her progress, but really to get some much-needed advice.

"You're playing with fire, you know," Tansy told him. "Living on the edge is only for people with no real responsibilities. Those kids need you."

"So does the ranch. How can I keep it without additional capital?"

"Get a job that doesn't have the risks of rodeo."

"Where?" he asked belligerently.

"Take down this number."

She gave it to him and he jotted it down with a pencil. "What is it?"

"It's Ted Regan's number," she replied. "He still needs somebody to manage his ranch in Jacobsville while he's in Europe. It won't be a permanent job, but it would keep you going until you decide what else you'd like to do with your life."

"Jacobsville."

"That's right. It's a small town, but close enough to Houston that you could bring the kids to see me. You'd have time to spend with them. You'd have a second chance, Emmett."

He could use one, but he didn't want to admit it. "That's an idea." He didn't add that it was going to get him closer to Melody than San Antonio was. He didn't know why it exhilarated him to think of being close enough to see her when he liked, but it did.

"Call Ted and talk to him," Tansy suggested.

"I suppose it wouldn't hurt."

It didn't. Ted Regan knew Emmett's reputation in rodeo and he didn't need to ask for credentials or qualifications. He offered Emmett the job on the spot, at a regular salary that was twice what he was pulling down on the rodeo circuit.

"Besides, it may turn into a full-time job," Ted continued in his deep, Texas drawl. "My present manager just quit. I don't know if I can spread myself thin enough to manage the ranch and keep up with my purebred business. I'm buying and selling cattle like hotcakes. I haven't got time for the day-to-day routine of ranching."

That was what worried Emmett. If he left his own ranch, he'd have to let Whit manage it for him. Whit was good, but could he hold it together?

"We'll have to talk about that later, but I will think about the offer," Emmett promised. "And thanks, I'll take the job."

"I'm glad," Ted replied. "I know you'll do it right." He gave Emmett a date to report and concluded the fine points of the agreement.

When he hung up, Emmett called the kids together and sat down with them.

"We're going to move to Jacobsville and I'm going to manage a ranch there," he began.

Guy glared at his father with pale, angry eyes in a face as lean and strong as Emmett's. "Well, I'm not moving to Jacobsville," he said curtly. "I like it here."

Amy took her cue from her eldest brother, whose pale eyes dared her to go against him. "Me, too," Amy said quickly, although not as belligerently. "I'm not going, either, Emmett!"

Emmett looked at Polk. Polk didn't say a word. He just looked at the other two, grinned and nodded.

CHAPTER FIVE

ONLY A WEEK AGO, Emmett might have lost his temper and said some unpleasant things to the kids. But he'd mellowed just a little since his concussion. He was sure he could handle the children's mutiny. He smiled smugly. It was just a matter of outsmarting them.

"There are horses there," he remarked. "Lots of horses. You could each have one of your own."

"We live on a ranch, Emmett," Amy reminded him. "We already have a horse each."

"There's the Astrodome in Houston," he added.

"There's the Alamo here," Guy said.

"And the place where they film all the movies, outside town," Polk added.

"All our friends are here," Amy wailed.

He was losing ground. He began to lose some self-confidence. "You can make new friends," he told them. "There are lots of kids in Jacobsville."

"We don't want new friends." Amy began to cry.

"Oh, stop that!" Emmett groaned. He glared at all three of them. "Listen, don't you want us to be a family?" he asked.

Amy stopped crying. Her eyes were red but they lifted bravely. "A family?" she echoed.

"Yes, a family!" He pushed back his unruly dark hair from his broad forehead. "I haven't been much of a father since your mother left us," he confessed curtly. "I want us to spend more time together. I want to be able to stay at home with you. If I take this job, I won't be away all the time at rodeos. I'll be home at night, all the time, and on weekends. We can do things together."

Guy stared at him warily. "You mean, things like going to movies and goofy golf and baseball games? Things like that?" he said slowly, hardly able to believe that his father actually might want to spend any time with them. That wasn't the impression he'd been giving since their mother had left.

"Yes," Emmett said. "And if you had problems that you needed to talk to me about, I'd be there."

"What about Mrs. Ray?"

"She's resigning," Emmett said sadly. "She says she's reached the age where she needs peace and quiet and flowers to grow. So we'd have to replace her even if we stay here."

Guy and Amy and Polk exchanged resigned glances. They didn't want the risk of a housekeeper they couldn't control. There was always that one chance in a million that their father might come up with someone they couldn't frighten or intimidate.

"Melody could stay with us, couldn't she?" Amy asked suddenly.

"Sure!" Polk agreed, beaming.

Guy's complexion went pale. He muttered something under his breath and got up and went to the window to stare out it. He knew for certain that Melody wouldn't want him around, even if she did like the other two. She'd never forgive him for what he'd done to her cat. Besides, he reminded himself forcibly, he didn't like her. It was her fault that he didn't have a mother anymore.

Emmett found the suggestion warming, if impractical. He'd done a lot of thinking about Melody himself. "Melody has a job," Emmett said. It surprised him that the kids found it so easy to picture Melody as part of their lives. It surprised him even more that he did, too.

"Jacobsville isn't very big, is it?" Guy asked without looking at his father. "There's not much to do there, I guess."

"You're old enough to start learning how to manage a ranch," Emmett told him. "You can come around with me and learn the ropes."

Guy's usually taciturn face brightened. He turned. "I could?"

"Yes." Emmett's eyes narrowed. "I'll have to turn things over to you one day," he added. "You might as well know one end of a rope from the other when the time comes."

Guy felt as if he'd been offered a new start with his father. It was a good feeling. Guy looked at his siblings. "I'll go," he said, his expression warning them that they'd better agree.

Amy and Polk stood close together. "I guess it would be nice to have you at home all the time, Emmett," Amy said softly. "It would be 'specially nice if you didn't have to ride any more mean horses."

"We don't want you to die, Dad," Polk agreed solemnly. "You're sort of all we've got."

Emmett's lean face hardened. "Maybe you're sort of all I've got, too. Ever think of it like that?"

Guy looked uncomfortable and Polk just smiled. But Amy slid onto his lap and hugged him. She looked up with soft, loving eyes. "I'm glad you're our daddy, Emmett," she said.

At that moment, so was he. Very, very glad.

IT COULDN'T LAST, of course, all that peace and affection. They moved to Jacobsville and they hadn't been in the big sprawling ranch house two hours when the cook started screaming bloody murder and ran out of the house with her apron over her head.

"What's the matter?" Emmett called.

"There's a snake in the sink! There's a snake in the sink!"

"Oh, for God's sake, woman, what kind of snake is it?" Emmett grumbled absently, more concerned about the books he'd been going over than this gray-haired woman's hysterics over some small reptile.

"It's twenty feet long!"

"This is Texas," Emmett explained patiently. "There aren't any twenty-foot-long snakes here. You're thinking of boa constrictors and pythons. They come from the jungle."

"Hey, Dad, look what we found in the barn!" Guy called, grinning.

He came out with a huge black-and-white striped snake. It wasn't twenty feet long, but it was at least six.

"Aaaaahhhhhhhhh!" the cook screamed and started running again.

"Go put it back in the barn," Emmett told them.

"But it's just a king snake," Polk protested.

"And he's very friendly, Emmett," Amy agreed.

"Put it back in the barn or she'll never come back. I'll have to cook and we'll starve," he explained, gesturing toward the figure growing smaller in the distance. He scowled. "As it is, I'll have to run her to the ground in the truck. Never saw anyone run that fast!"

"Spoilsport," Guy muttered. He petted the snake, which didn't seem to mind being handled in the least. "Come on, Teddy. It's back to the corn bin for you, I guess. I had hoped we could let him sleep with us. In case there were any mice inside," he said, justifying his reply.

Emmett could see the woman's face if she started to make up a bed and found the snake with its head on the pillow.

"Better not," he replied. "I'll load my pistol. If you see a mouse, I'll shoot it for you."

"The snake's a better bet, the way you shoot," Guy drawled.

Emmett glowered at him, but the boy just grinned. He and the other kids took the snake out to the barn. Half a mile down the road, Emmett caught up with the cook and part-time housekeeper, Mrs. Jenson. After swearing that the kids would never do any such thing again, he coaxed her into coming back and finishing those delicious salmon croquettes she'd started to make.

It was a hard adjustment, being home all the time. Emmett discovered that fatherhood wasn't something he could take for granted anymore. He had to work at it. All the problems the children had at school—problems that poor Mrs. Ray had handled before—were now dumped squarely in his lap.

Polk had a terrible time with fractions, and refused to do them at all in school. Amy had attitude problems and fought with her classmates. Guy was belligerent with his teachers and wouldn't mind spending hours and hours at in-school suspension. All these problems with teachers erupted in Emmett's face, now that he had sole charge of the children.

"Why can't you kids just go to school and get educated like other children do?" he asked. He had notes from three angry teachers in his hand, and he was waving them at the children while they watched television and pretended to listen.

"It's not my fault I can't do fractions. The teacher says I'm not mathematical," Polk said with a proud smile.

"And I have a bad attitude, on account of I don't have a mommy and my daddy is never home and I need discipline and attention," Amy said smartly.

That stung. Emmett brushed it off and tried to pretend he hadn't heard it. "What's your excuse?" Emmett asked Guy.

Guy shrugged. "Beats me. Mrs. Bartley seems to have trouble relating to me or something."

Emmett's eyes narrowed. "That wouldn't have anything to do with the mouse you stuck in her purse before lunch yesterday?"

"Awww, Dad, it was only a little mouse!"

"You have to stop that sort of thing," Emmett said firmly. "We need a little more discipline around here, I can see that right now."

"You bet, Emmett," Amy agreed readily. She propped her hands under her chin and stared at him. "He's right, isn't he, guys?" she asked her brothers.

"It isn't our fault that the educational system is in chaos," Polk reported. "We're just the innocent victims of bureaucracy."

Guy nodded. "That's right."

Emmett sat down and crossed his long legs. "Victims or not, I'll thank you to start minding your manners at school. Or I might just forget to pay the electric bill. How would you watch television then?" he concluded smugly.

Amy sighed. "Well, Emmett, I guess we'd just have to watch it by candlelight."

MELODY HAD PUT the children and Emmett forcibly out of her mind several times over the weeks that followed. Christmas came and went. She exchanged cards and presents with Randy and Adell, but it was still a lonely time.

It disturbed her that she kept staring at dark-haired men because they looked a little like Emmett. Re-

membering how he'd kissed her before he went back
to San Antonio didn't help her nerves, either. She
seemed to walk around in a perpetual state of ner-
vousness, jumping when people came into the office.

"You are a case," Kit said, shaking her head when
Melody leaped back from the filing cabinet as she
came into the office after work.

"Nerves," Melody agreed. "I have nerves. It
comes from mollycoddling nervous investors all
day. It's a wonder I haven't shaken my desk apart."

"Work is all it is, hmm?" Kit asked.

"Of course," Melody replied.

The dark-haired woman only smiled. "Have
you heard that Emmett and the kids moved to Jacobsville?"

Melody stopped filing and stared at her. "They
did?"

"Emmett's accident must have made him do some
hard thinking about his life. He phoned Logan last
night and said he's given up rodeo to manage Ted
Regan's cattle ranch in Jacobsville."

"Has he sold his own ranch?"

"He hired a manager. I suppose he'll make more
than enough to keep his own place going until the
economy gets a bit better. Meanwhile, he's having
plenty of time with his kids."

"They all need that," Melody replied. "Guy especially."

"You don't like Guy, do you?"

"I don't really dislike him. But he hates me. He

can't forget that I helped his mother leave. I can't say I blame him. Divorce is hard on little children."

"It's hard on any kind of children, even big ones," Kit replied. "Why don't you go home? I'll take over here until Logan's ready to leave."

"How nice of you!"

"Well, not really. I enjoy spending time with my husband. Since we both work at different jobs now, every second is precious."

Melody envied her that happiness, but she didn't mind an early night. She said so.

"You're doing a terrific job here," Kit said before she left. "We both appreciate you."

Melody grinned. "You're only saying that because I don't wear blouses cut to my knees or have a breathy voice."

"That, too." Kit chuckled.

Melody waved and went back to her lonely apartment. A telephone call from her brother shocked her speechless.

"You never phone me," she reminded Randy. "I even had to call you at Christmas. Is something wrong?"

"You know me pretty well, don't you? It's not that anything is wrong. It's just that…we have a sort of awkward situation," he began slowly.

"Randy?" she persisted.

There was an audible sigh. "I don't know how to tell you, and you can't tell anyone…especially not Logan or Tansy. Not yet."

"Why not?"

"Because if it gets back to Emmett, I don't know what we'll do!"

She was getting worried. "Randy, what is it?" she said proddingly.

"Well, it's like this. Adell's pregnant."

MELODY REMEMBERED BELATEDLY congratulating her brother, but the news was a complication that wasn't going to make things easier for Emmett and the kids. A new child in a mixed family always brought turmoil. It was a shame, too, when Emmett and the kids had just gotten settled into a new life in Jacobsville.

On the other hand, she was going to be an aunt again, and a real one this time, because Randy was her own blood. It would be his first child. She couldn't be sad about that. But she hurt for Emmett. It wasn't going to be easy for him to learn that his ex-wife was pregnant by the man who'd taken her from him. It was going to cause all sorts of problems.

EMMETT STOPPED OUTSIDE Logan's office and hesitated. He hadn't wanted to come here, but Melody was playing on his senses. He'd missed her. Christmas, even with the kids, had been oddly lonely for him this year. There was a hollow place inside him that a casual date couldn't fill any longer. He'd brooded over what to do about it, and he'd finally come to the conclusion that he needed to see Melody again, to make sure he wasn't overreacting to her.

He'd looked for days for an excuse to show up here. He'd finally found one, in the guise of letting

Logan invest some money for him. But he hadn't telephoned first. He wanted to know if Melody was as attracted to him as he was to her. The element of surprise was going to tell him that.

He opened the door and walked in. She was typing at the computer. She didn't see him at first, not until he closed the door and the sound distracted her.

She looked up with her usual welcoming smile for clients, but it fell short when she saw the man in the gray suit and Stetson standing just inside the door.

"Emmett!" she said involuntarily.

The light in her eyes couldn't lie. Emmett smiled, because she was glad to see him and it showed. He liked the way she looked in that figure-hugging beige dress, with her long hair in a neat French braid and her dark eyes warm in her freckled face.

"Hello," he replied. He moved close to the desk, feeling his body throb, his heart race as he drank in the sight and scent of her from scant inches away. His voice dropped an octave involuntarily in reaction. "You look well."

"I am. I'm fine. How about you?" she asked worriedly.

"No more problems. I have a hard head," he replied. His eyes slid over her face and down to the mouth he'd possessed briefly so long ago. It made him hungry to remember how eager and willing she'd been.

"Emmett!"

The exclamation came from Logan, who'd walked

out with a letter to find his cousin standing over his flustered secretary.

"Hello, Logan," Emmett said, extending a hand.

"You look prosperous," Logan murmured with a smile. "What brings you to Houston?"

"I needed some advice. I was about to make an appointment…"

"No need for that. I'm not busy right now. Come on in." He handed the letter to Melody and tried not to notice that her hands were trembling. Emmett obviously had a powerful effect on her.

"I wanted to see you about some investments," Emmett said when they were sitting in Logan's office.

"Imagine that," Logan said thoughtfully. "You said you didn't trust the stock market."

"I've changed," the other man replied doggedly.

"Indeed you have. How is it, being a full-time father?"

Emmett tossed his hat onto a nearby chair. "It's hell," he said flatly. "I get all the hassles now. I never realized how much trouble three little kids could be. In fact, they're never out of trouble."

"Now that you're home at night, that will change, I imagine," came the droll reply. "You've spent a lot of time avoiding them."

"You know why."

Logan nodded. "Yes, I do. Are you finding your way out of the pit, Emmett?" he asked kindly.

Emmett ran a lean hand through his thick, dark hair. "Maybe. I don't know. A lot of things have changed since I had the fall. Maybe I was looking at it all the wrong way."

"Divorce isn't easy on anyone," Logan said quietly. "It would kill me if Kit left me, for any reason. I don't know if I could take it if it was for another man."

"That's how I felt. I thought I loved Adell," he said heavily. "I really did. But now I'm not sure it wasn't just hurt pride."

"Having her run out in the middle of the night with the other man involved couldn't have helped."

"It didn't. I guess maybe I understand why she did it now, though. She isn't a fighter," he added, echoing the words Melody had spoken. "She probably figured I'd play on her sympathy and talk her out of it if I had the chance." He smiled faintly. "That's what would have happened. She never could stand up to me in a fight." He leaned back. "It's all water under the bridge. I have to go on living. So does she. I want to make some provisions for the kids, in case anything happens to me. That's really why I'm here. I've got a little spare cash and I want to put it where it can grow."

Logan considered it for a moment, his eyes narrowed. "All right. I've got a few ideas. How long are you going to be in town?"

"Until tomorrow," came the surprising answer. "Mrs. Jenson is living in, so that she can watch the kids while I'm away. I…have a few other things to do while I'm in town."

"Where can I reach you?"

Emmett gave him the number at his hotel. "Until six," he said. "I may have plans for the evening."

"Oh," Logan said with a chuckle. "Confinement getting to you, is it? I gather the plans have something to do with a woman."

"Well, yes."

"From what I remember, the kids would make any sort of relationship impossible. I haven't forgotten that they were trying to take off the door of the bathroom when Kit and I were in there, at your ranch."

Emmett grinned at the darkly accusing stare. "So they did. Good thing the screwdriver was too big, wasn't it?"

Logan gave in to laughter. Emmett was as incorrigible as his kids.

HE SHOWED THE other man out, but Emmett seemed strangely reluctant to leave. Perhaps he wanted to tell Melody something about the children, Logan decided, so he said his goodbyes and went back into his office.

Melody was typing nonsense into the computer, because Emmett's stare made her too nervous to function.

"Is there something you needed to ask me?" she said finally, dark eyes lifting to his.

"Yes," he said with a husky laugh. "What are you doing for dinner?"

Doing for dinner. Doing for dinner. The words passed through her mind with very little effect. She stared at him blankly. The telephone rang loudly and she jumped, fumbling the receiver all over the desk before she finally got it to her ear and gave the correct response.

"I'll put you through to Mr. Deverell," she said breathlessly, and buzzed Logan to give the caller's identity.

When she put the receiver back down, she was still very visibly shaken.

Emmett had his Stetson by the brim and he was watching her with a half-amused look that glittered in his green eyes. "Looking for excuses not to go?" he asked softly.

"Oh, no!" she replied huskily. "But why?"

"Why not?"

Her pulse started to run away. She wanted to refuse. She should. But somehow she couldn't. "I... what time?" she asked.

"Six."

"This isn't a good idea, you know," she said. "I'm still Randy's sister, and the past hasn't changed. Not at all."

He moved closer to the desk and his lean hand toyed with a notepad on its paper-littered surface. His pale green eyes searched her dark ones quietly. "That's true. Maybe I've changed. I enjoy your company. I want to take you out for a meal. That's all," he added flatly. "You won't have to fight me off over dessert and coffee."

She laughed nervously. "That was the last thought in my mind."

He didn't believe that. But she relaxed, and he felt

glad that he'd said it. He didn't want to make her uneasy. She'd been too much on his mind lately and he wanted to find a way to purge her from it. Perhaps closer acquaintance would solve the problem for him. Often women who seemed nice weren't, and they couldn't keep up the act when a man took the time to get to know them.

Melody was relieved by his blunt statement. There had been a time or two when she had found herself having to talk her way out of a difficult situation.

"I'll see you at six, then," he said.

He stuck the Stetson back on his head and went to the door. He paused there and turned. "I'm rabidly old-fashioned in one respect. I like dresses."

She grinned impishly. "Yes, but how do you look in a dress?" she asked curiously.

His pale eyes splintered with good humor. "Wear what you damned well please, then," he mused. "See you later."

MELODY OWNED ONE nice dress. It was black with a silvery draped bodice and spaghetti straps. It flattered her full-figured body without making her sexiness blatant. She coiled her hair around the top of her head and wore more makeup than usual. The final touch was high heels. Most men she dated were her height or shorter. But Emmett was very tall, and she could get away with wearing high heels when she went out with him. She liked the way she felt when she was dressed up; very feminine and sensuous.

Now, she wondered, why should she think of herself as sensuous? She had to douse that thought before Emmett read it in her face. She didn't want any complications.

He was prompt. The doorbell sounded exactly at six. She opened the door and there he was, very elegant in dark slacks and a white dinner jacket with a red carnation in the buttonhole of his lapel. The stark white contrasted handsomely with his lean, dark face and dark hair. He had on a cream-colored Stetson to set off the elegance.

"You look very nice," she said huskily.

"Stole my line," he mused, grinning at her. "Ready to go?"

"I'll just get my wrap and my purse."

She draped a black mantilla over her shoulders and picked up her small black crepe purse. She checked to make sure Alistair had water and cat food. He was curled up on the couch asleep, so she didn't disturb him.

Emmett waited while she locked the door before he took her hand in his and led her along the corridor.

If someone had told her that holding hands could be a powerful aphrodisiac she might have laughed, but with Emmett, it was. His lean, strong hand curled into her fingers with confident possession. Beside him she felt protected and unexpectedly feminine. She couldn't remember ever feeling that way with another date.

He saw her expression as he led her into the empty elevator and pushed the down button. He'd let go of her hand to do that. Now he leaned elegantly against the rail inside the elevator as it started to move and just watched her, registering the conflicting emotions that washed over her face.

The tension between them was chaotic. She could barely breathe as she met his eyes and felt her knees go weak.

"You look lovely," he said, his voice deep, his eyes faintly glittery. "Black provides a backdrop for all the color in your hair and your face." His eyes fell to her draped bodice and lingered there, making her feel shivery all over.

"How do you like Jacobsville, you and the children?" she asked quickly, hoping to distract him.

"What? Oh, so far, so good. It's no picnic, but I think we're all getting the hang of it. It's going to be the best thing that ever happened to the children," he added quietly. "I honestly didn't realize how much out of hand they'd gotten."

He looked broody for a minute, and Melody wondered if there wasn't more to it than that. But before she could voice her opinions, the elevator door opened and they were on their way out.

He stopped, taking her hand back in his and holding it warmly while he searched her eyes. "I like it better like this. Don't you?" he asked softly, and he didn't smile. His eyes dropped to her mouth. "For now," he added, very gently.

CHAPTER SIX

THE COOL AIR on her face felt good as they left the apartment house and walked down the street. Melody was still vibrating from the heady experience of being on a date with Emmett. He, on the other hand, seemed perfectly nonchalant. Her heart was racing like a mad thing while they walked, hand in hand.

He led her to the car and unlocked it, but when he partially opened her door, he stood still, so that she couldn't get past him. She was so close that she could smell his tangy cologne, feel the warm strength of his body. It made her react in an unexpected way, and she moved back against the car a little self-consciously.

"You're nervous of me. Why?" he asked.

She twisted her bag in her hands and laughed. "I'm not, really." She shrugged. "It's just that it's been a long time since I've been out for the evening."

He tilted her face up to his quiet eyes. His thumb smoothed against her chin and her full lower lip, making sensation after sensation wash over her. She wasn't fooling him. He read quite accurately her helpless physical response to him. Whatever else she was, she wasn't experienced. That was unique to a man who deliberately chose women for their so-

phistication and disinterest in involvement. Melody
was different.

"That's the only reason?" he asked, probing softly.

She couldn't hide her expression quickly enough.
"Well...maybe not the only one," she said demurely.

He smiled with pure delight. He bent and his lips
brushed gently across her wide forehead. She smelled
of soap and skin cream and floral cologne. The mingled scents appealed to his senses. "There's nothing
to worry about," he said quietly. "Nothing at all."
He moved away from her then, still good-natured.
"I hope you like a smorgasbord of choices. This restaurant has international fare."

The change from tenderness to companionship
was unsettling, but Melody managed the shift. "I
love international fare," she said.

He opened the car door the rest of the way and
helped her inside. All the way to the restaurant, the
most intimate thing he discussed was the stock market and the state of the economy. By the time they
disembarked, Melody could have been forgiven for
thinking she'd dreamed that gentle kiss in the parking lot.

It wasn't a terribly ritzy place to eat. The food
was very good and moderately priced, but Melody
didn't have to worry if her clothes were good enough
to wear to it. The thought made her smile.

Emmett cocked an eyebrow. "Private thoughts?"

"I was just glad that I'm properly dressed for this
place, without being underdressed," she confessed on
a laugh. "I don't have the wardrobe for those French

restaurants where they don't even bother to put the prices on the menus."

He chuckled. "I've eaten in a couple of those," he replied. "I never felt very comfortable in them, though. My idea of a good lunch is a McDonald's hamburger."

"Good old Scottish cooking," she mused, tongue-in-cheek.

He laughed with her as he sampled his rare steak. "You're remarkably good-humored."

"Oh, I like laughter," she told him. "Life is too short to go around with a long face complaining about everything."

He studied her over a bite of nicely browned steak. "You manage to work for my cousin without complaints?"

"Well…not many," she said. "And he's my cousin, too, you know."

His eyes grew somber and they fell to his plate. "So he is."

"You look so remote." She hesitated. "Oh, I see. You were thinking that Adell was related to him by marriage, and she's still related to him because she's married to Randy—" She broke off, flushing.

He put down his fork. His appetite had gone. He'd thought he was getting over Adell's defection, but apparently the wounds were still open.

"I'm sorry," she said with a grimace. "I've ruined it all by bringing them up, haven't I?" She laid down her own fork. "It won't work, Emmett," she said suddenly, without stopping to choose her words.

"There are too many scars for us to be able to get along. You're never going to be able to forget about Randy and Adell." That was true—and he didn't even know what she did, either, about Adell being pregnant. She felt guilty.

He lifted his eyes to her face. It made him angry that she'd assumed that he was romantically interested in her. It made him more angry that he'd actually been thinking along those lines until she'd dragged Randy and Adell into the conversation.

He lashed out in frustration. "Aren't you taking too much for granted? My God, this was only a dinner invitation, not a proposal of marriage!" he said angrily. His eyes calmed. "Or is that what you thought I might be considering by asking you out?" He smiled at her embarrassment without humor. "Do I really seem the sort of man who can't wait to get married a second time?"

She had to force down the hopes she'd been nursing since his invitation to this meal. He obviously had cold feet about any relationship between them, and he was hiding it in sarcasm. She knew that as surely as if he'd told her so.

"Of course not," she lied. "That isn't what I was thinking at all. I only meant that taking me out isn't a good idea."

"For once, we agree on something." He lifted his coffee cup to his firm lips, averting his gaze. He must have been out of his mind to have come up to Houston in the first place. Asking Melody out had been another temporary mental aberration. He had enough trouble already without rushing out to search for more.

"Are you finished?" he asked when he'd drained his cup.

She was glad she hadn't wanted dessert. He seemed to be in a flaming rush to leave. She was eager to oblige him. The evening had been an unmitigated disaster!

He drove her back to her apartment in a furious silence, without even tuning in a song on the radio to break the tension. Melody didn't feel any more inclined toward conversation than he seemed to.

She rode up in the elevator beside him without looking to the side. He paused at her door, sighing angrily.

"Thank you for an interesting evening," she said tightly.

"It was gratitude for keeping the kids," he said, his words as clipped as her own. "That's all. It was a belated thank-you for kindnesses rendered."

"And accepted in the same vein," she said. "No complications wanted."

"That's right, and you remember it," he said through his teeth. "You're the last damned complication I need right now!"

"Did I offer to be one?" she asked, aghast.

"Whether you did or not is beside the point! I've got kids who can't get along with anyone because they don't get any love at home. Their father doesn't give a damn about them and their mother ran away with your damned brother!"

The anger she'd felt was suddenly gone as she saw through the furious words to the hurt beneath it. He was wounded. She wondered if he knew how obvious it was, and decided that he didn't. Her dark eyes lost their glare and became gentle. She reached out with unexpected bravery and took one of his big, lean hands in hers.

"Come inside and have some coffee, Emmett," she said gently. "You can tell me all about it."

He must be daft. He kept telling himself he was as he let her lead him like a lamb into the softly lit kitchen.

He perched himself on her tallest stool and watched broodingly while she filled the coffeemaker and turned it on.

She sat down at the counter next to him, her mantilla and purse deposited on the kitchen table until she had time to move them.

"What's wrong with the children?" she asked.

He sighed heavily. "Polk won't try to do his math. Guy can't get along with his teacher. Amy can't get along with anybody, and her teacher sends me this damned note that says she doesn't get enough attention at home."

"And you're doing the best you can, only nobody knows it but you, and those words hurt."

He lifted narrowed, wounded eyes to hers. "Yes, it hurts," he said flatly. "I've done my best to provide for them. All I've had since Adell walked out is a housekeeper. Now, I'm trying to put things right, but I can't do it overnight!"

She smoothed her fingers gently over the backs of his strong, lean hands. "Why don't you write Amy's teacher a note and tell her that," she suggested. "Teachers don't read minds, you know. They have to be told about problems. They're people, too, just like you and me. They can make allowances, when they know the situation."

He relaxed. His tall, broad-shouldered form seemed to slump. "I'm tired," he said. "It's a shock. New surroundings, new people, a new job with more responsibilities than I've had in years and the kids on top of it. I guess I got snarled up in it all."

"It's perfectly understandable. Don't the kids like it better, having you home?"

"I don't know. Guy's still standoffish. I've tried to get him interested in things around the ranch, but he's shying away from me. He's not adjusting very well to school, because the teacher wants him to mind and he won't. He can't seem to conform, and his temper is his worst enemy. Amy and Polk aren't much better, but at least I can handle them when they're not driving school officials batty."

"Better them than you?" she teased.

He chuckled reluctantly. "Not really. I'll have to bone up on fractions and spend some time with Polk. Maybe I just haven't found the right tack with Guy yet. He likes ranching, but we don't have much in common outside it."

"Emmett, hasn't it occurred to you that these problems could be nothing more than pleas for attention?" she asked. "Randy and I used to get into all sorts of trouble when Dad got too wrapped up in Mother's illness to notice us. It's a child's nature to want to be loved, to have proof of that love."

"Not only a child's, Melody," he said unexpectedly. His eyes searched hers from much too close. "Even adults can go off the deep end when no one gives a damn about them."

"You know the kids love you."

"I know." His chest rose and fell heavily and his eyes grew intimate, holding hers for much longer than necessary, making her own pulse race.

"The, uh, the coffee's ready, I think," she said. Her voice sounded husky, even shaky. She dragged her eyes away from his and went to get the coffee.

She took down cups and saucers from the cabinet, and while she got the coffee service together, Emmett moved around the living room, restless and unsettled. His eyes searched out the books in her bookcase, the framed prints on the wall. He seemed to be noticing everything, taking inventory of her likes and dislikes.

He was thumbing through a volume of poetry when she put the coffee things on the dining-room table.

He put the book down and joined her at the table. She put cream and sugar into hers. He left his own black.

"I've got some cookies around here somewhere," she offered.

"No need. I don't have much of a sweet tooth," he said. He stared into his coffee. "How did you know?"

"Know what?"

He looked up with a rueful smile. "That I needed to talk about the kids."

"You picked a fight for no reason," she murmured dryly. "I used to have a friend in school who did the same thing. She never said what was bothering her. She picked fights until I made her tell me." She fingered the rim of her coffee cup. "Or maybe you didn't exactly pick a fight for no reason," she added sadly. "You aren't over Randy and Adell, really."

He moved restlessly in the chair. "It's going to take time."

Her eyes lifted to his. He didn't know that Adell was pregnant. How was she going to tell him? How could she tell him?

He saw that curious expression and scowled. "There's something," he said slowly. "Something you're holding back. What is it?"

She averted her gaze to the coffee cup. "Nothing."

"Now you sound like one of the kids." He moved her coffee cup out of her reach and caught her hand in his over the small table. "Out with it. You made me talk when I didn't want to. It's your turn."

"Emmett…"

He nodded reassuringly. "Come on."

She winced. Her big, dark eyes were full of sadness, sorrow. "Adell…is pregnant."

He didn't react at all for a minute. He let go of her hand and sat back in his chair. He let out a long, rough breath. "Well."

"You'd have found out sooner or later. I didn't want to have to be the one to tell you."

He looked at her. "You didn't? Why?" he asked, letting the shock of what he'd learned pass over him for the moment.

"You resent me enough already because of my brother," she said miserably.

His eyes searched her wan, sad face. "Do I?" he wondered aloud. It didn't feel like hatred. No, not at all.

He drained his coffee cup, and she took it, and hers, into the kitchen. She felt terrible. Working helped sometimes, so she busied herself loading the dishwasher. There wasn't much, but she'd saved last night's pots and pans to make a load. Behind her, she felt Emmett's eyes and could only imagine the torment he must be feeling. She wanted to console him, but she didn't know how.

After a minute, Emmett got up and poised himself against the kitchen counter to watch her work. He didn't want to think about Adell being pregnant by her new husband. He wasn't going to let himself do that now. Later would be time enough.

Melody was graceful for such a tall woman, he thought reluctantly, watching her hands as she put the dishes into the dishwasher.

She noticed the look she was getting. It made her tingle. He'd long since taken off his dinner jacket and tie and Stetson. His long-sleeved, pristine white shirt was partially unbuttoned and the sleeves were rolled up. He looked elegant and rakish, and Melody was surprised that he seemed to find her so interesting. He'd been married, and she knew very well that women still chased him. He had more experience than any man she'd ever dated. It made her nervous to remember how vulnerable she was with him, how easily he could overrule her and take anything he wanted. She hoped her unease didn't show too much.

"You're efficient," he remarked.

She smiled. "Oh, I'm very domestic. I had to learn early. My mother was an invalid for years before she and Dad died. Randy and I would have starved if I hadn't been able to cook."

His face closed up at the mention of his ex-wife's new husband.

Melody put detergent into the dishwasher and started it running. Her eyes flicked to Emmett and away. "Yes, I know, you hate my brother as much as you hate me."

His green eyes were completely without hostility for once as he studied her. The black dress she was wearing suited her fair complexion. Its fit emphasized her full breasts and hips and small waist, and the milky-white softness of her shoulders with their scattering of freckles. He liked what he saw when he looked at her, even if it was against his better judgment.

"I don't hate you," he said quietly.

"Pull the other one, Emmett."

She'd turned and was starting out the door when he moved with surprising speed and blocked her way. "I like the way you say my name. Say it again."

His arm was across the doorway, almost touching the tips of her breasts. She tensed at the sensual threat of it. "This isn't wise," she said seriously, meeting his green eyes levelly.

One eye narrowed. His gaze on her face was intent, curious. "Isn't it? Maybe not. We're years apart—almost a generation. Funny, I always thought you were older. I don't know why. You seem very mature for a woman just barely out of her teens."

"I had to grow up fast. May I get by, please?"

He could see her breathing quicken. "Why are you afraid of me?"

Her eyes darted up and down again. Her cheeks colored. "Am I?"

He reached out and caught her by the waist. He tugged, pulling her slowly to him, so that her mouth was poised just under his.

"Maybe intimidated is a better choice of words," he murmured. His hands slid up her rib cage with slow sensuality, making her flinch at the sudden pleasure of their touch. "I know a hell of a lot more than you do about this, don't I, little one?" His breath was warm on her parted lips. "Is that what's wrong?"

"Yes," she whispered breathlessly.

He looked at her mouth instead of her eyes. It trembled, pink and soft like some pastel flower, waiting to be touched. She was so young, he thought. She really was off-limits to a man his age.

But even as he thought it, his lips moved the scant inches necessary to bring them right down over her whispered gasp, and took possession of that petal-pink mouth.

She grasped his shirtfront and stiffened in surprise.

"Shh," he whispered against her lips while he worked with sensuous mastery at parting them. "You're safe. You're perfectly safe. There won't be anything to regret. Relax for me."

She'd been kissed. She'd been kissed plenty of times, and even by him! There was certainly no reason why Emmett's mouth should be so different from any other man's.

But, it was. Her whole body felt as if it contracted while Emmett's warm, strong arms enveloped her and his tongue slowly, tenderly impaled her mouth as it had once before. She stiffened again as the throbbing pleasure began to make her feel unwanted, unwelcome sensations. She fought them.

He felt the resistance, as slight as it was, and lifted his dark head.

"You're still holding back from me," he said, his voice tender if a little unsteady. "I'm not going to hurt you."

"It makes me feel funny," she replied dizzily.

His nose brushed lazily against hers. "Where?"

"In my stomach…"

"Good," he whispered. His lips eased back down and brushed hers apart, teasing them to make her mouth follow his in a sensual daze. His hands slid to her hips and contracted in a strangely arousing rhythm, pulling and pushing, brushing her legs against his.

She shivered. He felt that and lifted his head to search her wide, curious eyes.

"You're so young," he said quietly. He took a slow, steadying breath. "And so responsive that I'm likely to take advantage of it."

Desire had her in its grip. She wasn't afraid. She was hungry. "How?" she asked in a breathless whisper, and her eyes clung to his hard mouth as she spoke. "What will you do to me?"

His fingers eased up her rib cage and came to rest against the soft swell of her breasts. He nibbled at her mouth. One lean hand slowly cupped her and began to caress her with tender mastery. She started to stiffen until the dark delight of it made her go boneless in his embrace. She could have resisted his desire, but not her own. He was years beyond her in experience, and she reacted with helpless curiosity and need.

He nibbled tenderly at her lower lip. "I know. It's forbidden territory, isn't it?" he whispered into her parting lips. "Nice girls don't let men do this. Except that they do, Melody," he breathed as he drew her even closer. "This is part and parcel of being human." His thumb drew suddenly, tenderly, across her taut nipple, a fiery touch that caused her whole body to clench. Her nails bit into him and she gasped. "If I hurt you, I want to know it," he whispered. "Because it's only meant to arouse, not to bruise."

She shivered, but she didn't back away. She felt

as if she had pulses where she'd never suspected, throbbing and hot. "It didn't hurt, Emmett," she admitted huskily, although she was too shy to look at him. She closed her eyes and hid them against his shirtfront. "Do it again."

He hadn't expected this kind of honesty, or as much cooperation. It ate at his control. His hand swallowed her, making magic on her body. She gave in without a sound, and he felt ten feet taller. He paused just long enough to unfasten his shirt halfway down his chest and drag her hand inside it, against the damp tangle of hair over the warm, hard muscles.

The feel of his body like that made her pulse throb. "You're hairy," she whispered.

"I'm like this all over," he whispered roughly. His hand moved down to her hips. The other one joined it. He pulled her into the blatant arousal of his body and held her there firmly but gently. "It's all right. Be still," he said when she tried unsuccessfully to pull away. He searched her face, finding shy curiosity there. "Have you never felt a man's body in full arousal before?"

"No," she managed to say, embarrassed.

"There's a first time for everything," he said softly, lowering his head. "I need oblivion and you need teaching. Think of it as a…reciprocal exchange."

"It isn't a good idea," she said unsteadily.

"I know. But it will be sweet."

And it was. The sweetest kind of exchange, savagely tender and violently arousing.

Her nails thrust gently into the hair at the back of his head while he kissed her and slowly caressed her breasts with hands that held a faint tremor at the license they were being given so generously.

In turn, she was learning about his body, enjoying the feel of the thick mat of hair over warm, firm muscles. She smoothed her hands sensually up and down his chest with delight while he taught her the intricacies of openmouthed kissing. By the time he began to brush against her rhythmically with his hips, she was whimpering with the same desire that was riding him. But it couldn't go on. He was fast reaching the point of no return, and seducing her was impossible.

She felt swollen from head to toe, throbbing, when he finally lifted his head to look into her misty, half-closed eyes. He was more aroused than he could remember being in recent years. His body throbbed painfully with the need for release.

He pushed her hips away from his and took her face in his hands before he kissed her again, with growing tenderness.

She started to move closer, but he caught her by the waist and kept her away.

Her eyes asked the question that her swollen lips wouldn't form.

"Does the term 'playing with fire' ring any chimes?" he asked with forced, husky laughter.

"I don't care," she said unsteadily. Her face colored, but she didn't look away. "I like the way you feel."

His face tautened. "I like the way you feel, too, but

a few minutes of feverish sex isn't going to improve our situation. And I did promise you that there would be nothing to regret." He forced himself to let her go and move away. He lit a cigarette. He hardly smoked these days, but he needed something to steady his nerves.

"A few minutes of feverish sex?" she said with a feeble attempt at humor as she leaned back against the counter and stared at him from a face that held lingering traces of desire.

He glanced at her and laughed, too. "Yes, well, it may be crude, but it was all I could think of at the time. I had to save you from yourself. Not to mention, from me." His eyes were bold on her breasts, assessing their taut peaks before his gaze lifted again to her flushed, excited face. "You're a quick study."

"Is that what I am?"

"That, and alarmingly innocent, for all your response just now," he added, the laughter leaving his eyes, to be replaced with quiet introspection. "Why are you still a virgin, Melody?"

She didn't bother to deny it. She knew all too well from what Kit had told her that he was definitely no novice. Women apparently fell over themselves trying to climb into bed with him. "I'm oversized and old-fashioned and plain, didn't you notice?" she asked, stung by the question.

"Don't take offense," he said quietly. "It wasn't a sarcastic question. If you want to know the truth," he added, his voice going sensual and soft, and his green eyes glittery, as he looked at her, "it excites me to the point of madness."

She drew a slow breath. "That's a new observation," she replied. "Most people think I'm crazy or fanatically careful. The truth is that nobody ever put on enough pressure to make me careless."

"Until now?" he asked gently.

She started to deny it, but that was pointless. He knew. She saw it in his eyes.

"Until now," she echoed.

He lifted the cigarette to his lips and blew out a faint cloud of smoke. Half angrily, he turned on the faucet and held the barely touched cigarette under it, extinguishing it. He tossed the finished remains into the trash can and stood staring down at it.

"I used to smoke a pack a day. I've lost my enthusiasm for it. Addiction is unwise." He turned and stared at her intently. "Any kind of addiction."

"Smoking is bad for you. I never even tried it."

"Good for you." He took the almost full package out of his pocket and dropped that into the trash can, too. "I have to go."

She didn't want that. She felt a sudden, acute sense of loss that was puzzling.

She moved out of the kitchen and preceded him to the front door. But when she would have opened it, his big, lean hand flattened on its surface and prevented her.

"What are you doing Sunday?" he asked abruptly, and against his better judgment.

CHAPTER SEVEN

MELODY FELT THE floor giving way under her feet, and realized that it was because her heart was beating so fast. For a minute she thought he might be joking. But he didn't look as if he were, and there was a new softness in his green eyes.

"Why?" Her voice sounded like a croak.

He'd buttoned his shirt and put his dinner jacket back on. He finished with his tie and picked up his Stetson before he answered her. "I want you to spend the day with us so that I can show you the ranch," he said quietly. "Amy and Polk have talked about you since we left here. They actually asked if you could come and look after them when our housekeeper quit in San Antonio," he added with a smile. "They think you're great."

"I think they're great, too." She hesitated. "I'd love to. But Guy wouldn't like it."

"I know," he said easily. "Guy's been distrustful of everyone since his mother left." He grimaced, remembering what she'd told him about Adell. "I wouldn't dare tell him she's pregnant—him or the other kids. Not until I have time to prepare them."

"They'll adjust," she said softly. "It's amazing

what people, even little people, can do when they have to."

"I guess so." He searched her dark eyes for a long time and laughed softly. "I hated you that night you helped Adell meet Randy at the airport to leave me," he recalled. "I said some terrible things to you. I guess I scared you pretty good, too, when I went after Randy." He shifted restlessly. "I'm sorry."

The belated apology was unexpected, as was the invitation to Jacobsville.

"People in pain lash out," she said simply. "I understood."

"All the same, you backed away from me when I first came to town with the kids."

"Self-protection," she mused. "Survival instinct."

"Yes, well I notice that it's done a nosedive tonight," he murmured, letting his eyes fall to the wrinkled black fabric of her bodice that his exploring hands had disturbed.

She cleared her throat. "What time Sunday?"

"I'll pick you up about ten. Or do you go to church?"

"I do, usually. But I'll play hooky Sunday. I could drive down," she added.

"I hate the idea of having you on the roads alone," he said. "It's a good long drive from Jacobsville to Houston."

She smiled. He was being protective. She didn't mind one bit. It was nice to be cared about, to have someone worry about her welfare. These days, that was unusual.

"Okay," she said gently.

His chest rose and fell heavily. He smiled back at her. "Can you ride?"

"A little."

"Play checkers?"

She blew on her nails and buffed them on her dress. "World champion class," she informed him.

He lifted an eyebrow. "Well, we'll see about that!"

She grinned. "Okay." Her eyes narrowed. "You'll be sure you take matches and ropes away from those kids before I get there?"

"I'll confiscate everything incendiary," he swore, hand over his heart. "Also sharp objects, blunt instruments and listening devices."

"They sound like a renegade branch of the CIA."

He leaned close. "They are. Juvenile division."

She laughed delightedly. "They're good kids, Emmett," she said. "All three of them."

"Guy was honestly sorry about the cat," he said with emphasis. "He's never done cruel things. Mischievous, yes, but they always drew the line at deliberately hurting people. He learned something from it."

"I'm glad."

"Sunday, then?"

She nodded. Her eyes sketched his face with soft hunger. He returned the look, but he didn't touch her again. It was a wrench, because he wanted to. The feel of her body in his hands had made him weak-kneed. His eyes slowly dragged over her and he felt himself going taut. He had to get out of here before he did something stupid.

"I have to go. Good night," he said softly.

"Good night."

He opened the door and turned, silhouetted in the hall light. "Wear jeans and boots," he cautioned. "If we go riding, it's safer."

"I'll remember."

He winked at her, producing an odd jerky sensation in the region of her heart. Then he tipped his Stetson down over his thick, dark hair and walked away, whistling to himself.

Melody closed the door reluctantly. She could have stood watching him all the way to the elevator with the greatest pleasure.

AMY AND POLK had been looking forward to Melody's visit all week. When she drove up with Emmett, they opened her car door and ran into her arms, laughing and talking together. Guy didn't move off the porch. He stood there, a little belligerent, with his hands tight in his jeans pockets, glaring.

Melody noticed him there, and thought how like his father he looked. It wounded her that she and Guy were enemies. It was going to make any relationship she tried to form with Emmett impossible. Emmett probably knew it, too, she thought. But perhaps friendship was all he had in mind. Then she remembered the way he'd kissed her and what he'd said about her innocence. No. Friendship wouldn't be all of it.

Fielding Amy and Polk, Emmett opened the door for all of them. Mrs. Jenson, looking harassed, stayed just long enough to meet Melody and then beat a hasty retreat to the kitchen.

"What did you do, try to tie her to the television?" Emmett asked his angelic brood.

"Not at all, Emmett," Amy assured him, smiling up at them. "Melody, how do you like our new house?"

"It's very nice, Amy," Melody replied. "Hello, Guy," she added coolly.

Guy only shrugged and didn't look at her.

He pretended to be watching television intently while Polk and Amy showed Melody all their treasures and school papers. Just as if she was already their mother, he thought bitterly. Well, he wasn't going to show her anything of his! Melody hated him, and he certainly hated her. She wasn't his mother. She wasn't ever going to be!

He glanced at her from his pale eyes, and his mind began working. It wasn't certain yet. He had time. He had to remember that, and not panic because his father had brought her down to the ranch. He could get her right out of his father's life if he just kept his head. The one thing he couldn't afford to do was let things get serious between them. His mother would come back one day. She'd get tired of her new husband and come home, and they'd all be a family again. Guy was sure of it. He just had to stop his father from getting involved with any other woman until that happened. And he would, too.

Melody was blissfully unaware of Guy's plotting, and frankly glad when he wandered off later to play with his dog, Barney.

"We can go riding after lunch, if you like," Emmett said, smiling at her while Amy and Polk turned their attention back to a nature special on television.

"I'd like that."

"Come on. I'll show you my horses." He held out his hand. She put hers into it, tingling at the contact. He looked good, she thought, in jeans and a blue-checked shirt and boots. He was tall and lean and she loved looking at him, touching him.

He was doing some looking of his own. She was wearing yellow jeans and a matching yellow knit sweater that suited her fair complexion. She walked just in front of him toward the front porch and his eyes narrowed on the fit of those jeans. He had to do some quick mental exercises to stop the physical reaction his interest provoked.

"It's beautiful here," she said, gazing lovingly around at the long, bare horizon and the white-fenced acreage thick with red-coated cattle. There were live oak and pecan trees all around the house, along with pines and thick glossy-leaved bushes.

"I guess it is. I miss my own place." He stuck his hands into his pockets and stared out at the barn. "I guess this place will be lush and green when spring comes. Right now, it looks a bit barren. And there's no mesquite," he muttered.

"Don't tell me you miss the thorns on the mesquite," she teased.

The light in her face made him hungry for things he didn't realize he wanted. He took his hands out of his pockets and captured one of her hands in his. "Come on and see the horses."

"Okay!"

He smiled and led her out to the barn. A small calf was resting in a stall by himself. Emmett explained that the calf's mother had died and he was malnourished before he'd been found. They were feeding him up before they went through the process of trying to pair him with a foster mother.

Down the aisle from the calf in a separate section of the huge barn, he had several saddle horses and a stud Appaloosa stallion in separate quarters. The stallion wasn't kept with the other horses. Emmett explained that it was because he was too volatile.

"I love Apps," he said wistfully, gazing at the big animal, which was mostly splashy red with white spots. "They're beautiful, but they have unpredictable qualities."

"Just like people," she teased.

He glanced down at her from under the wide brim of his gray working hat. "Just like people," he agreed. He let his eyes run down her body boldly. "You bother me in tight jeans. I didn't know you were going to look so sexy."

She laughed self-consciously. "Well, I never," she murmured.

"I know you've never," he murmured dryly. "That's another thing that excites me."

"You'll turn my head if you aren't careful," she said, trying to lighten the atmosphere.

"I'm tired of being careful." He drew up a booted foot and rested it on the lowest rung of a gate. "In between work and more work, you're all I think about lately," he said matter-of-factly, watching her with glittery green eyes. "I don't look at other women. I haven't slept with anyone since long before I got thrown off that bronc."

She was almost afraid to ask, but she had to know. "Because of...me?"

He nodded slowly. "Because of you." He sighed heavily. "Melody, you're barely twenty. It's a hell of a jump from your age to mine, and I've got a built-in family. I can't seduce you because my conscience won't let me. I can't stay away from you because you're obsessing me. Know that old saying about being caught between a rock and a hard place? I don't have any trouble understanding it these days."

She met his eyes steadily. "You want to sleep with me."

He frowned slightly, his expression whimsical. "I hadn't thought about sleeping, exactly," he said meaningfully. He scowled and his eyes narrowed thoughtfully. "On the other hand, I wouldn't mind holding you all night in my arms. I haven't wanted to do that since I was courting Adell." He pushed his hat back from his forehead, and his level stare didn't waver. "In fact, to be brutally frank, what I wanted to do with Adell was pretty limited. It's... different with you."

That was nice. She began to smile. She felt a delicious kindling of joy deep inside herself. He had to care a little, for there to be a difference. She wanted him, too, but it was much more than a physical need. The thought of lying close in his arms all night gave her a warm, comforting sort of pleasure.

"You don't wear pajamas," she said absently.

His eyebrows went up.

She flushed, remembering how he looked without clothes. "Sorry! I guess my mind was wandering."

"Oh? Where was it wandering?"

She traced the grain of the wood on the gate. "I was thinking about sleeping with you," she said quietly. "I haven't been held in a long time. Not…by anyone who cared about me."

"Neither have I."

She glanced at him. "Oh?" she said with a cold, speaking look, because she'd heard about the rodeo groupies of the past year.

His broad shoulders lifted and fell. "Being held in a sexual frenzy isn't the same." He scowled. "And I think there has to be more to a marriage than good sex. That's new for me. Adell and I had nothing in common except desire and a love of children."

"That's pretty important, isn't it?" she asked.

"Yes. But common interests, mutual respect—those things make a relationship last." He smiled wistfully, studying her. "Funny, I could never talk to Adell the way I can to you. She liked sex, but she was ice-cold in the daylight, as if it embarrassed her that she had physical needs."

"I think a lot of women are like that," she said.

He tilted her chin up. "Are you going to be?" he asked, smiling indulgently. "Will you want the lights out the first time?"

She considered that. "I haven't let anybody see me without my clothes, except my doctor," she said. "I think it will be embarrassing, and I'll be self-conscious, because I'm big and a little overweight…"

He touched her mouth with a lean forefinger. He wasn't smiling. "You aren't overweight or oversized. You look like a woman should," he said. "I don't know why you think men should go lusting after skin and bones. There are exceptions, but most of us like a well-rounded figure with big breasts."

She flushed, but he wouldn't let her look away.

"Don't be embarrassed," he said gently. "There's nothing wrong with you. Nothing at all."

"Thanks," she said huskily. It was unusual to feel smaller than an Amazon. She smiled at him. Her eyes turned toward the doors of the barn, toward the outside, which was sunlit and peaceful. "It must be nice to live on a ranch," she said with unconscious wistfulness. "I know it's hard work, but you're so far away from technology."

He laughed uproariously.

"What's so funny?"

"Wait until you see the mainframe computer in my office," he mused dryly. "Not to mention the state-of-the-art jet printer, the fax machine, the color hand scanner, the photocopier and the modem."

She stared at him blankly.

"I have to buy and sell cattle, keep up with sales reports, tally information about the herds and the cross-breeding program. I'm in constant contact with breeders and buyers, the National Cattlemen's Association, the Texas branch of it, not to mention veterinarians and state officials—"

"But you raise cattle, don't you?" she faltered.

"Raising cattle is big business these days, honey," he said, the endearment, which he never used, coming so naturally with her that he hardly noticed he'd said it.

She noticed, though. Her face colored and her eyes brightened.

He touched her hair, fingering its thick, elegant length in the French plait. He wondered how it would feel to run his fingers through its thick, loosened strands at night. She didn't usually wear it down. "Honey," he repeated. "It's an endearment that suits you. Your hair looks like wildflower honey in spots, all golden and glowing in the sunlight, Melody."

As he spoke, he moved closer and his head began to bend. He brushed his mouth over hers until he coaxed it to open. Then he kissed her with piercing hunger, with possession.

Seconds later, she was riveted to every inch of him, held so close that she could feel him in an intimacy they'd only shared once before.

"God!" He ground out the single word, and his hand slipped under her yellow knit sweater to raid her soft femininity. He kissed her hungrily for a long few seconds and then lifted his head to look into her dazed eyes while his hand felt for the catch to her bra and snapped it with practiced efficiency.

He glanced around them to make sure they weren't being observed. Then, while he watched her, his hand moved up to softly caress her bare breast. He felt it swell, felt its tip go hard and hot in his damp palm.

"Your breasts are very full," he whispered huskily. "I love touching them like this."

"Emmett," she protested weakly, and hid her face against his chest.

She was shy, but not at all inhibited or coquettish. He loved that honesty. His lean hand covered her completely, and he searched for her mouth until he found it.

She felt hot all over. Shaky. Throbbing with a kind of fever. She moaned faintly.

"Yes," he said roughly. "It isn't enough, is it?"

His hands went to the hem of the sweater and abruptly pushed it up, along with her loose bra. Then he stood and stared at her with an expression she'd never seen on a man's face before. She blushed, because certainly no man had ever looked at her bare breasts before.

"Baby," he said unsteadily, "you are a walking, blushing work of art!"

He made her feel beautiful. She watched him watching her and couldn't manage to feel any embarrassment. His eyes were explicit and very, very flattering.

His hands shook as he forced himself to pull the

fabric down. He couldn't be sure those kids weren't hiding out somewhere nearby and he could lose his head much too easily if he did what he wanted to.

Her misty eyes asked a question.

He avoided meeting them while he reached behind her and refastened the bra under the cover of her sweater.

"I don't have a lot of control with you," he confessed quietly. "I don't want to push my luck and spoil things."

"You only looked at me," she whispered.

"That wasn't all I wanted to do, though," he said bluntly. He met her eyes. "I wanted to put my mouth on your breasts and taste you with my tongue and my teeth. And if I'd done that, I'd have taken you standing up, right here."

She stared at him blankly. "You would…bite me?" she asked uncertainly.

He laughed at her expression. "Not like that, for God's sake! I'd nibble you." He shook his head, because she so obviously didn't understand. "Melody, you're incredible. Just incredible. Have you done anything with a man beyond kissing him?"

She glowered at him. "Does it matter?"

"Yes, it does. I don't want to scare you."

"Did I act scared?" she asked, big-eyed.

He smiled, delighted. "No."

"I'm not afraid of you. I'm a little intimidated because I've never felt anything so overpowering before. But I enjoy having you touch me." She lowered her eyes to his broad chest. "I...would like to make love to you, Emmett."

He didn't say anything. After a minute, she was horrified that she'd gone too far, said too much, been too blatant.

She started to turn away, but he caught her softly rounded chin and turned her face back to his.

"I want that, too," he said tautly. "And that complicates things royally. I have three children. You might have noticed...?"

"They're pretty hard to miss," she agreed.

"And then there's the very obvious fact of your virginity." He brushed at his jeans. "Listen, I know it isn't modern or sophisticated, but I was raised to think of innocence as something too special to make an entertainment of. Do you understand? My parents always said that a decent man didn't make a plaything of an innocent woman, not when there were so many around who knew the score and weren't looking for marriage. But if a man seduced a virgin, he married her and made her the mother of his children. I'm afraid I still feel that way. I don't sleep with women who aren't experienced. Not ever."

"I see." She shivered a little, wrapping her arms around her chest. He was telling her that they had no future. She'd hoped. How she'd hoped! But she had to retain as much of her pride as she could. She forced a smile. "Well, no harm done. Do you think we could have some coffee?"

He felt her pain as if it had been his own. Amazing, he thought, that she cared so much that his words could wound her. He discovered that he couldn't bear to hurt her.

He pulled her into his arms and held her, feeling her stiff posture. He knew what to do about that. His hand slid sensuously down to her hips and moved her against him in a slow, sweet rotation.

She tried to move away, but he wouldn't let her.

"This hasn't happened with anyone since I first found you working in Logan's office," he whispered at her ear. "Do you feel how capable I am right now? I don't even have to work up to wanting you. I touch you, and I can take you. You'd have to be a man to appreciate how sweet that immediate response is."

"You just got through saying…"

"That I don't sleep with virgins," he finished for her. He smiled against her forehead. "That's right. Why don't you rip my shirt open and kiss me to death? You could push me down in the aisle here and ravish me, if you liked."

"Emmett," she said uncertainly, lifting her face to his.

"I'll get something to use the first few months," he said matter-of-factly, "so that you have plenty of time to decide whether or not you want to let me make you pregnant."

She stopped breathing. Her eyes went wide and shocked, and her heart began beating against her rib cage. "Wh-what?"

"Three is probably too many already," he murmured. "And the world is certainly overpopulated. But I would love to give you a baby," he whispered.

"I may not be the best father around, and I've got a lot to learn, but I love kids. We could have just one together, with honey-brown hair," he added thoughtfully, studying her. "That would be unique. Wouldn't you like to touch me?" he added huskily, dragging her hand to his chest. "I'd like it."

"Emmett, I can't get pregnant!"

"Yes, you can," he said. "It's easy. All we have to do is not use anything when we make love." He lifted his head and frowned down at her. "Didn't you take health classes in school?"

"That's not what I meant! I can't go around getting pregnant!"

"You can if you're married," he reminded her.

"I'm not married!"

"You will be." He bent his head and kissed her, slowly and with a deepening hunger. "I can't wait long, either," he said unsteadily. "Some men can go for months without sex, but I can't. I have to have it. I've abstained since just before Kit and Logan got married, when I first realized that I wanted you. But it's been a long, dry spell, Melody." He moaned against her mouth. His hands became insistent. "Very long."

She melted into him. It wasn't a conscious decision, but she wanted him so badly that she couldn't manage any reasons to tell him she wouldn't marry him. The kids, the consequences, all took a backseat to his throbbing need and her desperation to satisfy it.

"I'll marry you," she said huskily. "I'm probably

crazy, and I know you are, and I don't know how I'll manage being a mother to three kids when one of them hates me. But I guess I'll cope, if you're actually proposing and not kidding around."

He lifted his head and searched her eyes. His hands on her hips were firm and bold. He ground her belly into his in blatant need. "Does it feel like I'm joking?" he asked unsteadily.

"No."

He brushed her lips with his and whispered something so explicit that she flushed and buried her face in his hot throat.

"Shocked that I can talk to you that way?" he asked roughly. "I'll make you like it, though. I'll make you like what I was talking about, too."

She pressed closer. Her legs trembled. "I know that," she breathed.

His head lifted. He searched her eyes. "Once you agree, there won't be any going back."

"No."

"Okay, then. We'll go and tell the kids."

"Not yet," she pleaded. "Not for at least a week or two. I want you to be sure, Emmett."

"I already am," he said quietly. It was quick, maybe too quick, but he didn't have a thought of hesitating. What he knew about her was more than enough. They'd have a good life together. He cared for her and he knew it was mutual.

"For the children," she hedged. "Let's give them a little time. Just a little, to get used to seeing us together, and doing things with them, before we hit them with it."

He groaned. "How much do you think I can stand?"

She smiled gently. "I'll be very careful not to make it any worse for you than it is."

He sighed roughly. "All right. But just a week or two."

She nodded. "That's fine."

CHAPTER EIGHT

MELODY WENT THROUGH the next two weeks in a kind of daze. She'd never felt as close to anyone as she felt toward Emmett and Amy and Polk. They went riding and to movies and ball games. They went to rodeos. They watched new releases on the VCR at her apartment and on his at the ranch. All the while, they grew closer as they talked about themselves and their hopes and dreams.

There was nothing physical. Emmett was restrained to the point of madness, only kissing her lightly when he took her home. He never deepened the kisses or touched her or made suggestive remarks. Except for the way he looked at her now, they might have been nothing more than friends.

The one sadness Melody had was that Guy was more withdrawn than ever, and she couldn't help but think he was plotting against them. Amy and Polk had looked worried a time or two, as if they had something on their minds. Melody was tempted to try to pry it out of them, but there was never an opportunity.

Guy did find one way to irritate her. He found every photograph he had of his mother and put them all in plain view. He talked about Adell at every opportunity. Behind the irritating behavior was fear, but it didn't help Melody to know it. Guy had become her enemy, and she didn't know how to deal with him.

"You aren't giving Melody a chance, are you?" Emmett asked Guy late one evening after he'd taken Melody home and Amy and Polk had gone to bed.

Guy didn't look at him. "I thought you still loved my mother."

He frowned. "What?"

Guy shifted on the chair. "You were real mad when she went away, but you used to talk about her all the time. I know you miss her. So do we." He looked up at his father. "Why don't you tell her you want her to come back? She might. Maybe she doesn't like her husband. Maybe she'd like a reason to come back!"

Emmett couldn't tell him about Adell's pregnancy. It would be the last straw for the boy right now. He grimaced. He hadn't known that Guy was nursing such futile hopes. No wonder he was resentful of Melody and upset about her being around all the time.

"Son," he began slowly, "you have to understand that sometimes even people who care about each other can't live together."

"But you and my mother did," Guy returned. "You were happy, I know you were!"

That was desperation. Guy was growing up so fast, Emmett wasn't sure how to handle it. All that rodeoing, when his kids had needed him and he'd turned away from them, was coming back to haunt him now.

"Your mother wasn't happy with me," Emmett said quietly. "That's the root of the whole matter. She loves Randy," he added, gritting his teeth as he made the grudging admission. "There is no chance, whatsoever, that she'll ever divorce him and come back to us. You have to accept that."

"No!" Guy stood up. "She's my mother! She didn't want to go, you made her! You were never home!"

Emmett tightened the rein on his temper. "That's true," he said quietly. "Maybe my actions helped her make the decision. But the fact is, if she'd loved me, she'd never have left me. You don't run away from people you love."

Guy's lower lip trembled. "She didn't love me?"

"Not you! Me!"

Guy averted his eyes. "I don't like Melody. Does she have to keep coming around here?" he said, changing the subject.

"I'm going to marry her."

Guy looked horrified. He gaped at his father. "You can't! You can't do that! What about Mom?"

"Your mother is married," he said flatly. "I'm sure she still loves you and Amy and Polk, but she won't be coming back. You're going to have to take it like a man and learn to live with it. Life isn't a cartoon or a movie. Things don't always work out to a happy ending."

"I don't want Melody here!" Guy said harshly. "She's not going to be my mother!"

Emmett felt exasperated. Arguing was getting him nowhere. He stood up abruptly. "I'll marry whom I please," he said flatly. "If you don't like it, that's tough. But you'd better not give her any trouble," he added with quiet menace. "If her cat disappears again, or anything happens to her that upsets her, I'll hold you responsible."

Guy flushed, averting his head. The cat haunted him. He couldn't tell his father how sick he'd been when he knew Alistair might have died because of him.

"I won't bother her stupid cat," he said shortly.

Emmett sighed wearily. "The other kids love her," he said. "She's kind and gentle and if you'd give her half a chance, she'd care about you, too. But you're the original tough guy, aren't you?" his father asked. "You're Mr. Cool. Nobody is going to get close to you. Not even me."

Guy averted his eyes.

"I've done everything I can think of to reach you," Emmett continued. "Including involving you in the routine of running a ranch, but you're too busy or there's a television program on or you have to play with Barney."

"You're only doing it because she isn't around," Guy said icily. "You'd rather be with her than me."

Emmett smiled half amusedly. "When you're a few years older, the reason will become perfectly obvious to you."

Guy flushed. "I know about girls. There's this one at school, but she thinks I'm ugly and stupid. She said so, in front of her girlfriends. I hate girls!" He stuck his hands into his jeans and glared at his father. "Especially Melody!"

Emmett could only barely remember being eleven years old and hating girls. He smiled faintly. "Well, I'm marrying her whether you like it or not," he said pleasantly.

Guy turned and stormed off into his room and slammed the door. Emmett lifted an eyebrow. Parenting, he decided, was not a job for the weakhearted. He was going to have to find some way to get to that boy, while there was still time.

THE NEXT WEEKEND, Emmett and Melody made a formal announcement to Amy and Polk. They knew. Guy had told them already, and they were unusually reserved, glancing at their older brother uncertainly.

"Will you live with us, Melody?" Amy asked.

"Yes," Melody said quietly. "I hope we'll be good friends. I don't have a family, you know," she added without looking at them. "Only my brother."

"Yeah, her brother who stole our mother!" Guy burst out. "Well, I don't want you here…!"

"Go to your room," Emmett said. His voice was low and very quiet, but the look in his eyes made Guy obey without another word.

"Guy said you'll be mean to us," Amy told Melody worriedly. "He said you were only pretending to be nice until you hooked Emmett."

Melody went down on her knees in front of the little girl and studied the green eyes in the softly tanned thin face framed by pigtails.

"Amy, do you know how you feel with different people? I mean, you feel happy around some, and nervous and unhappy around others?"

Amy frowned. "I guess so."

"Well, sometimes when we don't know people very well, we have to trust our feelings about them. I can't promise you that I'll never be angry, that I'll never lose my temper, that I'll never hurt your feelings. I'm just a person, and I'm not perfect. But I'll love you a lot, if you'll let me," she added with a smile. "All of you. I know I'll never be your real mother, but I can be your friend and you can be mine."

Amy seemed to accept that, and to relax. She smiled. "Polk and I think you're the greatest. Guy just doesn't want you around because he thinks Emmett and our mother will get married again someday." She grimaced. "But they won't."

Melody wondered at the wisdom in that small voice. Amy was something of a conundrum. At times she seemed much older than her eight years.

"Do you love Emmett?" Amy asked out of the blue.

Melody blushed, embarrassed.

"Yes. Do you?" Polk seconded, joining Amy, his eyes large under the spectacles as he smiled at her.

Emmett pursed his lips, and his eyes twinkled. "That's it, kids, make her tell you!"

Melody glared at him. "You can be quiet."

"I want to know," he persisted. He chuckled softly. "Never mind, then. I'll find out for myself, later."

That went right over Amy's and Polk's heads, thank goodness. They began to talk about school and soon afterward, supper was put on the table. Guy's was taken to his room by an irritable Mrs. Jenson, because he refused to come out.

The boy's behavior was the one regret in Melody's mind when Emmett left the kids with Mrs. Jenson and drove her back to Houston.

"He isn't going to accept it," she said, when they were in her apartment and the door was closed. She looked up at Emmett worriedly. "I can't come between you and your son... Emmett!"

He'd lifted her off the floor in midspeech and carried her without a word into the dark bedroom. He laid her gently on the coverlet and slid onto it beside her. When she tried to speak, his mouth covered her protesting lips. Seconds later, she couldn't speak at all.

Guy and his attitude were forgotten in the slow, tender moments that followed. Emmett eased her out of her dress and slip so gently that she hardly noticed, and his warm mouth moved slowly over every inch of her, kindling unmanageable sensations that quickly made her writhe and moan.

Her eyes grew accustomed to the semidarkness, so that when he removed her bra, she could see his eyes glitter as he looked at her.

"Sometimes I think I dreamed you," he said huskily. Then his head bent, and what he'd once described to her began to happen all at once. His warm mouth nibbled tenderly at her taut nipples before it moved hungrily over the swollen softness around them. He held her and caressed her to the point of madness, and when his hands invaded the most intimate part of her, she was helpless, enslaved.

He whirled her body against the length of his and enveloped her while he kissed her mouth into submission. The abrasion of his jeans and shirt against her unclothed skin was as exciting as the mouth that was tutoring her own.

She clung to him when he lifted his head. He was breathing roughly and his chest was shaking with the beat of his heart. Against her stomach, she could feel the hard, impatient maleness of him.

"Emmett?" she whispered unsteadily.

"Do you want me?" he asked in a harsh, husky tone.

"Oh, yes," she said honestly.

"All of me, right now?"

"Yes!"

He sat up, and it was an effort. His hand shot out and the room exploded in light.

For a shocked instant, Melody lay on the coverlet disoriented. Then she saw him looking at her body, at the soft pink nudity that her thin white briefs did nothing to disguise, at the taut, swollen evidence of her desire. She went scarlet and began to lift her hands to her breasts to hide them.

He shook his head, and his hands caught hers.

"You're mine," he said quietly. "We're engaged. That gives me the right to look at you like this. In fact, it gives me a few other rights that I'm damned tempted to exercise." His hot gaze fell to her stomach and lower, to her long, elegant legs. His hand followed his eyes, and she gasped and moved restlessly, helplessly, on the coverlet.

He eased down, his face somber, almost stern, as his fingers trespassed gently past the elastic band. He touched her and she fought him, wincing.

"Easy," he said gently. "It isn't supposed to hurt."

"It…does!"

He bent and brushed his lips tenderly against her wild eyes, her cheeks, her trembling mouth. "You're frightened. There's no need. None at all. When it happens, it will be as easy as falling into water, as easy as breathing. Your body is soft and elastic here," he whispered. "It will absorb mine, like a glove absorbing a hand."

The analogy made her shiver. He kissed her flickering eyelids, tracing her long lashes with his tongue. "I don't want you to be afraid of me. I promise that I won't hurt you, in any way."

She looked at him worriedly, her eyes big and uncertain.

He nodded. "I suppose I knew all along that it would take more than words." He reached over and turned off the lamp before he slid alongside her again. "It will be easier for you in the dark, won't it?" he whispered.

She didn't understand what he meant until it

began. The soft, stroking motion kindled explosive
feelings in her untried body. She tried to fight them
at first, but the tide of pleasure he induced was as
overwhelming as life itself. She gave in to it, gloried
in it, wept and writhed and moaned in an anguish of
hot, building tension that finally splintered into the
most incredible surge of pleasure she'd ever imagined in her wildest dreams.

He gathered her close and held her trembling
body, fighting his own demons even as he banished
hers. His lips smoothed over her hot face, tenderly
calming her.

"That, magnified," he whispered at her ear, "is
what I'm going to give you on our wedding night."

She clung to him, dazed. "I never dreamed...!"

"You're more than I ever hoped for," he said quietly, cradling her in his arms. "You don't tease or
play games, do you? And you're not ashamed to feel
what I can give you, or to admit that you do feel it."

She touched his lean cheek and felt the muscles
taut in it. "I like to think I'll be able to give it back,
when I know how," she murmured shyly.

He kissed her with aching tenderness. "You will,"
he said quietly. "Lovemaking should be mutual. I
won't ever take my pleasure at your expense."

He was a surprisingly considerate man. She had
a fleeting glimpse of him as a lover, and her body
moved unconsciously on the coverlet.

"I want you, too, very badly," he said, feeling
and understanding the movement. "But we'll wait
until after we're married. I don't want a tarnished

memory of our first loving. Hors d'oeuvres, on the other hand," he murmured wickedly, "are perfectly permissible."

He bent and nuzzled his mouth over her breast, feeling her instant response, hearing her urgent cry.

It couldn't last. He was too hungry for her, and the risk grew by the minute. Finally he groaned and got to his feet, shivering a little with the effort.

"I'd better go home while I still can," he mused wryly. "Don't get up. And try not to faint. I'm going to turn on the light."

She would have protested at the beginning, but it didn't matter now. He knew her almost as well as a lover.

The light came on and she lay there, letting him look at her. The briefs he'd stripped from her were tossed onto the foot of the bed. There was nothing between her and his narrow, hungry green eyes.

"I hope you don't believe in divorce," he said in a faintly strangled tone. "Because you'd have to change your name and move to the jungle to escape me."

She stretched deliberately, glorying in the growing tautness of his lean, fit body. She could imagine how it was going to feel grinding into hers, and her lips parted on a rush of breath.

"That goes double for you," she whispered. "You'll belong to me, too, when we're married."

"It's more than desire for you, isn't it?" he asked quietly.

"Yes."

He searched her eyes. "For me, too, Melody," he

replied. "It's more than enough to start with. I'll arrange the ceremony for next Saturday."

"All right."

"I'll make sure I've got what we need to keep you from getting pregnant right away," he added.

"I can see the doctor and get him to put me on the pill," she began.

He sat down on the bed beside her, his eyes troubled. He drew the cover over her prone body with a rueful, reluctant smile. "Too much temptation can kill even a strong man," he said dryly. The smile faded. "Listen, I know the pill is pretty foolproof, and everybody says it's safe. But I feel uncomfortable about letting you take chances with your health."

"If I don't take the pill... Well, I've heard that some men don't like using what they have to use," she said hesitantly.

He touched her face tenderly. "Well, I'm not some men," he replied honestly. "And I believe pregnancy shouldn't be an accident."

"I know." She traced his hand where it lay on the cover beside her head. "The kids will need time, too, to get used to me before we start creating new complications."

"In the meanwhile, I can take care of it."

"If you're that worried about the pill, you can come with me and talk to the doctor yourself," she said. "There are other ways."

"How do you feel about it?" he asked.

She flushed and averted her eyes.

He turned her face back. "It's too serious an issue to evade because of modesty. How do you feel about it?"

She searched his hard face. "I'm not afraid to take the pill. I don't think it's so risky. And I want to be... very, very close to you when we love each other," she said huskily. "As close as we can get when we fit together."

His face went ruddy. He actually shivered.

"Oh, Emmett, I want you...!" She drew him down and kissed him with helpless urgency, feeling him throw off the covers as he levered himself over her. His knee urged her legs apart and he slid between them, shaking as he pushed down, letting her feel him in total intimacy.

He groaned harshly, his body stilling suddenly as the danger of the situation cut through his desire for her.

Her body was new to pleasure and hungry for it. He understood her headlong rush toward it, but he had to protect her from a danger she still didn't understand.

"Lie still. Lord, baby, please...!"

His hands forced her a few inches away from his tormented body. She moaned, but he persisted. "Melody, it hurts me." He ground out the words.

She lay still, curious. Her big eyes found the pallor of his face even as she felt him tremble.

"Hurts?" she asked uncertainly.

He dragged her hand up against him. "Here," he said huskily. "It hurts like hell. You've got to stop moving against me. All right?"

"Yes." But she didn't move her hand, even when his withdrew. She moved back a little and looked down with open curiosity.

He saw her expression and sighed heavily. "All right. Here."

He rolled over onto his back and lay there, stoically letting her look and touch and experience him. He shivered a little, but her touch soothed more than it wounded.

She drew away almost at once, embarrassed by her own boldness, and smiled at him.

He threw the coverlet at her. She understood without words, wrapping herself up in it to remove the threat with a wicked smile on her face.

"Witch," he accused.

"You liked it," she said right back.

He stretched, winced and put his hands under his head while he studied her. His body began to relax, but slowly.

"When you're through having anatomy lessons, I'll leave," he said pointedly.

Her eyebrows lifted. "You call this an anatomy lesson?" she asked with mock surprise. "When I'm totally nude and you're lying there with all your clothes on?"

"I'm modest," he informed her.

She pursed her lips and stared at his jeans. "Take them off. I dare you."

He laughed with pure delight. "No! Damn it, woman, have you no shame?"

"Shame is for people who don't want to have sex

with other people." She leaned closer, fanning the coverlet between her breasts. "I'm famished!" she whispered with a mock leer.

He chuckled at her uninhibited display. "Come here, you torment."

He pulled her down and kissed her, but with slow, sweet tenderness, not passion. "I adore you," he whispered. "And I take it back about the jungle. If you ever want to get away from me, it had better be Mars."

"I'll keep that in mind." She kissed him back. "I really don't mind taking the pill."

He nodded. "It's your body. It has to be your decision." He smiled ruefully. "Having just discovered you, I don't want to risk losing you."

That made her feel warm all over. "You won't," she said softly. She pushed back his thick, dark hair. "Can I love you?"

He threw his arms out to either side and closed his eyes. "Go ahead."

She hit him. "You know what I mean."

He searched her face for a long moment. "You're serious."

"Yes." She traced his chin and then his mouth as her eyes levered back up to hold his.

He smoothed his hands over her shoulders, under the coverlet, savoring her magnolia-petal skin. "Love is important to a woman, isn't it?" he asked with faint cynicism.

"It's important to most men, too," she said softly. Her eyes were warm and steady, without deceit. "I'm going to love you anyway. I just thought it would be polite to ask. But if you're going to be difficult about it, just pretend you don't notice that I'm crazy about you."

He sighed and smiled. "It would be pretty difficult to miss. Even your breasts blush when I look at you."

"They do not... Emmett!"

She made a grab for the cover, but it was too late. "See?" he asked, nodding toward the faint ruddy color below her collarbone. But the smile faded almost at once. He touched her reverently. "You are so incredibly lovely," he whispered, almost choking on the emotion he felt. He closed his eyes and dragged himself off the bed. "I have to go. Now. Immediately. Without delay."

She had to fight back a smile at his desperate look. She pulled the cover back around her and got up, looking so smug that he glowered at her.

"Proud of yourself?" he muttered, blatantly aroused and with no way to hide it from the new wisdom in her twinkling brown eyes.

She glanced down and back up. "Yep," she said, grinning.

He laughed defeatedly, shaking his head. "I'm out of here."

"Until Saturday," she reminded him pertly as she walked with him to the door. "After that, you're mine!"

"And you're mine," he returned. He caught the doorknob and glanced down at her with quiet introspection, taking in her flushed face, her swollen mouth, her joy-filled eyes. His soul seemed to clench at the pleasure it gave him to want her.

She saw that tension and understood it. "I won't ever hurt you," she said suddenly, dead serious. "But I'll love you until it hurts. If you really don't want that, you'd better say so now. Once I've lived with you, I honestly don't know if I can let go…"

He pressed his fingers against her lips. "You won't have to," he said quietly. "Love doesn't come with money-back guarantees. It's a risk. We'll take it together."

"All right."

He sighed gently, and he smiled at her. "Sleep well."

"No, I won't," she said.

"Neither will I." His eyes darkened. "I do want you so desperately," he said huskily, emotion throbbing in his voice.

"Then stay with me," she invited quietly.

"I want to," he said fervently. "But we'll do things properly. Not for our sakes, but for the children's. A white wedding may be old-fashioned in this unstructured society, but I want one for us."

She smiled at him. "So do I. But I'd do anything for you."

Incredible, the burst of inner light he felt at the words. He smiled, a little dazedly as he let it ripple through him. "Anything?" he murmured.

She studied him. "Well, almost anything. I wouldn't kiss a snake or eat a chocolate-covered ant for you."

He bent and kissed her quickly. "Okay. No kissing snakes and eating ants. Now good night!"

"Good night."

He winked at her and went out the door. She locked it behind him. On second thought, she mused privately, if it wasn't a venomous snake, and she could keep her eyes closed while she kissed it...

EMMETT HAD JUST finished arranging the small service when Guy came into his office, his hands in his back pockets, looking repentant but still belligerent.

"Well?" Emmett asked curtly.

Guy's thin shoulders rose and fell. "I'm sorry," he said stiffly.

"For what?"

"What I said. The way I acted." Guy stared at the floor. "My mom really won't come back?"

"No."

He took a slow, audible breath before he glanced at his father. "But she didn't go away because of me?"

"Of course not," Emmett said. "She loves all you kids. If you want to know, I wouldn't let her near you after she left," he confessed heavily. "I was wrong, too. Dead wrong. If you want to see her, talk to her, it's all right."

Guy didn't say anything for a minute. "Melody hates me, doesn't she?"

"No. It isn't in her nature to hate people," Emmett said quietly. "But you haven't gone out of your way to endear yourself to her, either."

"Yeah. She won't forget about the cat, I guess."

"If you meet her halfway, it won't matter at all," Emmett said. "You have to compromise. I'm a hell of a bad teacher, in that respect, but I'm learning. We'll both have to learn."

"Okay. I'll try."

Emmett smiled. "And you might reconsider getting used to the business side of ranch work," he added.

Guy shrugged. "I guess I could." He glanced warily at his father. Emmett looked pretty different lately. He looked happy.

"Things going better at school, are they?"

"Since I beat up Buddy Haskell, they're going great," Guy said simply.

"You what?"

"He made a remark about smelly ranchers who walk around all day in cow…well, in manure." Guy corrected himself, grinning. "He said you smelled like that, so I pasted him one. The teacher was too busy talking to the other teachers to even notice." He chuckled. "He told her he walked into a door."

Emmett looked skyward. "Now, listen, here…"

"Homework to do," Guy said quickly. "Have to get on it, right now. I'm helping Polk with fractions." He frowned. "Isn't it amazing that he can do multiplication in his head but he can't add a fourth and a half?"

"He'll be a rocket scientist one day," Emmett replied.

"God help us if he can't do fractions by then," Guy mused. He left his father sitting there and went to get his books.

Emmett felt a glimmer of hope that Guy would change his attitude. If Guy came around, it would be clear sailing for sure. Except that Adell was pregnant, and he should have told the boy. Well, there was no need, and plenty of time for him to find it out. Plenty of time, now.

CHAPTER NINE

THE WEDDING WAS held at the local Methodist church. Ted Regan came down for it, and so did Tansy, Logan and Kit Deverell. Amy was flower girl and Polk carried the rings on a pillow. Guy sat stiffly on the pew reserved for family, having declined belligerently any sort of participation in the wedding.

Despite the talk he'd had with his father, he'd still hoped that his mother might come along at the last minute and stop the service, say that she was wrong, that she loved his father and wanted to marry him again. But it didn't happen. Nobody wanted him, he thought suddenly. His mother had run away and never even phoned or written, and now his dad wanted somebody's company besides his. He glanced at his brother and sister, so radiant at the thought of their new stepmother. He'd have to make the most of it. He was sorry that he'd made things so hard for Melody. He hoped that his dad was right, and she didn't have a vengeful nature.

As he watched, Emmett spoke the words, put the ring on Melody's finger and lifted her short veil. He looked at her for a long, long time before he finally bent and kissed her. It was the gentlest kiss she'd ever had from him, one of respect and affection and delight. She gave it back in the same way, brimming with joy.

After the service, Ted Regan stopped long enough to congratulate them. Having heard him called "old man Regan," Melody's first glimpse of him was a surprise. He wasn't old, but he did have prematurely silver hair, a great shock of it, combed to one side. He had pale blue eyes and a long, lean, very tanned face. He reminded her of the actor, Randolph Scott, an impression that was emphasized when he spoke in a slow Texas drawl.

"Can't say I've ever wanted to marry anybody," Ted mused, "but I guess it's all right for some people. Best of luck. Don't even think about going back to San Antonio," he added as he shook Emmett's hand and his blue eyes glittered like cold steel. "I'll hunt you down and drag you back here at the end of a rope if you even try. You've accomplished more in a month than any other foreman I've hired accomplished in a year. I'll even give you a half interest in the place if that's what it takes to keep you."

Emmett felt a foot taller. Marrying Melody was delight enough, but praise from tight-lipped Ted Regan was something of a rarity and accepted with pride.

"Thanks," Emmett told the other man, who was as tall and fit as he was himself, despite the fact that Ted was almost forty years old. "I like my job a lot. I can't think of anything that would make me quit at the moment." He frowned. "Maybe if a cow fell in the well…"

"I don't think you could stuff a calf down that wellhead," Ted reminded him. "Unless it was cooked and ground up."

"Point taken. I'll stay for a spell."

"Good." He clamped his white Stetson back on his head and tilted it at a rakish angle. "I'm off to Colorado for the national cattlemen's meeting. More damned politics than horses in the industry these days." He walked off, shaking his head.

"He's never married? Really?" Melody asked her new husband as she watched the tall man walk away.

"They say there isn't a woman in south Texas brave enough," Emmett said under his breath. "He's very pleasant in company, but he can scorch leather when he's upset. We've got two old cowboys who hide in the barn every time he stops by to check the books!"

"You don't," she implored.

He chuckled, drawing her against his side as they moved lazily toward the car where the kids were waiting. "Oh, Ted and I get along pretty well. Peas in a pod, you know." He glanced at her mischievously. "Or didn't you know that I can scorch leather, too, on occasion?"

She leaned closer. "I'll settle for having you scorch me tonight," she whispered.

He drew in a breath. "Lady, that kind of talk will get you ravished on the hood of the car," he said with an uncomfortable look. "Shame on you, saying such things to a man, and near a church, too!"

"No better place for it," she said gently. "We're married. With my body, I thee worship…?" She wiggled her hand with the plain gold band she'd asked for on her third finger under his nose.

"Shameless," he repeated.

"Yes. And tonight you'll be on your knees giving thanks that I am," she said smugly.

He glanced at her. "You'll be the one on your knees, begging for mercy."

She grinned at him. "Promise?" She wiggled her eyebrows.

He laughed out loud and hugged her. Probably she was bluffing, but he didn't mind at all. He'd never been so happy in all his life. Except for Guy's attitude, he amended, watching the boy's faintly reticent stare as they approached him.

Guy's face set in familiar lines, unsmiling and resentful, and Emmett lost his temper at that look, not realizing that Guy was nervous and intimidated because he wanted to congratulate them but was uncertain of the reaction he was going to get from Melody.

Emmett wasn't about to let the boy put a damper on Melody's wedding day. Best way to avoid trouble was with a good strong offensive, he thought. "Put a sock in it," he told Guy when he opened his mouth to speak. "Or you can go and pay a visit to that military school we've talked about."

Melody was shocked at the threat and the expression it produced on Guy's face.

She started to protest, but Emmett stopped her.

"I've given you more rope than you've earned," he told Guy coldly. "I won't plead with you anymore. Melody is my wife. If you can't accept that, a good private school is the best answer. I enjoyed it. You might, too."

Guy's pallor was obvious. He swallowed. "I don't want to go away to school," he said heavily.

"That's your only other option," Emmett said.

Guy's head lifted with what pride he could manage. "I'm ready to go home when you are." He glanced at Melody and away. "Congratulations," he said in a ghostly tone, and turned to get into the backseat with an excited Amy and Polk.

Melody's heart ached for his wounded pride. "Oh, Emmett…!" she moaned.

He averted his gaze from her pleading eyes. "Some boys take a firm hand," he said curtly. "I've been too lenient with all three of them, and they've gone wild. It's never pleasant to get the upper hand back once you've lost it." He looked at her. "I won't hurt the boy. I won't send him away unless I have to. But you must see that allowing him to persecute you and dictate to me is impossible. He's only eleven years old."

"I know. But…"

He bent and kissed her gently. "It will take time. We both knew that from the beginning. Stop trying to gulp down the future. We haven't begun."

"All right. I'll try."

She wasn't going to give up, though. She'd wait

until he was less tense and then approach him about Guy. She really couldn't let him send the boy away before she'd even tried to make friends with him. It was Guy's home as well as Emmett's and hers. The look on the boy's face haunted her.

They took the kids home and a beaming Mrs. Jenson congratulated them while Melody changed into a simple gray dress for travel. They were going to have a three-day honeymoon down in Cancún. The kids were bitterly disappointed that they couldn't go, but Melody promised Amy and Polk that they'd go as a family very soon. Amy had remarked that she guessed newly married people did need a little time alone. A remark that sent Emmett into gales of laughter.

Guy didn't speak to his father. Melody stopped just in front of him as Emmett was saying goodbye to the other kids.

"He won't do it" was all she said. She smiled. "It will be all right, you know."

Guy was shocked. He couldn't even speak. He hadn't expected her to say anything to him after the way he'd treated her. Now he needed to talk, and he couldn't.

It was too late, anyway. She was gone, with his father.

"They look nice together, don't you think?" Amy asked with a sigh. She glared at Guy. "You're going to get it when Emmett gets back. You were awful at their wedding."

"I'm not going to get it, but you are if you don't watch your mouth," Guy said, daring her.

"Will you two stop fighting? Look, Alistair likes to play with a string!" Polk called, dangling a string while the cat played with it.

The big tabby was staying at the ranch, and Mrs. Jenson had ironclad orders not to let him out. Guy went to stand by Polk and Amy while he watched the cat. He hoped Alistair had a forgiving nature, as well as Melody, or things could get real hectic here.

CANCÚN WAS A VISION. The colors of the sea and the blistering white of the beach, the modern Mexican architecture with exaggerated Mayan motifs made a potpourri of images that Melody found fascinating. She'd been to Mexico before, but never to this particular part of it. Despite the crowd of tourists, she drank in the atmosphere with delight.

Emmett looked good in white swimming trunks. She admired his long, tanned legs with covetous eyes, not to mention his broad, hair-matted chest and arms and flat stomach. He was delicious, and a lot of other women seemed to think so, because they kept walking by with their flabby, white-skinned husbands, staring unashamedly at him.

"One more time, lady, and I'm going to leap up and crown you with my tanning lotion," Melody muttered under her breath.

"What was that?" Emmett asked without opening his eyes.

"That skinny brunette. She keeps walking by, leering at you."

"My, my, are you jealous?" he teased.

She stared at him without blinking. "Why don't you go back to the room with me and find out?"

His heart began to beat wildly. "We've only been here an hour or so. I thought you might be too tired," he said gently.

She shook her head very slowly. Her long hair was loosened, blowing softly in the ocean breeze. She searched his green eyes. "I want you," she whispered.

His body reacted sharply and he laughed with self-conscious delight. "Damn it, woman…!"

"Recite multiplication tables," she whispered with a gleeful smile.

He glared at her. "You'd better have packed something that prevents multiplication, because I forgot to."

"I did." She'd decided on the pill, despite his objections, because she felt it was the safest way to prevent a child until they were ready. She stood up, holding out her hand. "I've waited twenty years," she murmured dryly. "I do hope you're going to be worth it."

He got to his feet, his pale eyes shimmering with a kind of knowledge that made her blush. "Honey, I can guarantee it."

He took her hand and they went back to the room in a tense, delicious silence.

SHE WENT STRAIGHT into his arms the minute the door closed, determined not to admit that she was nervous of him this way. It was broad daylight, but waiting until tonight would have inhibited both of them. Besides, she thought as she lifted her face to look at him, she loved him. It would be all right, as long as he didn't compare her with any of his past lovers. She hoped that she was going to be enough for him, because despite her bravado, she felt vaguely inadequate.

But that fear was quickly forgotten when he bent to kiss her, and the heat of his body and the skill of his mouth and hands turned her nervous response into sensual fever.

He eased her onto the bed and very efficiently moved everything out of his way, so that her nude body was cradled to his in the slow preliminary to their first loving.

"Shh," he whispered when she began to writhe and pull at him. "Not so fast, little one. Don't gulp it. Sip it. Slow down."

"It aches," she whispered unsteadily as his mouth teased and tormented hers. "I ache all over."

"So do I," he said on soft, unsteady laughter. "But we're building to one hell of an explosion, and it's too soon for you, despite what you think. No, don't touch me like that, not yet," he said softly, stilling her hand. "This is all for you. My turn will come later, when I've satisfied you to the tips of your pretty pink toes. Kiss me, sweetheart."

He coaxed her mouth back up to his and his hands moved again, tasting her body as his mouth tasted her lips, and then settled hungrily on her breasts and her soft, flat stomach, experiencing, exploring her, making her crazy for his possession.

"I can't…bear it…!" she whimpered finally, anguish in her wide, haunted eyes. "Oh, please…!"

"All right," he whispered tenderly, moving over her. "Gently, little one," he breathed. "Gently, gently."

He held her firmly, his face above hers, his muscular body cording as he positioned her and began to move down. He was afraid of hurting her, even as it excited him beyond bearing to be her first lover. But she didn't flinch, didn't fight. She lay there, shivering, her eyes open and fixed with pain and wonder on his taut face as he invaded the sweet, warm softness of her innocence and was slowly, painstakingly engulfed by it.

She flinched and he grimaced, stilling until she relaxed again. He could barely breathe. "Is it bad?" he managed to ask.

"It was. It's not now." She closed her eyes and willed her body to accept him. And it did, abruptly, and generously. She let out a long sigh of relief.

He moved as close as he could then, fighting a hellish surge of tense pleasure that begged for relief.

"It doesn't hurt anymore," she whispered shyly. Imagine, talking to a man while you were doing this!

"That's what you think," he groaned.

"Oh, Emmett," she breathed. She lifted to him, watching him shiver. She liked his reaction. She felt suddenly confident, all woman. She lifted again. He protested, but he didn't try to stop her. His face clenched and he breathed roughly. She loved him. It was going to be so beautiful.

"Witch!" he groaned.

"Do you like it?" she teased, moving sensually.

"I'll show you how much I like it," he breathed with a smiling threat. He whipped over onto his side, taking her with him. His strong, lean hands caught her hips and he laughed with something savage, untamed, in his pale eyes as he slid one long leg between both of hers and began to rock her in that deep intimacy.

She gasped as pleasure began to sting her body with bursts of throbbing heat.

"Did you think you could match me so quickly?" he whispered with passionate tenderness as he teased her mouth with his. And all the while, his hands pulled and pushed and teased while he invaded her trembling innocence. He watched her face the whole time, enjoying the stunned wonder of her dark eyes. "How does this feel?" he whispered.

She cried out at the shock of pleasure that came with the movement. Her hands caught at his powerful arms, but the great waves of sensation kept coming, faster and faster, his whole body an instrument of pleasure as he held her and quickly deepened his possession, laughing like a devil as he drove her down into the fires of fulfillment and watched her body splinter into ecstasy against the hard whip of his passion.

Only when she began to cry out in a hoarse, sobbing oblivion did he allow himself the delight of joining her in that lofty plane of mindless joy.

The explosions of pleasure surged through him like tidal waves, lifting, slamming into him, burning him in feverish delight. He called her name, again and again, clutching her to him as he gave in to satiation.

It wasn't like other times, other women. He shivered, but he couldn't stop. His lean hands pulled her into him, over him, and he moved helplessly under her soft, warm body, coaxing her mouth down to cover his as he began the rhythm all over again.

She hadn't imagined what it would be like. He was inexhaustible, incoherent in his passion, but the skill and mastery were beyond her dreams. He raised her to levels she couldn't have pictured, gave her endless ecstasy, made her alternately wanton and exhausted as the day turned finally to night.

When she was too tired to turn her head to kiss him, she fell into a deep, dreamless sleep.

A sweet smell and the feel of light disturbed her. Light shone into her eyes. She put up a hand and felt the warmth of sunlight filtering in through the venetian blinds.

She opened her eyes. Emmett was holding a warm pastry under her nose, letting her smell it.

"Hungry?" he asked softly, smiling at her.

He was fully dressed and she was wearing a sheer blue nightgown. She didn't remember putting it on, but she must have. She smiled back at him. "Starved. Oh!"

She moved and grimaced. He chuckled wickedly, because he knew why she'd grimaced.

"Are you sore?" he asked with mock sympathy.

"Yes, I'm sore," she murmured, blushing. "I hope your back is broken..."

He kissed her gently, stemming the words. "You're the best lover I've ever had," he whispered.

"But I couldn't be," she protested. "I didn't know anything."

"Yes, you did," he replied, kissing her eyelids shut. "You knew how to love me, and you did. It was the most beautiful, the most exquisitely fulfilling night of my life. Even Mars won't be far enough for you to run to get away from me now. I've just been farther out than that in your arms."

She sighed and snuggled closer to him. "Now I know what they meant, when they said it was like eating potato chips." She laughed delightedly. "Oh, Emmett, I like it!"

"I'm glad. So do I." He lifted his head and cocked a rueful eyebrow. "I suppose for a few days now we'll be good friends and companions."

She peered at him through her long lashes. "In health class, nobody ever said you got sore."

"That was my fault," he said, and looked guilty. "I should have stopped after the first time. I'm sorry. It had been a long time and you went to my head. But I should have had more control."

"I wasn't complaining," she said sincerely. "I loved it. I'd do it all over again if I could."

"So would I. That's the hell of it." He brushed his

mouth gently against hers. "Was it worth the wait?" he asked seriously, searching her soft, dark eyes.

"Yes," she whispered. "It was worth waiting all my life for."

"For me, too," he replied tersely. "My God, I never dreamed it would feel like that with you." He touched her face gently. "Mrs. Deverell," he said as he kissed her forehead with aching tenderness. "Mrs. Melody Deverell."

She looped her arms around his neck and nuzzled her face into his warm throat. "I'm still sleepy."

Her vulnerability made him strong, made him ache with tenderness. He bent and lifted her, carrying her to the armchair. He sat down with her in his lap and put down the pastry. Then he lifted a cup of hot coffee to her lips.

She sipped it, staring at him curiously.

"What do you want to do today?" he asked quietly.

"Stay with you."

He smiled. "What else?"

"Nothing," she said. "Only that." She reached up and put her lips gently to his. "I love you so much. More than anything or anyone in all the world." She kissed him again and felt him tremble.

He put the coffee cup down and turned her against his broad, bare chest. He held her gently, undemanding, for a long time, staring across her bright head to the window. "Go to sleep," he breathed at her temple. "I'll hold you while you sleep."

She smiled drowsily and curled closer to him, resting her cheek on his shoulder.

She slept and he watched her, fascinated by the color in her face, the soft sigh of her breath against his throat, the trusting, tender posture of her body in his arms. He thought that he'd never been so happy in all his life.

But with that feeling came a quiet regret that their first intimacy had been so turbulent. She'd given in to him, loved him, responded completely to his fierce ardor. He should have given her tenderness instead of raw passion. It was just that it had been so long and he'd wanted her so desperately. He couldn't hold back.

Now, looking down at her sleeping face, he felt an aching need to cradle her against him in bed and show her the most exquisite kind of tenderness.

Next time, he promised himself. The thing was, she wouldn't be capable of intimacy for several days; probably not until they went home again. He grimaced. Well. Better late than never. After a minute, he closed his eyes and fell asleep himself, wrapped in her warmth and love.

WHEN MELODY AND Emmett drove up at the front door of the ranch house, Guy was peering out the window. He'd worried himself sick about how he was going to keep Emmett from shipping him off to a military school. He didn't know how he was going to cope with so many changes at once. He was no longer part of his own family. Now he was going to be an outsider in Emmett and Melody's, an unwanted burden. Amy and Polk were ecstatic. They would accept

Melody and love her and be loved by her. He wasn't
sure that he could fit in. She might still be pretending to care about him, until she was settled with his
father. Some of his friends at school had stepparents.
He'd heard some terrible stories about that. Oh, why,
why, did people have to get divorced? he agonized.

Melody had hugged Amy and Polk and greeted
Mrs. Jenson. She came into the house, looking for
Guy. He glanced at her warily.

"How are you?" she asked.

He shrugged, painfully shy. She looked radiant.
It was a contrast of some magnitude to the way he
looked, and felt.

"Guy. You might at least say hello," Emmett said,
interfering all too quickly, his green eyes flashing.

"Hello," Guy replied, dropping his eyes.

Melody put her fingers against Emmett's hard
mouth. "Let's get our clothes changed. I want to pass
out the presents," she said, before Emmett could do
any more damage to her fragile relationship with
Guy. "I brought stuff for all of you," she told the
children. "Even Mrs. Jenson."

"Why, how sweet of you, Mrs. Deverell!" the
older woman exclaimed. She hadn't anticipated liking Emmett's young wife. But the woman was not
what she expected. She beamed. "I'll just fix some
coffee and cake."

She went off toward the kitchen with an excited
Amy and Polk, while Guy sat down on the sofa, idly
stroking Alistair. The cat seemed to like him. It was
forever following him around and purring. He was

glad something liked him. Even Amy and Polk had been resentful and unkind since the wedding. He felt alone in the world except for this cat he'd been so cruel to in the beginning.

"I'm glad you like me, Alistair," he told the tabby.

Alistair looked up with half-closed green eyes and purred even louder.

"YOU CAN'T BE cruel to him," Melody told Emmett gently when they were cloistered in the master bedroom. "He'll try. I know he will, and so will I. You can't expect him to be instantly happy, Emmett. It's hard for him. Really hard."

He sighed heavily, drawing her gently to him. "I'm impatient. Too impatient sometimes." He searched her soft eyes and something alien flared in his as he touched her face. "I can't bear the thought of letting anything or anyone hurt you," he said hesitantly. He drew her close, feeling her soft response to the words as he bent to kiss her. "I can't bear to let you out of my sight…"

She kissed him back, hungry for him because even though they'd been passionate lovers that one time, they hadn't been able to make love again because it had taken such a long time for her to recover from his ardor that first day.

His tall, powerful body began to vibrate, to harden. "I want you," he choked, and his mouth became insistent.

"Tonight," she promised, smiling at him. "Oh, Emmett, tonight…!"

WHEN THEY REJOINED the family, several hectic minutes later, Melody was flushed and shy and Emmett was grinding his teeth. But he looked at her with wonder and delight. It got better and better, he thought. The walls were thick, but she was still a little shy. He'd have to have a radio on or something tonight. Tonight. His body began to throb and he went off into the kitchen to see about coffee.

Melody passed out presents: a set of Mexican coins and a cup and string-tied ball toy for Amy; a book on the Mayans and a few replicated artifacts for Polk, who seemed bent on being an archaeologist. And for Guy, a serape and a pocketknife with a hand-carved handle.

Guy was speechless. He'd wanted a pocketknife of his own for ages, because he loved to whittle things out of wood. He was forever borrowing his father's. Melody had noticed. Imagine that, he thought regretfully. He'd been terrible to her, but she'd gone to a lot of trouble to buy something he really wanted.

He looked up at her, shyly.

"Do you like it?" she asked, frowning. "I wasn't sure…"

"It's great!" he said slowly. "Thanks."

"Don't abuse the privilege," Emmett told him firmly. "You can't use it to carve your initials in the walls or make devices of torture to use on unsuspecting tourists."

Guy grinned. "Sure, Dad."

It was the first time he'd seen the boy smile in weeks. He glanced at Melody and nodded. She'd known, and he hadn't, the way to his son's heart. He had a lot to learn about his own children and his new wife.

Amy tugged at his sleeve. "Emmett, it was very nice of you to think of us on your honeymoon," she said, smiling radiantly at him.

"It sure was!" Polk enthused. "Look at this atlatl," he said, displaying the use of the Aztec throwing stick that looked something like an arrow on a slab of bamboo. "Ancient Aztecs used to hunt with these, did you know?"

"I know about dinosaurs and Pleistocene animals," Emmett corrected him. "My minor was paleontology, not archaeology."

"Archaeology is a branch of anthropology," Polk said authoritatively. "I'm going to study it when I get out of high school. Just think, Dad, maybe I'll be the one to find the first Homo erectus remains in the United States!"

Emmett frowned. "There's no proof that Homo erectus ever set foot here."

"Yet," Polk said. And grinned.

Amy tugged on Emmett's sleeve again. "Emmett?"

"Hmm?" he murmured, still distracted by Polk's question.

"Are you and Melody going to have any babies?"

Emmett stared at her. "What?"

"Babies. You know. People have sex and they get babies." She grinned. "I learned about that on television. There was this movie and it showed what people do in bed together." She frowned. "Do you and Melody have sex?"

Melody went scarlet and Emmett actually blushed.

"Shut up, Amy!" Guy muttered. "Honest to God, are you ever going to grow up? Come on, let's go outside and play with Polk's atl-atl."

"It's mine! I didn't say you could play with it!" Polk raged, his glasses sparkling.

"I'll let you see my knife," Guy offered.

The smaller boy hesitated. "Well…"

Guy put an arm around Polk and led him toward the door. "Just think, Polk, I can whittle arrows for that atl-atl. If we set up a fort just down past the barn, we can lie in wait for that nasty-tempered old bull…"

"You shoot one arrow at that bull and I'll stop your allowance forever!" Emmett called after them.

"Aw, Dad!" Guy groaned.

"I mean it!"

Amy went with the boys, glowering at her father. "Emmett, you're not the same man since we moved down here. You never let us have fun anymore."

"Considering what you people call fun, it's a miracle I haven't had to bail all three of you out of jail!"

Amy just shook her head and went out behind the boys.

"See?" Melody told him. "Guy will come around. It will take time, that's all. He's already loosening up, didn't you notice?"

He had. Guy was much more like his old self, like the boy he'd been before Emmett ever saw Melody in Logan's office. He drew her close and kissed her softly. "All right. I give in." He eased her across his lap on the sofa and kissed her more thoroughly, feeling the warmth and tenderness of it right through his body.

"I love you," she whispered, smiling against his mouth.

"Kiss me…!"

He gathered her up and devoured her until they were both trembling. His mouth slid down to her throat and he held her, shivering. He was afraid. He'd never been so afraid. She possessed him, delighted him, made him whole. He'd lost his father, whom he idolized. His mother had killed herself. Adell had left him. If he lost Melody…!

"Emmett!" she protested gently, because his arms were bruising her.

He lifted his dark head and looked at her. The expression on his face, in his eyes, touched her deeply.

She reached up to press soft, tender kisses against his fearful eyes, his cheeks, his nose, his mouth until she felt him begin to relax. Then she drew back and searched his eyes.

"Emmett, I will never leave you," she whispered, and put her fingers over his mouth when he tried to speak. "Never," she repeated, understanding what was bothering him. She put her mouth against his and held on, feeling him shiver as he gathered her against him and kissed her with quiet desperation.

She knew then that he felt something powerful for her, even if he'd never said so. She smoothed his hair and lay quietly in his arms until the brunt of his passion was spent. Then she curled against him, trustingly, and sighed.

He stared over her head toward the door, a little less horrified than he'd been. How shocking, he thought, to discover so late in life that he'd never known what love was. At least, not until now.

CHAPTER TEN

EMMETT WANTED TO tell Melody what he felt. He wanted to shout it to the world. But he couldn't manage it. He felt choked up with the knowledge. He looked down at her and his heart seemed to swell to the point of bursting.

"You delight me," he whispered huskily. His hand touched her hair, her cheek. "Oh, God, I'd do anything for you…!"

She drew his mouth down to hers again and kissed him tenderly.

"Coffee's on," Mrs. Jenson said with a wicked smile as she came into the room with a tray. "I suppose you newlyweds would rather live on kisses than cake, but here it is, anyway. If you need anything else, just call."

"Thanks, Mrs. Jenson," Emmett murmured.

Melody shyly climbed off Emmett's lap to sit beside him on the sofa. "Yes, indeed, it looks delicious!" she said enthusiastically.

"Could you peek out the window occasionally?" Emmett called to Mrs. Jenson. "Just to make sure the kids aren't making shish kebab of any of old man Regan's cattle?"

"Why do you think the curtains aren't drawn?" she asked, tongue-in-cheek. "All the same, they're a nice bunch of kids. They went down to Mark Gary's cabin yesterday with a straggly bunch of old silk flowers they found. His dog got run over in the road and they felt sorry for him. Guy even offered to give him Barney because he was so upset."

Emmett was touched. He didn't seem to know his own kids at all. "That was nice of them."

"Yes, it was. They've got a lot of heart." She twisted her apron. "Of course, there was this one little incident while you were away."

"Little?" he asked hesitantly.

She shifted. "Well, you know how they feel about that inspector who comes out here—the one who yelled at Barney and made Amy cry? The one everybody in the county hates?"

Emmett's face hardened. "I had words with him about upsetting Amy."

"You weren't here," she pointed out. "He made a remark that Guy didn't like about that big Appaloosa stallion of yours that Guy adores. Then he made a couple of remarks about you."

"What did they do?" Emmett asked with resignation.

"Nothing really vicious…"

"What did they do?" he repeated.

She grimaced. "They put a potato in his tailpipe."

"Did he take it out?"

She cleared her throat. "He was too busy at the time."

"Doing what?"

"Trying to get the snake out of his front seat."

Emmett buried his face in his hands. "Oh, my God!" he wailed. "He'll shut us down for sure!"

"I don't think so."

There was hope? He lifted his head. "Why?"

"Well, the kids had some food coloring they got out of the cabinet. They sort of colored the snake up before they put it in the cab. I don't like snakes, you know, but it was real pretty. Sort of blue and pink and yellow and green, with polka dots." She shrugged. "It seems that the gentleman went back to his office and told them he'd been shut up in his car with a blue and pink and yellow and green polka-dotted snake by three midget commandos." She wiped her hands on her apron. "I hear he's having therapy. There's this new inspector. He's real nice, and he likes snakes. We, uh, didn't let him see Guy's, of course. The food coloring will wear off, eventually."

Emmett hadn't stopped laughing when she got back to the kitchen.

Melody could hardly contain herself. She hoped that the kids never got it in for her!

GUY WAS NERVOUS around his father. He hadn't forgotten the threat about military school, and there was the incident with the snake. He was sure Mrs. Jenson had mentioned it.

Because he was uncertain of his position now that Melody was in residence, he tried to keep out of everyone's way.

That night, an impatient Emmett hustled the kids to bed and turned off the television long before the news was due to come on.

He held out his hand, his eyes quiet and tender as they met Melody's.

"You look impatient, Mr. Deverell," she said demurely as he tugged her along the hall toward their bedroom.

"Impatient, desperate and a few other things. How I wish these walls were soundproof," he muttered under his breath. He closed the door and locked it before he turned on the radio by the bed to a country-western station. He looked down at Melody, who was blushing. He drew her against him and bent to brush his mouth sensuously over her own. "We're starving for each other," he whispered. "I don't want eavesdroppers, and we both get pretty vocal when we let go in bed."

"Yes." She shivered as his hands smoothed down her body. "It's been so long—!" Her voice broke.

"Eons." He lifted her onto the bed and followed her down.

Tenderness still wasn't possible, he thought as the room began to spin around them. Not yet…!

Later, when the anguish of wanting each other was spent, he aroused her again, but tenderly this time. He moved against her in a soft, sweet rhythm that was unlike anything they'd ever done together. All the while, he looked into her eyes and smoothed away her damp hair, kissed her forehead, her nose, her cheeks, her eyes. Until speech was no longer possible, he whispered broken endearments and praise.

When the spiral caught them, her body convulsed violently, despite the slow, gentle rhythm, and she began to sob under the warm crush of his mouth. The rainbow of sensation made her cry out and he was vaguely aware of the radio drowning out the sound as his muscles corded and his hips arched violently, convulsively, against her.

They were both shaking with reaction when the room came back into focus. She was crying softly, because the force of the ecstasy he'd given her had been devastating.

"I wanted to give you tenderness," he whispered with exhausted regret. "I wanted it to be soft and slow and gentle and I couldn't…!"

"But it was," she protested. She lifted up, resting her arm across his damp, throbbing chest as she looked down into his eyes. "Emmett, it was!"

"Not at the last," he said through his teeth.

"Oh. Then. Well, of course not," she murmured shyly. She smiled at him wickedly and laughed deep in her throat. "You lose control," she whispered. "I like to watch you cry out, and know that it's because of me, because of the pleasure you get from my body."

He touched her face with wonder. "I like to watch you for the same reason. Melody," he said quietly, "I never watched before. The pleasure I gave never mattered that much before."

"I'm glad." She drew her face gently against his, wrapping him up in the sweetness of her adoration. "I'd die for you, Emmett," she whispered.

He drew her down and enveloped her hungrily. His hands in her hair were unsteady as he used them to turn her head so that he could find her mouth. His lips trembled, too, with the rage of feeling she unleashed in him.

Incredible man, she thought dizzily. So much a man...

She eased her hips over his and coaxed his body into deep intimacy, pressing soft kisses over his hair-roughened chest as she shifted over him until he groaned. He lay like a pagan sacrifice, and she sat up, feeling the power of her own femininity as he writhed and moaned beneath the slow movement of her hips.

"I love you," she whispered, increasing the pressure. "I love you, Emmett, I love you!"

His lean hands bit into her hips and he arched, crying out helplessly as she fulfilled him and, in the process, herself. In the back of her mind she was grateful for the radio. If those kids had heard... She moved again and he lost the ability to think at all.

BREAKFAST WAS UNCOMFORTABLE for the whole next week.

"You sure must like country-western music a lot, Emmett," Amy muttered. "But does it have to be so loud?"

"All those wailing cowboys," Polk said with a shake of his unruly hair.

"Sounds more like rock music than country," Amy agreed.

Melody's face was scarlet. She didn't dare look at Emmett. The muffled laughter coming from the head of the table was bad enough.

"I'll try to keep the volume down," Emmett promised dryly. "It helps us sleep."

"That's right," Melody agreed.

"Bill Turner wants me to go hunting with him Saturday," Guy remarked. "We're going after squirrels."

"No," Melody said abruptly.

Guy glared at her. "I can go if I want to."

"No," she said flatly. "Emmett?"

He glanced at her and frowned. She was giving him muted signals that he didn't understand. But if she was that vehement about it, there had to be a reason.

"Dad?" Guy asked belligerently.

"Melody said no," Emmett replied. "Eat your eggs."

"She's not my mother!" Guy burst out. "She can't tell me what to do!"

"She's my wife, and the hell she can't tell you what to do! This is her house now, just as much as it's mine and Amy's and Polk's and yours!"

Guy got up from the table. "I hate her!" he raged. He turned and ran out of the house. He'd wanted to go hunting more than anything in the world. It would have been the first time he'd ever shot a rifle, ever hunted anything. He'd been sure Emmett would let him go, and now that interfering woman was telling him he couldn't and Emmett took her side against his! He hated her! He ran off into the small wooded glade past the barn and stayed there for the rest of the afternoon, refusing to budge even when Amy and Polk came to find him.

"Why didn't you want him to go?" Emmett asked Melody after Guy and the other two had gone. "Is it the thought of shooting a squirrel that bothers you?"

"It's the thought of Bill shooting him," she replied worriedly. "Emmett, the weekend before we married, Bill was out beyond the barn with a .22 rifle shooting wildly all around the place. He wasn't even aiming at anything. I yelled at him when one of the bullets whizzed past me and he stopped."

"Why didn't you tell me?" he demanded.

"He begged me not to. He said you might fire him." She looked up at him. "He promised he wouldn't do it again, and he hasn't, but he's careless and haphazard. Would you really trust Guy's life to somebody like that?"

"No, certainly not. I'll talk to Guy later."

"Thanks." She grimaced. "I guess I'm public enemy number one again," she said miserably.

"He'll understand when I explain it. All the same," he said with a glowering look, "he's not going to talk to you like that."

"Look at you bristle." She sighed, resting her chin on her hands. "A conceited woman would think you're head over heels in love with me."

He stared at her levelly. "I am head over heels in love with you," he said matter-of-factly.

Her breath stopped in her throat as she met the

soft sensuality of his eyes and got lost in their green depths. "You what?" she faltered.

"I love you," he repeated. "Adore you. Worship the ground you walk on." He grinned. "We could go into the bedroom and I could tell you some more. But it's broad daylight and the radio's unplugged. And Mrs. Jenson won't confuse wailing with country music," he added, tongue-in-cheek.

She blushed, laughing. "Well, you do your share of that, too. It isn't all me!"

"I know," he said shamelessly. He sighed warmly and smiled at her. "I like just looking at you with your clothes off. Being able to make love to you is a bonus."

"I used to think I was oversized and plain before you came along," she murmured.

"Not anymore, I'll wager," he murmured, staring pointedly at her breasts. "If you're oversized, long live big girls."

She laughed. "Emmett!"

He grimaced. "I have to go to work. I don't want to," he added, when he got up and paused to kiss her on his way out. "But I don't get paid for kissing you."

"Pity," she whispered. "When you do it so well!"

He chuckled. "So do you."

"Emmett?"

He paused. "Hmm?"

"I love you, too," she said solemnly.

He smiled. "You tell me that with your body, every time we love each other." He traced a line down her straight nose. "I was telling you, the same way, but you didn't realize it, did you?"

She shook her head. Her eyes blazed with feeling. "I could walk on a cloud…"

"So could I." He bent and kissed her very softly. "One day, when the sharp edge wears off the hunger, maybe I'll be able to make love to you as tenderly as I want to in my heart," he whispered. "Right now, I can't tone down the desire I feel for you. If I have any regret, it's that."

"Have I complained?" she asked softly. "I want you just as badly, Emmett. It will keep." She smiled. She beamed. "I didn't know you loved me!"

"Well, you do, now." He pulled his hat low over his eyes. "Don't let it go to your head just because I walk into fence posts staring at you like a lovestruck boy."

She put her hand over her heart, one of his favorite postures, and grinned back at him. "Would I do that?"

His green eyes glittered with mischief. "We'd better find a rock station to listen to tonight," he murmured dryly.

She laughed with pure delight as he winked and went out the door. She had the world, she thought. She had the whole world. Emmett loved her! Everything was going to be perfect now.

THE EUPHORIA LASTED until suppertime, when she went to feed Alistair. And she couldn't find him.

She looked through the house, in all his favorite

places, but he wasn't anywhere to be seen. It was cold outside and threatening rain. Surely he wouldn't have gone out voluntarily! He hated the outdoors. He hated getting wet even more.

Then she remembered that Guy had been angry with her. The last time he'd been angry with her, he'd let Alistair out, and she almost hadn't got him back. But the boy wouldn't be that cruel again, would he?

She came back into the dining room, white in the face and obviously troubled.

"What's wrong?" Emmett asked, pausing with a bowl of mashed potatoes in his hand and an uplifted spoon over his plate.

"Alistair's missing," she said unsteadily.

She didn't look at Guy, but everyone else did.

"I didn't let him out," Guy said. He felt frightened. He hadn't been near the big cat. He liked him, now. The last thing he'd ever want to do was hurt the animal. But everybody, including his father, was giving him looks like daggers. Everybody except Melody, who couldn't seem to look at him at all.

"I didn't!" Guy repeated. "I haven't even seen him today…!"

"You were mad because Melody didn't want you to go hunting with Bill," Emmett said curtly.

"I didn't let her cat out!" Guy got to his feet. "Dad, I'm not lying! I didn't do it! Why won't you believe me?"

"Because the last time you got mad at Melody, you turned him out into the streets of Houston," Emmett said icily. "And he wound up at the city pound, where instead of being put with new arrivals to be offered for adoption, he was accidentally mixed in a bunch scheduled for immediate termination!"

Melody's gasp was audible. Emmett had never told her that. She shivered, and Guy saw it, and felt sick all over again. She looked devastated. He was sorry he'd been so angry about Bill.

He'd complained to one of the cowboys about being deprived of the hunting trip, and the cowboy had told him, tongue-in-cheek, that Bill couldn't get anybody to go with him after he'd accidentally wounded his last hunting partner. He'd added that Bill had damned near accidentally shot Melody herself a couple of weeks back, too. Guy hadn't known that. It had surprised and then pleased him that Melody had argued about letting him go. He wanted to ask her about it over supper and apologize. He'd been about to, when Melody couldn't find Alistair. And right now Guy felt in danger of becoming the entrée instead of a fellow diner.

Emmett put the mashed potatoes down. "Let's go," he said, tossing his napkin onto the table. "Everybody outside. We're going to find Alistair if it takes all night. Then," he added with a cold glare at his eldest son, "you and I are going to have a long talk about the future."

"You can't send me to military school." Guy choked. "I won't go!"

"You'll go," Emmett said, and kept walking. Melody barely heard him. She was too frightened for Alistair to notice much of what was being said. Guy had seemed so friendly, until she'd argued over that hunting trip. He was never going to accept her. He hated her. He had to, in order to put her pet at risk a second time. She was devastated.

So was Guy. He was going to be banished because of something he hadn't even done. He was going to be sent away. Military school. Demerits. Uniforms. No sister and brother to play with. No ranch.

"No," he said to himself. "No, I won't go!"

The others had gone out the door. Guy rushed to his room and got the few things he couldn't do without, including his allowance. He went back through the house, his heart pounding like mad, into his father's study. There was a small telephone journal, where important numbers were kept. His mother's number was there. He'd always wanted to use it, but he hadn't had the nerve. Now he did. He had absolutely nothing left to lose.

The phone rang and rang, and Guy watched the door nervously, chewing on his lip. He didn't want to be caught. He had to get away, but he needed a place to go. His mother was his only hope. She loved him. He knew she did, even if his father didn't.

"Hello?"

"Mom?" His voice wavered. "Mom, it's me. Guy."

"Guy!" There was excitement in her soft voice. "How are you? Does your father know you're calling me?" she added hesitantly.

"Mom, he's got a new wife," he began.

"Yes, I know. Randy's sister." She didn't even sound upset. "Melody is sweet and kind. She'll be good to you. I'm happy that your father has finally found someone he can really love, Guy…"

"But she hates me," he wailed. "She blames me for stuff I don't do. Look, can I come and live with you? They don't really want me here!"

There was a pause. "Son, you know I'd love nothing better. I really would love to have you. But, you see… I'm pregnant. And I'm having a hard time. I can't really look after you right now, having to stay in bed so much. But after the baby comes…" she added. "Guy? Guy?"

There was nothing but a dial tone on the other end of the line.

Guy stood looking at the replaced receiver. His mother was pregnant. She was going to have a baby. Not his father's baby. Randy's baby. That meant she was certainly never going to come back. She would have another family of her own, Randy's children.

Now, Guy thought numbly, he had no one at all. His father was remarried and would have other children, too. His mother didn't want him. He had nobody in the whole world.

He turned and walked out the front door. The rain was starting to come down in sheets. It was cold, and his jacket wasn't waterproof, but he really didn't care. He had nothing left to lose. His home, his secure life, his father, his mother, his family were all nothing but memories. He was unwanted and unloved.

Well, he thought with bitter sorrow, perhaps he could make it alone. He had twenty dollars in his pocket and he didn't mind hard work. There had to be someplace he could go where nobody would care about his age.

He started walking across the field toward the main highway. He didn't look back.

"ALISTAIR!" MELODY WAILED. They'd been searching for half an hour, with no success at all. The big tabby cat hadn't turned up yet.

"You won't stop me this time," Emmett said angrily as they paused just inside the barn. "Guy won't be hurt by a little discipline. I'm going to enroll him in the same military school where I went when I was a boy."

"But he was getting used to me," Melody said miserably. "I know he was. I shouldn't have said anything about Bill…"

"And let him go off with the man and get killed?" He stared at her. "Melody, part of being a parent is knowing when to say no for a child's own good. You have to expect rebellion and tantrums, and not let yourself be swayed by them. Parenting is a rough job. Loving a child isn't enough. You have to prepare him to live in a hostile world."

"I guess there's more to it than I realized." She looked up at him. "Guy is so like you," she said gently. "I care about him. I don't want him to be hurt."

"Neither do I, but education isn't a punishment. I think he'll like it. I was homesick at first, but I loved it after the first two weeks. If he doesn't take to it," he added quietly, "he can come back home."

She smiled through her sadness. "You're a nice man."

"I'm a wet man," he replied. "Let's look for a few more minutes…"

"Emmett!" Amy shouted. "Emmett, he's here, he's here!"

"What?" He went into the barn, following her excited voice.

Emmett and Melody peered over into the corn crib and there, curled up on some hay, was a sleepy, purring Alistair.

"Oh, you monster!" Melody grumbled. She picked him up and cradled him close, murmuring softly to him.

"Found your cat, did you?" Larry, the eldest of the cowboys, asked with a smile. "Meant to tell you he'd got out, but we had a few head get lost and I had to go help hunt them. He ran out past me when I was talking to Ellie Jenson in the kitchen. Guess my spurs spooked him," he added ruefully. "No harm done, though, I suppose, was there? I'll be more careful next time, boss."

He tipped his hat and went to put up the tack he was carrying, water dripping off his hat.

Emmett and Melody exchanged horrified glances.

"Guy!" she whispered.

He drew in a deep breath. "Well, I guess I'll eat crow for a month," he muttered. "Come on. I might as well get it over with."

But it wasn't that easy. They went back into the house and the telephone was ringing off the hook.

Mrs. Jenson had gone home an hour earlier, and Guy was apparently unwilling to pick up the receiver.

Emmett grabbed it up. "Hello?"

"Emmett! Thank God! It's Adell," she said.

Hearing her voice threw him off balance. He'd avoided talking to her for two years. Now, it was like hearing any woman's voice.

"Hello, Adell," he said pleasantly. "What can I do for you?"

"It's Guy," she said. "I've been trying to get you for a half hour. Guy called, and he sounded pretty desperate. He wanted to come and live with me, but I blurted out about the baby, and he hung up. I'm so worried. I didn't mean to tell him like that, Emmett. I didn't mean it to sound as if I didn't love him or want him…!"

"It's all a misunderstanding," Emmett said gently. "Now don't worry. He's hiding in his room and we'll get it straightened out. He'll be fine."

"I knew it would be hard for the kids when you got married again, but Melody's so sweet," she said softly. "She's just what the four of you need. The boys will worship her when they get used to her, and so will Amy."

"They already do," he said. "I've been pretty bull-headed over this, Adell. I'm sorry."

"I did it the wrong way," she confessed. "I ran when I should have stood up and been honest with you. I guess if we'd really loved each other it would have been different. But I didn't know what love was until Randy came along." She hesitated. "I hope you know what I'm talking about."

"I do now," he said, staring quietly at Melody. "Oh, yes, I understand now."

"Let me know about Guy?"

"Of course. Adell, I'm glad for you and Randy, about the baby."

"We're ecstatic," she said. "I can hardly wait. A baby might be just the thing for the kids."

"You can bring it down to meet them when it's born," he said.

"Thanks. I will. But what I meant was if you and Melody had one of your own eventually, it would bring them closer to her."

He stared at Melody and flushed as the glory of fathering her child made his knees weak.

"Emmett?" Adell called.

"What? Oh. Yes. You can call the kids or write to them if you want," he said absently. "They can come and visit, too, when it's convenient. Or you and Randy can come down here. Tell him I won't hit him."

"He knows that. We both felt guilty over what he'd done to you, for a long time. I'm glad it worked out."

"So am I. I'll have Guy call you back."

"That would be nice. Tell him I love him, and that I didn't mean he wasn't welcome here."

"I will." He hung up, his eyes slow and warm on Melody's face. "Adell thinks I should make you pregnant," he mused.

She caught her breath. "Well!"

He moved toward her, and paused to frame her face in his big, lean hands. "I think I should, too," he whispered. "Not right away, not until we're really a family. But I'd like it very much if we had a child together, Melody." He bent and drew his lips softly over hers.

"So would I." She clung to him, giving him back the kiss. She smiled warmly. "But for now, we'd better tell Guy that he isn't going to be banished to Siberia."

"Good point."

They went to his room and knocked. There was no answer. With a rueful smile, Emmett pushed it open, but Guy wasn't there.

Emmett looked around. Some of Guy's favorite possessions were missing, including that whittling knife that Melody had given him. He looked at her with fear in his eyes.

"He's run away, hasn't he?" she asked with faint panic.

His face was grim. "I'm afraid that's just what he's done," he replied.

CHAPTER ELEVEN

JACOBSVILLE SEEMED TO be a long way from anywhere, Guy thought, huddled miserably in his jacket while rain poured down on his bare head and soaked his sneakers. He was cold and getting colder by the minute. He should have taken time to search for the raincoat he could never find, but he'd been afraid someone would try to stop him.

After a few wet minutes, he managed to flag down a family of Mexicans driving toward Houston. With his meager Spanish, painstakingly taught to him by his bilingual father, he made them understand that he was on his way to his family. They smiled and nodded and gestured him into the crowded car of smiling, welcoming faces. People, he thought, were generally pretty nice. He was pleasantly surprised. Too bad he couldn't say that for his own family. They'd probably find Melody's cat dead and nobody would speak to him for the rest of his life. It wasn't his fault, but he guessed maybe he deserved it for what he'd done in Houston.

The Mexican family stopped at Victoria to get gas, and Guy had second thoughts about continuing on to Houston. He might as well try to find a place to stay here. Victoria was big enough that he could get lost in it.

He found a vacant lot where a small building stood with its door ajar. It was still raining. He darted into the shack and came face-to-face with a couple of men who looked as if murder might be their favorite Sunday pastime.

IT TOOK FOREVER just to get the kids into Emmett's Bronco and strapped in. All the while, the rain was getting worse and Melody was chewing on her fingernails. They'd called the local police and a bolo went out over the air to law enforcement vehicles. Emmett had a CB unit and a scanner in the Bronco, and the scanner was turned on so that they'd hear immediately if Guy was spotted.

Emmett was actually able to track the boy down the highway at the end of the ranch road, until the footprints abruptly stopped.

He got back into the vehicle, his hat dripping water. "This is as far as he walked," he said tersely, turning toward Melody. "Thank God for thick mud and a light drizzling rain. I tracked him to the other side of the road. He's headed that way, toward Victoria."

He wheeled the vehicle around in the road and set off with grim determination toward the city.

"I hope to God whoever he was riding with needed gas, and that he found some decent person and not a pervert to get into the car with."

"He's a smart boy," Melody said gently, touching

his arm. "He'll be all right, Emmett. I know he will." She grimaced. "Oh, it's my fault!"

"No, it's not," he said tersely. "It takes a little work to turn five people into a family. It doesn't happen overnight, you know."

"I'm learning that. All the same, Guy's more important to me than Alistair, even if I do love the stupid cat," she added quietly, staring worriedly through the misty windshield.

It took forever to get into the city. Then Emmett stopped at the nearest gas station before he proceeded to the next few. They were almost at the far end of town before an attendant remembered a bareheaded boy in a leather bomber jacket and jeans and sneakers.

"He was pretty wet," the man said with a grin. "Came in with a family of Mexicans, but he didn't want to go on to Houston with them. I had to explain. Kid spoke really lousy Spanish," he murmured sheepishly.

"Did you see which way he went?"

"No. I'm sorry, but we got busy and I didn't notice. Can't have gotten far, though. It's only been ten or fifteen minutes, and he didn't hitch another ride, I'm sure of that."

"Thanks. Thanks a lot. Okay if I leave the Bronco here while we look for him?"

"Sure, it's okay! Just park it anywhere. I'll look out for it."

"Much obliged."

Emmett pulled it out of the way and parked it.

He turned to the others. "We're going to spread out and go over this area of town like tar paper. Amy, you go with Melody. Polk, with me. If you find him, sing out."

"All right, Emmett," Amy said politely. "We'll find him."

"God, I hope so," he said heavily. It was already dark. The streetlights were a blessing, but any city was dangerous at night. They had to find the boy soon, or they might never find him.

They piled out of the Bronco and Emmett paused to look hard at Melody. "Don't go anywhere you don't feel comfortable. I don't like having any of us out on these streets at night. Stay where it's lighted. If you get in trouble, scream. I'll hear you."

She smiled up at him. "Amy and I both will," she mused.

"I can scream good, Emmett," Amy said. "Want to hear me?"

"Not just yet, thanks," he murmured, tugging a pigtail. "Get going."

Melody and Amy went down one street, Emmett another. They met a policeman cruising by, and Emmett stopped to talk to him. He explained the situation.

"We got the bolo on the radio," the patrolman, an elderly man, replied. "We're watching for him. He's pretty safe if he's still in this area. Hope you find him."

"So do I," Emmett said quietly. "He's got the

wrong end of the stick. He thinks we don't care about him because we have to say no sometimes."

"Prisons are full of kids who never got said no to," the policeman mused. "Might tell him that."

"He'll get an earful, after he gets hugged half to death," Emmett said with a wry smile.

"That's how I raised my four. One's a lawyer now." With a twinkle in his eyes he added, "Of course, the others are respectable…"

Emmett laughed despite his fears and lifted his hand as the patrol car pulled away into the darkness.

DOWN THE STREET, Melody was huddled in her coat, drawing Amy closer as the rain began to fall again. She looked and looked, and found nothing. Finally, yielding to defeat, she turned and guided Amy back toward the service station.

The shack in the empty lot had caught her eye earlier, but she hadn't paid it much mind because she was sure Guy would be trying to make some distance.

Now, she wasn't so certain.

"Let's take a look in there, just in case," she told Amy. "Stay close."

"Okay, Melody."

They moved quickly toward the shack, and as they approached it, loud voices could be heard. There was a violent thumping noise, and the ramshackle door suddenly moved and Guy came tearing out of it. His face was bleeding and his jacket was half off.

A thin, dirty man was holding the half that was off, dragging at it.

"I said, I want the damned jacket!" the surly voice repeated.

"It's Guy!" Amy exclaimed.

"Yes." Melody's eyes blazed with anger. She was never so happy for her size. "Stay behind me," she called as she broke into a run.

Guy was fighting the man, but the other one had a stick and was raising it.

"You leave my son alone!" Melody yelled at them.

The men stopped suddenly and gaped at her. So did a shocked, delighted Guy. While they were gaping, she sailed right into the one who had Guy by the sleeve, performed a jump kick accompanied by a cry that would have made her instructor applaud and landed her foot squarely into the attacker's gut.

Guy barely had time for one astonished look at her threatening stance. Loosened by the man's collapse, Guy turned quickly to place a hard kick in the other man's groin before he could bring down the stick he was holding up and then planted a hard fist right into his cheek. The second man went down with a little cry of pain and landed unconscious.

"Are you all right?" Melody asked Guy, dragging him close to hug him. "Oh, you holy terror, if you ever do anything like this again...!" She was barely coherent, crying and mumbling, searching his face for cuts and bruises, brushing back his unruly damp hair. But the whole time she was holding him as his mother once had when he stumbled and fell, when he was hurt or afraid.

Big boys weren't supposed to like this sort of thing, of course, much less tolerate it. And he was going to twist away from her any minute now and make some curt remark. But just for a minute or so, it wouldn't hurt to be hugged and cried over.

"How did you do that?" he asked, aghast.

"Oh, that. Well, I have a belt in tae kwon do. Just a brown. I never finished my training."

"Just a brown!" He caught his breath. "That was great! Like watching Chuck Norris or Jean-Claude Van Damme," he added, naming his two idols. "Listen, could you teach me some of that?"

"You and the other kids, too," she promised. "Then next time, you'll be prepared." She grimaced as she studied him. "Listen, Alistair's fine, one of the men accidentally let him out," she said miserably, drawing back. "I'm so sorry. All of us are sorry for blaming you. For heaven's sake, you're more important than a cat, even if he was the only friend I had! Your father was frantic, and so were the rest of us!"

Guy felt strange. He sort of smiled and couldn't stop. "I'm all right." He looked down at the squirming, groaning men. "Uh, it might not be a bad idea if we leave," he suggested, taking her arm. "You and I were pretty much a match for them, but we've Amy to think about."

"You're right. I do wish I had a gun," she muttered, glaring at them.

"Can you shoot one?" Guy asked on the way down the street.

"Sure I can shoot," she said. "I've won awards."

"Really?"

"You still can't go hunting with Bill," she said curtly, glaring at him. "He'd kill you. He's not responsible with a gun. If you go hunting, I'll take you, or your father will. Or we'll all go. But I'm not shooting anything, even if I do go along, and I couldn't skin a squirrel if my life depended on it."

"We wouldn't go hunting to kill stuff," Guy said. "We'd go hunting so that we can grumble about how cold it was and how much big game got away. And so that we can sit and talk away from cars and horns and clocks."

"Oh."

He shrugged. "It would be all right if you came along, I guess. We could shoot at targets."

"I can shoot, too," Amy said. "I have a bow and arrow that Emmett made me."

"Polk can bring his atl-atl," Guy remarked. "We'd be the most dangerous family in the woods."

Melody laughed. She felt exhausted now. They came to the street where the service station sat on the corner, and there were Emmett and Polk coming toward them.

"Guy!" Emmett shouted.

The boy ran to him, and Emmett lifted him off the ground in a bear hug. "My God, you are something! I wish I'd hit you harder when you were a little kid!"

"I guess you should have, all right," Guy murmured, fighting tears. "I'm sorry, Dad…!"

"I'm sorry," Emmett corrected grimly. He put the boy down. "We're all sorry. If you had any idea how worried we were!" His green eyes began to glitter. "Son, if you ever, ever do anything like this to us again, I'll… I'll…!"

"He's trying to think up something bad enough to threaten you with," Melody translated, grinning at him. "It may take a while."

"Some men were beating up Guy, Emmett," Amy said excitedly. "Melody knocked one of them out, and Guy hit the other one. They're lying in the dirt back there."

"You'd better show me those men," Emmett said. The remark Amy had made about Melody went right over his head. He was incensed that anyone should hit his child. "Why were they beating on you?" Emmett asked slowly.

"They wanted my jacket," Guy said, grimacing. "I should have had better sense than to go in there in the first place, but I was wet and miserable and I didn't think. They were tramps, I think—maybe hitchhikers."

"Let's check this out, just in case," Emmett said, and he looked pretty dangerous, Guy thought as they walked together toward the shack. But a police car came by before they reached it. Emmett told the officer what had happened, and he was told that there had been some trouble with transients lately. He went to check, but the men were long gone. Which was just as well.

The fighting Deverells climbed back into their Bronco and went home.

A LITTLE LATER, with three exhausted kids tucked up in bed before they managed to rehash the exciting incident, Melody lay curled up in Emmett's hard arms, smiling with pure bliss after the most tender loving she'd ever known.

"This is what I wanted it to be on our wedding night," he said drowsily. "But I was too desperate for you." He bent and brushed his mouth lovingly over her soft lips, smiling warmly.

"When we get around to making a baby, I want it to be like it was tonight," she whispered into his warm throat. "We've never been closer than this."

"I know." He cradled her body to his and stretched lazily. "Guy's going to be Alistair's champion from now on, I imagine," he murmured.

"Friends to the end. Alistair's sleeping with him."

"He's your champion, too. You should have heard him telling Polk what you did to that tramp on his behalf." He glanced at her. "Polk told him what you said, about his being more important to you than Alistair. He's been strutting all night."

"He's a very special boy. But he's much more sensitive than he looks." She traced his thick eyebrows. "We'll have to remember that. Both of us. And no military school. If he goes, I'm going with him."

"For protection?"

"Laugh if you like, but I'm a brown belt in tae kwon do."

"What?"

She shrugged, smiling at his surprise. "Didn't you wonder how I was able to drop a man that size so easily? I didn't have anything else to do on long winter nights, so I enrolled in a Korean karate class. It was very educational."

"No wonder you didn't balk when I asked you to go with Amy to look for Guy. I worried about doing that. Men are going to feel protective about their women. It's their nature."

"I know that. I don't mind. Just as long as you know that I'm not helpless all the time." She rolled over and kissed his chest, feeling his breath catch as her lips pressed through the thick hair to the hard, warm flesh beneath it. "Of course," she whispered, "there are times when I really enjoy being helpless."

"Is this one of them?" he murmured, coaxing her mouth closer.

"I think so."

"Good. Let's be helpless together…"

He rolled her over and very quickly, the friendly banter turned to something much more serious and intense.

RANDY AND A very pregnant Adell came to visit two months later. The children accepted her condition without comment, and there were no problems.

By the time Emmett and his family drove Adell and Randy back to the airport, they were friends.

Randy, who looked so much like his sister, was obviously the end of Adell's rainbow.

"Nice to see them so happy," Emmett remarked as he and Melody watched the other couple walk off toward the loading ramp, arms close around each other.

"Yes, isn't it?" Melody asked with a sigh. "Emmett, I'm so happy I could burst."

"So am I." He bent to kiss her, very softly. "And the kids were so good, weren't they? I could hardly believe they were the same bunch that put on their Thanksgiving Indian costumes and attacked that car of Florida tourists that got lost on the place last week. We really are going to have to start enforcing some new codes of behavior."

"Oh, maybe not," Melody said. "They've been so good today..."

"Excuse me?"

A uniformed security guard with a grim expression tapped on Emmett's shoulder.

"Yes?" Emmett asked politely.

"Someone said those might be your kids...?"

He gestured toward the concourse. Emmett noticed three things. An empty pet carrier. A screaming, running woman. Three laughing children holding equal parts of an enormous, friendly python. It looked almost identical to a Far Side cartoon by Gary Larson that the twins had just been looking at in the book he'd bought them earlier...

Emmett didn't dare do what he felt like doing. Hysterical laughter was not going to help him. He looked at the security guard. He put his hand over his heart. "Officer," he said pleasantly, "I have never seen those kids before in my life…"

Melody gave him a glare that was good for two headaches and a lonely night, and went running down the concourse after the children.

* * * * *

A blizzard is keeping guests at Sterling Montana Guest Ranch, where a killer is lurking in the shadows.

Read on for a sneak preview of
Stroke of Luck *by* New York Times *and* USA TODAY
bestselling author B.J. Daniels.

"Bad luck always comes in threes."

Standing in the large kitchen of the Sterling Montana Guest Ranch, Will Sterling shot the woman an impatient look. "I don't have time for this right now, Dorothea."

"Just sayin'," Dorothea Brand muttered under her breath. The fifty-year-old housekeeper was short and stout with a helmet of dark hair and piercing dark eyes. She'd been a fixture on the ranch since Will and his brothers were kids, which made her invaluable, but also as bossy as an old mother hen.

After the Sterling boys had lost their mother, Dorothea had stepped in. Their father, Wyatt, had continued to run the guest ranch alone and then with the help of his sons until his death last year. For the first time, Will would finally be running the guest ranch without his father calling all the shots. He'd been looking forward to the challenge and to carrying on the family business.

But now his cook was laid up with a broken leg? He definitely didn't like the way the season was starting, Will thought as the housekeeper leaned against the counter, giving him one of her you're-going-to-regret-this looks as he considered who he could call.

As his brother Garrett brought in a box of supplies from town, Will asked, "Do you know anyone who can cook?"

"What about Poppy Carmichael?" Garrett suggested as he pulled a bottle of water from the refrigerator, opened it and took a long drink. "She's a caterer now."

Will frowned. "Poppy?" An image appeared of a girl with freckles, braces, skinned knees and reddish-brown hair in pigtails. "I haven't thought of Poppy in years. I thought she moved away."

"She did, but she came back about six months ago and started a catering business in Whitefish," Garrett said. "I only know because I ran into her at a party recently. The food was really good, if that helps."

"Wait, I remember her. Cute kid. Didn't her father work for the forest service?" their younger brother Shade asked as he also came into the kitchen with a box of supplies. He deposited the box inside the large pantry just off the kitchen. "Last box," he announced, dusting off his hands.

"You remember, Will. Poppy and her dad lived in the old forest service cabin a mile or so from here," Garrett said, grinning at him. "She used to ride her bike over here and help us with our chores. At least, that was her excuse."

Will avoided his brother's gaze. It wasn't like he'd ever forgotten.

"I just remember the day she decided to ride Lightning," Shade said. "She climbed up on the corral, and as the horse ran by, she jumped on it!" He shook his head, clearly filled with admiration. "I can't imagine what she thought she was going to do, riding him bareback." He laughed. "She stayed on a lot longer than I thought she would. But it's a wonder she didn't kill herself. The girl had grit. But I always wondered what possessed her to do that."

Garrett laughed and shot another look at Will. "She was trying to impress our brother."

"That poor little girl was smitten," Dorothea agreed as she narrowed her dark gaze at Will. "And you, being fifteen and full of yourself, often didn't give her the time of day. So what could possibly go wrong hiring her to cook for you?"

Don't miss
Stroke of Luck *by B.J. Daniels, available March 2019
wherever HQN Books and ebooks are sold.*

www.Harlequin.com

HQN™

Save **$1.00**
off the purchase of
Stroke of Luck
by B.J. Daniels.

Available wherever books are sold,
including most bookstores, supermarkets,
drugstores and discount stores.

Save **$1.00**

off the purchase of *Stroke of Luck* by B.J. Daniels.

Coupon valid until June 30, 2019.
Redeemable at participating outlets in U.S. and Canada only.
Limit one coupon per customer.

52616280

Canadian Retailers: Harlequin Enterprises Limited will pay the face value of this coupon plus 10.25¢ if submitted by customer for this product only. Any other use constitutes fraud. Coupon is nonassignable. Void if taxed, prohibited or restricted by law. Consumer must pay any government taxes. Void if copied. Inmar Promotional Services ("IPS") customers submit coupons and proof of sales to Harlequin Enterprises Limited, P.O. Box 31000, Scarborough, ON M1R 0E7, Canada. Non-IPS retailer—for reimbursement submit coupons and proof of sales directly to Harlequin Enterprises Limited, Retail Marketing Department, Bay Adelaide Centre, East Tower, 22 Adelaide Street West, 40th Floor, Toronto, Ontario M5H 4E3, Canada.

U.S. Retailers: Harlequin Enterprises Limited will pay the face value of this coupon plus 8¢ if submitted by customer for this product only. Any other use constitutes fraud. Coupon is nonassignable. Void if taxed, prohibited or restricted by law. Consumer must pay any government taxes. Void if copied. For reimbursement submit coupons and proof of sales directly to Harlequin Enterprises, Ltd 482, NCH Marketing Services, P.O. Box 880001, El Paso, TX 88588-0001, U.S.A. Cash value 1/100 cents.

5 65373 00076 2   (8100)0 12414

DPCOUP0119

If you love
DIANA PALMER
then you'll love these Western Romances...

Available March 2019

HQN™

Available March 2019

HARLEQUIN
SPECIAL EDITION

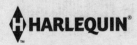

Looking for more satisfying love stories
with community and family at their core?

Check out **Harlequin® Special Edition**
and **Love Inspired®** books!

New books available every month!

CONNECT WITH US AT:

Facebook.com/groups/HarlequinConnection

Facebook.com/HarlequinBooks

Twitter.com/HarlequinBooks

Instagram.com/HarlequinBooks

Pinterest.com/HarlequinBooks

ReaderService.com

❖ HARLEQUIN®

**ROMANCE WHEN
YOU NEED IT**

HFGENRE2018

Reward the book lover in you!

Earn points on your purchase of new Harlequin books from participating retailers.

Turn your points into **FREE BOOKS** of your choice!

Join for FREE today at
www.HarlequinMyRewards.com.

Harlequin My Rewards is a free program (no fees) without any commitments or obligations.

MYR18